THE QUARRYGATE GAMBIT

THE STREETS OF MARADAINE
BOOK FOUR

MARSHALL RYAN MARESCA

PRAISE FOR MARSHALL RYAN MARESCA AND THE MARADAINE SAGA

"Maresca offers something beyond the usual high fantasy fare, with a wealth of unique and well-rounded characters, a vivid setting, and complicatedly intertwined social issues that feel especially timely."

— PUBLISHERS WEEKLY

"Marshall Ryan Maresca is one of the most ambitious fantasy authors to burst on the scene in the last decade."

— BLACK GATE MAGAZINE

"In one fast-paced, funny, highly readable novel after another, Maresca continues to build out every nook and alleyway of Maradaine, which is fast becoming one of the most richly detailed settings in fantasy."

— BARNES & NOBLE FANTASY BLOG

"This epic adventure is hard to put down, leaving readers curious about the future progression of these characters while smoothly setting up the next adventure."

— BOOKLIST

"Maresca has achieved something truly magnificent here."

— CASS MORRIS, AUTHOR OF *FROM UNSEEN FIRE*

"It's a story about morality, about sacrifice, about what people want from life. It's a fun story–there's quips, swordfights, chases through the streets. It's a compelling, convincing work of fantasy, and a worthy addition to the rich tapestry that is the works of Maradaine."

— SCI-FI AND FANTASY REVIEWS

"Highly recommend this series to anyone who loves high fantasy, political intrigue, magic, fantastic world building, and characters who you can root for."

— GIZMO'S REVIEWS

"Veranix is Batman, if Batman were a teenager and magically talented.... Action, adventure, and magic in a school setting will appeal to those who love *Harry Potter* and Patrick Rothfuss' *The Name of the Wind*."

— *LIBRARY JOURNAL* (STARRED)

"*The Thorn of Dentonhill* was a fast-paced read with action from start to finish. I loved every minute of it."

— SHORT AND SWEET REVIEWS

"Maresca brings the whole package, complete and well-constructed. If you're looking for something fun and adventurous for your next fantasy read, look no further than *The Thorn of Dentonhill*, an incredible start to a new series, from an author who is clearly on his way to great things."

— BIBLIOSANCTUM

ALSO BY
MARSHALL RYAN MARESCA

MARADAINE SAGA PHASE ONE

The Thorn of Dentonhill
The Alchemy of Chaos
The Imposters of Aventil

A Murder of Mages
An Import of Intrigue
A Parliament of Bodies

The Holver Alley Crew
Lady Henterman's Wardrobe
The Fenmere Job

Way of the Shield
Shield of the People
People of the City

THE DISPLACED DAUGHTERS
An Unintended Voyage

MARADAINE SAGA PHASE TWO

The Assassins of Consequence
The New King of Rose Street*

An Unkindness of Uncircled Mages*
A Pride of Partners*

The Quarrygate Gambit
The Andrendon Plan*

City of the Truth*
Truth of the Crown*

MARADAINE SAGA SHORTS
The Mystical Murders of Yin Mara
Hultichia
The Withered Boy
The Royal First Irregulars*
A Proper Lady of Society*

THE ZIAPARR CYCLE
The Velocity of Revolution

*- Forthcoming

THE QUARRYGATE GAMBIT

BOOK FOUR OF
THE STREETS OF MARADAINE

MARSHALL RYAN MARESCA

PREVIOUSLY IN MARADAINE

THE HOLVER ALLEY CREW (Maritan 27th–Joran 5th—mid-spring)

Asti and Verci Rynax—a broken spy and a brilliant gadgeteer—lost their home and shop to the Holver Alley fire, and gathered a crew to steal a statue for an unnamed buyer. They learned the fire was set on purpose, and have their revenge on the man who arranged the fire, only to learn he was part of a larger plot.

LADY HENTERMAN'S WARDROBE (Erescan 18th–24th—early summer)

Asti and Verci's investigation of the fire led them to Lord Henterman, and inadvertently to Liora Rand, the spy who betrayed Asti to the Poasians. Their final confrontation left Liora severely injured, but she was able to control Asti's broken mind, and escaped with a statue similar to the one they stole before. Major Grieson—Asti's old handler —confides in Asti that Liora is part of a corruption in Intelligence. Liora has been working with Major Altarn, and is also connected to the Brotherhood, Lord Sirath, and someone called Crenaxin, the Dragon.

THE FENMERE JOB (Oscan 13th–17th—early autumn)

Asti and Verci tried to keep Fenmere's Poasian smugglers from using their neighborhood as an entry point, which connected to the Firewing mage house that had been built in the wake of the Holver Alley fire. Veranix came to their neighborhood to cut off Fenmere, and after an initial misunderstanding with the Rynaxes, worked with them to stop Fenmere and the Firewings. Asti's mental state continued to deteriorate, drawing the attention of Poasian spies who believe he knows of a mysterious list. The brothers learned that a project behind the fire involves building underground machine carriages, and began a plan to infiltrate and sabotage the project.

PEOPLE OF THE CITY

(Oscan 25th–28th—early autumn)

Circumstances—partially directed by the mysterious Sister Myriem-- led Asti and Verci to team with the Thorn, Minox and Satrine and others—to a massive battle in St. Bridget's Square, where the brothers help defend their neighborhood against the Brotherhood, and gain some small bit of notoriety for it.

THE QUARRYGATE GAMBIT
Alasim 1215
Late Autumn

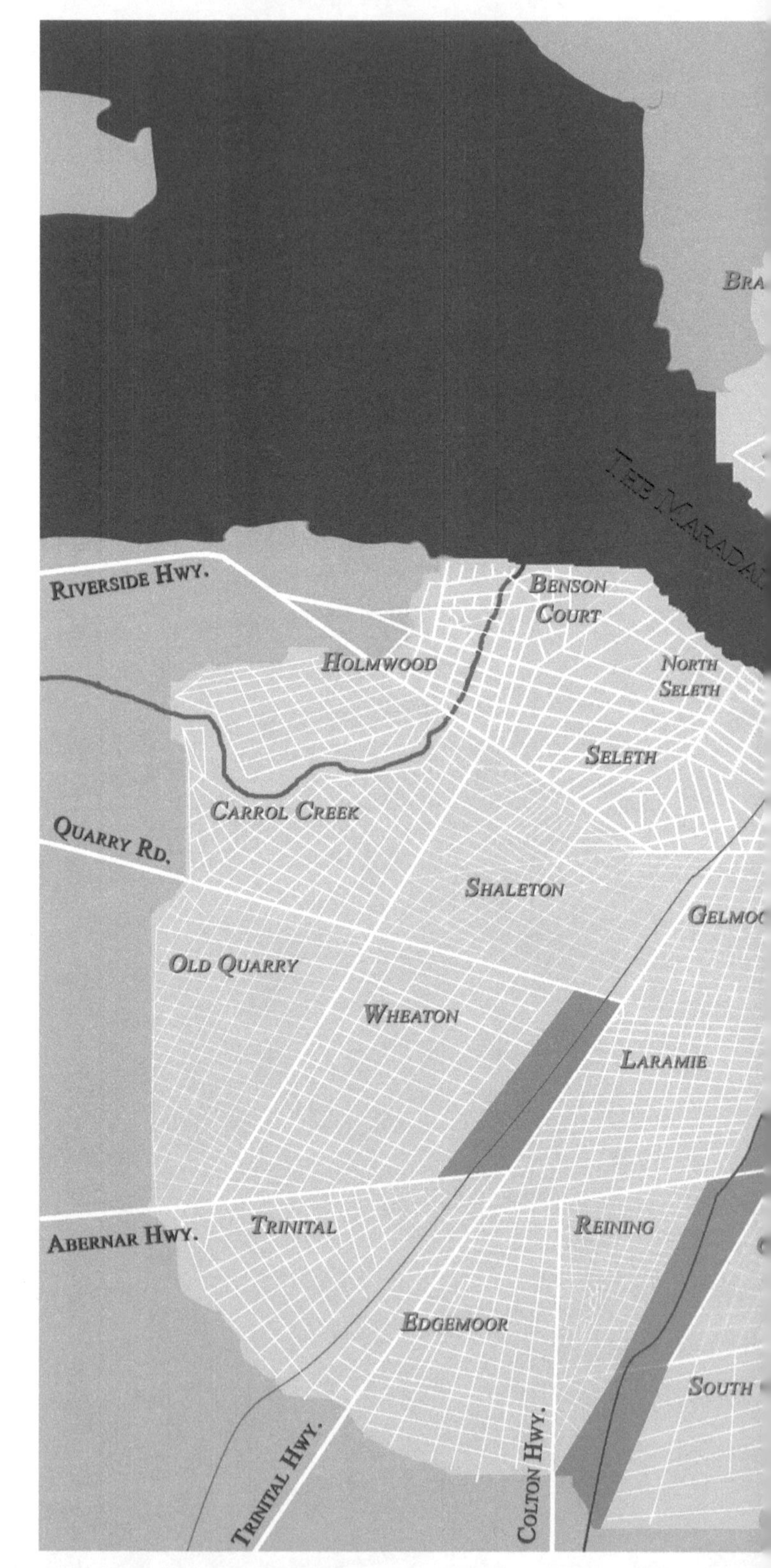

RIVERSIDE HWY.
BENSON COURT
HOLMWOOD
NORTH SELETH
SELETH
CARROL CREEK
QUARRY RD.
SHALETON
GELMOO
OLD QUARRY
WHEATON
LARAMIE
ABERNAR HWY.
TRINITAL
REINING
EDGEMOOR
SOUTH
TRINITAL HWY.
COLTON HWY.
THE MARADAI
BRA

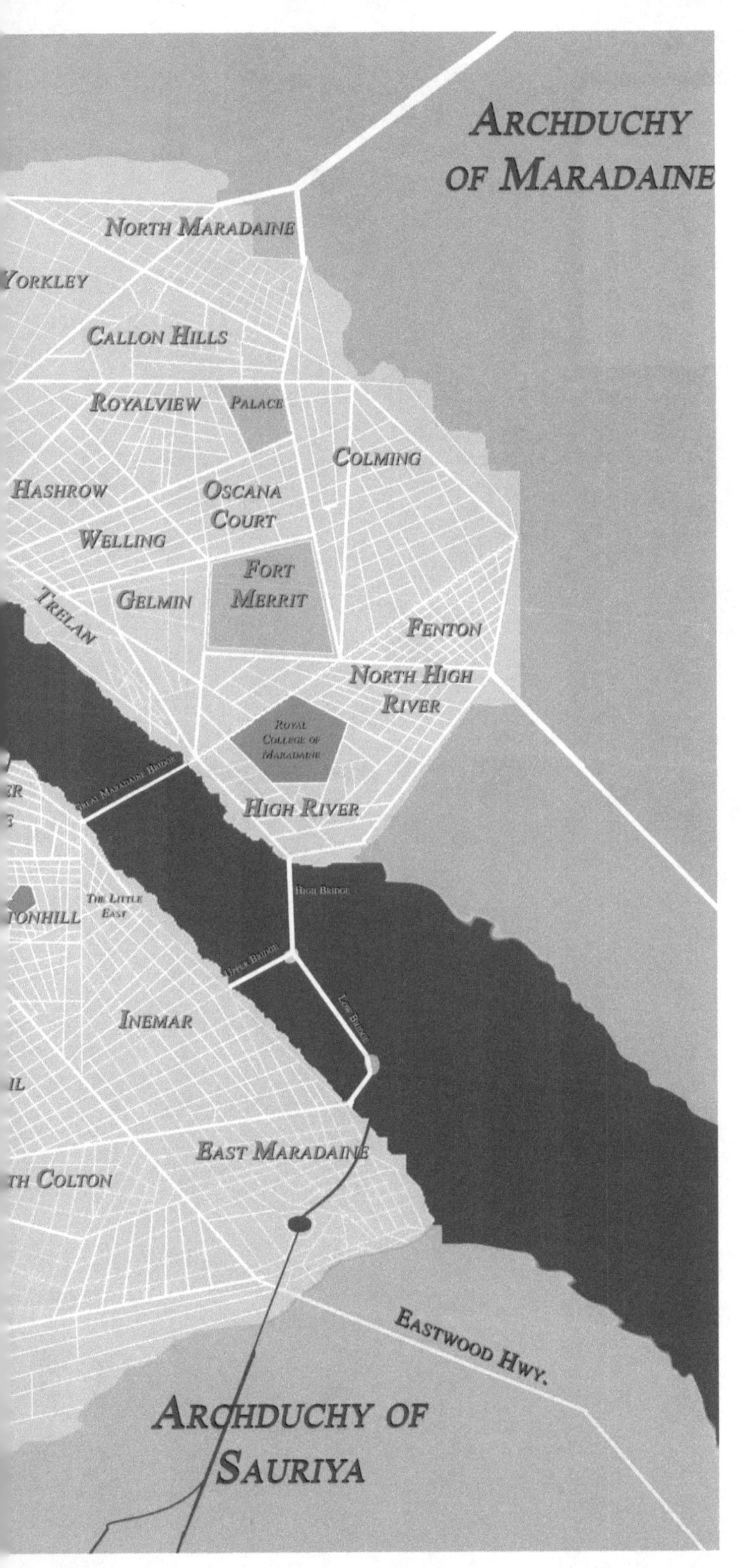

ARCHDUCHY OF MARADAINE
NORTH MARADAINE
YORKLEY
CALLON HILLS
ROYALVIEW
PALACE
COLMING
HASHROW
OSCANA COURT
WELLING
FORT MERRIT
GELMIN
TRELAN
FENTON
NORTH HIGH RIVER
ROYAL COLLEGE OF MARADAINE
GREAT MARADAINE BRIDGE
HIGH RIVER
ER
E
TONHILL
THE LITTLE EAST
HIGH BRIDGE
UPPER BRIDGE
IL
LONG BRIDGE
INEMAR
EAST MARADAINE
TH COLTON
EASTWOOD HWY.
ARCHDUCHY OF SAURIYA

THE MARADAINE RIVER
BENSON COURT
NORTH SELETH
SELETH
KELLER COVE
1 - Rynax Gadgeterium
2 - Kimber's Pub
3 - Oberick Warehouses
4 - Doc Gelson's Office
5 - Junk Avenue Bakery
6 - Elk Road Shack
7 - St. Bridget's Church
8 - Jonet's Clay Bowl
9 - The Firewing House
10 - The Milst St. Tavern
Heel Rd.
Bridget Road
Frost Road
Junk Avenue
Rabbit Road
Colt Road
Elk Road
West Birch
Fawcett Avenue
Ullen Road
Holver Alley
Kenner Ln
Scal Rd
Calder Way
Evans Ave.

PART I
ARRESTS OF JUBILATION

CHAPTER ONE

Asti Rynax's plan was going perfectly—every piece was in place, every one of his people were exactly where they were needed to be, doing exactly what they should. But there were so many details swimming in his head that as he crossed through the back alley to Frost Road he didn't even see the kid with the knife until it was right at his throat.

"Your coin, old man!"

"Old man, really?" Asti asked.

"You heard me!" the kid snapped. "Hand it over or I—"

"I mean, I only just turned twenty-seven," Asti said, keeping his voice even. Being called "old" was quite upsetting. "That's not really old at all, son."

"What are you on about?" the kid said, pressing his knife up on Asti's chin. "I told you, coin! Or I cut you!"

"See, you already showed me you don't want to," Asti said. "Else you'd just cut me and search my pockets as I bled."

"I'm serious!"

"So am I," Asti said. "I mean, who even taught you? You're not even holding it right."

"What?"

Asti didn't have time for this, but it really was just sad. No form, no technique.

"Look," Asti said, taking the kid's wrist and twisting it away from his neck. "You don't want me to be able to do that. And you let me for a couple reasons." The kid cried out and dropped the knife, which Asti caught in his off hand.

"Hey, ow!" the kid said as Asti kept his wrist in the lock.

"See, right, that hurts a lot," Asti said. "You got too close, and that means you had nothing to thrust with, and I could reach past your knife and grab you. Part of the point of having a blade, especially in a situation like this, is you're able to keep the other person at a distance. They don't close in on you because they don't want to get cut."

"The blazes are you on about?"

"I'm talking about technique, son," Asti said, releasing the kid and pushing him up against the brick wall. He looked at the blade, checking its edge with his thumb. Dull and nicked. "Did you really just grab any knife you could find and come out to an alley? Honestly, who does that?"

"I was just—"

"Look at this, all wrong," Asti said, showing the kid the blade. "Especially if you get in close, put it at someone's neck. You do that, you can only swipe fast to slice my throat, and this blade has no edge for slicing at all. At best you're going to scratch up someone's neck and just rise up their temper. Then you're in for it."

"What—"

This kid really had no idea what would happen if he rose up Asti's temper. The beast in his skull, it was simple to keep it held by a chain right now. He kept that thing in check every day, through fights or catastrophes where it howled to be let loose. While it wanted to gut this boy open were it allowed, Asti had no trouble holding it down. Certainly he saw no need to hurt this kid, who clearly had no one to teach him anything.

Asti threw the knife down the alley and drew out one of his own. "See, this one, I've kept honed." He put it in the kid's palm and then wrapped his fingers properly around the hilt. "Feel that, feel the weight in your hand like that, you've got a good grip."

"I don't—"

"And now—" Asti grabbed the kid's wrist and twisted. "See, you don't let go, you're still in control. Someone's got you like this, you throw a solid punch—you do know how to punch, don't you kid?"

"What is happening?" the kid asked, tears coming to his eyes.

"Saint Senea, I just want some standards," Asti said. "Is no one teaching you this—where are you coming from, kid?"

"I—"

"This alley isn't your patch, is it? I know most of the boys your age around here on sight." Blazes, he had some of them scouting for him right now. He shouldn't be wasting time with this. "Where are you from?"

"Benson Court?"

"Your people didn't teach you any of— Saints above, kid." He took a step back, taking a few coins out of his pocket. "I got somewhere to be right now, but you take this, you go back home for the night, stay out of North Seleth altogether, hear? You're going to get hurt doing this."

Asti put the coins in the kid's hand, only about a half a crown's worth in total, nothing really. The kid just stared at his hand. "What is happening?"

"Tomorrow, eight bells in the morning, you meet me at Kimber's around the corner, and I'll show you how to really use that knife."

"I'm keeping this knife?"

"Yeah, but don't try anything until I show you, you'll hurt yourself," Asti said. "I need to move, kid. Eight bells!"

Asti went on his way, the kid still standing dumbfounded as he left the alley and turned onto Frost. The sun was nearly set, the golden-red light drawn out over the cobblestone, drenching the street in warmth. For the most part, things had been good in this neighborhood over the past few months, and tonight the plans he and his brother Verci had been toiling over were coming to fruition.

"Final target is in sight, Mister Rynax," one kid said as he ran up. "We got boys keeping eyes on each one of them."

"Good work, kid," Asti said. "Get back out there and make sure everyone is getting steered where they need to, hear?"

"Heard, boss," the kid said, and he ran off. Asti went into

Kimber's Pub, a place that wasn't quite a home to him, but served as one enough times that he was comfortable with it. And it was the best place for this plan to go down. And unlike the last time he set up something to shake down here, this one shouldn't end with any broken tables or glasses.

At least not too many.

"Asti Rynax, there you are."

Asti was surprised to find Khejhaz Nafath, the Poasian spice merchant and double-crossing spy, here in Kimber's Pub. This was exactly the sort of place that Nafath never came into; Asti had barely even seen him out of his spice shop. And this was the absolute last place he needed to have this man right now. Nafath was an unpleasant sort on a good day when Asti wanted information out of him. Here and now, when Asti had a plan in motion, it was beyond inconvenient.

"Why are you even here?"

"I am hearing things, Asti Rynax, that make me very worried."

"As am I, and it's your voice," Asti said.

"I think you may be in danger."

"I'm pretty much always in danger, but it's nice to know you care," Asti said. Nafath had taken more of a focused interest in him in the past months, usually while keeping a respectful distance, and never before coming out to find him like this. Asti didn't like it, but he didn't deny that Nafath was usually worth listening to. "I don't have a lot of time, so how pressing is this?"

"I am not sure," Nafath said. "I hear whispers, they rarely come with timetables."

"Tonight I'm busy," Asti said. "If all goes well, then come meet me here tomorrow at eight—make that nine—bells, and you can tell me all about it."

Nafath thought on this for a moment, and then two other people came down from the room upstairs. He must have thought better of being in close proximity to so many Druth folk, and stepped away. "Tomorrow. But be wary, Asti."

"Always am," Asti said.

In the taproom, Kimber was shaking her head at Asti. "What did he want?"

"I neither know nor care," Asti said. "The important thing is he's not ruining the plan."

"This plan of yours better not wreck my place," she said.

"I will be here in the morning to help you clean," he said. "I'm expecting some meetings at eight and nine bells, respectively, but beyond that, I'm all yours."

Her usual warm smile turned a little sad. "You actually believe that, don't you?"

"Should I—"

"Doesn't matter," she said. "Help me move the tables where you need them."

"Of course," he said. He glanced to the door as it opened. Almer Cort, the chemist and apothecary, followed by actors and con men Pilsen Gin and Vellun Colsh, came in, dressed and ready for tonight. Perfect. "We better hurry. Verci and Raych will be here soon."

Kimber rolled her eyes. "I can't believe she agreed to this."

"Agreed?" Asti said. "She insisted."

VERCI HAD NOT BEEN PREPARED FOR HOW HEAVY THE CRATE WAS GOING to be. He certainly couldn't carry it alone, and since the contents were so delicate, he wouldn't dare.

"Easy, easy," Raych said as she was lifting her end. "Just a little further, and . . ."

"Is it in place to slide it?" he asked, sweat already on his brow. He had no idea it would weigh this much, or how Raych didn't seem to be struggling as much as he was.

"And there," she said, letting her side down on the back of the cart. "Go ahead." He pushed—saints how could it weigh this much—and slid it so it rested comfortably in the back of the cart.

"You couldn't get a horse to pull it?" Raych asked him as she came around.

"There was no way to get one without drawing more attention," he said. "People would wonder why we got a horse for this."

"People are going to wonder why you're pulling it, either way, dear," she said.

He sighed. "So I have to pull?"

"You most definitely have to pull, my love," she said with a laugh. She kissed him on his cheek as she threw a tarp over the crate. "That will only make it a little less conspicuous."

"You should go on ahead, then," Verci said.

"Nothing of the sort," she said. "I am walking right by your side, not taking my eyes off this thing. Besides, you will look conspicuous all by yourself, it's just your nature. You always look like you're up to something."

"Fair," he said. He often had been up to something. He still was, frankly, though not as blatantly in recent days.

"I've thought about it. If I'm walking with you, I can keep a hand on the crate, make sure it doesn't slide or bump, as that would be—"

"A disaster," Verci said.

"And absolute disaster. Plus—"

"The cover is making deliveries for the bakery," he conceded. "With you right with me, that's a lot more believable. Though hopefully no one asks."

"Better get moving, Asti is waiting."

Verci took off his vest and handed it to her. Wouldn't do to get it grimy and sweaty before the plan tonight. He was of half a mind to take off his shirt completely.

"Don't even," she said, clearly knowing what he was thinking.

"I can't be looking like a pig," he said.

"It suits me that you're not looking *too* handsome tonight," she said, raising her eyebrow. "Even tonight, I wouldn't want anyone else swooning over you."

He grabbed her by her waist and pulled her in, kissing her. "You're the only one I want swooning."

Her eyes danced a bit as they met his. "Oh, if only we had a bit more time right now."

"We'll make a bit of time later," he said. "Our own celebration."

"I like the way you think, Mister Rynax," she said.

"You damn well better, Missus Rynax," he said, and lifted up the handles of the cart and pulled it out into the street. Raych chuckled quietly to herself as they went, keeping her steadying hand on the crate, as promised. He wasn't sure if that would really help, but it was comforting—everything about her was comforting—to have her there walking alongside him tonight. He was glad to have her with him here, just the two of them, while her sister watched little Corsi for the night.

He was so lost in those thoughts he barely even noticed when Lieutenant Covrane walked right in front of him.

"Evening, Rynaxes," the constable said, with a tip of his cap. "This seems like a lot."

"It certainly is," Verci said.

"Quite a sizable crate you're hauling," he said. "What's that all about?"

"Breads for a few of the inns and pubs along the dock roads," Verci said.

"At this hour?"

"You would be astounded the demand for fresh bread for the suppers," Raych said.

"And you load it in a crate like this?"

"It actually keeps the warmth and moisture in balance," Raych said. "I would not have any bread of mine be dry or soggy."

"I guess you wouldn't, ma'am," he said.

"We need to be moving," Verci said as Covrane leaned in as if to smell the bread. He would not get that smell from the crate, and the whole game would be ruined.

"I imagine Helene is waiting for you, Lieutenant," Raych said. "She's probably quite eager to see you."

"And I her," he said with a grin. "I should be off, and won't keep you."

He went off, and Verci started pulling along again. "Well done."

"Thank you."

"We would have been skunked if he took a proper whiff of the crate."

"I imagine so," she said. "But what did your father say about a job getting 'skunked,' as you say?"

"To drive forward and get it done," Verci said.

"Capital advice. Drive on. We need to get there before it's too late."

"You're late."

Helene Kesser wanted to be annoyed at Jarret Covrane, she desperately wanted to, as he arrived at her front stoop a good ten minutes after the agreed upon time. Jarret had so many wonderful qualities, but being punctual to any planned rendezvous was never one of them.

She wanted to be annoyed, but something about his face tied all that up. She couldn't get mad looking at it.

"There was—"

"One more call or such, I know. Julien already went ahead."

"Do I have time to change?" he asked, crossing into the apartment. "Or do you want me to go in my uniform?"

"Be quick about it," she said, though he was already taking off his coat. In the past months, more than a few of his clothes had managed to stay here, which Helene's mother would have found positively scandalous. Helene didn't care about scandalous, though, she just cared about this shop, the apartment over the shop, her cousin Julien, and most improbably, this Constabulary lieutenant who was hanging his uniform coat up in her front room.

How she had ever fallen so completely for this man was beyond her. And the fact that he apparently felt the same way for her. Her, Helene Kesser, lifelong North Seleth screwup who was known by half the crime bosses in West Maradaine as being one of the best crossbow slingers south of the river, and also known as too much trouble to ever put on a job. She had run in more heists than she could count, and burned more bridges than she could remember.

And despite that, this constable, an upstanding statue of a man, had fallen for her.

In no small part due to the fact that he respected a good crossbow.

"So what is this even about again?" he called as he splashed water on his face.

"We're having dinner with a new importer Julien is excited about," she said. "Brings in Waish and Kieran cheeses, and Julien wants to lock down a deal with him."

Covrane came out, stripped to the waist. Saints, that took her breath every time. "So why doesn't he just do that? He needs us?"

"You know Julien."

"I do," Covrane said. "When it comes to your shop, and especially the subject of cheese, he's on top of it."

"Contracts and numbers fluster him," she said. "He gets really worried that without me there he'll trap us in a bad deal."

Covrane came in close. "So he wants you there, and you want me there." He kissed her, the sort of kiss that made her want to move to more things, and there was certainly no time for them to do anything like that, at least not before this dinner.

She pushed him away before she would have to pull him to the bed. "Get dressed, fool."

"Yes, ma'am," he said with a smile that made her blood rush. He quickly grabbed a shirt and coat and put them on, and he looked reasonably presentable. He still looked like a stick, even out of uniform, but nothing would change that.

"You've got to leave the belt here," she said.

"If I must," he said, taking off his patrol belt, with his handstick and crossbow, and left it on her table. "Ready?"

"What do you think?" she asked. "You haven't said anything about how I look?" She had bothered with face-painting for this evening, and was wearing a nice dress that had been used for some scouting gig or another. It may have been the one she wore the night they robbed and burned down Tyne's Emporium, designed with extra panels so Verci Rynax could hide the parts of a mini crossbow within it. She was not hiding any weapons tonight. All her crossbows were still in the apartment, safely away in their trunk. She hadn't had cause to use them in months.

Not since the night with the Fire mages.

"You look incredible, as always," he said, taking her gloved hand. She almost always wore the glove on that hand now, with the wooden insert to hide her missing finger. Not that the glove was any less conspicuous. But she preferred that was what people saw.

"Then let's not leave him waiting," she said. "I think we need to get out to the Little East."

"Do we need a cab?" he asked as they walked out.

"Good luck flagging one down on this street," she said. "Maybe walk to Keller Cove and catch one there, but—"

That was all she got out when some kid—some ratty street kid—just dashed through them both, snatched Covrane's coin bag, and was off down the street.

Helene was already running after him, and Covrane was three paces behind.

"Thought you said we'd walk," he called after her.

"Can't let that gutter snipe pull that," she said. Though when she was that kid's age, she'd dared exactly this sort of thing plenty of times.

"I could put out a call—"

"No one would come in this patch," she said. She thought Covrane would realize, even now, even after that big brawl in Saint Bridget's Square a couple months back—saints, she was glad she hadn't been nearby for that one—there were never many sticks in these blocks, and any whistle call would almost always go ignored. Especially at this hour.

She followed the kid around an alley, down a ways, and saw him slip into the back door of Kimber's Pub. She was so intent on that she didn't even notice Kennith Rill running from the other direction until she collided into him.

"Whoa," she said, bouncing off the dark chomik man. She would have landed flat on her backside if Covrane hadn't been right there to catch her. Kennith had stumbled back from the impact as well, caught and held stable by Jhoqull-Ra, the native-born Ch'omik woman he had been courting for some time.

"I—sorry, Hel," he said, brushing himself off. "Didn't see you there."

"Likewise," she said. But the fact that he had been running, too, running into the same alley from the other direction, that was just plain odd. "Why were you—"

"A *jhikwi* boy grabbed my bag and dashed here," Jhoqull said. She glanced at Covrane and nodded her head deferentially. "Your pardon, officer."

"Not on duty," he said. "But we shouldn't let those boys get away with either of our things." He went for the door into the pub.

"Boys," Helene muttered. Something did not sit right about this. She looked to Kennith, who was dressed in a clean suit, but that wasn't uncommon on a night where he was driving the carriage for the North Seleth Inn. "Where were you two headed?"

"Heading to the Little East to have supper with her cousins," Kennith said. "We were just on our way—"

"When the urchin grabbed a bag and ran," Helene said. Saints and sinners both, she couldn't believe it. "You know what this is, don't you?"

"I—" Kennith stammered. Covrane and Jhoqull had already gone in. She sighed and followed, Kennith right with her.

The back door led through a corridor past the water closets to the taproom, which was surprisingly empty. That was an absolute sign that something hinky was up. The taproom at Kimber's Pub was never empty.

"Where did they—" Covrane asked, glancing about.

"Something odd, indeed," Jhoqull said.

"Saints," Helene muttered. Raising her voice, she said, "Fine, you got us!"

At once, folks leaped out from behind the bar, from the kitchen, from behind tables, from everywhere.

"Surprise!"

Covrane, to his credit, jumped just a bit.

All around her, familiar faces. Kimber, smiling so broadly with such joy. Verci Rynax and his wife Raych, wheeling out a giant cake from the kitchens. Julien, grinning like an absolute fool. Almer Cort, Pilsen Gin, Vellun Colsh, and a dozen other faces she knew far too well. And more she didn't, including Ch'omik folks who were likely kin to Jhoqull.

And Asti Rynax, leaning against the doorway, looking as happy as his face would let him express. Which was only a hair of joy above "not angry."

"What is this?" Kennith asked.

Verci Rynax, looking far too smug, came up with a tray holding four glasses of wine.

"This is a celebration of each of you," he said, handing them all their glasses. "From all of us, your dear friends and neighbors, to raise a glass together to you, and for you, and wish hearty congratulations and blessings on your respective futures together so we can mark the jubilant occasion of your impending marriages. So raise glasses high, one and all, to the engagements of Helene Kesser and Jarret Covrane, and Kennith Rill and Jhoqull-Ra of House Gheqham, daughter of Hejha-Cha, daughter of Kecelle-Amra!"

The crowd all raised their glasses and cheered.

Blazing Verci Rynax. Always a flair for the rutting dramatic.

CHAPTER TWO

"So raise glasses high, one and all, to the engagement of Helene Kesser and Jarret Covrane, and Kennith Rill and Jhoqull-Ra of House Gheqham, daughter of Hejha-Cha, daughter of Kecelle-Amra!"

The crowd cheered, and Verci was quite pleased with how well the whole ploy had gone. Yes, Helene had figured out what was going on, but it was obvious she had just figured it out only moments before, so the whole affair was, by his definition, a masterful success. He actually would have been a little disappointed in Helene if she hadn't.

"Really, what is this?" Covrane asked, still holding his wineglass like he didn't know what to do with it.

"It's a party, Jarret," Helene growled. "For us. And Ken and Jho."

"Do not be so loose with my name," Jhoqull said. She grinned. "But you, Verci Rynax, I am impressed with your respect of my mothers."

Verci leaned in. "I did have to make sure to get it right, or those cousins of yours over there might have had issue."

"You don't want them to have issue," Kennith said. He grabbed Verci by the shoulder and pulled him in for an embrace. "Thank you for this, though."

"There is the matter of my coin purse," Covrane said.

"And my bag."

"Asti!" Verci called out.

"Boys!" Asti called in return. The two street urchins came out of hiding from behind the bar, sheepish grins on their faces, giving Covrane and Jhoqull back their things.

"Sorry, mister," the one kid said to Covrane.

Covrane crouched down and said, "Let's make that the last time you do that, son, all right?"

Helene shook her head. "Whose idea was this?"

"This was all Julien's idea," Verci said, pointing to the big guy.

Julien came over, taking Helene's hand and putting it on Covrane's. "I just wanted to do something special for you two. I didn't know how to do it, but Asti and Verci helped. And then when we heard that Ken and Jhoqull were getting promised . . ."

"Yes, who told you all that?" Jhoqull pointed to one of her cousins. "Deki-Ra, were you the one?"

"It was *Suhi* Anqra!" Deki-Ra laughed. "She wanted to know more about the *echimbep* you have spent time with!"

Verci chuckled. "She came to the bakery."

"Speaking of," Raych said, rolling out the fantastic cake she had made. "I think I may have outdone myself on this one."

Covrane burst out laughing. "Of course. Late delivery of bread, indeed."

"My apologies for the deception, Lieutenant."

"Most accepted, Missus Rynax," Covrane said.

Helene shook her head. "All this . . . really wasn't necessary."

Despite that, Verci was seeing the grandest smiles he had seen from her and Kennith for months. The two of them had suffered, probably the most, at the hands of the Firewings, and anything he could do to make their lives brighter, he would.

Verci had let them down that night. They—and Almer, who seemed much less troubled by his abuse from the mages—had fought to cover his escape, so he could rescue Raych. They had been captured and tortured for his sake, for his family, and he could never repay that debt.

But he would keep trying.

"Everything is necessary for you all," he said. He looked at the assembled crowd: the friends who had been at the core of this crew—this family—who had fought to protect North Seleth, the neighbors whom they had helped, folks he had known all his life, and the new faces like Jhoqull's relatives, and even Covrane's mother and grandmother, quietly talking by the doorway. Verci could even swear he saw Enanger Lesk limping part way down the stairs, and then turning back up. He was amazed the man had survived. But he was amazed any of them had survived this long, given the odds.

"I just want to say one thing," Verci said, taking a beer mug from the bar. "And then if anyone else wants to make a speech, they're welcome, but we do have a few musicians here tonight who've promised to play something lively and danceable, and I imagine you'd all prefer that to my ramblings."

"Yes!" someone called out.

"Go on!" Asti said.

Verci held up his mug and climbed up on a chair. "Just about everyone in this room, we all have been through some terrible hardship. The fire in Holver Alley. The riot on election night. The fight against the mages. Saint Bridget's Square."

Kimber muttered a quiet prayer and touched her forehead.

"And despite that, we are still here, and we have been blessed. Almer's shop, recovered from the fire. This pub here, still standing strong. Kesser's Meats and Cheeses. The Junk Avenue Bakery."

"The Rynax Gadgeterium!" Julien shouted.

"We are here, we are standing tonight to celebrate these two couples, because we have been a neighborhood together. We have stood strong together. And we have lost a few friends, too, and I hope that their judgments were kind, and the saints are letting them watch us now. But we have all been very blessed to be able to be together. Blessings of neighbors, blessings of friends, blessings of family."

"Are you crying, Verci?" Raych asked him.

He wiped the moisture from his face. "I just wanted to express how lucky I feel to be here with you all, and grateful that the saints have let an old th—" He remembered Covrane was here, and was still a constable. "And old scoundrel like me have such things. And thus—I'm sorry, one last thing—thus, Helene and Jarret, Kennith and Jhoqull, if you all can love each other even half as much as I love the people in this room, well . . . your marriages will be deeply blessed indeed."

He looked to Helene, whose eyes were watered up. "All right, you fool, get off that chair. There's apparently dancing to be done."

FOLKS WERE DANCING, PEOPLE LAUGHING, TALKING, EATING, DRINKING. Asti was glad to see it all. And Raych had been right, she truly had outdone herself with the cake. It had truly been a success, which was all Asti could ask for.

The band had started out playing a few well-worn tavern songs, the sort any West Maradaine folk know by heart, and people sang along and danced. Then when the band took a break, a couple of Jhoqull's family borrowed the instruments and played their own songs, which had the crowd completely stumped for a moment, until Jhoqull showed them how to dance to it.

"Quite unique festivities," Covrane's grandmother said in Asti's earshot. "I've not seen its like."

"Oh, I remember you throwing a few raucous dances in your day, Miss Josie," Pilsen Gin told her.

"I beg your pardon?" Covrane's grandmother asked. "You've taken yourself too familiar with me, sir."

"Too familiar, that's a laugh, you're still that box-girl at heart who'd—"

Asti jumped up and pulled Pilsen away from the woman before he said something inappropriate. "Apologies, ma'am, he mistakes faces sometimes."

"Hmm," the grandmother said. "I need to find my daughter, wherever she's gone off to."

"She's sitting over there with Almer," Asti said, pointing to the table. Though, from Almer's expression, Asti wondered if he was about to ruin the man's hopes by sending the old woman over.

"Asti, why are your hands on me?" Pilsen said.

"Let's get you over to the bar," Asti said, guiding him to a stool. "Kimber, can we get a soft cider here? Or even some tea?"

Kimber nodded and came over. "Pilsen, let me get you something, you just sit right there."

"Incredibly kind, madam, incredibly kind. Remind me why I know your face. Did you play Casseria in the production of *The Hawk of Erien* at the Whirly?"

Asti stepped back and found Vellun Colsh's absurdly pretty face far too close to Asti's. He must have dashed across the taproom.

"What are you doing to Pilsen?"

"I was getting him away from Covrane's grandmother," Asti said, lowering his voice and pulling Vellun to one side. "Saints, he thought she was Josie."

Vellun sighed. "He's been doing that more and more."

"How bad has he been?"

"Honestly?" Vellun asked. "As long as he has a show, when he's in performance, he's fine. He's tremendous. But the rest of the time, he's . . . the only people he remembers, a lot of the time, are people from his youth. He thinks I'm Rendell a lot of the time." Vellun's voice cracked a little on that. Asti only knew Rendell's name from Pop's stories of the old days, Pilsen's paramour forty years ago. Neither Pilsen nor Pop ever talked about how Rendell died back then.

"Sorry," Asti said.

"It's how it is," Vellun said. "But it's good to have him around people." Vellun went and sat next to Pilsen.

A glass of wine was put in Asti's hand.

"I didn't think I needed this," he said to Helene, who had put it there.

"Been watching you half the night," she said. "And if anyone did . . ."

"I'm sure your future husband doesn't need you watching me."

"Pff," Helene said. "He knows full well not to be jealous of you."

"Thanks," he said, going to his seat back at the table he had been alone at. Helene sat with him. "Should you be dancing?"

"My feet can only take so much," she said. "So you pull all this, just for me?"

"And Kennith and Jhoqull."

"And Jarret?"

"He's a good man," Asti said. Perhaps too good, at least to be in the same room as Asti for too long, but he was a decent man who had saved Raych when it mattered, and was good to Helene. Asti tried to have no feud with the man.

"For you to say that about a stick is a lot."

"I'm feeling generous tonight."

"All right," she said, moving her chair closer. "So all this, I know, is still just a front. A thoughtful one, but I know better."

"What do you think you know?"

"This," she said quietly. "All this, the whole reputable citizen act. It's just a part of your whole scheme for stopping the Andrendon thing, whatever that is. Don't tell me you're not still on it, you and Verci, because I know you must be."

"This has nothing to do with that," Asti said. "Honest."

"But there is a 'that,'" Helene pressed. "You are working a scheme on Andrendon."

"And you're going to be a constable's wife soon," Asti said. "And that's a far better thing for you than being messed up in our business."

"Your business is still my business," Helene said. "You don't need to fence me out."

"Helene, it's fine, you don't need to—"

"Asti," she said firmly, "I'll remind you that my gran was killed by this business. You don't need me for what you're working, fine, I know you'll call on me when you need a shot taken. But do not fence me out. Let me know you are handling it."

Asti nodded. Even with her marrying Covrane, he owed it to her to be straight. "It's in long ploy right now. The Andrendon involves money guys from goldsmith houses, and some folks in the City Council of Aldermen. We're still unraveling all the details for now."

"All right," she said. "How?"

"Verci and I are ingratiating ourselves with the college boys in the 'mechanical firm' who are designing and building what will become the Andrendon. Which will put us in a position to sabotage it, if the opportunity arrives." He sighed. "And if we decide it's right to do so."

"Why wouldn't it be? These folks—"

"These folks didn't care how many of us they killed to make this happen, and that I will reckon with, have no doubt," Asti said. "But . . . the Andrendon . . ." He wasn't quite sure how to explain it, he barely understood himself. Underground carriages with steam-pulled cables, and people would be able to ride all over the city in a snap. Building the damn thing, and then keeping it running, that would be jobs. Jobs in this neighborhood. "The thing itself, it might be a good thing for folks around here, in the long run."

"How could it, given the cost?"

"Like I said, the folks who burned us, they will be reckoned with. But the thing itself, it . . . I can't help but wonder if it isn't a real good idea, and if trying to sabotage it is the wrong move."

She scowled, but patted his shoulder. "I don't see how, but I do trust you here."

"Thanks."

"Now I should go save my soon-to-be mother-in-law from Almer," she laughed, getting up. "And for the love of the saints, give Kimber a dance at least, hmm?"

THE NIGHT HAD WORN DOWN, AND MANY PEOPLE HAD SAID THEIR goodnights and left, but Raych was enjoying a rare, carefree night in a pub, Corsi at her sister's. It had been far too long since she had done such a thing.

Plus it was delightful watching Verci, who had had just enough beers to join the band and show off his skill in belting out bar ballads. It had become something of a challenge, where he let the band pick any song they could think of, and he'd be able to join in without missing a beat. He was currently crooning one Raych had never even heard of, about the blessed skies over Korifina.

She wearily sat down next to Asti. "Where did he learn how to do that?" she asked.

"The real story?" Asti asked back.

She chuckled. "You know I always want the real story."

"When we were kids, Pop made sure we knew every street trick for hustling coin. Picking pockets, quick grifts, the whole barn. But he also made sure we knew the cleaner ones as well. So he taught us a whole mess of ballads and lover songs and call-ups and shants from every part of Druthal. And Verci had the better voice for it, as you can hear."

"Not you? I thought you mastered all sorts of skills."

"I can carry it, mind you, if I have to," he said. "My clean grift was doing charcoal sketches. I could do a sketch of a fellow and his sweetheart in two blinks, and sell it for a few ticks. But Verci could suss out where a man was from by his accent, and sing the exact song that would make him homesick, and easily get a half-crown in his hat."

"So why didn't you all keep doing that?"

"Pop said—and we were just boys, mind you—that we should know how to do honest work, if we had to, but it's a much more joyful life to not have to."

"Your father was a strange man," she said.

"There are times," Asti said, with a weary sigh, "that I would have preferred he had been a simple baker who taught us how to make bread."

"If you really want, you can come to the bakery and still learn."

"You'd have me there?" he asked, and for a moment there was a hint of a broken little boy in his voice.

She rested her hand on his. "We're family, Asti Rynax. That's not just something I say, all right?"

"All right."

"Who's wants to try and stump me?" Verci called out.

Raych looked up. "Can you do the 'Song of the Trerliana'?"

"Oh, hmm," Verci said, an exaggerated look of dismay on his face. "I mean, that's not even a Druth song. It's a folk piece from, what, the Myam Province of Acseria?" He took an instrument from one of the musicians. "Which, if you didn't know, is where my wife's family came from, so it would be absurd for me not to know it."

He started to pluck the strings and sing words Raych had known since she was a child, but had never heard from her husband's mouth.

"I am an honest man
Who loves the life I live
Full of love and joy and blessing

And the songs that I give."

Raych's heart leapt, and that took her up on her feet before she even realized she was doing it, and then turned and took Asti's hand, pulling him out to the floor.

She had always known the steps, mother would always dance them, back when her grandparents were around. For a moment, she was a little girl again, dancing with her mother and Lian, words and steps that were written on her heart.

And, to her amazement, Asti was right there with her, he knew the dance. Knew it like her father had, like he himself had growing up in Damyar. He swept her around the floor, every step perfect, while her husband's voice, his immaculate playing, filled her spirit in ways she had forgotten it could be.

By the last chorus, the rest of the musicians had picked up on the tune and the rhythm and were fully with him, filling the taproom with the sounds of her family.

The song ended, but her heart still pounded, her face flush as she whirled away from Asti in the final move, almost falling into a table. She laughed as Helene caught her, and she looked back to Asti, who was smiling broadly. She had never seen that on his face before. And Verci was radiant, the same joy on his face that was in her spirit.

"Still full of surprises," she told him.

"I always will be," Verci said.

Then the front door was kicked in, and men in uniform, crossbows raised, swarmed into bar.

"What is this—" Kimber started, and got one of them pointing a crossbow right in her face for it.

"Shut it!" one of the uniformed men shouted at her. "All of you, hands high, on your knees."

Asti and Verci followed those instructions faster than anyone, but Covrane stepped forward.

"Now just a moment here—"

That earned him the butt of a crossbow cracked across his nose.

"Jarret!" Helene shouted, leaping to grab him before he collapsed to the ground.

"Down on your knees, everyone!" the man who clobbered Covrane said.

"Officers," Asti said, with infuriating calm. "What seems to be the issue here?"

"Shut it, or you'll get it, too!" another of the uniforms said.

Raych complied, looking to Verci. He mouthed something to her, but she couldn't understand what he was trying to say. But he looked to Asti. Follow Asti's lead. He could handle this. He could tear these fellows up without even breaking a sweat, but yet he was on his knees, hands high, doing what he was told.

He was calm, she would be calm as well.

Another man came in, his uniform marked with epaulets.

"These the ones, Chief?" the one aiming at Kimber asked.

"Yes, indeed," the chief said. "My apologies, people. We are here to apprehend some very dangerous people who are wanted for plots against the Archduchy of Sauriya and the crown." He pointed to Asti and Verci. "Those two."

"What?" Verci asked. "I'm sorry but—"

A crossbow but cracked against his face. Raych wanted to scream, but she couldn't even breathe.

"We'll go quietly," Asti said.

"Wise," the chief said. "Also him, him, him, him, and him." He had pointed out Julien, Almer, Kennith, Pilsen, and Vellun.

"What?" Helene screeched.

"What is going—" Julien started.

"Just a damned minute here," Covrane said, his nose bleeding. The officer who had hit him raised his weapon to do it again, but this time Covrane caught it and tore it from the man's hands. The officer drew his sword in response. "I am a lieutenant in the city Constabulary!" Covrane roared at him.

"Lieutenant, this is a matter for the Archduchy," the chief said. "We're taking these men into custody, you do not need to involve yourself."

"Name their charges," Covrane said.

"Those are under seal," the chief said.

"We'll go quietly," Asti said firmly. He glared at everyone in the room, as if to send a message to each and every person there. "We'll give you no quarrel. This is clearly a misunderstanding that will be cleared up."

One of the officers took Asti's hands and shackled them behind his back, and did the same to Verci, Julien, Pilsen, Vellun, Almer, and Kennith. Jhoqull and her family all looked like they were ready to tear the Archduchy officers to shreds, Helene red with rage as Julien's eyes welled with tears. Kimber was weeping in terror.

Raych couldn't feel anything, could barely even hear or see. Her body was numb, like this wasn't real. It had to be a trick, some ploy. Was that why Asti was going quietly? Was that what Verci was trying to say to her?

The officers pulled the men out of the taproom, one by one. Verci was the last one they were taking out, and Raych's legs found their strength. She ran up to him, grabbed his whole body and kissed him, kissed him like she'd never see him again.

The knot in the pit of her stomach told her she wouldn't.

One of the officers pulled her off Verci and threw her to the floor.

"Hey!" Verci snapped, and that officer smacked him across his face. Verci looked up, blood on his lip and grinned an ever so vicious grin. "I'll remember you, friend, have no doubt."

Hands were on her arms and shoulders, Helene and Jhoqull helping her to her feet.

"Verci!" she shouted.

"I love you," he said calmly as they pulled him to the door. "It's going to be fine."

Then he was gone.

Raych's heart shattered into a thousand pieces, and if Helene and Jhoqull hadn't been holding her up, she would have melted into the floor.

CHAPTER THREE

Each of them were loaded into a different lockwagon, and Verci sat in the back of his, arms shackled behind his back, two guards with him, both with swords out. Whatever this was, they weren't playing around.

Uniforms were Archduchy Sheriffs, or at least excellent replicas. Same with the lockwagon and the shackles. Either these were the real thing, or someone with a lot of resources to spare was behind it.

Verci's fingers probed at the shackles. Could he get out of them? Yes, he could, but it would take dislocating his thumb, a trick he was never very good at. He didn't have anything handy to pick the lock, not that he could get to his hand without being noticed, else he'd take that route any day.

"What are you looking at?" one of his guards asked.

"The man who shoved my wife on the floor," Verci said. "Let me make it clear, that's going to have a reckoning, friend, one way or another."

"Is that what you think?"

"It's what I know."

Verci was of half a mind to dislocate his thumb, pull one hand free from the shackles, and clobber this man with them. Then take his sword, use it to skewer his companion, crack open the doors of the lockwagon, and jump out into the street.

He would if he was certain he could pull it off. He was a good enough fighter when he had to be, and could probably manage it, but he had had enough to drink that he knew his reflexes were off, but not enough to be foolhardy. Also, the others were each in their own lockwagon, and he didn't know where they were going. From what he could hear, they weren't even necessarily all taking the same route.

They were heading southwest, though. An Archduchy Sheriff Waystation would be outside the city, after all.

Asti said to go quietly, it would get sorted. Verci trusted in that.

Even still, he memorized the man's features, and would have that reckoning when the time came.

The wagon finally came to a halt, the door popped open, and several men came in to take Verci out. On some level he was flattered by the lengths they went to here. The building he was being brought into, it definitely looked like a real Sheriff Waystation. If this was a ruse, they were pulling out all the stops.

Two men gave him a quick search—for once he wasn't carrying any gadgets or weapons, but they did miss the screwtool he managed to get out of his pocket and palm—and then put him in a cell. A few minutes later, Asti was thrown in with him. Asti grabbed him in an embrace as soon as the door was shut.

"So, not how I expected our evening to end," Verci said when they pulled away.

"Likewise," Asti said, brushing himself off.

"I presume you decided to comply because it would have been too messy to fight in the middle of Kimber's, with several other people there."

"Mostly, but something is off," Asti said.

"You think?" Verci said. "We've not done anything that qualifies as crimes against the archduchy or crown. At least, I'm reasonably certain we haven't."

"These fellows seem to be the real deal," Asti said. "And they didn't give any sort of professional courtesy to Covrane."

"You think the problem here is one of courtesy?" Verci asked.

"There are a lot of problems here," Asti said. He moved closer, voice down. "They didn't name charges, which is odd. Even when pressed by Covrane."

"I've never heard of charges being under seal," Verci said. Law officers were supposed to follow the rules on that, telling someone what they were being arrested for. "What does that mean, they don't have to say what you're arrested for?"

"Archduchy Sheriffs have a little more latitude," Asti said. "I've not heard that term before, but Covrane didn't push back on it."

"So it likely is a legitimate term?"

"But there's more than not naming charges," Asti said, moving on. "They didn't name us. That chief sheriff, you seen him before?"

"No."

"Me either. But he walked into a room with at least twenty people and quickly picked out you and me, plus Ken, Almer, Vellun, Pilsen, and Julien. An extremely specific group of people, involved in the things we have done together. Who would know that?"

"But they didn't grab Helene," Verci said. "Or Raych, depending on which job we're talking about."

"Right. Or Jhoqull. So this has something to do with us, as a group, but excludes them. Just because they're women?"

"Can we rule out Josie, some sort of revenge?" Verci asked. The last time he had seen Josie Holt, still easily the biggest criminal boss in North Seleth, he and Raych had poisoned her for leverage.

"I'm not ruling out anything, but I don't think she has the kind of rattle to arrange something like this."

"Who does?"

"That is the question."

"Someone connected to Mendel Tyne?" Verci offered.

Asti thought about that. "Possible, but Vellun wasn't a part of that."

"Lord Henterman?" Verci offered. "We were all in on that."

"That opens up several other possibilities. Like *her*," Asti said. Verci understood, he meant Liora Rand, Asti's former partner in Intelligence, whose infiltration of Henterman's home had been ruined by their scheme.

"Does she have this kind of rattle?"

"Not that I'm aware of, but she is full of surprises."

"So," Verci said, glancing around. "I presume they took your knives."

"Missed one. You?"

"Screwtool is all I have, but that hallway isn't being walked, so I can probably spring the door in a few minutes, and it's three doors and eight guards between us and the outside, at least."

"And we don't know where the others are."

"So you don't want to crack out?"

Asti shook his head. "There's one of two things happening right now. We've been mistaken for someone else, or we've been targeted. Most likely both, that someone targeted us so we would be mistaken by the sheriffs. That they're the marks in a ploy to get at us."

"They put you and me together, away from the rest," Verci said. "Whoever is doing this wanted to give us a chance to talk."

"Maybe listening for a confession," Asti said. "Whatever this is, as of right now, we've not been charged, or even had our names used. If this is an error, we should ride it through and see what is happening before we make any sort of move. If this is just some terrible mistake, and we broke out—"

"We'd be on the run for good," Verci said.

"Last thing you want," Asti said. "And if this is some game or ploy on us, well, we need to know more to handle it. But make sure our friends are safe too. Whatever this is, none of them deserve to be dragged along."

"Nor did any of the folks who weren't taken."

Asti sighed, and nodded. "She's going to be all right. And we'll get you back home to her before you know it."

RAYCH DIDN'T KNOW WHAT SHE COULD DO, SO SHE SWEPT AND MOPPED the floors of Kimber's taproom. It was a concrete action she could manage, a task to focus on. Most of the other guests had left, though Kimber seemed far too stricken to do anything. She stumbled into the back rooms and shut the door behind her. Raych couldn't blame her. Part of her wanted to do that, wanted to fall to the floor and scream, but . . .

She needed to do something with her hands. She needed to move, to work, and if Kimber was in no state to clean up, she could do that.

Jhoqull seemed to be in the same mindset. She had made a point of thanking the other guests, getting them out the door, assuring folks that everything would be sorted.

Soon, it was just Raych, Jhoqull, Helene, and Covrane. He had been pressing ice and a cloth to his cracked nose, and was the only one who was expressing his frustration verbally, though he was coming at it from a very different place.

"No procedure, no writs," he said. "Under seal, my foot."

"Easy," Helene said as she packed more ice into a rag. Her voice was calm, but Raych could see her fists balled so tight the knuckles were white.

"Not to mention, they are not supposed to even take any action in the city without some kind of joint structure. Someone from my station-house should have at least, as a courtesy, been on the escort."

"Jarret—" Helene said.

"No, no," he said firmly. "Highly irregular. Charges not named, and . . . they never named your friends, either."

"What?" Raych asked. Not that she was able to focus her thoughts on anything but the concrete task of cleaning the floor.

He snapped his fingers, as if in revelation. "The chief, he walked in and just pointed—him, him, him—no names, no charges, no . . . I will file a complaint."

"How?" Helene asked. "With who?"

"With my captain, for one. I did take note of badge names on most of them. Chief Sheriff Rowls."

"Do you think that would help?" Helene asked.

"It's a path to answers," Covrane said. He went over to her to kiss her, and then winced. "I will find out exactly what is happening to your cousin, and the rest of your friends. Believe me, I will not let this slide." He gave her a gentle peck on her cheek, as if that's all he could manage without hurting his nose again, and left.

"Finally," Helene growled. She looked to Jhoqull. "I'm of a mind to do some violence."

"Agreed," Jhoqull said. "If I had any idea who to be violent toward."

"I'm not feeling particular at the moment."

"We can't be stupid," Raych said quietly.

"What?" Helene snapped.

Raych found herself drawn fully back into the reality of the moment, pulled in so hard it almost made her stumble. She braced herself with the mop.

"We can't be stupid about it," she said.

"Are you kidding me?" Helene asked. "Julien, Verci, Asti, Kennith, all of them . . . Are you going to pretend that they didn't just get arrested?"

"No," Raych said. Great prophets, she didn't want to hold herself together here, but it was clear someone had to, and it wasn't going to be Helene or Jhoqull. "But Asti didn't fight his way through that. Verci took his cue. We need to do the same, and not be stupid."

"And what does that mean?" Helene asked.

"It means we do not know who to be violent toward," Jhoqull said. "If I knew who we could charge against for our men, I would be there to fight at your shoulder. But we know nothing. Maybe your man will learn something in his crusade."

"Maybe," Helene said. "So, what then?"

Raych realized she was looking at her. "You want me to decide?"

"You said not to be stupid, and I'm afraid stupid is all I got," Helene said.

"Right," Raych said. What would Verci do here? Or Asti? They would make a plan, and then do something stupid when the plan fell apart. Raych had no idea, really, but that thing Covrane said struck an odd chord. "They weren't named, nor given charges. So we need to know more about what's going on before we can do anything else."

"All right, how?" Helene asked.

"You stay on Jarret, use him for as much information as we can get. In the morning I will raise a sinner's chorus at the Justice Advocate Office."

"We might want to look to acquiring our own lawyers as well,"

Jhoqull said. "And you did note that the ones taken were explicitly our fellows, who worked the jobs together at the warehouse a few months back."

"I did several jobs with those boys," Helene said. "So why them and not us?"

"We don't know that we're not the next targets," Jhoqull said. "This could be a ploy to isolate us."

"Looks like I'm carrying the hiphangers all the time again," Helene said.

That solidified things in Raych's mind. "Then we all go together, first to get your weapons from your place, and then we all stay above the Gadgeterium tonight." Verci had rigged their place with so many alarms, special locks, and other surprises, no one would get at them easily.

"And Kimber?" Helene asked.

Raych tried the door to Kimber's room. Latched. No response to their knocks. She was likely completely out.

"We'll latch up behind ourselves as we go, and . . . tomorrow we'll check on her as well." Raych had no idea what to even say, but she felt she needed to sound comforting, sound in control. "Tomorrow is a very busy day, so let's not waste any more time."

ASTI HAD MANAGED TO SLEEP RELATIVELY WELL IN THE CELL UNTIL dawn broke, when a few guards came in with bowls of watery porridge and weak tea. Asti ate it without complaint, as did Verci, and a few minutes later the guards came again to escort them out.

"I take it we have a hearing," Asti said to one of the guards.

"Shut it," the guard said.

"I just want to point out," Asti said, ignoring this command. "We've not been formally charged with anything, nor have any charges been named. So if anyone is in violation of the law, it would be you fellows."

"I ought to—" the guard said, pulling back his arm.

"Ooh, adding battery to unlawful abduction, very nice," Asti said.

"Think you're clever, Tacklin?" the guard said.

"Tacklin?" Asti asked.

The guard grabbed Asti's arm and pulled him down the hallway, with Verci being dragged along behind him. Through a few corridors, they were brought into a chamber and placed in two of seven chairs, and then shackled to the chairs.

"This seems extreme, even compared to last night," Verci muttered.

Then the others were all brought in. Almer was seated next to Asti as they were all shackled into place.

"What is this all about?" Almer asked. He had a fresh cut over his eye. "That's what I got for asking."

"Still trying to figure that out," Asti said. Though he wasn't sure what he would do if he did figure it out. If he had to pop his thumbs, pull out of the shackles, and fight his way out, so be it, but that wasn't how he'd prefer it. And what did the guard call him? Tacklin?

A man in a tight-buttoned suit came in with a pair of sheriffs and looked over the seven of them while thumbing through his documents.

"Yes, well done, Sheriff, well done, indeed."

"You're going to tell us what this is about?" Asti asked.

"Hmmph," the suited man said. "I guess you're going to attempt ignorance. So be it."

Another man came in from the back, this one in magistrate robes. So this was a hearing.

"All right, you pulled me out of bed early for this, so let's be about it," he muttered as he took his place at the desk in front of them. "And you are?"

"Ocklin Parette, from the Office of the Archduke's Protectors, sir," the suited man said, presenting papers to the magistrate.

"And your claim here is?"

"Honorable, presented before you here are the ringleaders of the Corvian Liberation Front, who have organized mayhem, murder, and destruction all along the Sauriyan coast. We are prepared to present no less than one hundred and seventy-four charges under seal for these seven men: Marin and Indlen Tacklin, Corrick File, Orritan Dale, Gendor and Callick Trentin, and Mahk'ken-ta."

"These are quite a lot of charges, indeed, Parette."

"Honorable," Asti said. For a moment, he debated how to play this, considering speaking with a more refined accent to address the magistrate. He dropped that idea, as honesty was his best weapon right now. "This is clearly a misunderstanding, as we are not those seven men. Those are not our names, and we are not part of the Corvian Liberation Front."

"Never even been to Corvia!" Julien cried.

"My name is Asti Rynax," Asti said, and then he identified the others. "You have the wrong men."

"As you can see, Honorable," Parette said, "among the charges are the forging of papers, crafting of aliases, and deception of identity."

"Mister Tacklin," the magistrate said to Asti firmly. "These are all serious charges."

"My name isn't Tacklin."

"You must admire the conviction," Parette said.

"Mister Tacklin," the magistrate said even firmer, "the charges under seal here are dire, and must be taken seriously. I cannot ignore that, and so I will accept this filing and have you all held for trial."

"Held?" Julien asked.

"Where is Justice Advocacy?" Asti asked, trying to remember the appropriate language here. "We have been severely mishandled and poorly treated, in addition to our alleged crimes going unnamed, all compounded by the fact we've been misidentified."

"This is not a trial, simply an assessment of finding, Mister Tacklin," the magistrate said. "However, Mister Parette, the Archduchy is obliged to send report to the Justice Advocate Office, as well as avail these gentlemen with counsel before trial proper, which will be held no later than fifty days from today."

"Of course, sir. I would request that these fellows are designated a great risk for flight and mayhem. They should be held in presumptive custody by the Archduchy."

That was not good.

"So noted. They will be held in presumptive custody for the fifty days prior to trial, and for its duration. However, we will not risk further potential for flight or mayhem by extended transport. So I rule said custody will occur within the city confines at Quarrygate Prison."

"As you see best, Honorable."

"Hold on," Verci said, getting to his feet. "We are not these men you're naming. You can't lock us for fifty days on a trumped-up sham! I am a businessman in Maradaine, I run a respectable shop, I have a wife, son—"

"You will have ample opportunity to prove your defense at trial," the magistrate said.

"I don't understand," Pilsen said. "I . . . seem to have forgotten my lines."

"This isn't a show, dear," Vellun said.

"No, I demand you listen!" Verci shouted. Three sheriffs started pummeling him with handsticks. Asti jumped up and did his best to block the blows, take the hits himself, but he couldn't get close enough.

"Gentlemen, no need for that," the magistrate scolded. "We can keep this civil."

The sheriffs backed away, and Asti helped Verci get to his feet.

"In the name of civility, sir," Asti said. "We are not the men the Archduchy claims we are."

"My hands are tied, Mister Tacklin, or Rynax, or whatever it is," the magistrate said. "Given the severity of charge, the injustice of you all staying in custody for fifty days to prove your innocence far outweighs the risk of possibly allowing seven of the most dangerous men in the Archduchy be at liberty. My judgment stands. Sheriffs, take them out of here and send them all to Quarrygate Prison."

PART II
THE BAKER'S DOZEN

CHAPTER FOUR

"Raych, I don't understand, what is going on?"

Raych had barely slept at all, and the last thing she needed was to deal with Lian and Hal making the situation even harder.

"I don't entirely know," Raych said, handing the baby back to Lian. "I wish I could explain it better to you both."

Hal bumbled about the kitchen, grabbing a pastry off the counter. "Well, explain it as best you can, including why *that* woman is in my parlor again."

"Hal, manners," Lian said.

Raych wasn't sure how to explain it, or what she even wanted to tell them. She was not a practiced liar.

"Raychelle," Jhoqull said, coming into the kitchen, her accent now flowing like quicksilver. "Tell them exactly what we know, which is sadly very little."

Raych sighed. "Last night, at the engagement party, Archduchy Sheriffs barged in and arrested Verci and Asti, as well as Julien, Kennith, and a few other friends. We don't know why."

"We cannot even say with certainty that they were sheriffs," Jhoqull said. "It is a situation that is smelling terrible."

"I knew it," Hal said. "I knew that Verci and his brother, they would come to a bad end. Bad sort, they were."

"Hal!"

"I'm not saying that because of their Kieran heritage, Lian, you know that. But you know they are trouble. We've seen it time and again, their street-corner antics."

"How dare you," Raych growled.

"I mean, really, Hal," Lian scolded. "For Archduchy Sheriffs to be involved, it would have to be something serious. Not street-corner antics."

"What were the charges?"

"We don't know," Raych said. "Lieutenant Covrane asked them to name charges, and they cracked his nose for his trouble."

"That's not proper," Hal said. "I don't believe it."

"That is what happened," Jhoqull said.

"Why is she here? In my home?" Hal asked.

"Halkirk Elman, you will cease your rude and improper behavior toward my sister and her friend, or may every prophet help me!"

Hal looked to Lian, shame creeping over his face. He turned back to Jhoqull, staring at the floor. "My apologies."

"It's not proper," Raych said. "Which makes me wonder what the real situation is. And I'm worried it was part of some ploy to isolate me, or Helene, or even Jhoqull, we don't know."

"I don't like it, Raych," Lian said. "I won't disparage your husband or his kin to your ears, but he clearly is a man who's made enemies, you can't deny that."

"No, I won't," Raych said. "But he is a good man, and you know his enemies are not." She pointed to the pamphlet titled *The Champions of Maradaine* that was on their parlor table. Though she had been part of the event described in that story, and she had trouble believing it had been real, let alone that Verci had somehow helped save the city. Even more incredible that someone wrote a whole story about it.

"Fanciful exaggeration to sell paper," Hal said. "Beasts and great lizards indeed."

"You have seen the damage to the square," Jhoqull said.

Hal sighed. "Yes, something happened at Saint Bridget, and I'm sure it was terrible, and Verci and Asti apparently were helpful to the proper authorities. But that doesn't change the sort of folk they are, and I think this arrest proves it."

"We really don't know anything about the arrest at all," Raych said. "Which is why I need to get to the Justice Advocate Office, perhaps employ our own lawyer."

"And I walk where she walks," Jhoqull said. "For her safety."

"You think you're in danger and you bring it to our home?"

"I need someone to watch Corsi while I do this," Raych said.

Lian nodded, holding the baby close to her chest. "Of course, I will. Should I still open up the bakery? Or at least go there? You always said it was a safer place."

"Stay here for now," Raych said. "If nothing else, let's keep Corsi somewhere stable and calm."

"Calm is something we can provide," Lian said.

"Which that little boy deserves," Hal added. On the hot looks from Lian and Jhoqull, he grabbed another pastry and left the kitchen.

Raych kissed her son's forehead. "Be good for your aunt, sweet."

Lian reached out and touched Raych's face. "Be careful, hmm? And steel yourself for the news to be bad."

"It's already bad," Raych said, kissing her sister's cheek. "But I know it's a mistake, and I'm going to go fight it."

HELENE FELT HER STOMACH REBEL AS SHE WALKED INTO THE KELLER Cove Constabulary stationhouse, an absolutely unnatural thing. Even over all these months of romance with Covrane, accepting his proposal, she hadn't yet stepped inside the building before today.

You're going to be a constabulary wife, she told herself. *You better get used to this sort thing.* Saints, what did being a Constabulary wife even mean? Was she going to be coming here more often once they lived together? Making dinners for his captain? Socials with the other wives? What would she even talk about with them? It wasn't like she could tell them stories of working jobs, or putting down a man four blocks away with a well-placed bolt.

"Can I help you, miss?" the woman at the desk asked.

"I'm here to see Lieutenant Covrane," Helene said.

"I don't know if he's about, but maybe someone else can help you? Is this about a crime report?"

"No, I—" Helene stumbled. She realized she had to say it. "I'm his intended."

"What?" the woman exclaimed. "Well, what an astounding surprise, you could knock my very breath out. I had no idea that Lieutenant Covrane even had intentions, let alone had declared them."

"Well, I—"

"Hey, Issie," she called to a clerk. "This lady here is engaged to Jarret."

"Nothing being," Issie said, coming over. "These are not your normal parts of town, are they Miss . . . Sorry, didn't catch it?"

"Kesser," Helene said. "Helene Kesser. And, no, I'm over in North Seleth. I run a cheese shop out th—"

"Cheese shop!" the front desk clerk exclaimed. "You remember, for Terrentin, Jarret brought everyone those fancy Acoran cheeses? Was that your doing, Miss Kesser?"

"We do carry those, yes—"

"Those were some rather fine cheeses, Miss Kesser," Issie said. "Can we take her out to tea? We should take her to tea."

"My manners," the front clerk said. She offered her hand. "Regilia Consance. I'm engaged to Lieutenant Endlin."

"Issanora Candle, engaged to Lieutenant Welling," Issie said. She lowered her voice to a mock whisper. "He's the captain's nephew!"

"Let me tell you, there were some whispers among the ladies about Jarret, they'll be happy to know they were wrong."

"But now we know why he was always 'patrolling' over in Seleth!"

Helene kept a smile on her face, but she wanted nothing more than to bury crossbow bolts in their throats. "So is he around?" she asked through tight teeth.

"Issie, take her up to his desk. Worst thing, you can wait for him there."

"Thank you," Helene said.

Issie led her down a corridor. "So Helene, or Hel, or . . ."

"Either is fine."

"How are you at cards?"

"Never much for them," Helene said.

"Some of the ladies here have a weekly game, if you'd like to join. They'd all love to know all about you."

"That's terribly kind," Helene said. "But at least for the immediate future I won't be able to."

"Oh?"

"A dear friend, her husband has run into a bit of a spot," Helene said, wishing she had paid more attention to those lessons Asti and Pilsen had given Mila about putting on a fake persona. Saying the right thing, trying to sound like a legit businesswoman instead of a westtown shotcracker. "Nothing too serious, I hope, but she is relying on my help during these times."

"Of course, oh the poor dear," Issie said. "I understand. But let me know when you can. And once we all get our bracelets, I hope we can all be good friends. Do you know when you're having a ceremony?"

"Haven't decided yet," Helene said.

Issie nodded. "We had to hold ours off, his family is in mourning, but hopefully soon. Maybe we'll do the same day, won't that be fun?"

"So fun," Helene said, wanting to bury a crossbow bolt in her own throat now.

"Here we are," Issie said, presenting the desk that Jarret was working diligently at. "Lieutenant, you have been keeping secrets from us."

"I what?" he asked, looking up. "Oh, Hel!"

"Morning," Helene said.

Jarret got up and kissed her on the cheek. "Thank you, Miss Candle."

"Any time, Lieutenant." She went off.

He sighed. "I hope that wasn't too awful for you."

"Well, Miss Candle and Miss Consance still have the same number of teeth they woke up with," Helene said. "So it was clearly tolerable."

"I was going to come out to check on you once I had something more concrete to tell you," he said. "But I'm afraid I've failed at that so far."

"How so?"

"Well, I've asked about there being any sort of formal writ filed by the Sheriffs to make an arrest in these neighborhoods, and I've sent word to the Seleth and Benson Court stationhouses. But no one in this house knows anything about the Archduchy sending folks in to make arrests."

"Is that unusual?"

"I'd call it peculiar," he said. "Also I've reached out to the Protector's Office, and the Justice Advocate Office, that I want to be informed about whatever charges are filed at Julien, or the Rynax brothers, or Kennith, or anyone with them. So far nothing, but I'm still asking about."

"Thank you."

"But as I said, it's all quite peculiar. Everything that happened last night, it's not strictly a violation of law or jurisdiction, but definitely one of courtesy. Not to mention . . ." He gestured at his face.

"Have you slept?"

"I caught a couple hours in the bunk here. You?"

"I stayed with Raych at her apartment."

"How is she. And . . . the Ch'omik girl, I forget . . ."

"Jhoqull," Helene said. "They're both even more upset than me."

"How upset are you?" He raised an eyebrow. "Forgive me, but you seem more put together than usual, even clam."

"An absolute facade," Helene said. "Frankly, if you've got someone down in holding you need to have beaten senseless, I'd love nothing more."

"I definitely do not," he said. "But I understand. I'm sorry I don't have more. But I'll come by later with anything I find."

"Come by the Gadgeterium," she said. "I . . . I'll be staying with Raych for the immediate future."

His face fell just a little, but he caught it before he showed real disappointment. "Of course, I completely understand."

"Hey," she said, taking his hand. "It's because she needs to feel safe."

"I really do completely understand," he said, squeezing her hand. "I'll keep pushing here, let you know what I find."

She pulled him to her and kissed him in a way that would probably be inappropriate for a Constabulary stationhouse work floor. Certainly that would be shocking to the Constabulary wives, but she didn't care. With Julien arrested and missing, with everything in a spiral, she needed some kind of anchor, and good, stable Jarret Covrane was exactly that.

"Find it soon," she whispered, and pushed him back down into his chair. She turned to the door, giving a wink to the gaping Issie as she left.

THE CLOSEST JUSTICE ADVOCATE OFFICE WAS IN SHALETON, THOUGH IT took Raych the better part of the day to even find that out, and then the whole afternoon was spent with her and Jhoqull crammed in a waiting room with twice as many people as could comfortably fit in there. Raych was wearing her most presentable, professional-looking dress, paired with a waistcoat and jacket, so she looked like a businesswoman of some substance. Jhoqull had agreed to wear a dress and coat of Raych's, though she was clearly put out by it. The Ch'omik woman looked quite charming in the outfit, though her fidgeting made it clear she was not comfortable with either long sleeves or tight collars.

"I would be mortified if my family saw me like this," Jhoqull whispered as they waited. "I am hiding my achievements."

"Is that what your tattoos are?" Raych asked. Some conversation, any, would be welcome. The crowded waiting room was filled mostly with women that Raych imagined were in situations not unlike theirs: seeking some form of justice for husbands or brothers or other loved ones. Some of them had their small children clutched close to them. Some of them were clearly ill, coughing or blotched with lesions. Raych tried to look at them all with sympathy, but also did her best to stay in a corner with only Jhoqull pressed close to her.

"They tell my story, what I've done, who I am." Jhoqull shifted her stance, bumping another woman, who made a disgusted noise and pulled away. "I do want to thank you for helping me with this aspect of things. I would not have made it to this office without you."

"I wish we weren't having to deal with this," Raych said. "But we're in this together."

"Shameful," the woman Jhoqull had jostled said. "She shouldn't even be here."

"We have our business here," Raych said. "Mind your own."

"And we have enough trouble without savages coming from across the world and clogging our streets."

"Am I the savage you refer to, ma'am?" Jhoqull asked.

"You should be locked up, put in a ship back to where you came from."

"How dare you," Raych said. "I have more than half a mind to box you down."

The crude woman squinted at Raych. "You too. You might have thought I can't tell, but I've got the look of you. Too many folks coming from all over and ruining this city."

"Ma'am, you have a very wrong idea," Jhoqull said calmly. "Were I the savage you accuse me of being, I would have already driven my thumbs into your skull to pop your eyes clean out. Were I that, I would have sliced you open from neck to nethers, and dressed you in a garland of your own innards. Were I that, I would not be engaged in civil conversation with a *dhotou mkenzoke* like yourself."

"What did you call me?" the woman shrieked. Looking at Raych she added, "You should keep your horse on a tighter rein."

"And you should keep your fool mouth shut," Raych said, pushing the woman against the wall. "Right now I'm not feeling anywhere near as civilized as my friend."

"Rynax?" someone called out. Raych saw some beleaguered clerk coming out from the offices. "Do we have a Missus Rynax?"

"Next time, stay quiet," Raych said, letting the woman go and heading inside.

"Right this way, we'll have someone see you now," the clerk said as he led them down a hallway. "I apologize for the wait, but . . ."

"It's fine," Raych said.

"Try not to start fights with petty fools," Jhoqull said quietly. "It does not help our situation, and could get us arrested as well."

"You're right," Raych said. "She just needled my hair."

"I cannot afford to be seen as anything less than civil," Jhoqull said. "And I cannot afford for my company to do otherwise."

"I'm sorry," Raych said.

"I appreciate your awareness."

They were led into an office where a young man—saints, so young he couldn't possibly have his letters—was looking through a pile of papers.

"Which is this one?" he asked the clerk.

"Rynax, and . . . I don't know, they're together."

"Right," the young man said. "I'm Mister Pindlenight, I'll be looking into this case you say you have." He picked up the sheet that Raych had filled out when they first arrived. "Now, Missus Rynax and Miss . . . Juckel?"

"Jhoqull."

"My apologies, sit," he said, gesturing to the two chairs that were about the only flat surface not covered in paperwork. "Hmm, yes. You're inquiring on behalf of husband and intended and five others they were arrested with, yes?"

"Yes, I put all their names there," Raych said.

"And you spelled those names correctly?"

"Yes, of course," Raych said.

"I needed to ask, needed to," he said. "And these arrests occurred in North Seleth, at . . . Kimber's Public on Frost Avenue? And the arresting officers were not City Constabulary, but Sheriffs of the Archduchy of Sauriya, with the lead officer being Chief Sheriff Rowls? And you're certain of that information?"

"Yes, quite," Raych said.

"Well, it's that I've scoured through our records here, there's been nothing brought to any courts in any of the western precincts with men with these names. I've put in a records mandate with the Sheriffs, and they don't have any arrests of these men on record."

"That's impossible, we were there, we saw it."

"I'm just telling you what I have here. Of course, clerks misplace records, not everything gets sent, though we have people on hand in each stationhouse and court to observe all proceedings, but nothing for arrests or charges on your husband or his associates."

"And what of Chief Rowls?" Jhoqull asked. "Does he have his records, have they been checked?"

"I've sent out a letter to the Sheriffs' city representative, asking for full disclosure of Rowls's activity . . . last night, it was?"

"Yes."

"And once I get that, it should clear some matters up."

"When will that be?" Raych asked, her heart falling into her stomach.

"Honestly, it will probably take the better part of a week for a response. That's just typical with the Archduchy. I'll reach out to the Archduke's Justice Office as well, but . . . the main office for that is in Kyst, and . . . it will take even longer."

"So where is my husband?" Raych asked. "Where are any of them?"

"I don't know," he said. "Listen, I believe you. I believe this happened. But I don't have any information that can verify it. And certainly nothing that can help you right now, ma'am."

"What can you do?"

He sighed. "As I said, I've send in a request for Rowls's activity, I will have my clerks go through all the court filings—everything in the city has to go into Central Filing, but it may take a few days—and check each stationhouse log, Quarrygate entries . . ."

"Quarrygate?" Jhoqull asked, her voice going up sharply. "How could that happen without trial or sentence?"

"It's called 'presumptive custody.' It's sometimes used before the trial when the accused is considered to be a great risk. We try to argue against it, but often get overruled by magistrates. I doubt your men are there, at least not without a proper hearing, but I will keep at it, as best I can. Beyond that, I can't help you. Come back in five days, and—"

"Five days?" Raych asked. Impossible. Horrifying. One night had already been torture. Five days?

"Papers need time to be copied, get filed, go to where they are going, and then my clerks here are already overworked. And . . . you saw the lobby out there. There's only so much I can do."

"Thank you," Jhoqull said, pulling Raych to her feet. Raych couldn't speak or respond, and just let Jhoqull take her. "We will return and hope for better news."

"Thank you, and, again, I'm so sorry I don't have more for you."

"It is understood," Jhoqull said. "Come now, Raychelle, we are walking out."

Raych didn't even register the walk out of the building, she just became aware they were back outside, Jhoqull leading them down the street back toward North Seleth.

"They're just . . . gone? Lost?" Raych said.

"Or they were lost on purpose," Jhoqull said.

"Why did you take us out of there?"

"Nothing else we could say would have changed things, nor did that man need further prodding. We need him to be well disposed enough to us that he continues his search. We leave thankful and polite, hopefully he feels some pity. That is all we can hope for from there."

"Then what?" Raych asked.

"I do not know," Jhoqull said. "I was hoping you and Helene could find an answer, as I am completely without them."

CHAPTER FIVE

After another night of no sleep, no news, and hearing Raych cry through the night, Helene considered trying to open the cheese shop for the day. But just the process of opening things up made her want to cry, scream, and punch things, so she abandoned the idea and locked everything back up again. She knew there was no point in going to the stationhouse again and harassing Covrane. He'd have reached out if there had been any news. Raych and Jhoqull were going to try to find a lawyer and check in with Jhoqull's family. There was nowhere to go, nothing to do, so she went to Kimber's. If nothing else, a few beers would drown her rage.

Kimber was wiping down the bar in the taproom while some kid swept the floor.

"Drop me a pint of your dark and get another one ready," Helene said as she sat down.

"I guess there's no point in asking how you're holding up," Kimber said as she pulled a few drafts from the tap. She gave one to Helene and kept the other for herself, clinking the glasses as Helene picked hers up.

"Health and prosperity," Helene said emptily, and drank down half the glass in one go. Kimber matched her and beyond, finishing hers completely. "So that's new for you."

"It's not been my best day," Kimber said, refilling her glass. "Especially if you're coming in here, that look on your face."

"Sorry it took me this long to come."

"So is there bad news, or just none?"

Helene finished her beer and gave the glass over. "Nothing. We don't know a damn thing."

"How is Raych? And Kennith's girl, Jhoqull?."

Helene shrugged. "We're all looking for answers and not getting any."

"Do we even know what they were arrested for, or why?"

"We haven't even been able to get proof they have been arrested. Constabulary knows nothing, at least Jarret doesn't. Raych has been to the Justice Advocate Office, nothing. She's hunting down a lawyer today." Helene's voice cracked. Kimber's hand found Helene's and squeezed.

"He's going to be all right."

"You know, this is the longest I've been apart from Jules since his accident?" Helene said. "I've never gone two sunsets without seeing him and here we are, I don't even know where he is."

"Asti and Verci are with him. They'll take care of him."

"You really think so?"

Kimber chuckled, even though her eyes were watering. "You see that kid cleaning the floor?"

"He's new?"

"He came in here yesterday, eight bells in the morning, said that some guy told him to come, he'd teach him to use a knife properly. Described Asti to the hair."

"Where'd he meet Asti?"

"I asked him, he said he tried to rob Asti, and Asti took the knife from him, told him he was doing it all wrong, and to come in the morning and learn something proper. Have you ever heard anything so wild?"

Helene burst out laughing. "That is . . . the most Asti thing I've ever heard," she said.

"So I told him he had a job here if he needed money. The only thing I could think to do."

"You always were one for taking in strays."

"Asti most of all," Kimber said. "Just so you know, I'm not . . . I don't fool myself about him. He doesn't love me, I know. And he doesn't want love from me."

"I don't think he trusts himself to let anyone love him," Helene said.

"No," Kimber said. "But by every saint, does he need it, because he hates himself so much. So I give him as much as he's willing to take. And . . . I've always had a thing for lost causes."

"You still have Nange up in a room, I see," Helene said. Enanger Lesk should have died after Asti carved him up, but he managed to make a slow recovery. And he had nothing left, his whole gang was gone.

"Asti said to keep him until he was well enough to be out on his own, so I did," Kimber said. "Asti takes in the strays as well."

"Thank the saints for that," Helene said. "But this arrest business, it has to be something done by his enemies. Our enemies. It's the only sense of it I can make."

"Because of the things you all have done since the fire?"

"Exactly," Helene said. "But why arrest the boys and leave me on my own?"

Kimber took the empty glass away. "In that case, maybe this is your limit. If someone comes for you, you need your wits."

"I don't even know what to expect," Helene said. "At this point, we're just waiting, but we're probably going to exhaust every legal recourse."

Kimber snorted. "Then, my dear, I think you know what the next step is for you."

Raych had not been prepared for Helene to stumble into the Gadgeterium, having clearly been in her cups, let alone make such a nonsensical declaration.

"What?" Raych asked.

"We," Helene said, taking a moment to focus herself on Raych. "We . . . we need . . ."

"How much did you drink?"

"Two beers," Helene said. "At Kimber's. Then she said I was done, so I went to the Fuergan restaurant and had a few little glasses of their house whiskey, which . . . is terrible, at least the first couple. But then they also make this thing with layers of pastry and a cream and something green and—"

"Helene," Raych said, bringing her into the back room. "Why did you get drunk?"

"What else am I going to do?" Helene asked.

"Someone could still be coming for us—"

"No one is coming for us," Helene said. "If they were, they would have. Whatever this is about, we're irrelevant to the scheme."

"How can you think that?"

"Because that's what I'm seeing here," Helene said. "Listen, if this was a ploy aimed at us, to grab you or me while keeping Asti and Verci out of the game, they would have taken their opportunity already. Or if it was a ploy that needed us, it would have reared its head. But it's not."

"I don't understand."

"All right," Helene said, sitting down on the floor. "Let me explain. If you kidnap Asti Rynax because you want to grab something he'd protect—you have to know there's only a short amount of time to take advantage of that. You're not going to neutralize him and then wait two days, because you would risk that he'd break out and kill you before that. So whatever this is about, we're not the target. We're not the concern. So we need to figure out how to become a concern." Helene's expression made it clear she had lost her train of thought at the end of her diatribe.

"I don't understand." Raych knew she was saying that again, but she didn't know what else to say. She had barely been able to think straight the last two days, and some part of her wished she could let herself get as ripping drunk as Helene was. "How do we become a concern?"

"I'm still trying to figure it out," Helene said. "I'm never one for plans. Tell me a plan, stick me on a rooftop, and I can do whatever you need . . . I'm useless on my own."

"Helene," Raych said, sitting down in front of her. "You came in here all fired up on something, but I don't know what. Explain it. We need an illegal recourse?"

"Did you hire a lawyer?" Helene asked.

"They weren't interested because I don't know where Verci and the others are, and can't even prove they were arrested. And I can't afford to hire them to do the investigative work to find the boys."

"Right. Constabulary is no help, lawyers no help, the Justice Advocate Office no help. Legal recourses are done. So, illegal recourses. We can't investigate, so who can?"

The door flew open, and Raych jumped up, grabbing the closest of Verci's devices and holding it up as a weapon. Which was ridiculous, as it was a bottle-popper, and it was Jhoqull at the door.

"I think I know where they are."

Helene hopped up on her feet, surprisingly steady. "Where?"

"Quarrygate," Jhoqull said.

"I mean, that's a reasonable guess, but we have no idea," Raych said. "But even still, wouldn't the Justice Advocate Office have heard?"

"They don't hear what I did."

"How did you hear?" Helene asked.

"I've checked in with the family. They have all reached out, ears open around the city. Just about every Ch'omik in Maradaine knows about what happened the other night, and have been learning what they could. So, a cousin of a cousin works in a boarder house out southwest. And a good swipe of the folks living in that house are guards at Quarrygate."

"All right," Raych said.

"So this kin overheard talk about a fight in the prison yard they had to stop. Gang boys going after, as they said, 'chomie and pirie' who were together, and then a big guy got involved and they had to put him in the box."

"In the what?" Helene roared.

Raych was a step behind with the math of it. Could it be true? Kennith with either Verci or Asti, and then Julien. At least three of them together, too much of a coincidence to otherwise ignore.

"So why haven't we heard through official channels?"

"Because the official channels don't rutting care," Helene snapped. "They put Julie in what?"

"I don't know," Jhoqull said. "This is through a few sets of ears, so the details might have been lost. The point is, it's likely the boys are there. So what do we do?"

"Go back to the Justice Advo—"

"No," Helene said. "If they're already in there, it's without a trial or counsel. Shady sewage. Like I said, no legal recourse will help us."

"But if we know—"

"You'll be buried in paper. And it won't help the boys."

"We don't know—"

"We know it won't help them. Look, if they're there, then they were either really arrested by Archduchy Sheriffs, or by someone who could manipulate or control the Sheriffs. You think a lawyer we could hire, or the Justice Advocate Office could handle that?" Even through her drunken slurring, Helene was on target with her words. She was right, and Raych hated that.

"So what do we do?" Raych asked. She looked to Jhoqull.

"I have no idea, unless you want me to call the family to fight."

"We're not going to storm Quarrygate," Raych said.

"But we do need . . ." Helene laughed. "What was it, what I said when I came in?"

"An illegal resource."

"We need someone who can fight a dirty fight for us," Helene said. "We need to go to Josie Holt."

That was it. The thing Raych had feared Helene had meant from the start.

JUST FINDING JOSIE HAD BEEN A BIT OF A CHALLENGE. THE WOMAN knew how to stay hidden, and she was no longer at the pub where Raych had last seen her. That place was now boarded up completely.

Helene had gone to Enanger Lesk, since he used to work for her, and his main advice was, "Find Ia, who usually is running the Honey Hut. If anyone is still close to Josie, it's her."

Raych did not want to go to the Honey Hut, certainly, but Helene made it clear that it was the best option to talk to Josie, and that was the best option for the help they needed.

Raych dressed in the same smart dress she had worn to see the lawyers. If nothing else, she'd look professional and composed. Jhoqull had assembled an outfit that looked somewhat like a Druth summer dress, but had taken off the sleeves, and wore her leather vest over it, buttoned tight almost like a corset. Helene dressed in her usual dark purple ensemble that she wore for most of the runs she had done with Verci. Her "business attire" when her business was being on a roof with a crossbow. Two crossbows dangled at her hips. But the strangest part of her outfit was a green cap, which didn't match the rest remotely.

"What is that hat?" Raych asked.

"A message," Helene said. "We need to go through Ia, so I wanted to remind her who I am."

"And who is that?" Jhoqull asked.

"The woman who knocked her on her backside and took her damned hat."

Raych wasn't going to argue with that. Great Prophets, Ia Estäan was a tower of a woman. She certainly terrified Raych, so having both Helene and Jhoqull at her side for this was absolutely critical.

The Honey Hut was not very busy when they arrived, since it was the middle of the day, and most fellows didn't get their randy on until the sun had set, at least. They came in to find a number of women, all dressed relatively respectfully, slouching about in the front parlor. Raych wasn't sure what she had expected, but it had been a bit more salacious than this.

"Well," one of the women said, walking up. "This almost feels like a trap. We agree to service one of you ladies and then the constables pour in and arrest us all for moral degeneracy."

"Not looking for that," Raych said. "We would like a word with Miss Estäen if she's available."

"Miss Estäen?" the woman asked. "Isn't that proper?"

Helene stepped up. "Just tell Ia that we need to talk to her. Tell her it's Helene Kesser and two friends."

"Fine," the woman said, and she went off to the back of the house. In a few moments, Ia strode out, an absolute statue. Hair like the sun, skin like snow, and as she approached, she was so tall that Raych only came up to her bosom.

"Are you looking for work, Kesser? You think men will pay for this, *sjat*?"

"Not looking to work for you," Helene said. "We need to talk to the Old Lady."

"Who is we? You and the dark bit and the poisoner?"

"Sorry about that," Raych said.

"Don't apologize to her," Helene said.

"No, I like that," Ia said. "She made me vomit my guts and worse for two days, I thought I was going to die. An apology is the least."

"Please," Raych said. "We need to speak to Missus Holt."

"So you come to me," Ia said. She looked Helene up and down. "Oh, yes, very good, Hel. You want to scrap me here in my own house?"

"If I got to."

"And this one," she said, pointing to Jhoqull. "You would be a good fight, I think, *sjat*?"

"Test at your convenience," Jhoqull said.

"I may, I may. And then the Rynax woman. I will say this about you, miss, you did make a very good pie. Even with the poison, quite tasty."

"Are you going to get the Old Lady or not?" Helene asked.

Ia pursed her lips in thought. "What could it be that brings the three of you to my place needing to talk to Missus Holt? This is very interesting, *sjat*? I want to hear it. But . . ." She reached out and grabbed the hat off of Helene's head. "I want my rutting hat back."

Helene bristled, but Raych grabbed her arm. "Fine, you can have it," Raych said. "Just, please."

"Payra, take them to the kitchen. Have Missus Rynax make some tea for all the girls while she waits. I will see if Missus Holt wants to talk to you."

The kitchen was dreary and dismal, but Raych, despite the glares from Helene, went to work on a pot of tea. She didn't know what else to do while waiting, and since she was here to beg for help, she might as well be amiable. If that meant making tea, perfect. If they had the ingredients in this kitchen—which was in a state, how did these ladies eat?—she would make cookies or cakes. Anything to curry some favor. It was the absolute least to do. Jhoqull and Helene both sat and watched her, shaking their heads.

"You handle things your way, I'll do mine," Raych said.

Raych finished the tea and brought it out to the ladies in the parlor, who were all very kind and appreciative. She returned to the kitchen to find Ia standing there, looming protectively over Josie Holt, now sitting in one of the chairs.

"Well, Raychelle Rynax," Josie said. "It has been a little bit, hasn't it?"

"Ma'am," Raych said,

"I would normally like some tea myself, but last time you made me something, well, it wasn't all it was presented to be, was it?"

"I suppose not, ma'am."

"You see, Hel?" Josie said. "She understands deference."

"You earn some deference, you'll get some."

"No need to be salty, Helene."

"I still think you stole from us, so I'll bring the salt."

"I did what the neighborhood needed. As I always do."

"Speaking of," Raych said, sitting down.

"Yes, the Rynax boys are in trouble, I hear. Same with your cousin, and Almer, Kennith, Pilsen and his boy. Ia, do I have that count right?"

"Sjat."

"Quite the predicament."

"They're in Quarrygate, we think," Helene said. "We need to get them out."

"That's a tall order."

"One I think you can help with, though," Raych said.

"I would have to find out what I can do. But let's say I'm inclined—and I somewhat am, as Ken and Pilsen haven't irritated me much. They probably don't deserve whatever business this is. Not even Julien."

"None of them do," Raych said.

"I need to investigate, but my gut tells me the Rynax boys have been up to something, no? And perhaps they earned this being visited upon them all."

"But can you help?" Jhoqull said brusquely. "Or do you just talk in games?"

"She's a fire, I like that," Josie said. "Now, I probably can. But I have to ask, what is in it for me?"

"What do you want?" Raych asked.

"Oh, my," Josie said. "Is this an open offer? Whatever I want?"

"Within reason," Raych said. "We're not going to work here for you."

"If that's what I wanted, you would," Josie said. "But I have no need for unenthusiastic doxies with mediocre skills. But do you know what? Just the other day, a job crossed my desk. A job I would really like to get done. At one time, it's exactly the sort of job I'd call on Asti and Verci Rynax for."

"So get them all out, and they'll do it," Helene said.

"No, that's not what I'm thinking," Josie said. "I think I can't get it done as an Asti and Verci Rynax job. Not on the schedule I need, and not on empty promises. I need it done now." She chuckled and leaned back in her chair.

"So maybe, if you truly are desperate enough, it's a Raych Rynax job."

CHAPTER SIX

"Are you rutting kidding me?" Helene asked. She couldn't believe Josie was even suggesting it. "She's not her husband."

"No," Josie said. "But Nange's boys had abducted her, and she got away from her lockup all on her own. She outfoxed me with that pie trick. Not to mention she's probably strong enough to even beat Ia on a pull-fight."

"She is not one of us," Helene said. "Blazes, I'm barely that—"

Josie scoffed. "You're North Seleth in your blood, Helene. Your pop was shooting in crack jobs for as long as I've known, and I don't even want to get into what your gran used to do back in the day."

"So, fine," Helene said. "You give me a target, a list of targets, and I'll put bolts in their skulls all day long. You want that? I'll do that. Every rival you have, lying in their own blood by sunrise tomorrow."

"Very bold promises," Josie said. "I almost wish that was a practical thing I needed." She turned to Raych. "I mean, if five years ago, Helene had shown that kind of drive, that kind of hustle? With her talent she'd be the most sought-after assassin in the city. Able to name her price."

"I'm telling you now," Helene said, leaning into Josie's face. "You need work done, talk to me."

"I'm also talking to Raych," Josie said. "If I'm helping the three of you here, then I am talking to all of you. I'm going to need all of you to be working with me for what I need done."

"You don't even know what we can do," Jhoqull said.

"I have some inkling," Josie said. "And I am fascinated by the . . . motivational power of this situation. Look how enterprising it made Helene. Ready to start a murder spree, just before marrying a constable at that. Astounding."

Helene pounded the table. "Do you want to see what kind of spree I'll go on if something happens to Julien?"

Raych touched Helene's arm, drawing her back down to her chair. Then, in a choked whisper, asked, "What's the job?"

"You can't be serious, Raych."

More assertively, "What's the job, Missus Holt?"

"There it is," Josie said. "Like I said, motivation. Love to see it."

"Just tell us what you want," Raych said.

"I'm so glad you've seen things my way, is all."

"The job," Helene stressed.

Josie snapped her fingers, and Ia handed her an envelope. Josie pulled out sheets with charcoal sketches on them. "Have any of you been to the Druth History Museum?"

"I did not know there was such a thing," Jhoqull said.

"North side of the city, near The Royal College of Maradaine. I've not gone, but I have heard good things."

"What about the museum?" Raych asked.

"You want us to rob a museum?" Helene could not believe this sewage.

"Specifically, five paintings, all ninth century, painted by Maricon Noile." Josie laid out the sketches. "Crude renderings, so you know what you need to look for. I don't expect you to be art experts or anything."

Helene glanced at the pictures: a battle on a river, a guy on a throne, a battle on a cliff, two old ladies, a bunch of men at a table. "The blazes is this?"

"I think it's called the Noile Pentaptych, but I'm also not an expert. Ia, are you?"

"Not for old Druth paintings."

"Yes, we don't know. But there are interested parties who would want the complete set for their private collections. And all five are currently on display at the Druth History Museum."

"The catch?" Raych asked.

"The catch would be that all five will be leaving the museum in five days, and returning to their individual homes in various museums in Vargox. The Pentaptych being together in one place is an incredible opportunity, which I'll pass on to you."

"Why?" Helene asked.

"Because when it comes down to it, while such a theft would be quite the plum for my reputation, I don't need it. Not like you need my help. So that's my price."

"We could just knock down a goldsmith house, or, blazes, rob one of the other southside bosses, and . . ."

"I don't want money, Helene," Josie said firmly. "I want the paintings. You get me all five paintings, and I will bend my will toward returning all your men to you. Fair?"

"And if we fail?" Raych asked.

"Then I won't. You'll see no further consequences from me. Though I imagine such a failure would have its own consequences."

"How do you expect me to do this?" Raych asked.

"Us," Helene said. She put her hand on Raych's shoulder. This was madness, but she'd at least put on a good front for the Old Lady.

"I mean, I imagine you do what Asti and Verci would do. Put together a crew, make a plan. I mean, they're your family, right? You must know them."

"Sure," Raych said. "I've got my crew right here."

"Absolutely. I mean, a crack shot like Helene? Can't hurt. And every good job can use a carriage driver, which is just a slice of this one's talents." She pointed to Jhoqull. "Of course I know what you can do, you're in my patch, I make it my business."

"Fine," Raych said.

"I'll even lend you Ia if you need an extra set of strong arms."

"Really?" Ia asked.

"If they need you, be cooperative," Josie said. "But we'll see what you come up with."

"What do you really want?" Helene asked. This seemed like just a strange lark to the Old Lady.

"My father used to say, 'with enough power, even the dog will dance.' And after all the grief you and yours gave me . . . oh, I want to see you all dance. I honestly don't expect you to succeed, ladies. But I do hope it will be entertaining to watch."

"STEAL PAINTINGS," RAYCH SAID FOR THE NINTH TIME THAT NIGHT. After an afternoon of baking in an attempt to clear her head enough to think this through properly, she had given up and decided to take Helene's advice and lose a bit of herself in a bottle of wine. "How in the name of every prophet are we supposed to do that?"

Helene, sprawled out on the floor of the Rynax family apartment, laughed drily. "I don't think we're supposed to at all. I think Josie just wanted to make us squirm." She had started on the wine as soon as they had returned to the apartment above the Gadgeterium. She had, at least, brought several bottles, as well as an armful of meat and cheeses from her shop. Between that and the breads, cakes, and pastries Raych had prepared, they were, if nothing else, well-fortified for their misery.

"We are but as bait to her," Jhoqull said. She sat at the table, taking it easy on the wine but devouring spiced cakes. "Our suffering is her joy."

"Basically," Helene said, "going to her was a mistake."

"She was our only option," Raych said.

"Which means this robbery is also our only option," Jhoqull said. "I am game for the attempt, if it brings me closer to reuniting with Kennith. I imagine you feel the same."

Helene said up. "You really want to try to steal these paintings?"

"I would think, we should at least understand what it might entail before we decide to fail from the outset."

Raych slathered some delightfully pungent soft cheese on her bread. "Fine, so what would Asti and Verci do here? Make a plan?"

"Make a plan and tell us what to do," Helene said.

"And put together a team," Raych said.

"Crew," Helene corrected her. "Asti is very particular about correct terms."

"Of course he is."

"We have a crew," Jhoqull said. "Do we not?"

"What do we have?" Helene asked.

"Assets," Raych said, forcing herself to think through the wine haze. "First off, we have you, Helene Kesser, crack shot with a crossbow. You can trim a man's beard from three blocks away."

"I do appreciate a good buttering," Helene said.

"And Jhoqull-Ra. You can drive a wagon or carriage, and you can fix them too, and you can cast or shape whatever we might need in your forge."

"And I am not useless in a brawl," Jhoqull said.

"Unlike me," Raych said. "I have ovens and know-how of all forms of bakery, and that's about it."

"You also have a dozen or so Verci Rynax gadgets at your disposal. The whole inventory of the Gadgeterium."

"I don't know what any of it does. Or at least most of it."

"We can figure it out," Helene said. "If nothing else there's some good scopes for roof scouting. And I can roof scout. Any good job needs a roof scout."

"See, that's something I didn't know. What else?"

"I mean," Helene got up from the floor. "I never deal with this part."

"Yeah, but you've been a part of it," Raych said. "What else?"

"The whole scout. From the roof, from the ground, figure out what it is you need to steal, where it's vulnerable, what the gaps in the security are, how to take advantage of that . . ."

"How do we do that?"

"I don't know," Helene said. "Asti and Verci were good at that, and I would do what they told me."

"But they would talk about it in front of you," Raych pressed.

"I honestly didn't listen. They had this whole thing with cute names for ploys and stories about stuff they did years ago and I just tuned it out. The only one who paid attention was—oh."

"What?" Raych asked, standing up a little too quickly.

"I don't know how to plan something like this," Helene said. "But I know who might."

THE FALL SEMESTER AT THE UNIVERSITY OF MARADAINE HAD BEEN going perfectly well, at least from an academic standpoint. Mila Kendish was doing just fine in all of her classes, top marks all around. She found that she could easily do all her reading and coursework while still keeping her instincts sharp.

From a personal standpoint, it had been a bit more chaotic. Keeping her instincts sharp meant that most of her time in the woman's college was spent keeping her fellow dormmates at a certain degree of distance. She knew all about them, more than they realized she knew, because she was constantly watching them, learning their comings and goings, figuring out their secrets, and keeping a tally of every bit of leverage she might need to use. Not that she planned to need leverage on any of them, but she'd rather have it and never need it over needing it and not having it.

There had been some excitement for the first few weeks helping Veranix in his fight against Fenmere, but that had cooled down since that terrible day last month. He wasn't being the Thorn anymore, and he didn't need a Rose by his side, at least on the streets. While their romantic moments hadn't stopped since then, they had certainly taken on a different flavor. She was still enjoying it, but now she had a guard up around him that she didn't before.

Her guard was constantly up. Mila Kendish, University Student was a mask she was wearing almost every waking moment, because no one here could really know Mila Kendish, West Maradaine Street Rat, also known as Miss Bessie, also known as Jendly Marskin, also known as the Rose. Pickpocket, thief, killer. No one here could handle it.

No one but Kaiana Nell.

Mila would hesitate to call Kaiana a friend, strictly speaking. When they first met, Kaiana had been nearly hostile. But they had settled into a reasonable rhythm when they were both helping Veranix, and since then they had found a certain degree of mutual kinship in shared experience.

Around Kaiana, Mila could drop the mask.

And in the past few weeks, they had found themselves meeting for lunch every other day. This was in part because now that Kaiana had her father living in her apartment, she needed someone she could drop her mask around as well.

The Crying Baby, an ironically quiet pub right off the west side of campus, was a perfect place where they could meet up, talk plainly, and not be seen by anyone they knew from school. For some reason, students almost never came to any of the restaurants out of the west gates. Something about how going west meant going lower class. But for a West Maradaine girl like Mila, and a half-Napolic girl like Kaiana, there was no problem.

Kaiana was already waiting with three ciders on the table when Mila got there. Three ciders, and someone else sitting there.

"Missus Rynax," Mila said as she approached to the table. "What are you doing out here, and . . . you know Kaiana?"

"That whole business with the Brotherhood you missed," Kaiana said. "We met after some cultists tried to take over her husband's shop."

"Quite unpleasant," Raych Rynax said with a weak smile. "I came out here to look for you, and ran into Miss Nell on campus, she said she was coming to meet you for lunch, and . . . here we are."

Mila sat down, curious but concerned. "All right, why are you looking for me?"

"Well . . ." Raych looked nervously at Kaiana.

"She knows everything," Mila said. "Go on."

"Asti and Verci have been arrested," Raych said. "Along with Kennith, Almer, Julien, Pilsen, and . . . Pilsen's friend, the pretty one."

"Vellun," Mila said, trying to take that in. Asti and Verci arrested? Did they screw up a job? They didn't go down fighting? "What happened? What were they up to?"

"That's just it, nothing," Raych said. "It was a party at Kimber's for Helene's engagement—"

"Her what?"

"To Lieutenant Covrane."

Mila picked up her cider and downed it. "I have clearly missed too much. We'll come back to that. Having a party, constables bust in—"

"Archduchy Sheriffs, actually."

That was unexpected, but Mila took it in. "And charged them with what?"

"They wouldn't say. We haven't really heard anything, but we think they're all in Quarrygate."

"Sorry, Kai," Mila said, taking Kaiana's cider and drinking it. Kaiana signaled for more to come to the table. "So, what's next? Justice Advocate, trial? And then . . . are you just here to let me know?"

"No," Raych said. "Helene and Jhoqull and I, we . . . we've been trying everything, and when none of our options worked out we . . ."

Mila could sense exactly where this was going. "You went to Josie Holt for help."

"Right."

"So what's the catch?"

"The catch is, she . . ." Raych looked around the room again, and then leaned in and whispered. "She wants me to steal paintings from the Druth History Museum."

"She what the where?" Mila asked.

"Miss," Kaiana called out to the server. "Make that six more ciders."

"How are you supposed to do that? You don't know about—" Then the gears clicked. "That's why you're here."

"I don't even know where to start with this, and Jho and Helene, they . . . they've got skills but . . ."

"But I'm the one who actually learned this stuff." Mila shook her head. "Kai, you don't need to . . ."

"No magic or saint could get me from this table," Kaiana said.

"Raych," Mila said, taking her hand. "You know damn well I'm going to be there for those boys. If you need a plan to rob the . . . what?"

"The Druth History Museum," Raych said.

"Saints above," Mila said. "Certainly aiming big for this. All right, if that's the target the Old Lady wants hit, so be it. I have class in an hour, but after that I'll get to work."

"We," Kaiana said.

"Kai," Mila said. "You don't need to be a part of this."

"I appreciate the gesture," Raych said. "But you don't need to get involved in our own troubles. This is personal for us."

"I know," Kaiana said calmly. "I want to help you because it isn't personal for me. Missus Rynax, you're in a state, I can tell by looking at you that you haven't slept proper in days. Mila, the vein in your forehead is throbbing. And the other two you mentioned, I bet they're just as invested."

"It's family for all of us," Raych said.

"So you need someone who isn't, who can have a little perspective. I know more than a bit about that, trust me."

"We'll come to the bakery tonight after a bit of legwork," Mila said.

"The Gadgeterium," Raych said. "That's where we're all . . . it's just better protected . . ."

"Of course," Mila said.

Raych got up, looking even more flustered. "I should check on the bakery, though, and my sister, and . . . thank you, Mila, and . . ."

"Hey," Mila said, taking her hand again. "Like you said, this is family. I have you, all right? We'll be there tonight."

"Thank you," Raych said with tears in her eyes.

"Now sit down and eat a meal made by someone else," Mila said. "I will cover it."

"Yes, thank you," Raych said, taking her seat again.

"And we're settled on this business with the museum. Job is driving forward," Mila said. "So now, I want to hear all about Helene and this rutting constable."

CHAPTER SEVEN

Raych had spent the remainder of the afternoon working in her apartment over the Gadgeterium, splitting her time between cooking, cataloguing Verci's devices, and briefly reading Asti's journals. The last one, she had discovered when she dared to look through his rooms to see what he had on hand that might be of use. There had been a trunk under the bed, filled with handwritten notebooks, and curiosity compelled her to open them up.

As soon as she did, she felt she had committed an atrocious violation. They were filled with his personal observations, an almost daily practice, that included mentions of "the beast" and "Liora," how loud or quiet they were, how much they wanted to compel him to do horrible things. She knew he was a troubled man, but she had no idea how truly shattered it was inside his mind, how much he faced a daily battle with his own demons.

That was a word they didn't use here in Maradaine, but it was a recurring theme in the Acserian faith. Raych's own practices of her faith had always been, at best, spurious. Her father had never been a believer, that was why they had left Damyar. But as children she and Lian had read the entire Acseram, mostly to please their grandmother, so she knew the principles of the faith well enough. Demons served the same function as the sinners did in the Druth church, a source of temptation and torment. Asti's writing made it clear exactly how tormented he was, every single day, and she was in awe at how well he had been hiding it.

Raych put the books back in the trunk and slid them back under the bed, and returned to her other tasks. She did, though, take a belt with the pair of knives, the one that matched Verci's bandolier of darts. Both had belonged to their father, and as much as the idea terrified her, she accepted that one day they both might go to Corsi. Not that she wished her son would have anything to do with the life his grandfather had raised Verci and Asti in. But he should still know his legacy, where he came from, and own the things that were his due.

Also, Raych wasn't sure if she would need the weapons on this job. Not that she really knew how to use either, just like she really didn't understand the collection of Verci's inventions that she had laid out on the apartment floor. But she wanted a full sense of the assets she had on hand for this mad task.

Helene and Jhoqull arrived shortly before sunset, both bearing more food, and this time no wine. Raych had insisted on that point, they needed to have clear heads from here on out. Jhoqull had brought some type of Ch'omik chilled tea, which she confirmed had nothing fermented in it whatsoever.

As Raych finished laying food out on the table, there was a knock on the door. She checked the lenshole, just to be sure, but it was exactly as she had expected: Mila and Kaiana. Both of them were dressed like the lawyers at the Justice Advocate Office, and were carrying briefs filled with papers.

Helene looked Mila up and down as she came in. "Looks like they feed you well at that school."

"And it looks like the constable rolls you pretty well."

Helene gasped, and then grabbed Mila in an embrace, pulling her further inside.

"Hello," Kaiana said, warily crossing into the apartment.

"This is Kaiana," Mila said, introducing her to Helene and Jhoqull. "She works on campus, as well as working with the Thorn. She's got a good head and can stay calm in trouble."

"I like the sound of that," Jhoqull said.

"Sit, sit," Raych said, guiding everyone to the table. "Let's get started."

Mila chuckled. "Asti and Verci don't usually do this with a meal."

"Well, this is my way."

"It's probably a better way," Mila said.

"Do . . . do you all mind if I say an Acserian prayer before we start?" Raych asked.

"I'm open to any help we can get," Helene said. "I've been whispering to Saint Senea for days."

Jhoqull responded only by taking Raych's hand and squeezing it affectionately.

"It's your table, Missus Rynax," Kaiana said.

"Thank you," Raych said. "And it's just Raych." Closing her eyes, she said. "Blessed god, look upon our souls, see that we strive toward a task of danger and transgression. We do this not from a place of greed or wrath, but from love, so please bless our acts from the place in which it comes. Fix your blessing on our hearts so we may face the test ahead. In the name of each of your prophets who have come, and the ones you will still send us."

Then Jhoqull looked upward and said, in an almost musical voice, *"Yar mzu ti thayar thavarj mluwa va, mwemye mpyi va, mill wep bloll pe zin njhu mlukh til mnyi mra, zinywul zin mri ikh jhini umru mzu nya."*

"What did that mean?" Kaiana asked when she was done.

"I was calling to many mothers past to guide us and stand with us in our task," Jhoqull said. Looking to Helene, she said, "Any help, yes?"

"Absolutely," Helene said.

"So," Mila said as they started to eat, "Kaiana and I have already done some research. She went through information in the university library and the planning charts, and I worked my charms in some of the city offices. Turns out a few of the folks there really missed me. Or rather, Jendly."

"And what did you learn?" Raych asked.

"First off," Kaiana said, taking out a notebook. "The Noile Pentaptych, five paintings in a sequence, painted by Maricon Noile from 875 to 878. Depicting the five foundational moments in what was, at the time, the Kingdom of Oblune. Noile is considered the greatest painter of the era—at least, posthumously."

"What?" Helene asked.

"He was largely ignored as a madman in his lifetime, impoverished into his old age. His daughter took care of him as best she could, but after he died his debts were so great, all his belongings, including stacks of his paintings, were gathered up and auctioned off in bulk."

"That's tragic," Raych said.

"It wasn't for another fifty years until the art-loving nobility in Vargox discovered his works—those that survived—and started hailing him as a genius. Then his style was imitated across all of Druthal for another century, which art historians call the Noilic Period."

"So the paintings are a big deal," Helene said.

"Beyond a big deal," Kaiana said. "The five of them together are considered Noile's masterwork—the only complete series that still exists—and held up as some of the most important artifacts of cultural heritage in the Archduchy of Oblune, perhaps even all of Druthal."

"So people will notice them missing," Raych said. She was regretting disallowing wine at this meeting.

"That's the big challenge here," Mila said. "Now, to our advantage, the museum was built using an existing building, a guesthouse that used to belong to the Royal College that was converted into the museum."

"Why is that to our advantage?" Jhoqull asked.

Mila grinned, pulling out a chart. "Because it means the building wasn't built to be secure. Lots of soft points." She pointed out on the chart. "Assuming this is accurate, we've got both sewer points and other access tunnels at a few points. There was a whole period in the tenth and eleventh centuries when folks in Maradaine were just wild about building underground."

"That's the truth," Kaiana said quietly.

"So we've got possible access to basement areas here, and here," Mila said, pointing out on the map. "Unless it's bricked over, in which . . . Almer is with the boys in the prison, right?"

"Presumably," Raych said. "He was arrested."

She turned to Kaiana. "Do we still have boom powder left? Vee won't miss it."

"I'd have to check."

"If you have any of Almer's stuff, bring it in," Helene said.

"We can add it to our assets," Raych said. She pointed to the pile of gadgets and weapons. "Plus all that."

Mila looked at that. "All right, that's pretty good. What other assets do we have?"

Jhoqull raised an eyebrow. "I've been taking care of Ken's horses at the inn, and there's also the carriages he's got in the barn. All of them."

"Do any of us know how to operate that spring-powered one?" Mila asked.

"I think I can drive it," Jhoqull said. "And any of the others, sure."

"And if we need another body, especially a strong one, we can bring in Ia," Helene said.

"I thought you hate her."

"I do. But she could be useful. And you want to know our assets."

Mila shrugged. "If we want a distraction, there's worse choices than a six-foot blond woman."

Raych stood up and looked at the charts. "In looks like the building has a few entrances."

"At least by that," Mila said. "Main ones, a couple side once, a loading door that can handle a full carriage with an alley exit."

"So what's next?" Raych asked.

"Now we need to confirm what we're looking at. Full scout, eyes on the ground." Mila pointed to Helene. "And on the roofs."

"You're thinking you'll need me on the roofs?"

"I want your eyes up there tomorrow. I want you to especially watch all the streets around the museum, how things move. What's the foot traffic, who's vending on the walkways. Jhoqull, you're going to do the same thing on the ground." Mila pulled out a map of the city. "We're out of our territory with this one, and we want to get back here, on our side of the river, and the bridges are choke points where we can be trapped. We need exit routes, escape plans, and contingencies. I want to know our best routes in case we have fire coming after us."

"Will we?" Raych asked.

"I don't know. We need to know what it looks like inside. So tomorrow, you, Kaiana, and I are visiting the museum."

"All right," Raych said, swallowing hard. If this is what it took to get Verci home, she'd do it. She couldn't imagine what he was going through right now.

"All of these buildings are very tall."

Helene realized as she walked through Victory Square, that she had never really been across the river, and the north side of Maradaine was a completely different city. She had seen it from across the river, but had never been particularly interested in going there. Short of her hunting ventures into the woods past Carrol Creek, she had barely ever left the limits of the south part of Maradaine.

"What do you reckon that is, ten floors?" Helene asked Jhoqull. The Ch'omik woman was dressed in very Druth clothes now, matching Helene's look of a work dress and heavy coat. The wind on this side of the river was bitter, and once they were there, Jhoqull stopped complaining about covering up her arms.

"I have no sense of that," Jhoqull said, looking up briefly. They kept their way walking through Victory Square, doing their best to not looking like they were scouting the area for escape routes. "But why are we all the way up here? The museum is several blocks south of here. We would want to escape toward the river, no? This is the wrong way."

"It is the wrong way, but like you said, these buildings are very tall, and that gives us a great view down. That one looks good."

"For height, yes, very tall," Jhoqull said. "But we cannot get in easily." She pointed to the front door, where a man in a uniform that was reminiscent of military or constabulary, but not either, was standing watch. "He will not let us in there."

"Back doors?" Helene asked.

"Possibly, but I have my suspicions about those. Come." They made their way through the alley to the side, where there were service doors. "As I suspected, they cannot even be opened from the outside." And the back alley was blocked by a locked gate.

"This is one of those moments where the Rynaxes shine," Helene told Jhoqull. "Either crack that door, or the gate, or climb up to the that balcony a few floors up."

"None of those are in my skillset."

"I'm mostly a shooting girl," Helene said. "But I was paying attention when they dressed me up for some of those grifts." Across Victory Square, she noted the Henson's Majestic store, a grand sort of place, she had heard, where swells and rich ladies could buy all sorts of clothes, jewelry, perfume, and whatever else. Not the sort of place she would ever go. But she did notice women coming out carrying wrapped packages and parcels. "Wait here, I've got an idea."

Helene went around back to the employees' entrance, and walked right past two people smoking their pipes inside. She walked through a back room work floor, dozens of folks organizing boxes, unloading crates, moving in and out to the shop floor. The place was chaos, which was just what she needed. She moved quickly, grabbing an apron off a hook, a paperboard off a desk, a dress, a box of pins and measuring line from a worktable, all while the full plan came together in her head.

She walked right up to someone who looked nominally in charge—at least in vest and cravat instead of work clothes—and launched right into a speech, full confidence.

"Listen," she said as soon as she was in his face. "Some idiot spilled tea on my orders for one of the alterations I need to do. I lost everything, the measurements, even the woman's name."

"I, um . . . I'm not sure . . ."

"Look, I'll take the shouting for it, I shouldn't have had my paperwork in the tea room—"

"No, you certainly shouldn't have."

"I just need to get new measurements for this woman—it's . . . blazes, you know . . ."

"Language, miss, even in the back rooms."

"Right, sorry," she said. "Her name is . . . you know, that bossy lady who lives in the tower across the street. The one with the cat?"

"Are you talking about Missus Alsterton?"

"That's the one," Helene said. "If this isn't ready by tomorrow, she's going to bring the wrath of the sinners on me."

"That sounds like your problem," the man said. "It's not my department, but I will make sure your supervisor does know about your negligence, miss—" He looked at her with stern questioning.

"Kendish," Helene said. "I will do better, sir."

"See to it."

He went off, and Helene went right out the back door.

"Hey, where you going with that?" one of the smokers asked her.

"Always some crisis to solve!" she called back to him. "They don't pay me enough for this."

Helene went back across the street, walking past Jhoqull. "Follow me."

"Oh, this will be interesting," Jhoqull said. "Did you steal a dress?"

"I'll put it back."

"Is this typical for you?"

"Just got to get in the door," Helene said. They approached the uniformed guard at the door.

"Can I help you ladies?" he asked dubiously.

"I hope so," Helene said. "I have had a day, my friend. Some fool spilled tea on my measurements for Missus Alsterton's new gown, and it's completely illegible. So my assistant and I need to go up and get new measurements of her."

"That's Missus Alsterton's gown?" he asked, looking at the dress.

"This, oh, saints, no," Helene said. "This is a fitter dress to measure from. Can you imagine, they would just let me carry her gown across the street?"

"No, I could not," he said.

"Believe me, I would rather not," Helene said. "When she brings her cat to the store, it makes me sneeze something fierce. I can't imagine what it would be like in her apartments."

He chuckled. "I understand." He opened the gate and let them in. "Ninth floor west."

"A thousand blessings, sir," Jhoqull said as they entered. They went through the lobby and made their way up the stairs. "That was, in fact, interesting."

"A name, a story, and confidence," Helene said. "Mila is better at that, and Pilsen was an absolutely master in his day."

"How did you know about the cat?"

"That was the detail that got me the name," Helene said. "I just hope no one named Miss Kendish actually works at that store."

"How is that store?"

"Busy in the back rooms," Helene said. "Which made that grift I just pulled work in the first place."

"Give me a moment," Jhoqull said after a few more flights. "How tall is this cursed building?"

"I think it's ten or eleven floors. You don't have anything like this in whatever city you came from?"

"Paht'kira," Jhoqull said. "Watchtowers and beacons, yes. But nothing that people live in."

"Do you miss it?"

"I miss seeing the sunrise over the bay," Jhoqull said. "The light, the land, it's golden in a way you never see here. And that there's no winter there."

"I hear we're in for a rough one this year. At least, that's what Jarret says."

"And this man you're marrying," Jhoqull said, pointing at the stolen dress. "What would he say of all this business?"

"Best not to think about it," Helene said. "Let's get to the roof."

The roof was pretty easy to reach, and Helene found a perch spot looking southwest. She got out her lensescope and started looking.

"Would you want to shoot from here?"

"Saints, no. Even with the Rainmaker, I couldn't hit anything near the museum. But the view is impressive, no?"

"I suppose," Jhoqull said.

Helene got out the map Mila had given her. "Mila wanted to know how the streets flowed, the best routes to escape from the museum. And we can see all that from up here."

"Indeed," Jhoqull said. "And there are quite a few people and carriages clustered at the intersection by the bridge."

"That bridge is a mess," Helene said.

"Too much of a choke point for a good escape."

"All the roads are a tangled mess between the museum and the water," Helene said. "Streets at odd angles, dead ends, not a good straight run to the river."

"Saint Orrick Street?" Jhoqull offered, pointing at the map.

"To get to the bridge, which—"

"Choke point, yes."

Helene didn't like it. "I don't see a good way if we have to run."

"I concur," Jhoqull said. "But that is the information Mila needs, yes?"

"Right," Helene said. She looked through her scope, and made some notes on the map. Jhoqull tapped her shoulder and reached for the scope. Helene passed it over. "You seeing something?"

"Perhaps nothing," Jhoqull said. "But there are a few dockhouses on the river that are also livery stables."

"You have an idea?"

"Not yet," Jhoqull said. "If you've learned what you can, we should get back to the street, and check for those sewer entrances Mila wanted us to find."

"Joy," Helene said. "She puts us on that, while she walks through the museum."

"It seems to be the right tasks for the right people, given who we have," Jhoqull said with a shrug. "Come, let us be about it. And return the dress."

"Yes, return the dress," Helene said. No need to get some innocent stranger fired over that. The last thing Helene needed was that on her conscience. It was already heavy enough.

MILA FOUND HERSELF HOLDING HER BREATH SEVERAL TIMES IN THE Druth History Museum. It really was an incredible place, like nothing she had ever seen before. Even on the University of Maradaine campus, where she had fully explored the library, as well as some of the archives, there was nothing that matched the majesty of the museum.

She had nearly forgotten the purpose of coming here, she was so entranced. The front hall—a wide, sweeping, circular gallery with winding stairs up to the second floor—had portraits of all the kings of Druthal for the past twelve hundred years. There were rooms dedicated to the Imperial years before the Free Era, to various wars, the Reunification, everything. There was a wall-size portrait of all the Grand Ten together, which was at odds with what Mila had read in terms of historical accuracy.

Their whole walk through, Mila kept a map in her head. Doors, rooms, stairs, windows. Guard spots, checkpoints. Discreetly mounted mirrors giving a wide view of the room. Spiderwire catches and jangle bells. Lockdown gates between galleries.

She had wandered away from Kai and Raych to check out the water closets as possible points of entry, as well as examine a few doors marked for employees to see how easy they were to open. She figured she was the best one of the three of them to take that risk. She and Kaiana had worn University of Maradaine uniforms, which Mila felt made them both effectively invisible, though Mila more so than Kaiana could be.

Mila had dressed Raych so she looked more professional class, in one of her Jendly Marskin outfits, and told her to make her own walk through away from them. It was best not to have her seen with them. Her and Kaiana together, any guard seeing them—and there were guards in dark blue suits, looking more like lawyers than sticks—they were a pair of students, that didn't look strange at all.

After getting a sense of those possibilities—there was a back room that connected to the loading dock—she found Kaiana in a room dedicated to the Island Wars. She was standing in front of one display: a woven basket and fishing net, in a glass case.

"What's this?" Mila asked.

Kaiana pointed to the plaque. "Native goods made by the Gotapa of Bintral Island."

"Is that . . . ?" Mila let it hang.

"It's entirely possible my mother made these," Kaiana said softly. "There's a display there showing the eight different battles on Bintral, and then the final evacuation. That's when my father took me."

"Are you all right?" Mila asked. "Should we get out of here, or . . ."

Kaiana shook her head. "It's fine, I just . . . come on, we want to be in here."

Kaiana led Mila into the Feature Gallery, a grand octagonal room, which was highlighting the Shattered Kingdoms, the period where Druthal was as many as twelve different nations, depending on who was winning which war at the time. Raych was in here, really looking at the Noile Pentaptych taking up one entire wall.

Four doorways into this room, all of them with crashdown gates. Blue-suited guards at each doorway. Watch mirrors in the ceiling. And a glass sunwindow, with wrought-iron lattice bars over it. Mila had already paced it out—the shortest route in or out was at least three rooms, and thus three places for gates to be dropped, and that was assuming one of the employee doors led straight to the loading dock.

She and Kaiana walked up to the Pentaptych, standing near Raych.

"You two head out," she whispered.

"And what are you going to do?" Raych asked quietly.

"Change clothes, do another pass through here, then watch what happens when they close at seven bells," Mila said. "I'll be back at the Gadgeterium tonight, and we'll break down what we know."

"Right," Raych said. Her attention was still on the Pentaptych. "It really is something powerful, isn't it?"

Mila wasn't sure what to say to that. The paintings were impressive, easily the boldest in color, evocative in style, of any that were shown here. "Take different routes out when you leave, take your time. Give no sense you were overly focused on this room."

"You think they noticed?" Raych asked.

"Probably not, but best not to push it."

Raych and Kaiana both walked away from the Pentaptych, Raych moving out of the room completely, and Kaiana lingering around glass cases about the Republic of Acora.

Mila took one more look at the paintings, and then looked up at the ceiling, confirming her suspicion. Another crashdown gate, just in front of this wall. So these paintings could be locked off from the rest of the room, probably just with a lever release. Another wrinkle in the plan she was forming.

It wasn't a plan, not yet. Just pieces of ideas, but she would have to scout the building more. It depended how many guards worked the night. But every instinct screamed that it would be nearly impossible to get these five paintings out of here.

MILA WALKED INTO THE APARTMENT OVER THE GADGETERIUM. "All right, this isn't looking great, so tell me what you know."

Helene and Jhoqull were at the table, both using Verci's tools. Helene was tuning a crossbow, while Jhoqull had a different device that Mila couldn't recognize. Kaiana was sprawled out on the floor with the charts and maps.

"There's no good road to get home," Helene said. "Bridges are hard choke points, and if we have anything where we need to shake pursuit, that's a loss."

"Unless we stay on the north side to cool it down," Mila said.

"We'd need a safehouse to cool in," Helene said. "Do you have one?"

"No," Mila said. "And we don't have a lot of budget to play with on this, right, and . . . where is Raych?"

"She went to the bakery after the museum," Kaiana said. "Said to meet her here."

"She may have also stopped by her sister's home," Jhoqull offered. "She has barely seen her son these past few days."

Mila couldn't begrudge Raych doing that. "It's fine. But, all right, we should see if we can get some sort of safehouse on the north side, at least as a place to stash gear, lay low."

"It's not a full safehouse, but there is a dockhouse with a livery stable and boat slips."

"So we could keep horses and a boat there?" Mila asked. "Do we have either?"

"There are Ken's horses at the inn, but we could rent horses there, as a way to pull a carriage without having to worry about his horses getting stuck on the north side."

"Will it be a problem using strange horses?" Kaiana asked.

"I can manage."

"But," Helene said, "if we can get to the river at the dockhouse, we can then go by boat across the river, no choke."

"No choke, but yes, River Patrol."

"If it comes to that."

"I'd prefer not to have any pursuit, regardless," Mila said. She pulled some papers out of her pocket. "There're no great paths from the outside to the paintings. And once the museum closes, they latch all the doors, drop all the crashdown gates for the night, and keep guards at every door."

"You're thinking a night job?"

"Best chance is a quiet in and out. Ideally through the sunwindow, but that's got serious metal covering the windows. Plus the paintings have their own crashdown gate probably protecting them."

"That's a lot of metal to cut," Helene said.

"So how would we do that?" Kaiana said.

"That's the challenge," Mila said. She looked down at the various gadgets on the floor. "One of these is a line climber, so I think we can get up to the roof with little trouble. From there—can we get into Almer's shop?"

"Maybe," Helene offered. "But would you know what to look for?"

"What are you thinking?" Kaiana asked.

"One of the acids, burn through the grates?"

"Could work," Helene said.

"What could work?" Raych asked as she came in the door. She was carrying her baby, and something about her seemed almost lighter.

"The room with the paintings has a sunwindow, but it's got a heavy iron grate. I'm thinking a midnight crack, climb up to the roof, burn through the grate, drop down, pull out with the paintings, and make off in the night, hoping you don't set off any jangle bells in the process."

"Sounds like a lot of problem points," Raych said.

"It definitely does, and we've got, what, three nights before the paintings are taken away?"

"Right," Raych said. "But we are doing the job in the early evening, two nights from now."

That confused Mila. "Why are we doing that?"

Raych handed the baby to Helene—who didn't seem to realize she was going to take it until it was too late—and then pulled a paper out of her pocket. She handed it to Mila.

"The day after tomorrow, there's a grand reception in the museum.

Several of the elite of Maradaine will be there, doors open at six bells. Celebrating the art of the Shattered Kingdoms Era, with the Noile Pentaptych as the highlight."

"You want to do it then?" Mila asked, completely confused. "But there will be hundreds of people there."

"Exactly," Raych said with a sly smile. "So there will be two things there. First of them is confusion."

Kaiana snapped her fingers. "A lot of people means the guards have their eyes on a lot."

"Easy to distract, sure, but that's still a hard play to make," Mila said. "And how are we even to get in there?"

"Because of the second thing," Raych said. "There will be food."

CHAPTER EIGHT

Raych was feeling the heat of the other four women staring at her. "All right, break this down," Mila said. "How does that help us?"

"We have two big assets here that we've been ignoring," Raych said. "The bakery and the cheese shop."

"Because with those, you could provide food for the party, and that's an in," Kaiana said. "Is that right?"

"I can see that," Mila said, scratching at her chin. "But surely they would have hired caterers already, right?"

"They have," Raych said. "And when I was working my way out of the museum, I found myself walking near a couple of the administrators talking about the party and the catering plans for it. And they've hired three different companies to cover everything."

Mila's eyes went wide; she understood. "That's really good."

"Why is that good?" Jhoqull asked.

Raych smiled. "Three different companies doing the job means that no single person will be in charge of every employee working the party. Each of them will have their own people."

"And," Mila said, "anyone who spots someone they don't recognize will assume they work for a different company."

"No one will notice a few more women in the right outfits," Raych said confidently.

Helene chuckled. "So we need the right outfits, maybe some paperwork?"

"What are the three companies?" Mila asked.

"Delilah's Delights, The Savory Ladle, and Pickled Perfection," Raych said. "All north side."

"All right, Helene and I will go out tonight and do a crack job on those places, get uniforms and paperwork."

"We will?" Helene asked.

"Come on, you and I, we can do that in our sleep," Mila said. "It's not like any of them will have spiderwire or crashdown gates."

Helene shrugged. "It's not like I'm getting much sleep anyway."

"There's a girl," Mila said.

"That gets us inside," Jhoqull said. "And then?"

"Also they're bringing in more guards to work the event. So there would be guards who won't know each other. Those suits, we should be able to get something that looks just right."

"They're pretty simple, right," Mila said. "But I don't think any of us could pull that off. I didn't see any women guards."

"I was thinking Ia," Raych said.

Helene screwed her face in thought. "She's rutting tall enough, sure, and keeps her hair short. You'd have to wrap her chest pretty damn tight, though. Ain't no way she'd be confused for a man otherwise."

"So we have Ia pretending to be a guard, us with the food," Jhoqull said. "And where does that get us besides in the building?"

"I'm not completely sure yet," Raych said, looking to Mila. "Here's where I need your brain, but . . . this is my main idea. When I bring the pastries and breads out from the kitchen to the shop floor, I have a large rolling rack. You've seen it, right?"

"I suppose," Mila said.

"It's designed to carry several of my large baking trays at once." She went out into the hall and got the one she had brought from the bakery and put down so she could open the door. She brought it back in the apartment and held it up for them. "How big would you say that is?"

Mila and Kaiana both came closer, and looked at each other, and back to Raych.

"That looks about the exact size of each of the paintings," Kaiana said.

"With the right plan—some distraction and confusion—we could just roll the paintings out the doors."

"The only question remains," Jhoqull said pointedly, "what happens once we are outside those doors? How far can we get?"

"Working on that," Mila said.

Raych put the tray down, and took her child back from Helene. She needed to keep thinking as well. This had to work, they had to pull it off. It might be Verci's only chance. It terrified her to wonder what he was going through right now.

Helene's apartment was so quiet. She hadn't been opening the shop for the past couple days, and without the familiar sounds of Julien lumbering about, humming as he prepared sandwiches, the emptiness of her home was thick as curdled cream.

She had told herself she was staying with Raych during all this for Raych's sake, to help her get through this without Verci. But she needed that sense of other people around her just as much.

She wouldn't have even come back to the apartment tonight if she didn't need her gear to make the run at the catering shops with Mila tonight. She didn't know why Mila wanted her to go along, but she supposed the kid needed someone to watch her back, and Helene was the only one who had any experience with this sort of thing. Not that Helene had much experience with plain old windowcrack jobs. Burgling wasn't exactly her skill, but she had been along for a few. Usually as the lookout, covering the escapes. But she could still climb a gutter and crack a window as needed. Almost no one grew up in North Seleth without learning those vital skills.

Dark coat, slacks, boots, she put those in a knapsack. She switched to her dark leather gloves, and then realized she hadn't worn those in some time. She had no false finger in place in that one. She sighed. Hopefully, no one would see her tonight, there was no reason to hide her mutilation.

She contemplated her crossbows. Tonight was just supposed to be a couple slip-in jobs. Quiet and nimble. The hiphangers were best for that. She checked them over, put them in the knapsack, and closed it up. That should do.

She was nearly out the door when there was a familiar series of raps upon it.

Helene knew that knock all too well.

She put the rucksack in the closet and opened the door.

"I took a chance and came by," Covrane said. He held up a newsprint-wrapped bundle. "Crackle and tang?"

Helene chuckled despite herself. He was so damnably good-hearted. "I should eat," she said. "Come in."

He brought the bundle to the table and unwrapped it. Covrane knew how much she loved the batter-fried fish sandwiches from the shop around the corner from his stationhouse, since they had perfected their version of the spiced cabbage dressing that made the damn things irresistible. She and Julien had tried in vain to replicate it, but never could get it right.

"This is something of a peace offering," Covrane said as she sat down.

"I didn't know we were at war," she said.

"We're not, but . . . I still have absolutely nothing to report on what's happened to Julien and the others, and I—" he stammered.

"It's all right," she said.

"I feel guilty, I've let you down."

"You really haven't," she said. "I know that . . . this trouble is far beyond any of us."

"You know?" he asked, with a bit of a point to his voice. "Have you learned something?"

"Nothing solid," she said.

"Yeah, but . . . if you have something, maybe it's something I could use to learn more. Find out what happened to them."

"And then what?" she asked. She sounded harsher than she had intended it too, and took another bite of her sandwich, hoping to cover up her anger with it.

"And then . . . well, you'd know what you could do. Have some options, I suppose."

She chewed silently for a moment and swallowed hard. "Folks like me never have options, Jarret. That's why things like this happen."

"Folks like you?"

"Can we just eat?" she asked. "I am really glad you brought this over."

"But folks like you, I mean . . ." He sputtered for a moment and put his sandwich down. "You are going to be married to an officer in the Constabulary. I have some small amount of influence, and connection. Once we find out what happened, we can talk to the Justice Advocate Office, to a private lawyer, blazes, I have friends in the Protector's Office, they can talk to the Archduchy, and . . ."

"And what? Julien has been arrested, Jarret. Same with Asti and Verci, and the others, and they have been vanished. Out of the legitimate system you're talking about. They aren't in there."

"So what do you mean?"

"I mean that . . . that . . ." She took another bite and mumbled the rest under her breath. "That a legitimate system isn't the answer."

"So something illegitimate, then?"

"Who do you think I am?" she asked him. "Who do you think I've always been?"

"Listen, I've never . . . I have *never* interrogated you about your past, nor the pasts of your friends. And let me tell you, making these inquiries, the name 'Rynax' raised some eyebrows. There is history there with them, with their father."

"And their father leads to mine. And Julien's. It's all the same history in this part of town."

"I didn't say that."

"Then you made a choice not to look."

He sighed and looked down at the table, unable to meet her eyes. "Maybe."

"Then, Jarret?" she asked. "If you love me, keep making that choice. Keep making it for a few more days."

"Why are you asking this of me?"

"Because while I love you, Julien is my whole life, and you need to understand that."

"I do, of course," he said.

"And I am going to do whatever I have to do get him home, do you understand? Whatever it takes."

"Hel, you can't mean—"

She took off her glove and put her four-fingered hand on the table. Forced him to look at it. Forced him to understand just an ounce of what she had endured, and what she still would.

"Whatever it takes, Jarret. Even if it breaks your heart. Even if it breaks mine."

He was silent for an excruciating two minutes. "We . . . we should finish these before they get too cold. And maybe some ciders? But I think that's all I have time for tonight. I'm sure . . . I'm sure you have plenty to take care of tonight."

Helene relaxed in her chair. "That's a great idea." She took another bite of her sandwich. "In a few days, if all goes well, we'll have some real answers, and we can put this all behind us."

He nodded and went to the icebox, getting the ciders. "That sounds really good. If everything works out, you and Julien should come have dinner at my mother's."

"That would be wonderful," she said.

He sat down and took hold of her hand. This was the first time she had ever left her hand bare in front of him, let him hold it. "I do love you, Helene, and I trust that you know what's the best thing for you and yours. If you need anything, anything in my power . . ."

"I know, Jarret," she said, holding up her bottle to his. "Here's hoping I won't."

She knew, from here on out, if she did need something in his power, that meant things had already gone horribly wrong. And she refused to let that happen.

CHAPTER NINE

Raych was in the bakery at dawn. Great prophets, she hadn't been in here for a few days, and there were already paper jobs pasted completely over front door, as if the store had been abandoned for months. But she didn't have time to worry about that. In a few days, everything would be back to normal. In a few days, everything would go fine. Verci would be home, and the bakery and the Gadgeterium would be open for business again, and everything would be fine.

She wouldn't open the bakery today, but there was plenty to do. She needed to take an inventory of what she had in her stores, and then figure out what she could make with what she had on hand, add in what supplies she could get today—or tomorrow morning at the latest—and then write that up and get it to Mila so she could forge the paperwork she needed, and then also start the baking process and...

She sat down on the floor of the bakery, too overwhelmed to even move. How in the blazes was she going to get all this done in the next two days? The other ladies were handling a lot—Jhoqull on the carriage and Verci's gadgets, Helene on getting Ia to come along, Mila and Kai on forging papers and uniforms, and she . . . she just had to bake.

But it was too much.

"Come on, let's see what we can find for today—oh!"

Raych looked up to see her sister, carrying Corsi on one hip. "Lian, what are you . . ."

"Are we opening today?" Lian asked. "This little man was having trouble sleeping, so since I was up, I thought we'd come down here to—"

Raych jumped to her feet and took her son out of her sister's arms. "Oh my, I've missed you, baby," she said, kissing his sweet face. "Have you been good for your aunt? Have you been waking her up?"

He responded by grabbing her face and squeezing her cheeks affectionately.

"He's been lovely," Lian said. "A bit fussy tonight, probably missing his mother."

"And she missed him," Raych said. She sighed. "But there's going to be a few more days before . . ." She didn't know how to finish that sentence.

"Hey, hey," Lian said, touching her face. "If you need a few more days, I'm here, whatever it is."

"Whatever it is," Raych repeated. "Prophets, if you only knew."

"You can tell me," Lian said. "Do you need anything from me? Honestly, whatever it is. I know your husband is in some real trouble, and I know that I've not been the most welcoming of sisters to him—"

"Not at all," Raych said.

"But he is your husband, so he's my brother," Lian said. "And so is his brother, even if he is a lunatic. He's still our lunatic."

"This is new from you."

Lian chuckled. "I was in a market a week ago, and someone was giving me trouble about the price, and this woman came over and said, 'Don't you swindle her, she's kin to the Rynax boys.' And the shopkeep gasped, and dropped a whole crown off his price. 'Let Asti know I did that for you.'"

Raych chuckled. "That happens a lot."

"And I said, 'I don't want a favor because you're afraid of Asti Rynax.' Very haughty, I'm sure I sounded. And the fellow paled, saying, 'Afraid? No, ma'am, just grateful. He saved my daughter, saved my shop in that trouble.'"

"Folks around here know," Raych said.

"And I'm learning," Lian said. "So what do you need?"

Raych handed her son back to Lian. "I'm going to tell you, but you swear, swear on our mother's blood, that you will not tell another soul. You will take this to your very test, do you hear?"

"Yes," Lian said, without a hint of equivocation.

"So, Verci and Asti and some other friends were arrested."

"Right, I knew that, but why?"

"We don't know why, but we think they are being held in Quarrygate, maybe under false names."

"How is that possible?"

"It's just an idea, and it's based on a lot of rumors and whispers. But I believe it, it *fits*."

"All right."

"So we—Helene and Jhoqull and I—we went to Missus Holt for help."

"Who is that?"

"Basically, anything gray in this part of town, anything that the law isn't a part of, Missus Holt has her finger in it. And she's known the boys from way back."

"Hmm," Lian said. "So the kind of help that won't come cheap."

Raych started to laugh. "No, not cheap at all. She's made a ridiculous demand, and I . . . I said yes."

Lian sighed and nodded her head. "So what did you say yes to?"

"Stealing five paintings from the Druth History Museum?" Raych said, racing the words out as fast as she could.

Lian's eyes went wide, and she bit her lip hard. Raych watched her as Lian stepped back, like she was trying to find any words to say, or just get her breath.

Finally, she said, "And how, exactly, are you expected to do that?"

"By infiltrating an event as caterers, so I have to bake a lot of pastries by tomorrow to deliver in the rolling racks which we'll use to get the paintings out?"

"Oh?" Lian asked. "So, to be clear, this is a pastry baking job?"

"It definitely is, and I have to get working . . ."

Lian had already put Corsi in his playpen and was grabbing her apron. "We need to get working. There's no way you'll be able to do this on your own."

"Lian, are you sure . . ."

"This is a very deep problem that you are in, dear sister," Lian said. "And you reminded me just now that, sooner or later, I will face my test before God. I will not stand before my maker and say that I abandoned my sister when she was at her lowest." She kissed Raych on the cheek, which was already wet with tears. "Come on, let's get to work."

Raych had been quite pleased with how the work had been going. It felt good to be back in the kitchen, Lian by her side, Corsi happily playing or napping without any care in the world. Almost back to normal. She nearly expected Verci to just stroll in the back door as if nothing had been amiss, that infuriating grin on his face.

She had not expected Mila to pop out of the pantry as if she had been hiding there all day.

"We have a problem," Mila said as she came out.

"Sweet prophets!" Lian shouted, almost dropping the pastry tray.

"Oh!" Mila said, seeing Lian. "I mean, there's not a problem, it's just—"

"She knows," Raych told her. "Where the blazes did you come from?"

"This bakery was the Old Lady's, remember? There's all kinds of passages in and out of her old safehouse down there."

"I thought Verci locked those down."

"He did," Mila said. "But I helped him do it, so I know how to unlock them."

"Yes, but why—"

"Because we have a problem. Right now there's a couple constables —and maybe a marshal, I'm not sure—sitting in a wagon outside the Gadgeterium."

"What does that mean?" Lian asked.

"I'm not entirely sure, but I wouldn't risk going in there, at least not through the front door."

"So I can't go home?" Raych asked.

"I wouldn't," Mila said. "There's also two fellows keeping an eye on this door. Not in uniform, but they've got that stick feeling to them, you know?"

"I trust you on this," Raych said. "So we can't leave?"

"Not through the door or the alley, but I've got a way out for you down there." She sighed heavily. "I'm afraid that's not all."

"Where else?"

"Helene's shop, and Jhoqull's forge."

"Does this mean someone is onto us?" Helene asked.

"We're going to prison!" Lian cried.

"We've not done anything but make pastries," Raych said. "So calm down. Is that all?"

"Near as I can tell, no one is watching me or Kaiana, so whoever is keeping tabs, it's about the three of you, not our plan."

Raych pulled another tray of perfect pastries out of the oven. "So what do we do?"

"Well, we were going to meet at the Gadgeterium to break down the plan, make sure everyone knows their job, make sure we have everything we need. We still need to do that. Plus probably just lay low for the night."

"Right, but where?"

"My house?" Lian offered.

"What about Hal?"

"Hal will have to accept it."

"That can work if we can get word out," Raych said. "How do we do that?"

"Kai had an idea of how to get Jhoqull out of her place without being noticed or followed, so I'm going to trust her on that. I've still got to get to Helene somehow, and then I'll get all our gear out of the Gadgeterium."

"I set all the traps and alarms when I left."

"Again, I know where they are," Mila said. "If you're ready to go, I can lead you through the tunnels and get you out near Elk."

"Just about done," Raych said. "Help put those on the cooling racks, and we can start covering the rest up for tomorrow."

Lian looked very concerned. "How are we going to load this all up for the mission—"

"Job," Raych and Mila said in unison.

"Job, yes, if we can't get out the door, bring the wagon in the alley and all?"

"Working on that," Mila said. "But we need to hurry so I can get to the others with the change in plans. Once we're done and out, can you get Ia?"

Raych nodded. "You sure we need her?"

"I'm not happy about it, but she is damn perfect for this."

"Fine. Seven bells at Lian's house. 61 Colt Road."

"And me?" Lian asked.

"Tell Hal you're having several guests for dinner."

MILA HAD NEVER BEEN TO LIAN'S HOUSE BEFORE, WHICH WAS A perfectly respectable narrowhouse on Colt, looking about the same as every other house on this block, each one crammed in together with barely a breath of an alleyway between it and its neighbor.

A good portion of her afternoon involved getting a warning to Helene, and then getting together the gear and supplies they would need, and stashing them in the old safehouse they had established with Josie, back when they had all been together. Asti had declared that place as burned, unsafe, but since they were working for Josie again on this one, so Mila figured there was no risk. It was the most useful place they could use right now, and practicality had to win the day. There were still supplies for disguises, some of Verci's gadgets—including one that was perfect for tonight—and one of the carriages that he and Kennith had been working on.

When she had met up with Kaiana and Jhoqull—Kai had gotten her past her watchdogs with help from a couple of Jho's cousins and a pretty simple outfit swap trick—and told them of the changes in plans. Jhoqull was very excited about the carriage in the safehouse.

"That is perfect, I must go there immediately."

Mila didn't question it, and told them how to get in.

It was nearly half past seven bells when she got to Lian's house, having collected the last things from the Gadgeterium in the cover of night. She had taken an indirect route to make sure she hadn't picked up a tail, changed clothes to her school uniform behind an alley backhouse, and then again walked a full lap around Colt Road to make sure no one was watching or following. If they were, they were good enough for her not to notice, so she went up the stoop and knocked.

The door flew open, a portly man with a ruddy face there, holding Corsi on his hip.

"Another! Please tell me you're the last."

"I don't know who's here already, sir, so I can't answer that."

"At least you look respectable," he said, craning his neck outside to look around. "Saints only know what the neighbors must be thinking right now."

"Hopefully nothing, sir," she said. "May I?"

"Yes, yes, let's not stand here making a scene," he said. "Come in, miss—?"

"Kendish. Mila Kendish." She realized she had slipped into her University accent, which was absurd, but had become habit whenever she was in uniform.

He led her into the house, where the rest of the crew were already sitting around a table, which was loaded with food and wine bottles, as well as notes and sketches.

"Sorry I'm late," Mila said. "I was securing the last of what we need."

Helene got up from the table, handing Mila a glass of wine. "And we appreciate that. Especially me."

"You?" Mila asked.

"I think the extra scrutiny is on me," Helene said. Lowering to a whisper. "From Covrane."

"Are . . . are you all right?"

"It'll be fine," Helene said, her face saying otherwise. "Sit."

"All right, talk me through it," Kaiana was saying, looking over the notes on the table as she slathered soft cheese on her bread.

"Who is this one?" Ia asked, pointing at Kaiana. She was looming in the corner of the room, like a great blond statue.

"I'm the common sense," Kaiana said.

"She's probably done as many stupid things in the streets of Aventil as all of us have here," Mila said. "I've worked with her, and she's sharp as knives."

Kaiana smiled. "And I'm used to folks charging in with no plan, so this is a delight."

"Her job is to look over everything and tell us what's stupid," Raych said.

"And she knows what's stupid?" Lian asked. She still looked terrified.

Lian's husband walked through to the kitchen, muttering the whole way. "Folks from so many places here, like a customs check."

"Thank you, Hal," Lian said to her husband, in a tone that seemed to quiet him.

Kaiana scowled at him, but then looked to Lian. "I've survived quite a bit of stupid, so I have a good eye for it."

"Fair enough," Ia said. "So give us the plan, *sjat,* so the island girl can tell us how dumb it is."

"Right," Raych said. "So we have a guard uniform for Ia, caterer uniforms for me, Lian, and Kaiana, and a fancy dress for Mila and Helene."

"And swap clothes hidden under those outfits," Mila said. "And Jhoqull—"

"I have three different outfits, it seems," she said. "I will spend as much time changing clothes as anything."

"Mila comes in front with the forged invite," Raych said. "And she's got the smokers and flashers strapped under her dress."

"So you're carrying those in?" Ia asked.

"The advantage of us being in fancy dress," Mila said. "Hel and I are going to have a couple Rynax gadgets strapped to our legs."

"And none of the guards will search you there, *sjat.*"

Raych continued, "Ia is there first, then the three of us arrive next in the bakery wagon with our pastry trays, which we bring in the service entrance. That's where the other caterers will enter."

"So how do we not get called out by the real caterers?" Kaiana asked. "We're wearing their uniforms, right? They should know we aren't working for them."

"There's three different companies hired to provide the food and serve," Mila said. "But I learned that all of them will be dressed the same, because the organizers want it to look seamless. So on our end, that means the people working it expect not to know everyone else."

"Really?" Kaiana asked. "Surely someone is overseeing it . . ."

"I know this one," Lian said. "I did a few jobs like that back before I married Hal—for that friend of father's, the one with the strange eye?"

"Mister Kenickila," Raych said.

"Right. In practice, there is a floor boss directing things, but usually they don't know who is who either, and it's a lot of just working with strangers and doing your best to get each other's rhythm."

"Head down, keep busy, if someone asks for something, say 'Right away' and get out of their eyesight," Raych offered.

Kaiana nodded her acceptance.

"From there, we load the trays onto the racks, and roll it through like we're going to the main buffet. In the rest of the gallery, Mila and Helene plant smokers and boom powder drops."

"Right, when those go off, we all move," Kaiana said.

"Ia helps drive folks away from the sound and smoke, into the gallery with the paintings, here." Raych points on the map. "Mila will be yelling about fires, and help drive folks in there."

"Everyone?" Kaiana asked.

Mila spoke up. "Just enough people for witnesses, enough for chaos. Then Jhoqull makes her move from the roof."

"I have climbed up there with this contraption," she said, holding up a device. "And I attach another to bars on the sunwindow, which will break the window in a dramatic shattering of glass."

"Helene's cue," Raych said.

"It seems overly dramatic," Helene said.

"It needs to be. It needs to scare people and keep their attention as the crashdown gates come down."

"How do we know they will?" Kaiana asked.

"They're supposed to whenever something like this happens. In a pinch, Ia pulls it herself. The point is, that gallery is locked down, and Helene puts on the show."

"Fancy dress off, mask on," Helene said. "It's ludicrous."

"She holds up the whole place with her crossbows, while Jhoqull sends down the cracker."

"Another of Verci's devices," Kaiana confirmed.

"That'll rip off the gate protecting the paintings," Raych said. "She takes them down, wraps them in a bundle, and from up on the roof, Jhoqull uses the springwinch to fly Hel and the bundle up through the window, and they belay to the street, where the spring-powered carriage awaits."

"A big messy robbery," Kaiana said. "Surely will get the guards and Constabulary in pursuit."

"That's exactly the idea," Raych said. "They'll pursue the spring carriage, flying off mad down the street with no one in it. Loaded with boom powder, it will explode in a fiery wreck several blocks away."

"And you three have swapped the paintings for the pastry trays, which are now on the tray rack," Mila said, as Hal came back through, muttering and shaking his head more.

"We have to do that in the cover of more smoke bombs?" Lian asked.

"We should practice that some," Kaiana said.

"Right, do it blindfolded a few times," Mila said. "And then as Helene escapes, I make a screaming scene—and I'm sure other guests will as well—and Ia opens the crashdown gates if no other guards do, and makes sure the rack gets out."

"And while she and everyone else cry and shout about this dangerous woman who robbed the paintings, we quietly roll the pastry rack back out to the loading dock and onto our real escape wagon, where Jhoqull and Helene are waiting."

"Well," Kaiana said. "I've done stupider, I can say that."

"You think it'll work?" Lian asked.

"A lot rides on her doing her part," Kaiana said, looking to Ia. "What's her motivation in this? We need her to let us all out, right?"

"Ia?" Raych asked. "Why are you here?"

"I work for the Old Lady, and she wants the paintings. If I don't help, then no paintings, *y jorar*? I am doing what the Old Lady needs, this is what she needs."

"Good enough for me," Raych said. "So, if everything goes well, the seven of us . . ."

"Eight, I think."

Mila looked to the new voice by the entryway, as all heads whipped in that direction, where stood a woman, resplendent in richly embroidered green; everything from her boots to her cap absolutely screamed of wealth.

"What?" Raych almost shouted.

"It seems you are all pointed toward misadventure," the woman said. "And my days have been so dreadfully boring of late, I would adore a small part of that."

CHAPTER TEN

Helene couldn't believe who was standing there.

"Lady Melania?" she asked.

"Sorry, she just barged right in," Hal said, standing fecklessly behind her.

"I'm so glad you recognized me this time, dear," Lady Melania said. "You walked right past me yesterday like we weren't old friends, but I didn't make a thing of it at the time, as you seemed frightfully busy. But I soon realized you were up to some delightful foolery, and I was determined to discover more. And I decided now was as good a moment to announce my intention to throw my hat in with you."

She took off her cap and tossed it on the table.

"Hel, who is this woman?" Raych asked.

"I am being dreadfully rude, forgive, I so rarely get to have any fun," Lady Melania said. "Lady Melania Landron of Canthen Hall."

Lian got to her feet and attempted a stumbling sort of curtsey.

"Oh, none of that," Lady Melania said. "Of course I know Helene, we met in the forest a few months ago, and you, young lady, were at Lord Henterman's party in disguise. I've not properly met the rest, but I did see you on campus trimming hedges last spring."

"I mean, I would have been," Kaiana said, "but how could you possibly remember that?"

That struck a chord with Helene. "Because she remembers everything."

"I'm glad you recalled, because, honestly," Lady Melania said, "sometimes I am astounded at how most of you even function."

"She's the one who got you and Asti out of Henterman's," Mila said.

"She's catching up, delightful," Melania said.

Raych stood up and walked warily up to Lady Melania. "So you discovered what we're doing?"

"Well, I don't know all the details, but I've worked out a bit. Helene here did a delightful little gambit the other day at the Grand when I was buying some gloves, and of course I was curious what she was doing on the north side of town."

"And you've been following me since?"

"More stalking than following. You and your friends here were taking such care to be clandestine I didn't want to ruin it for you."

"But . . . you want to help?" Raych asked, clearly incredulous. "Because, its, well . . ."

"Crime?" Melania asked, her voice rising in excitement. "I know I should be against that sort of thing, but I've at least pieced together that your cause is terribly desperate, that you are not the sort of ladies who would normally engage in this level of enterprise, and your target is the Museum of History, which means the people most hurt by your success are members of the nobility that I feel somewhat antipathetic toward. So my inclination to further your success is immense."

"I need more wine," Mila said, refilling her glass.

"So," Melania said taking Raych's hands and leading her back to the chairs, "you are at the center of this, I'm gathering. Tell me what, tell me why, tell me all."

Raych looked up at Helene. "Can we trust her? Or is she mad?"

"I think yes to both?" Helene said.

"Fair," Melania said. She looked hard at Helene, and then back at Raych. "Absolutely, there are so many things I have endured, and I cannot forget them, so madness might be a blessing. Ordeals, my friend, ordeals like you would not wish, etched upon my skull. But this is not about me, but about trouble you are in."

"My husband—" Raych said, her voice cracking.

"Her husband is . . . ?"

"Verci, the—"

"The brother of your other friend. Yes, handsome man there."

"The two of them were arrested and, we think, are in Quarrygate. The person who can help them wants five paintings at the history museum. So, we're—"

"Stealing the paintings?" Melania gasped and covered her mouth. "Delightful. Capital. Entirely for it. How can I help?"

Raych looked over to Mila. "How can she help?"

Helene poured her wine and sat down. "I think I know how."

RAYCH WOKE UP, NOT EVEN QUITE REMEMBERING HOW SHE HAD managed to fall asleep. At some point when Helene and Mila and that woman—there was no chance she was actual nobility, was there?—had kept going on about the plan, adding details to it, that she couldn't keep her eyes open any longer.

Someone must have carried her up the stairs and put her in the spare bedroom, Corsi nestled in her arms next to her.

"Morning, you," she said to him quietly. "Good to see you."

Corsi touched her face and gurgled.

"Yes, I agree," she said, and kissed his little face several times. She scooped him up and took him downstairs.

The sitting room was still a mess of plates and glasses and papers with notes. Clearly no one had taken the time to straighten up after everything was concluded. What was the conclusion? Details swirled in her memory. Mila had added some new elements to the plan, which struck Raych as overly complicated, but there had been some point made about complicated being critical for them to get away.

Raych knew that was true, understood it all—every though her consciousness had been decidedly fading by that point in the night—but she still struggled to keep it all in her head. She placed Corsi in his seat in the kitchen, and then got to work tidying the mess. The least she could do.

Lian was down after a few minutes. "We should probably leave that, there's so much to do today."

"Leave a mess in the kitchen?" Raych asked. "What has become of my sister?"

"I suppose I'm embracing degeneracy this week," Lian said. She crouched down in front of Corsi and kissed his forehead. "What's our plan for him today?"

Several choice profanities crossed Raych's mind. "He needs to be here with Hal, I suppose."

"Hal isn't going to be here," Hal said, coming into the kitchen as he buttoned up his vest. "Hal has a job he needs to go to, no matter what other shadiness is occurring today."

"Hal," Lian said sternly. "We need you to participate."

"I was accomplice enough by not calling the constables last night, thank you," he said. "Including Miss Kesser's intended! What would he think?"

"Let that be Helene's problem," Raych said. But she had seen Helene's jaw tighten every time he had been mentioned.

"I have been content to. And I am . . ." He grimaced as he settled on the right word. "Tolerant of my wife and her sister being involved in all of this, because you all insist that this is a matter of larger justice. Which, I don't understand, but *fine*."

"Good, then you can do your part by staying with Corsi."

"I still have to go to work!" Hal snapped. "I'm sorry, dear, but . . . by my saints, someone has to still do some honest labor. If for nothing else, so I can afford the lawyer you will need when you get arrested."

"I have an idea," Raych said. "Lian, you head over to the bakery, get the last parts of the work done. You remember how to get in there?"

"Yes," Lian said. She chuckled. "It's very useful! I'm going to take that route in all the time! No rain, no tough boys shouting at me."

"Good. And Hal, you work until, what, six bells?"

"Yes, that's right."

"Excellent. I'll bring Corsi over to Kimber's and ask her to watch him until then. And you will go there after work to get him, and take him back here."

"I will do what?" Hal asked, his voice going up.

"You'll get your nephew from Kimber's, like she said, Hal," Lian said.

Hal frowned. "Fine. As you say."

"Good," Lian said. "I trust you'll care for him like he was your own son."

"Yes, of course," Hal said. "I don't approve of this, but I will not neglect him." He crouched down in front of Corsi. "You and I will have an excellent night, young man."

Corsi giggled and grabbed at Hal's face.

"Excellent," Raych said, scooping him out of the chair. "Then we all have a very busy day ahead of us. So let's be about it."

KIMBER'S WAS QUIET, AS RAYCH IMAGINED IT MUST BE IN THE mornings. Kimber herself was sitting at a table in the taproom, going through her books, while a young man was organizing glasses behind the bar.

"Everything adding up?" Raych asked.

Kimber looked up and jumped to her feet, putting her arms around Raych in a tight embrace.

"Tell me what you need," Kimber whispered in her ear. "I've been so worried about you, praying for you."

"I appreciate the prayers," Raych said, returning the embrace as best she could with Corsi on her hip.

"I did not thank you for taking care of my place—taking care of me —that night. It meant a lot to me, especially since . . . since you . . ."

"It's fine," Raych said. "I had to do something to be busy."

"I understand," Kimber said. "And I'm so sorry, I was . . . I had no business being more upset than you."

"You had every business feeling what you felt," Raych said. Frankly, she didn't quite understand exactly what the relationship or arrangement was between Asti and Kimber, but it was clear they had a bond of affection, in as much as Asti could be capable of one. "You're as much family in all of this."

"Too kind for you to say," Kimber said. "Do you need something? Tea? Breakfast?"

"No, thank you," Raych said. "I do need a favor."

"It's yours."

Kimber's immediate response, her bright smile, it was a weight off of Raych's chest.

"Can you watch Corsi for the day?" Raych asked. "I have to—"

"Absolutely," Kimber said, taking him from Raych. "More than happy to, and you do not need to explain why."

"I appreciate that."

Kimber gave a sly smile. "I would imagine that my ignorance is better for everyone involved. Happy to keep it that way."

"It does make this less awkward."

"I've learned a few things keeping Asti under my roof from time to time." Kimber tickled Corsi under his chin. "You're going to be a very good boy for Auntie Kimber, yes?"

"Yes, he is," Raych said, kissing Corsi on the forehead.

"Do you know when you'll be back?" Kimber asked. "If . . . if it's not until tomorrow or . . . later . . . I understand."

"My sister's husband will be around to collect him this evening. Probably at half past six bells or so."

"Good, good," Kimber said. "Nothing to worry about, then."

"Nothing at all," Raych said. "Everything will be fine."

Kimber took Raych's hand and squeezed, warm with affection. "It will. Faith will manage."

"Thank you." She kissed Corsi one more time. "Mama loves you, little man. Be good."

She left the taproom, pulling her lips tight and trying to keep herself from crying. She didn't need to be a mess right now. She needed to focus on the tasks of the day, to achieve this mad, impossible plan, and get Verci home.

She was so intent on not crying, she didn't even notice when the Poasian man got right up to her.

"Missus Rynax," he purred. "What a glorious fortune to run into you."

"I'm very busy," she said, trying to step out of his way.

"I am certain, yes, you surely must have quite a lot on your mind."

"Thank you," she said, continuing to walk away.

He kept pace with her. "Thus I fully understand that you've elected not to procure spices for your business from my shop. My . . . inventory is not to everyone's taste."

"Correct."

"But should you find a need, please send someone to speak with me. Your husband's brother, for example. I would definitely enjoy speaking with him. Very soon, hopefully."

Raych stopped and spun back to him. "Are you cruel, sir? Or just an idiot?"

That stopped him, and his porcelain expression cracked with genuine surprise. "I do not believe either, ma'am."

"Whatever your game is today, you must know that Asti isn't available," she said.

"I know he's been avoiding me."

"He's been arrested. And vanished in the process."

The Poasian fellow made some ugly noises in his native tongue. "Deeply inconvenient."

"I'm so sorry it inconveniences you, sir," she said.

"Me, him, the city, the world," he said. "I was already quite concerned, and if circumstances are in motion, then it's rather urgent."

Raych sighed. "If you have some message for Asti, please, drop your subterfuge and tell me plainly."

"I'm afraid subterfuge is all I have right now," he said. "But I can do something plain."

He took out a notebook and charcoal stylus from his pocket and wrote a few words down. He tore the page out and handed it to her.

"What is this?" she asked, looking at the Poasian script.

"Next time you see Asti, give that to him."

"What if I never see him?" she asked. "What if something terrible happened to him?"

"Then I advise you go about your business with joy, Missus Rynax," he said. "For we could face deeply dark days very soon."

He tapped his head in an odd salute, and went off.

Raych shoved the paper in her pocket. It was the least of her concerns right now. And she could only imagine it would be the least of Asti's as well.

"ALL RIGHT, WHERE ARE WE WITH ALL THE THINGS?" MILA ASKED AS she came into the old safehouse. Everyone else was already there, which made her a little upset. She had wanted to be there earlier, double-check everything herself, but she didn't think she could also miss her morning classes. The best way to get away with something like this was to treat the day of the gig like it was a normal day.

"You're late," Helene said. She was stripped down to her chemise and skivs, strapping gadgets onto her thigh with Lady Melania offering advice.

Lady Melania. That was something that Mila still couldn't wrap her head around. But it did give them a lot of options. Part of the challenge of Mila's plan was that it required putting several key elements they would need for the night into position, and Jhoqull would have had do have done it. So much of the original plan put a lot of different tasks on Jhoqull's shoulders.

Lady Melania had relieved some of that, as she was able to hire porters and drivers to perform various innocuous tasks that they would never suspect were part of the plan.

"I had classes this morning," Mila said.

"Good for you, darling," Lady Melania said, as she was having her dress done up by a woman Mila had never seen before.

"Who is that?" Mila asked.

"This is Tarena, my lady's maid. There's no way we could get into these outfits correctly without her."

"And that's . . . all right?" Mila asked, looking to Helene, and then to Raych, who was working with her sister to stack trays of pastries.

"She says it is," Raych said, her voice more than a little strained.

Lady Melania looked to her maid. "Tarena, are you all right assisting with this criminal plan?"

"As you need, mistress," Tarena said. She looked up to Mila. "I am exceedingly well compensated by my lady, and she has earned my loyalty with blood. If she told me she was marching into the blazes to fight every sinner, I would dress and arm her just the same."

"Well then," Helene said.

"This is my bespoke battle gown," Lady Melania said. "It's designed for me to duel in."

"And if my lady is not properly dressed, she could be injured," Tarena said.

"So she is your *avubhap*," Jhoqull said. "When I was Jhoqull-Ta, I served as *avubhap* for Bajant-Kla, keeping her blades sharp and buckling her into her armor."

"Apt comparison," Lady Melania said.

"So, you're nearly dressed," Mila said. "I imagine Helene and I need to work on that."

"I am ready," Ia said, strolling over. She was in a guard's uniform, and however she bound herself under the coat, between that and the cap covering her hair, she certainly could pass as a man. "I can help you dress."

Kaiana, in her server uniform, came over from the delivery carriage, which she and Jhoqull had mocked up from one of the ones that had been left behind here. "We're almost loaded up."

"And you can handle driving that one?" Jhoqull asked.

"I can handle the horses," Kaiana said. "I lived in a stable for a few years."

Jhoqull shrugged.

"The rest of you better get moving soon," Helene said.

"Just . . . go?" Raych asked. "Don't you all usually do a thing?"

"A thing?" Lian asked.

"Is there some task we're all needed for?" Lady Melania asked.

"She means the pre-gig ritual," Mila said. "When we did the Emporium, Kennith made that *cha'dach* stuff, and we did some ritual about naming our fathers."

"Kennith did not make you proper *cha'dach*, I can tell you that," Jhoqull said. "And I would not make that for you. Your tongues could not handle it."

"Mercy," Helene said. "Ken's was spicy enough."

"Nor is that ritual for you. It is *barely* for Kennith, and I need . . . I need . . ." Her voice choked for a moment. "I will speak to him shortly on the subject."

"You will," Helene said.

"So, no on the *cha'dach*," Mila said.

"Is there something else?" Raych asked. "Shouldn't we do something else? For luck?"

"A toast or such?" Kaiana asked. "I noticed there was some wine back there."

"I saw that wine, and I would not recommend it," Lady Melania said. "I imagine if it was in this hotbox all summer, it surely turned."

"I have something," Ia said, and she went into the other room. She emerged with several glasses and a dark bottle, pouring out clear liquid.

"What is this?" Raych asked.

"If I'm not mistaken," Lady Melania said, picking up her glass and holding it up to the lamp light. "It's *ynyk vynæ*. The 'ice wine' of the Bardinic continent."

"I have a friend on a ship who brings me a few bottles from time to time."

"But what is it?" Mila asked.

"It'll make you strong, *sjat*," Ia said.

"Strength and luck," Helene said. She picked up a glass and held it up, and the rest of the ladies did the same.

"The honor is to you, Missus Rynax," Lady Melania said. "You are the hostess of this party."

Raych held up her glass. "May the prophets and saints bless us, may our foremothers watch over us, may our winds be with us, may our destinies be fruitful, and may fortune be in our feet."

"*Ziheyar njidhu i,*" Jhoqull said.

"*Tü gä cecjmysa kjyrorak,*" Ia added.

They all drank down, and Mila felt her throat burn and freeze at the same time.

"Sweet saints above," she wheezed out.

"It does have some bite," Helene said.

"But one to savor," Lady Melania said, with a wistful smile. "Thank you, Miss Estäan, and all of you, for that memory."

"Are we each to our places?" Raych asked.

"The bells press on," Mila said. "You all know where you need to be."

With nods and quiet acknowledgments, most of them left, save Helene and Lady Melania's maid, who brought over the dresses Mila and Helene were to be wearing. "My lady says I'm to make sure your disguise is impeccable."

"I've never been dressed before," Mila said. "I need to first attach the devices I'm hiding."

"Of course. Miss Kesser?"

"I guess I'm ready to be dressed," Helene said.

As Tarena got to work, Mila asked, "That . . . that thing Lady Melania says about not forgetting? Does she really remember everything?"

"I have never known her to falter in that."

"How is that possible?" Helene asked. "If you're comfortable saying, that is."

Tarena clucked her tongue for a moment. "I do not think my lady's mind is like any other. She once told me that she is always in every day she ever lived. Not that she merely remembers it, but she is always living it all."

"What does that mean?" Mila asked.

"I only know what she has said, I don't profess to understand it. But I think . . . I know that my lady has had some very bad days indeed. So I am grateful to you all for providing her with a good day to be in."

"Here's hoping it is a good day," Mila said.

"Are you ready to do this?" Helene asked.

"What is it the boys always say?" Mila said. "Just keep driving forward. So on we go."

CHAPTER ELEVEN

The journey across the river in the delivery wagon was slow, deliberately so, as they had planned an indirect route through Inemar and across the Upper Bridge, through High River, and around the Royal College so they ultimately approached the museum from the north. Which made perfect sense—all the other legitimate caterers were north of the museum, but it made the ride feel unending. Raych found herself in a cold sweat the whole ride. Was this how Verci felt when he was about to do something like this? How did he ever stand it?

The worst part was actually crossing the bridge. Raych had crossed into the north side of the city plenty of times, but this time she actually counted out how long it took. How many moments they had to stop the cart because the traffic had backed up. How long it truly was.

Even if they got out of the museum with the paintings, they still had to get back across this river with them, and even though Mila had a plan—a wild, mad plan—being on the bridge made her heart freeze. If the plan went wrong and they ended up out here, it was a trap with nowhere to go.

She closed her eyes. There is a plan. They won't be trapped. It's going to work. Verci needed it to work.

She needed it to work.

They reached the museum, where there were several other wagons and carts and folks in the same uniforms as they were wearing. It was actually perfect—they didn't stand out at all.

Kaiana pulled up the wagon, and Lian and Raych hopped out and started to unload the racks. This wasn't their first time getting racks full of pastries off of a wagon—they had done it with Dad several times—so they handled their business with practiced ease. Once they had those unloaded, they wheeled them up the ramp right behind other serving folks doing just the same thing.

"Hold up, which one's this?" an officious man at the door asked them.

"Pastries," Raych said. "And savory tarts."

"Pastries and savory tarts? Where did we—"

"I've got the invoices right here, Mister—?"

"Farratin," he said with a snort. "You should be aware that I am in charge of this event and making sure it goes smoothly."

"Excellent work, sir," she said. "Can we bring these in?"

"I wasn't informed of savory tarts," he said, looking at the papers she handed him. "But this appears to be in order." He waved them in.

"Where do we put our wagon and horses once we finish?" Kaiana asked him.

He looked at Kaiana with a hint of disdain. "Are you server or stable girl?"

"I just work the job I'm given, sir. They said deliver and work the event, so here I am."

He sighed. "This is what I'm dealing with. You were supposed to have separate drivers to take the wagons away."

"Our boss didn't tell us that," Raych said. "He doesn't like to—"

"I will be having words," Farratin said, looking at the invoice. "At least he's not trying to charge for three servers and a driver. Livery one block to the west."

"Thank you," Kaiana said.

"And make sure you wash up before you're serving, too," he said to Kaiana as she went back to the cart. "Can't have you smelling like a stable."

"Thank you, sir!" Kaiana said as she got the horses moving.

"Don't you two gawk, get on it," he said. His attention then went to the next set of folks delivering food.

"So we're in," Lian said. "That actually worked."

"It did," Raych said. "So let's keep at it."

"Right."

They wheeled the racks in further, finding a spot to merge in with the other servers and caterers. They didn't stand out, which was what mattered.

But the cart would be a block away in a livery. That added a wrinkle to the plan. Not too much, Raych assured herself, but still a wrinkle.

Either way, what would Verci say? "Drive forward." She muttered that to herself as she got to work.

HELENE HAD PUT ON PLENTY OF COSTUMES AND DISGUISES OVER THE past few months, including the dress she wore to the Henterman party. But this dress was perfect, and what an astounding difference it was to wear a dress that fit properly, and to be dressed by a lady's maid who knew what she was doing. She knew she should not get used to such luxury, but she could certainly see the appeal.

"We're approaching the museum," Jhoqull said. She was driving the carriage, dressed like any other cab driver in town with a high hat, suspenders, and cravat.

"You doing all right?" she asked.

"I am telling my line of mothers that I am not hiding my deeds out of shame, that tonight I go into battle, serving a cause, and to serve I must hide who I am. I hope they understand."

"This sort of gig isn't done in Ch'omikTaa?"

"If we needed to take something held in a stronghold there, we would walk up and attack, and if we win, we claim our prize. If we lose, we die. It is very simple."

"We definitely don't do simple here."

"I have noticed," Jhoqull said. "Especially since I seem to have several separate jobs of varying complexity."

"Sorry about that," Helene said. "You're the one on the outside for this."

"I am aware of why it is a necessity. And I am explaining that to my ancestors."

"You're going to do fine," Helene said. "But if something goes wrong, you should . . ." She wasn't sure how to best phrase this. "If we're skunked, and you can get away, then get away."

"Never," Jhoqull said. "I can accept deception and trickery for a noble cause, but not cowardice. I will not abandon any of you in this endeavor."

"Someone has to stay free if it goes wrong."

"I did not say I would be caught. I said I would not abandon you."

Helene chuckled. "Fair enough."

"We are arriving," Jhoqull said, pulling the carriage to a stop. "May fortune be at your back."

"And yours," Helene said, hoping that was the right response.

Helene got out of the carriage, where she was one of several well-dressed people arriving. She noticed some of the ladies were making a point of stopping in front of a group of folks who were clearly not guests, nor servers or guards. Members of the press. Lady Melania had prepared her for them, the first step in what she had to do upon arrival.

She strode over, locking eyes with one of the charcoal sketchers.

"So, I've arrived," she said with as much confidence as she could muster. Lady Melania had given her a script here. "Georgine Hullock, of the Erien Hullocks, and that's not Lady Hullock—we're the ones with money, not titles."

"All right," the sketcher said, looking over at the other journalists with a bit of confusion. "If you can give me a stance, I can get your look down."

"Brilliant," Helene said. The sketch was part of the plan, especially since between her wig and her face painting, she was completely unrecognizable as herself. But they wanted Georgine Hullock remembered right now.

"Got it," the sketcher said. "Enjoy the party."

"Oh, I will," Helene said. She pointed an accusing finger at one of the journalists. "That's Hullock, with two l's and a c-k."

"Yes, ma'am."

She strode up the steps into the lobby, where there were several fancy folks in glamorous outfits, all chatting in small groups, while the servers went about with trays of food and drinks.

There was Ia, in her guard uniform at one of the entranceways. Fit right in. And in the next room she spotted Raych's sister making her rounds with a tray. So they were inside, doing their job. Perfect.

She looked up the winding staircase to the next level, where Lady Melania was chatting up several people.

Time for her next bit of the script.

"So, this is the high society of Maradaine," she said in a loud voice as she grabbed a glass of wine off the tray of a passing servant. "I don't know why I expected better."

A couple nearby stepped back in shock at that, and then the woman stammered a moment. "Sorry, I don't believe we've been acquainted."

"We have not," Helene said. "So which are you, old titles or new money?"

"Well," the woman said, her hand to her chest.

The man shook his head. "I don't know where you were taught manners, ma'am."

"Guess I wasn't," Helene said, slugging the wine. "Now if you'll excuse me."

She walked off, hearing whispers of "Who is that woman?" "Where is she from?" "I heard her say she's from Erien." "Georgine Hullock."

This plan was absurd, but Lady Melania said there was no way she could blend in, so she needed to make a point of being an outsider. "They expect new money to be rude, so milk that for every drop."

"And get that name in people's mouths," Mila had said. "When the night is over, the only thing people will remember is Georgine Hullock."

Mila had also said something about making a lie so bright no one could see the truth, but that didn't matter.

Right now her job was to be rude, not fit in, and be remembered. She could do that. Pretending to keep sipping her wine, she made her way through the gallery. She didn't want to go straight to the hall with the Pentaptych, not just yet, but she did want to know how to get there without getting lost.

Last thing she needed was to mess this up by turning the wrong corner.

She walked through, stopping in front of one painting to make a comment to those viewing it about buying it, and noticed Kaiana making her rounds.

Except something was wrong. Her eyes were locked on someone across the room, and she looked scared as all blazes. Then she turned in a hurry and darted out.

Helene had to trust that she and the others could work it out. She glanced where Kai was looking—two young women, a blond one in a uniform Helene didn't recognize—with a sword at her hip—and a Waishen-haired girl in a green dress. Helene had no idea why that would spook Kaiana, but if they might be a problem, it was best to steer clear.

While she had attention to draw right now, and the last thing she needed was the wrong attention.

Mila worked her way through the party, surrounded by the upper classes of Maradaine—people with noble titles and important jobs—and was feeling more than a little pleased with herself with how well she was doing in this situation. Her dress fit, no one was raising an eyebrow at her accent, nor at her manners. She was not the girl in a stolen dress stumbling through Tyne's Emporium anymore. Looking back, she was astounded she even got through the door like that. It was comically amateur.

Seeing that everyone else was in place in the museum—save Jhoqull, who was hopefully getting into position on the roof—it was up to her to put everything into motion. No time to waste now.

She made her way to the closest water closet to the exhibit hall and latched the door. Then she lifted up the bustle of her dress and removed the packs strapped to her legs, putting them on the counter.

Mila took a moment just to look at the counter—clean, gorgeous white marble. Glancing around, this was the finest, cleanest water closet she had ever seen. Even the scent of piss and sewage was masked by floral oils. It was amazing how some people lived.

She opened up the packs—smokers and flashers of Verci's design, with Almer's chemicals. Saints, she hoped they were doing all right, wherever they were. As well as Asti. If they were in Quarrygate, she worried that Asti couldn't hold himself together there.

No, you're being foolish. Asti can hold it together anywhere. That's what he does.

Now, Julien, or Vellun? Those two would certainly be in trouble. But they'd have Asti and Verci to take care of them.

Saints, Asti and Verci were probably running the place by now.

Still, they needed help, Raych and Helene needed her, so she needed to get to work.

All of these devices had a wind timer. Turn the crank, it starts clicking, and in a about a quarter bell, smoke and flashes. Simple as that. But once she turned them, the game was underway. No turning back.

She took them out of the packs, strapped the packs back on her legs, hoping she wouldn't need the weapons or other gadgets in there, and took a few slow breaths to calm herself down.

She needed to be calm for this moment.

"Here we go," she whispered, and turned the crank on each of them, and then slid them into her dress sleeves, her bodice, and palmed the last one in her left hand. She unlatched the door and stepped back into the party.

Immediately, someone came right up to her.

"Miss Marskin, I thought that was you."

She pursed her lips, hoping to show confusion while she tried to place the face. Someone in the city records office, surely.

"I'm afraid you're in error, sir," she said, going full Scallic with her accent. She had been doing that in her persona the whole time already, but the surge of fear made her thicken it even further now. "We've never been introduced."

"No, surely," he said. "Darius, isn't this just the very image of Miss Marskin?"

Another man came over, and it clicked. Darius and Mellin. Two officials from street records that she had plied with pastries several times in the past.

"Most definitely," Darius said.

"I almost wish I was this acquaintance of yours," she said. "She's quite lucky to have two such handsome men in her knowledge."

"Well, now," Mellin said. "That's very kind, miss . . . ?"

"Miss Nerina Gessin of Nerifon," Lady Melania said, gliding over. "You'll forgive me, gentlemen, if I draw her away, but I did promise her mother I would keep a sharp eye on her. She's on mission to the Cathedral this season."

"Oh, my," Darius said. "How are you finding Maradaine, miss?"

"It is a jewel, but a cold one," Mila said. "But I do love the flavors of the northern cuisine. My lady, I see those trays are coming around again."

"I can't deny her," Lady Melania said, taking Mila's arm. "Your pardon, gentles."

They were a few steps away when Lady Melania started whispering at her. "They knew you, didn't they?"

"In one of my other personas," Mila said. "I think we slipped through it, though."

"Be careful," Lady Melania said. Mila noticed she had a remarkable ability to do speak while keeping her mouth in a fixed smile. "We don't need the wrong kind of recognition right now."

"Will they remember me with you?"

"The last thing I worry about is what other people remember."

"The charges are wound, I need to get them in place," Mila said as they passed by a bust of some king or other historical figure. She dropped the palmed smoker behind the bust without losing pace. "I need to move."

"Give me a couple," Lady Melania said. "I can help make up the difference."

"Won't you get seen?" Mila asked as she slipped three of them from her sleeve into her hand and passed them over to her.

"Never worry about that," Melania said. "I can walk through a herd of deer and not startle them. These folks are nowhere near as observant. Go." They split off in opposite directions, and Mila quietly placed more of the smokers and flashers in discreet places around the museum. There didn't need to be much strategy in their placement, as long as they weren't in the gallery with the paintings.

All were placed except the last one, which she secreted out of her bodice, and palmed in her left hand. This one was the starter, the one that would go off first, and that needed to be in the right hands.

There was Helene standing in front of a statue and talking loudly about the atrocities the man did that weren't taught in schools.

"Surely, Miss Hullock, even if that is true, which I am dubious . . ."

"The books are written by the men, sir, and they leave out these truths." Helene looked like she was having too much fun in her role. Mila almost envied her in this one.

Mila walked by with the slightest bump as she passed, dropping the flasher into Helene's hand.

It was going to be her show now.

Mila kept walking, now heading to the gallery with the paintings. But standing in her path, holding a tray and sweating profusely, was Kaiana. Her face told a whole story.

"Problem?" Mila whispered as she took a pastry off Kaiana's tray.

"A small one," Kaiana said. "There's a Tarian in the gallery right now."

"A Tarian?" Mila glanced into the gallery. "Where is he?"

"She," Kaiana said. "And the real problem is, see, we've met before."

CHAPTER TWELVE

Time was precious, and Raych couldn't waste a moment of it. On the warning from Kaiana and Mila, she had to act as everyone else was getting into position.

"Go with Lian to move the rolling trays in this direction," she told Kaiana. "The most important thing is having everyone in place. I'll figure out the Tarian girl."

Raych came back to the main gallery, noticing Mila and Lady Melania were in there already, getting in place. Ia was also taking position by one of the crashdown gates.

She carried her tray of sausage pastries through, walking up behind the Tarian girl and her young Waishen-haired companion.

"Now this one," the Waishen-haired girl said, pointing at the painting they were standing in front of—not one of the Pentaptych. "Surely this one stirs something in you, Jerinne."

"Stirs?" the Tarian asked. "I mean, the imagery is striking, but . . . I suppose it has historical meaning that I don't recognize."

"Don't recognize?"

"Try to remember, Rian, that my only real historical education has been Dayne throwing books at me."

"All right, so, this painting is about the fall of Free Opiska in—"

The girl—Rian—went on while Raych's mind raced. Jerinne, she said the Tarian's name was. That meant this was surely Jerinne Fendall, the same girl in the pamphlet. The same girl who fought with Asti and Verci in Saint Bridget's Square. She was part of all that business, and even though she was certain the boys had held back details, they spoke of her glowingly.

Jerinne Fendall would be a problem if she was in the gallery once things started. The plan relied on people being scared, it relied on Lady Melania being the most daring person in the room.

Jerinne Fendall was the sort of person who stepped up. She was a hero, in every sense, and if she was still in the gallery in five minutes, surely she would take charge in stopping Helene in her play.

And she would absolutely stop Helene. Just standing next to this Rian girl, she held her body with power and grace. She'd have Helene on the floor in seconds, and the plan would end right there.

Then, as Raych offered pastries to someone else, she saw it in Jerinne's eyes. Her eyes were completely focused on Rian. Entranced.

Raych glanced around the room again. Lian and Kaiana were coming in now. She didn't have any more time. She had to do something immediately.

As Jerinne and Rian moved away from the painting, she saw a couple walking past and with that, opportunity. She moved toward that couple—specifically the woman carrying a glass of red wine—and stumbled in her step, knocking her tray into the wineglass while falling on the floor.

"Oh, my dear," she said humbly. "I'm so sorry, my feet just got fumbled and . . ."

"Well, I cannot believe this," the woman with the wineglass said. "Of all the incompetence!"

"I'm so sorry," Raych said. "Please forgive me, and . . . oh dear saints, miss."

She pointed to Rian's dress, now covered with red wine.

"Is this ruined?" Rian asked, looking down at herself. "I . . . I can't . . ."

Jerinne took her hand. "Come on, let's get you to the washroom." And they went out the door.

"And I am going to speak to your superior," the wine-carrying woman's companion said. "We will make sure you never work something like this again."

"Oh no, please don't . . ." Raych said, since she had to put on the show. But they stormed off as well. And in this moment, the attention of the room was on her, which was perfect. No one would even see what Helene was about to do.

The Tarian girl was out of the gallery. Everyone and everything was in place. And Helene was unbuckling the skirts of her dress.

This was the moment. The show was about to start.

Kaiana's eyes went wide, and she glanced back and forth at Raych and Helene, and then went right out of the gallery. The blazes was she doing?

Raych didn't have time to find out. Helene threw the flasher across the room, which burst with light and thunder through the gallery. Then more blast and burst of smoke started throughout the museum.

They were committed now.

THE FLASHERS BLASTED WITH MORE NOISE THAN MILA WAS EXPECTING, but it got people screaming and running, and that's what mattered most. With the smokers filling the halls up, no one could see where they were running and who was screaming, which was all the better.

As predicted, the crashdown gates came down once the chaos started. Every exit from the gallery was blocked, despite the dozen or so patrons in here. Mila noted Ia right outside, having pulled one of the crashdown levers.

The gate went down in front of the Pentaptych, as well.

Glancing around, putting panic on her face for the performance, she noted Raych and Lian were here with one of their carts. No sign of Kaiana. Had she slipped out? Had something happened to her? That wasn't part of the plan. A problem, hopefully not too big of one.

Lady Melania was here, coming up to Mila and taking her arm.

"You all right, girl?" she asked, playing her part.

"Oh, saints what's happening?" Mila played along. "Oh, my what is this?"

Someone else screamed, and that was because Helene had leaped onto one of the benches. She had removed her dress, and was now in violet short pants and matching waistcoat and top, and she had put on a mask to cover her face. She had crossbows on both hips, and was holding her favorite.

"All right, listen up!" she shouted. "You're all in here with me, so if you aren't looking to get a bolt in your chest, you're going to do things *exactly like I say*!"

More screaming.

"Do you understand me?" she shouted. She aimed one crossbow at Mila. "Girl, do you understand me?"

"Yes, ma'am," Mila said.

"Then get on the floor! All of you, on the floor!"

Mila dropped on the ground.

"Face down! Kiss the floor like a lover! Flat palms on the ground!"

Mila provided a good example, as did several others. Some of the gentlemen did not, nor did Lady Melania.

"How dare you, miss!" one called at her.

"Do you have any idea who I am?" Helene snapped back.

"Georgine Hullock!" another man said. "She's Georgine Hullock!"

"Damn right I am," Helene said.

"You think you're going to hold us all on your own?" the first man asked.

"Depends which one of you wants to eat my quarrels," she said. She glanced up, and drew out one of Verci's other gadgets from her belt. "And besides, I'm not alone."

On the cue, the sunwindow window shattered.

Helene aimed Verci's device to the iron grate on the sunwindow and fired. A line shot up and hooked onto the grate. At the same time, there was a great crunching sound as parts of the grate cracked open and fell to the ground with a resounding crash.

Jhoqull—dressed and masked like Helene—slid down the line to the ground.

"I knew it!" Lady Melania called out. "It's the Wicked Daughters!"

SO FAR, WITH THE EXCEPTION OF KAIANA LEAVING THE GALLERY, THINGS had gone to plan. The smoke and flashes triggered alarm and gates, and Raych was in the center gallery with Lian and the tray cart. Mila and Lady Melania were in position, and Helene had successfully taken control of the room as Jhoqull came in through the sunwindow.

Most importantly, they were in a room that was locked down, with no guards inside, and enough patrons to be reliable witnesses, but not enough to be a problem.

"I knew it!" Lady Melania called out. "It's the Wicked Daughters!"

And now Lady Melania was taking care of several more parts of the plan—elements that originally would have fallen to Mila on her own, but having Lady Melania on their crew gave the whole thing an air of legitimacy they otherwise would have lacked.

Lady Melania was a known member of Maradaine high society, so her ability to bear witness and report what happened later would be far more powerful than Mila-in-character would have. But the noblewoman was about to serve a far more specific role.

"So the real challenge in the crucial moment where Helene and Jhoqull are actually robbing the gallery is accounting for random heroism," Mila had said.

"Meaning?" Lian had asked.

"We've got two intimidating, armed women taking charge of the room, and committing a crime, and hopefully no guards in the room. But that means some random guest may decide they're going to step up and play the hero. If that happens, the best case is we have someone Helene has to subdue. That means maybe they get hurt. Maybe killed. And at worst, they completely skunk the plan."

"Killing a member of high society would be quite the skunk," Helene said.

"How do we account for that?" Raych asked.

"You give them a hero," Mila said.

"And in this case, one they already know," Lady Melania said.

At that point, Lady Melania told a few stories of her own history, making her the perfect candidate for the job: a member of the nobility, both within high society but considered eccentric by its members, whose eccentricity had taken the form of chasing bounties in the city and countryside. Everyone knew she didn't need the money, but enjoyed the thrill of it.

A perfect hero in this moment.

"So you've heard of us?" Helene asked her. "We should be flattered, shouldn't we, sister?"

"Tremendously, sister," Jhoqull said. She had flattened her accent in an attempt to sound Druth, but it was not her best skill.

"Heard of you, yes," Lady Melania said. "You and the price on your heads."

"Shame you can't claim it."

"Oh, can't I?" Lady Melania sprang forward, moving toward a gentleman who was drawing a sword from his cane. She took the weapon out of his hand. "Thank you, Nigel, very helpful."

Helene snapped a shot at her, which Lady Melania ably parried.

"Work the gate," Helene ordered Jhoqull. "I have her."

Helene and Lady Melania launched into a spirited fight, which Raych would have loved to keep watching. It was incredibly seeing the two of them go at it, even knowing it was all theater. Helene moved with brutal intention, Lady Melania with practiced grace, neither of them able to land a blow, but absolutely no sense that either of them were holding back. She would have thought they had practiced a perfect choreography for weeks to achieve what they were improvising with pure instinct and body language.

But she couldn't keep watching, it was almost time for her to step up. Jhoqull had opened up a sack with another of Verci's devices, and inserted the mouth of it in a gap of the gate covering the paintings. Then she quickly assembled the parts of a telescoping pole and put it in the other end of the device.

"That's solid iron, you'll never break it!" one of the patrons said.

"Your friends haven't remembered their studies," Helene taunted as whipped a wild shot in the direction of that patron. She aimed to miss, but he didn't know that.

Jhoqull grabbed the pole, angled high in the air. "Read your

Jinentux. 'The strength of the hand is measured in the length of the lever!'"

She pulled down the pole with all her weight, and the gate shattered open.

"You two!" Jhoqull said, pointing at Raych and Lian. "Get those paintings down!"

Raych and Lian made frightened noises and complied, taking the five paintings of the Pentaptych off the wall and stacking them on a wide piece of sailcloth that Jhoqull had laid out on the floor. Once the five paintings were in place, Jhoqull wrapped it in a bundle and tied it shut with a cord.

"Sister, time to stop playing with your prey!" she called to Helene.

She was right in more ways than one: the guards were outside the crashdown gate, starting to get it open. They'd be in here in a moment.

"This has been fun," Helene said. "But it's time for us to run, darling."

She dodged Lady Melania's sword thrust and reached into the pocket of her waistcoat, pulling out a handful of smokers and flashes, slamming them on the ground.

The room erupted in smoke, and this was the moment for Raych and Lian to move. Covered in smoke, Raych jumped on the bundle and undid the cord, taking out the paintings. Lian was right there with five empty trays from the cart, and put them in place, taking the paintings from Raych. Then in the space of a breath, Raych tied the bundle back up.

And in that moment, Helene and Jhoqull were in position. With the snap of another of Verci's inventions, just as the smoke was clearing, the two of them and the wrapped bundle went flying up to the sunwindow. As the gates to the room opened up and several guards ran in, they were both through the broken window, and pulling the bundle through.

"Farewell!" Helene shouted. "Tell everyone about the time you saw the Wicked Daughters in action!"

And then they were out of sight.

CHAPTER THIRTEEN

Helene and Jhoqull flew off the side of the museum, belaying down to the ground with the bundle of trays over Jhoqull's shoulder. Helene had to admit, she hadn't had quite so much fun in some time. A terrible thing to be thinking in this moment, as they were far from out of danger, and far from succeeding with the plan.

Right now, she was in the most dangerous part of the plan.

"Where are we at?" she asked Jhoqull.

"This way," Jhoqull said, pointing to the alley. The old carriage was there, the one they used for the Tyne job. "Let's move!"

"We need an audience, first," Helene said, loading the bundle in the back of the carriage. "The whole point is that they give chase."

"I am aware of the point," Jhoqull said. She got up in the driver's seat. "The other point is to not be captured."

"Fair," Helene said as she got on the running board. "Plus we need to—"

"Save your words," Jhoqull said, taking the reins. She snapped the horses to, and they started off into the street. Behind them, at the museum, there was plenty of shouting and whistles. Helene looked back, seeing several guards running toward them.

"We've been seen now," Helene said. "Some speed would be good now."

"It would be, yes," Jhoqull shot back. She whipped at the horses and started swearing at them in Ch'omik.

"Those aren't Ken's horses," Helene said, realizing that they were uncooperatively just going at a pleasant trot right now. The first group of guards were likely to catch them on foot.

"Khenta will be angry enough over what we are doing to this carriage," Jhoqull said. "If I got his horses confiscated or killed, he would not forgive any of us."

Helene has some choice swears of her own. "Did you rent them?"

"And we are not getting our safety fee back, I can tell you that."

Helene pulled out one of the hiphangers, holding on to the bar of the carriage as she took aim at the guard who was keeping pace. Four more guards behind him, and a block or so farther back, horsepatrol constables were coming. "Not my biggest concern! Go faster!"

"I am trying!" She swore again, and there was a bit of a surge, only just enough to keep the first guard from catching their back rail. Helene aimed and took her shot. She grazed his leg—impossible to aim clean with this damn thing bumping along the cobblestone—and he stumbled enough to lose pace.

"How far do we have to go?" Helene asked. Jhoqull didn't, answer, but pulled her reins to get the horses to take a turn north, and then snapped them again.

Leading the chase north now. Good.

"Are we on the right road?"

"Yes," Jhoqull said. "Two more blocks."

The museum guards had slowed down in their run, still trying to keep up, but clearly getting winded. But the constables on horses were thundering up, and those horses were not the lumbering messes these rented ones were.

"Running out of time!"

"Pull the handle!"

Helene reached into the window and pulled the handle inside the carriage, which opened up a trap in the back, releasing a load of marbles, caltrops, smokers, and flashers.

At the same time, Jhoqull pulled the two levers she had. One released the horses from the yoke, and they were immediately off to the left, crashing into carts on the walkway.

The other released the spring drive.

Now the carriage was off like a shot, as blasts of smoke and light burst behind them.

Jhoqull jumped onto the runner next to Helene.

"Ready?"

"Not remotely, but—"

Jhoqull grabbed Helene's arm and leaped from the runner, just as they passed a narrow alley. The carriage, and its parade of trailing chaos, kept racing along as they hit the ground, rolling and crashing into the alley wall. Helene was a bit dazed, but Jhoqull was on her feet in a moment, grabbing Helene's hand and dragging her through the alley.

"How long until—"

The answer to Helene's question came before she could finish answering it, as the thundering boom echoed from behind them, with enough force that Helene stumbled and nearly fell on her face. She wouldn't have been able to keep running if Jhoqull hadn't been here, pulling her along.

But if she had nearly fallen over, here in the alley, surely out on the street, all the guards and constables that had been chasing them had all been knocked onto their backsides. Helene had wondered if they had put too much boom powder in the carriage, but it was too late to do anything about that now. They had only a few moments, where their pursuers were confused, blind, and deafened, to get away.

And there was a vegetable cart at the end of the alley, blocking their escape.

"Jho, we need to—" Helene shouted.

"Just jump!" Jhoqull leaped into the vegetable cart, and Helene followed suit, landing on a pile of radishes and turnips.

"What are we—"

Jhoqull grabbed Helene's face, covering her mouth, and in that same moment, Helene saw a pair of Ch'omik men covering them with a tarp. Then the end of the cart was lifted up, and they started to roll calmly down the street, away from the chaos they just created.

"You didn't tell me about this," Helene whispered when Jhoqull released her mouth.

"It occurred to me we needed another element for our escape, so I asked some cousins to be in place here."

"Not bad," Helene said. "Though a turnip in my back is not helping, with the dozens of other bruises I got doing this."

"That cannot be helped," Jhoqull said. "Though something else occurs to me, a flaw in our escape here."

"And now you're bringing it up?"

"We should have acquired a pair of dead bodies to put in the carriage, to be found once they go through the wreckage."

"That's deeply morbid."

"I am saying, if the goal is to get our pursuers to believe that we were killed and the paintings destroyed in the explosion, giving them some bones would sell that particular narrative."

"I think we did quite a lot," Helene said. "The last thing we needed was to also dig through a hospital ward for corpses."

"Perhaps so."

"It doesn't matter if they think we—or rather, the Wicked Daughters—"

"That is a quite good name, I must say."

"If the Daughters are presumed dead or not. Our job was to focus all the attention on us. Now that's done, and the guards and constables chased us several blocks away from the museum. Hopefully Raych and the others will be able to quietly roll the paintings out the door now."

"My cousins will take us a few blocks to an enclave house. We change out of these costumes there, and then go to the meet-up."

"Right," Helene said. Even if Raych got out with the paintings, they still had to get across the river with them.

Helene and Jhoqull were off, the guards had seen them fly off out the sunwindow, and the crashdown gates were open. Guards now poured into the gallery, going to the patrons inside and checking them over, ushering them out.

Mila knew this was her cue.

She ran up to the guards who were approaching Raych and Lian, with their tray cart loaded with the paintings. The last thing they needed was the guards to take a close look at them.

"Thank every saint and every blessing that they give you finally got in here!" she shouted, throwing her body on them. "It was awful, just a nightmare. A nightmare! Those terrible, terrible women were horrible! Please stop them!"

"Miss, it's all right . . ." one guard said, trying to signal one of his other men to get her out of the gallery.

"It's not all right! How could something like this happen here! How could something like this happen to us? I cannot even *fathom* . . ." She was laying the Scallic accent on extremely thick, but she wanted to keep their attention, keep their focus, stay rooted in their memories.

"Darling," Lady Melania said, swooning over to them, putting her body between the guards and Raych and Lian, who were rolling the cart out the door that Ia was at. Ia was in position there, waving people out, trying to look like she was not too focused on Raych and Lian and the cart. Lady Melania continued. "Darling, you need to breathe, you need to be calm . . ."

"Calm!" Mila shouted. "Saints above, look at you, my lady! You've been savaged! Assaulted!"

"Ma'am," the guards said, looking at Lady Melania. "You'll have to relinquish the weapon."

"This?" Lady Melania said, looking and the sword cane in her hand. "My apologies. I grabbed it off of Lord Nigel in the heat of . . . Nigel! Nigel, come here."

"Those terrible women," Lord Nigel said, shaking his head as he took the cane from Lady Melania. "You should have let me handle it."

"Nigel, darling, I've seen you with that. You would have been killed."

"Not at all—"

"Nigel, in these matters, pride only leads to injury. Namely, yours."

"But you're hurt," Mila said.

"And mostly in my pride that I was bested by that scoundrel."

"My lords and ladies!" the guard said. "We must get you out of here, secure the room."

Mila continued playing her hysteria. "But the thieves! They took the paintings and escaped!"

"They're being pursued, now please—you two! Where are you going?"

The guard was focused on Raych and Lian, still pushing the tray cart, now out in the hallway outside the gallery.

"Sir?" Raych asked. "We . . . we just wanted to get out of here."

"And what is that?"

"We were serving pastries from it, sir," Raych offered.

"Those terrible thieves abused them as well," Lord Nigel offered.

"You can't just roll that out of here, there's been a robbery!" the guard said. He looked to Ia. "You just let them out of here with that?"

"I . . . I didn't think anything of it," Ia said, trying her best attempt to sound like a man, but making no attempt to cover her Bardinic accent.

"What's your name, son?"

"Hassär Cjenik, sir," she said.

"Cjenik, you can't just . . . they haven't left your sight, have they?"

"Are we in trouble, sir?" Lian asked.

Mila grabbed Lady Melania's arm and squeezed. They weren't letting Raych and Lian just roll the cart out.

"Those women have been frightened, and they aren't paid enough to also be abused by you, sir," Lady Melania said.

"I'm not . . . I not abusing them, my lady." The guard shook his head. "I understand things have been a fright, but we need to get this room cleared, and make sure nothing else is missing, *and* that nothing is leaving the room that shouldn't." He looked to one of the other guards. "Jackin, did you see the caterers."

"Saw them go out there with, uh, Cjenik I guess. I wasn't watching close, but I think they hadn't gone far."

"Are you new, Cjenik?"

"First night," Ia said.

"Protocol, Cjenik. Jackin, get these people out of here."

"Come along," Jackin said, ushering Mila and Lady Melania toward the door.

"They're just caterers," Ia said. "Working the job like us."

"Keep your jaw shut, Cjenik, or this will also be your last night."

Ia nodded.

"My good man, there is no need for such coarse behavior," Lady Melania said as they were led into the next room. Now a few guards were standing around Raych, Lian, and the tray cart.

"We'd really like to go," Lian said, her voice cracking.

"We just need to make sure everything is in order," the lead guard said. He went up to the cart and pulled a tray out.

Pastries.

Then he checked the rest.

All pastries.

"Is that enough?" Raych asked.

He waved them off. "Go check in with Mister Farratin before you leave. The rest of you, I want you do give an account to one of the guards, and then you can be on your way."

Raych and Lian wheeled the cart past the guards, moving to the doorway near Mila, and Raych gave her the slightest wink.

Mila finally let the grip she had on Lady Melania's arm relax, and the noblewoman patted her hand in response.

"Please, sir," Lady Melania said. "If you need us to bear witness, let us do so with all haste. My companion here has had the most terrible fright, and she needs to lie down."

RAYCH COULD ALMOST LET HERSELF BREATHE AS THEY WHEELED THE cart into the loading dock. She had been absolutely terrified that Kaiana had improvised right before the crashdown gates dropped in the gallery, but it had been incredibly smart of her. She had been ready with the other tray cart—loaded entirely with pastries—and in position for them to trade carts the moment they were out of the gallery. When the guards stopped them, Kai was already out of sight with the paintings in her cart.

Now they were on their way to the loading dock, ignored by everyone as they made their way there. Whispers of shock and concern were all around them, and there was already a story circulating of the vicious "Wicked Daughters" who had taken the Noile Pentaptych and escaped.

Everyone was talking about it.

No one was watching them.

"Ladies," they heard as they entered the loading dock, where the various caterers and servers were all in a frenzied state of packing things up and trying to get out. Mister Farratin was coming right up to them. "I am given to understand that you were in the midst of the . . . unpleasantness."

"Rather," Raych said. She looked to Lian, who truly was pale and sweating, and absolute mess. "My associate here was very shaken by the whole ordeal."

"Yes, of course," Farratin said. "We are obviously sending all servers off, there will be no further festivities."

Lian spoke up, her voice a rasp. "We will be paid for the entire event, correct?"

Farratin scowled and nodded. "Yes, of course. Make sure your paperwork is in that box over there, all accounts will be settled before month's end."

"I appreciate that, sir," Raych said.

"Though I do say, that . . . foreign girl you came with, what is she, Turjin?"

Let his misconception help cover their tracks. "Yes, what about her?" Raych asked.

"Terribly rude girl, I must say. Flew through here and didn't mind a single thing I asked her."

"She was probably in a hurry to get our wagon, I imagine. But I'll speak to her about her manners."

"Appreciated."

Lian and Raych wheeled their tray cart out the door, where they saw Kaiana on their wagon, already queued up in the alley to load up and leave.

They wheeled over to her and loaded their cart in.

"Are we set?" Raych asked.

"Set. Everything we need is here," Kaiana said.

"You gave us a fright," Lian said. "You should have let us know."

"There wasn't time," Kaiana said. "I'm very sorry, but I realized that one of us should be outside and in place to switch carts quick."

"It was good thinking," Raych said. "We wouldn't have gotten out without that."

Now all that remained was getting the paintings across the river.

They drove through the streets quietly, taking a route that led them around away from the Constabulary blockades at the bridges and major roads, down to the dockhouse in Trelan where Jhoqull had rented a slip and had a boat waiting.

"About time," Helene said as they pulled in. She and Jhoqull were completely out of their Wicked Daughters outfits now, dressed completely unremarkably like shopworkers. No one would look twice at them.

"You're the one who got the fast exit," Raych said. "The rest of us had to work our way out."

"Did you have any problems?" Kaiana asked as she checked on the horses.

"Jumping out of a carriage that's racing down the street with spring power isn't something I recommend," Helene said. "I could stand to raid Doc Gelson's medicine bag and sleep for a week."

"I just need a few glasses of wine," Lian said. "My nerves are a wreck."

"Same," Raych said. "You were great. All of you."

Helene pulled the paintings out of the tray cart. "I suppose they are nice enough, but it's amazing they're worth the trouble."

Raych came over and really looked at the paintings and Helene placed them on the stable floor. She didn't know much about history, let alone this particular part of Druth history, but there was something powerful to the images these paintings held, the story they told. Her attention focused on the one depicting two older women. The women didn't seem to be ladies of noble birth or necessarily historical note. But their faces held such sadness, such pain, depicted with such truth.

"I don't think I've ever held something quite so extraordinary in my own hands," she said as she picked it up.

The others all stood around her and quietly took a moment simply feeling its power.

"Come on," she said. "We need to get these off their frames, and carefully."

"Don't do that. In fact, all of you hold fast."

They turned to the door to see the Tarian girl.

CHAPTER FOURTEEN

"Easy," Raych said, holding her hands out, hoping this young Tarian girl wouldn't do anything rash.

"Hold fast," the girl—Jerinne—said.

"She's unarmed," Helene said.

"And?" Jhoqull offered.

"And there's five of us," Helene said.

"She's a Tarian," Kaiana said.

"Five of us."

"Six!" Ia came through the doorway of the boathouse, a flurry of fists. She threw a series of punches that would have been devastating, had any of them landed. Jerinne ably dodged them, with practiced ease, and then caught Ia's wrist, flipping her onto her back.

"You were saying?" she said, pressing a boot onto Ia's chest. "Don't make me hurt you."

"You don't have to," Raych said.

"How'd she even find us?" Jhoqull asked.

Jerinne pointed to Kaiana. "I've been following since I saw you hurry out of the museum. I wasn't sure, I didn't want to be right, but . . . here you are, with the paintings."

"It's not what you think," Kaiana said.

"You didn't just pull off an elaborate theft of five valuable paintings?" she asked. Her eyes focused on Raych. "And you, you spilled that wine on Rian."

"Had to get you out of the room," Raych said.

"Sorry to ruin it for you."

"Listen, you're not going to stop us," Raych said.

"I don't want to hurt you all," Jerinne said. "Don't mistake that for not being willing to."

"Well, that's very aggressive."

Jerinne turned to the doorway, where Lady Melania and Mila were standing with the young Waishen-haired girl, Rian, Melania's arm protectively around her.

"Don't you think, my dear?" Lady Melania asked Rian.

"That's her job sometimes," Rian said quietly.

"That's very good, young lady," Lady Melania said. "Indeed, sometimes we all have to do unpleasant things for our job. I'm sure you've seen that."

"What . . . what are you doing here?" Jerinne asked, her attention entirely on Rian. "You shouldn't be here, it's not safe—"

"She's perfectly safe," Lady Melania said, squeezing the girl's shoulder. "She was very worried that she had lost track of you, and I offered to help her find you. A bit thoughtless of you to escort a lovely young woman to an event and leave her. But we all make mistakes, don't we?"

"What is going on?" Rian asked. "Should we get my mother?"

Kaiana tapped Raych's shoulder. "Her mother."

Raych made the connection. "The rest of you, break down the frames. We need to get moving."

"No, no," Jerinne said, who struggled slightly to keep Ia pinned to the floor with her foot. "And tell your man to stop."

"Ia, stop. And you let her up, she's not going to try to fight you." Raych cautiously took a step forward. "None of us are, but you must not stop us from what we have to do."

"You're fooling yourself if you think—"

"I know who you are, Jerinne Fendall. You're a hero."

Jerinne raised an eyebrow. "So you read some pamphlets. Or she told you." She pointed to Kaiana, who was getting started with the work of getting the paintings out of the frames. "Stop it!"

"I did read that pamphlet, yes. But I also lived it."

"What are you talking about?"

"You met her in the tunnels under the city, right?" Raych asked her, pointing to Kaiana. "And you sent her to get help, from Inspector Satrine Rainey."

"Mother!" Rian said.

"Yes, that's right," Raych said. "And do you know where she and Satrine went after that?"

"To Saint Bridget's Square . . ."

"No," Raych said. "To my house. Because they needed my husband, Verci."

"Verci's you're . . . no. You just read that."

"My name is Raych Rynax," she said. "And I know that after the fight in Saint Bridget's Square, the seven of you who fought together there went to the Fuergan restaurant. That's not in the pamphlet."

"All right," Jerinne said, stepping off Ia and jumping back, maintaining a defense stance. "Let's assume you are Verci's wife, that doesn't excuse—"

"Verci is in trouble," Raych said. "Him and Asti both, and other friends of ours. The only way to help them, the only way to save them is with these paintings."

"How?"

"That was the demand made on us," Raych said.

"Like a ransom?" Jerinne said. "There has to be another way."

"Look at me, Miss Fendall," Lady Melania said. "Do you know me?"

"Not directly," Jerinne said. "I may have seen you at some events."

"You have, and I could enumerate exactly which ones. But you have seen me there. I am a member of noted society in this city."

"Yes, I suppose."

"Do you think I would be party to this if it was just some random burglary? If it was anything other than just and necessary?"

"I don't know you well enough to say."

"I know something about you, though," Lady Melania said. "I know that you understand that what is just and right isn't always in line with matters of law." She gave a glance at Rian.

"This is for a good cause," Raych urged. "We could have done this a dozen different ways, ways that got more people hurt. But we didn't want to do that. We just need the paintings, to help our families. And if you don't believe me, go get her mother. If nothing else, if I'm getting arrested, I'd like it to be a friendly face."

Jerinne face was filled with doubt. She looked to Rian. "What do you think?"

"I think they're telling the truth, Jer," Rian said. She pointed to Kaiana, working on deframing the paintings with the others. "She did come to our apartment that night."

"You know who I work with," Kaiana said. "He's not exactly in line with the law, either."

Jerinne frowned. "Is this connected with the Brotherhood and all that?"

"I can't honestly say," Raych said. "I do know that whoever behind this is powerful."

"Tarian," Lady Melania said, "on the honor of my title, I pledge to you, this is just. If you demand, I'll prove it by trial of combat."

"No one does that anymore," Jerinne said. "Don't be absurd."

"Jerinne," Rian urged.

Jerinne pointed a finger at all of them. "Ladies . . . and you, sir . . ."

"I'm not a man," Ia said, taking her hat off.

"Ladies," Jerinne repeated. "I am not comfortable with this, but . . . but Miss Rainey needs to be escorted home. When I get there, I will tell the inspector to check on Verci and Asti. And if her investigation does not satisfy, I will entreat her to be on the hunt for every one of you. Even you, my lady."

"As you say, good Tarian," Lady Melania said. "Take your friend home."

"Come on," Jerinne said, offering her arm to Rian. She gave one last harsh look to Raych, and they were gone.

"We should not waste any more time," Mila said, stripping off her costume. She went to the trunk Jhoqull had planted here in the morning when she brought the boat. Clothes and other gear they would need for the last part. She started passing out the outfits, including the fishwife dresses and aprons she gave to Raych and Lian.

"No, you should not," Lady Melania. "You are all set for your plan to traverse the river?"

"Are we?" Raych asked, looking at the others. Helene gathered the painting canvases and rolled them together, putting them in a quiver-like tube. She then put another piece on top of it, and clamped it shut.

"Watertight," she said, holding up Verci's invention. "I tested it five times."

"And Verci swears that thing will keep you from freezing in the river," Mila said to Kaiana, indicating the sleek, body-tight outfit she was putting on.

"Is that sealskin?" Ia asked, touching it. "Yes, very good."

"So what do we have to do?" Lian asked. "Raych and I are just rowing the boat across the river?"

"Draw as little attention as possible. Just two fishwives returning home to Keller Cove after delivering to the north shore. Very normal." Mila walked over to the boat, and pointed to Verci's crankbox which had been installed in the bottom. "Just one of you has to keep cranking that so Kai can breathe."

"And you can swim the river?" Lian asked Kaiana.

"I was born next to the ocean," Kaiana said, picking up the helmet that connected to the device. "I swam before I walked."

"And the rest of you should start walking across the bridges, at your own pace," Mila said. She was dressed like a professional clerk now, and Helene and Ia were all dressed as shop workers, Jhoqull like a drover. All of them, unremarkable.

"I'll bring the wagon and trunk back," Jhoqull said. "I'll take High River bridge."

"The rest of us take the Great Bridge," Mila said. "I'll meet you two in Keller Cove."

"I'll tell the Old Lady to expect you," Ia said.

"Then you are set," Lady Melania said. "I am grateful to have made excellent memories with you all. When you need my help, please do not hesitate. Helene, stay sharp."

"And you, my lady," Helene said.

She left, and with quiet nods, the rest did as well. Kaiana strapped the waterproof quiver over her back, put on the air helmet, and jumped into the dark water. Raych and Lian got into the boat, and while Lian started rowing, Raych got to pumping air to Kaiana.

"Quite the night," Lian said. "But at least it's a beautiful one."

On the river, as Lian rowed, there was a quiet calm Raych hadn't felt in some time. She looked up at the stars and hoped, prayed to prophets and saints, that all of this would be for some good, and that Verci would be all right.

RIVER PATROL STOPPED THE BOAT JUST BEFORE THE KELLER COVE docks, but only gave them a quick glance to see they had nothing of value in the hold, and let them pull into the dock and tie off without question.

Raych and Lian got out of the boat, and found their way to the spot Mila had noted in one of the boathouses, where Kaiana emerged from the water. Quickly they got her out of the breathing helmet and sealskin outfit and into dry clothes, packed all their gear and the quiver of paintings into a satchel. Raych carried it over her shoulder and the three of them calmly walked down the street and through the neighborhood to North Seleth.

They came into Kimber's and took seats at a table, noting it was a quiet night there. The new boy cleaning tables, Doc Gelson nursing a drink in the back. Kimber came over with beers for all of them.

"Everything all right?" she asked Raych.

"Everything is fine," Raych said. "Did Hal come for Corsi?"

"He did, right on time," Kimber said. "And Corsi was a jewel the whole day."

"I'm very glad to hear it."

Kimber went back behind the bar.

"Now?" Lian asked.

"I wait for Helene and Jhoqull, and we'll go to Missus Holt. You can go home, if you want."

"No," Lian said. "Hal can take care of things for a while. I think I deserve more than a couple glasses of wine. You agree, Miss Nell?"

"Quite," Kaiana said. "Though I have to say, that actually was a glorious swim. I feel fantastic."

"Then let Hal stay with his nephew for a bit," Raych said. "Helene and Jhoqull are here. We'll be back in a little bit."

"I am certain we'll be here," Lian said.

Raych took the satchel and joined Helene and Jhoqull at the door, and they made their way to the Elk Road Shack, where Ia had already prepared the way for them to meet with Missus Holt. Upon arrival, there were quite a few gang boys and other heavies gathered about in there. All eyes were on them until Ia came over from the back.

"Come on, ladies," she said. As she led them down a back hallway, she said. "This was fun, you know. Missus Holt wanted me on this to make sure you didn't rabbit on the thing, but . . . no, I enjoyed working with you."

"Hopefully we won't make a habit of it," Raych said. "You were very good, Ia, just . . . this isn't the usual kind of night I want."

"I understand," Ia said. "Still, after tonight, we are bound. My arm is yours, *sjat*. Even you, Kesser."

"You're not too bad either, *sjat*." Helene said.

"Next time someone else fights the Tarian, though. Here we are." She opened the door to a warm, richly furnished office. Missus Holt sat behind a desk, and as they came in, she got up and made her way around to a table.

"Damn, Josie," Helene said. "This looks like you're putting down roots."

"Hiding away wasn't serving me like it used to," she said, leaning on her cane. "Things are changing, and I need to have a presence. You have something for me?"

"We do," Raych said. She took the waterproof container out of the satchel, opened its latches, and pulled out the canvases. Carefully she laid them out on the table. Josie put on a pair of spectacles and came close to them.

"Oh . . . oh my, they're glorious. Absolutely glorious. I am amazed at this, ladies. Truly. I didn't think you could do it."

"Then why'd you ask us to?"

"Two reasons, mostly," Josie said, taking her cane and coming back to the desk. "One of which is deeply personal. Did you read anything about Maricon Noile in all this?"

"Mila did some research," Raych said. "He wasn't successful in life, and his paintings weren't really celebrated until fifty years later."

"Indeed. Getting his work noticed in the art circles of Oblune, that was the lifelong pursuit of his daughter. She still had a few of his paintings then, and she worked tirelessly to get them noticed, and when she finally did, that meant several people were sitting on masterpieces. But Noile's daughter also died in poverty, and when his granddaughter tried to reclaim their property, or at least claim some of the wealth of her legacy, she failed. But she kept records. Kept journals." She gestured to Ia, who left the room.

"All right," Raych said, not sure where this was going.

"She eventually came to Maradaine, where she passed those on to her own granddaughter, who married a man named Holt, and eventually . . ." Josie took some leather journals out of from the desk drawer. "My mother passed them to me."

"Wait," Helene said. "You wanted these because—"

"Because they should be mine," Josie said. "And finally, they are back with my family, where they belong."

"This was just for you?" Raych asked.

"Restoring the legacy of her mother's mothers is notable," Jhoqull said. "That is a task that will please my mother's mothers."

"But we did all this just for you."

"You wanted something for you, it's only fair," Josie said. "And I am very grateful, Raychelle."

"Grateful enough to get my husband out of the prison?" Raych asked.

"And Julien and the others?"

"If I could, I absolutely would," Josie said. "Sadly, I can tell you that they aren't in Quarrygate. Not all of them."

"What?" Raych asked. "Where are they, then?"

The door opened, and Ia came in with Julien, Kennith, and Vellun. All of them looked in poor shape. Julien's face was pale, sickly. Vellun looked absolutely shattered. Kennith looked the worst of the three of them, his face with several cuts and bruises.

They were here. Jhoqull and Helene jumped up and embraced Kennith and Julien.

But just the three of them.

"What is this?" Raych asked. "Where were they?"

"They were in Quarrygate," Josie said. "They escaped and made their way up here, and my people got them off the street."

"Escaped?" Raych asked. Just these three? Her heart was trying to break out of her chest. "What about the others? Where's Verci?"

"Verci got us out," Vellun said, quietly. He looked so crushed, like he could barely manage to say even that.

"Verci did? Then where is he?" Helene asked. "And where was Asti in all this?"

"We hadn't seen Asti in days," Julien said. "And Verci . . ." He trailed off, eyes full of guilt.

"Where is he?" Raych asked again, nearly hysterical. "What happened to Verci?"

PART III
THE QUARRYGATE ESCAPE

CHAPTER FIFTEEN

Seven days ago . . .

They had been separated again for the ride to Quarrygate. Everything about this was baffling. Every explanation Verci came up with was even more insidious. It was impossible that this was merely a strange misunderstanding. At best, there really was a Corvian Liberation Seven, and someone had set them up to be patsies for reasons yet unknown. After the hearing, there was no chance to confer with Asti about it and make a plan. Now they were each in separate lockwagons on their way to the prison.

Whoever had put them in this mess clearly knew that Asti and Verci wouldn't attempt to escape without the others. As long as they didn't know where the others were or how to break everyone out, they wouldn't dare try.

And, damnit, the bastards were right. As much as he wanted to spring his way out of these manacles and fight his way out of the wagon, he couldn't go back home and look Helene in the eye and tell her he had left Julien behind. Or any of the rest.

Whatever was at play here, the only way to suss it out was to run it through. But once they were in the prison, he and Asti would work it out, come up with a plan.

The wagon came to a halt, and the guards let him out. Stepping into the yard, it was clear he was being unloaded already within the prison walls, as were the others. Crossbow-laden guards stayed between them all, forcing them to be at a distance.

"Everyone all right?" Verci called out.

"Do we seem rutting all right?" Kennith snapped.

"Of course you're not," Asti said. "But are you hurt?"

"What is all this about?" Vellun asked. "Is this one of your damned schemes?"

"Easy, pretty, easy," Pilsen said. "They didn't plan this. Even they would never make a plan that involved being in here."

"Hush up, the lot of you!"

"My name isn't Corrick," Julien said. "Why did they say my name is Corrick?"

"We'll get it all sorted, all right?" Asti said, calmly. "We stick together, and we work it out, hmm?"

A couple uniformed men came out to them. "All right!" the one in the lead shouted. "Welcome to your new home, gentlemen, I trust you'll find the accommodations to your liking! I'm going to tell you how this is going to go, and I'm going to tell you once, and then you're going to do it like I told you. If that is, in fact, how it goes, in an hour's time you'll each be in your cells in your wards, ready to join the rest of the population for lunch, and won't have any fresh bruises. If you do not do things like I tell you, I can promise you a different result. Am I clear?"

They all looked around at each other, then to him.

"Now, when I ask, 'Am I clear?', I expect to hear a 'yes' from you lot, because I know I am speaking simple words you understand, and I know from your papers here that you all speak Trade and none of you have bad ears or bad brains."

"That's not true," Julien said.

The lead guard stepped up to Julien. "What's that big fella?"

"My brain is pretty bad. But your papers aren't about me, they're wrong, so it's not true."

The lead guard chuckled, and started laughing loudly. "That is a first, let me tell you, I've been here eleven years, and no one, *no one*, has ever flat out said he has a bad brain. And there were plenty who came through these doors who did, but ain't no one just admitted it like that. So, normally, I'd have these boys make a rutting example of you, but just this once, I'll let you pass because you made me laugh."

He snapped a finger at one guard, who drew out a handstick and slammed it into Vellun's ribs. The lead pointed to Vellun, now doubled over.

"This one is too rutting pretty, though, so he gets your wailing this time. So, now, I ask again, am I clear?"

"Yes!" Vellun said, and Verci quickly joined the others in doing the same.

"Much better," the lead said. "Now, here's what'll happen. I'm going to blow a whistle, and when I do, the guards while remove your shackles. Then you all strip down to nothing, hear? I want to see tenders dangling. And then you walk through that door, and a couple fellows are gonna search every spot you've got, places on your body you've never seen. None of you are sneaking in a knife or nothing on my watch. A sew-up is also gonna look you over, make sure you've got nothing festering on you. Then they will send you under the well spigot, get you good and clean, and give you your grays. Any of you cause a hint of dustup, give my fellows the slightest breath of trouble, then we're back on that fresh bruises conversation I mentioned earlier. And to be clear, one of you steps out of line, you all will pay for it. Am I clear?"

"Yes," Asti said firmly, looking at the rest as if to send a message. Verci joined the others in the chorus.

"Grand," the lead said. He took out his whistle and blew, and the other guards came to remove their shackles.

They went through the motions just like he told them. Verci stripped down, went inside, made no complaints as several hands poked and prodded him in every which way, shoved him under the water and scrubbed him like a stone floor. Skin red and raw, he was pushed into the next chamber, where he was handed a pullover shirt and slacks. Rough and scratchy, and while they were certainly gray, they were clearly not dyed or intended to be that. If anything, it was undyed wool that and simply gotten so dingy faded it had just become gray.

Verci put the clothes on, since it was too chilly to do anything else, and in a few minutes they all stood together, shivering and damp in the same clothes. Julien's didn't really fit him at all.

"All right," the lead said, looking at his papers. "I want to congratulate you all for doing that very smartly. You keep that up, you'll do quite well here."

He walked in front of them all, and made a few gestures to his men. "Now, the brothers, Marin and Indlen." He pointed to Asti and Verci.

"Am I Marin?" Asti asked.

"I guess I look more like an Indlen," Verci said.

"See, this is the not smart thing," the lead guard said. "You two are the main instigators, I'm told, so we'll be separating you."

"What?" Asti asked.

"Can't have you boys plotting, no," the lead said. "So, Marin, you'll be headed to Ward Four with your friend Orritan." He pointed at Almer, and a pair of guards grabbed each of them and took them toward one door into the main prison.

"We'll work it out!" Asti shouted as they took him out of the room.

"Now, Indlen," the lead said. "You and the rest of yours will be in Ward Seven. I think you'll do well there, if you all keep being smart like you just did." He chuckled and pointed to Julien. "Except he's got a bad brain. Hope it doesn't get you all into trouble. Hope none of you do. Because, you never know what sort of trouble in Ward Seven might, you know, spill over to Ward Four. Or the other way around?" He came in close to Verci, whispering in his ear. "Am I clear, Mister Tacklin?"

"Yes, clear," Verci said.

"Grand," he said. "Well, gents, take them in, and give them all the tour."

Once they were settled in Ward Seven, Verci had seen only Julien for most of the rest of the day. He and Julien were put in the same bunkroom, but the others were elsewhere, and the guards—plentiful throughout the ward—barked at him when he tried to seek them out.

He saw the rest at dinner, but even there, he couldn't approach them. Sitting with your bunkroom was strictly enforced, and when Verci tried to go check in with Kennith, he was threatened with a handstick across the jaw.

"You got mates in other bunkrooms?" Hobely asked. One of their bunkmates, an older fellow, with faded ink on his arm from one of the gangs from the east side of Maradaine. "You can see them when we get yard time tomorrow."

"We didn't today?" Verci asked.

"Some boys made a mess the other day, and we lost our privilege for a few. Tomorrow it's supposed to be back up."

"How long have you been here?" Julien asked him.

"I lost count some time back," Hobely said. "What year is it?"

"It's 1215," Verci said.

"Then it's been fourteen years," Hobely said.

"Verci, I can't be here fourteen years," Julien said.

"I know, I know," Verci said.

"What's your sentence?" one of other bunkmates asked.

"We haven't even had a trial," Verci said. "Being held until it, and it's all a bung-up."

"They all say it's a bung-up, Tacklin," one of the other old-timers said.

"What kind of name is Tacklin for a pirie?" another asked.

"It's not," Verci said.

"Oh, is that the bung-up you're claiming?" Hobely asked. Laughing, he added, "I swear, you got the wrong man!"

"They do," Julien said. "My name isn't . . . ." He frowned. "I don't even remember what name they called me."

"Corrick File," Verci said. "Get it in your head, at least so they don't try to break your knees when you don't answer to it."

"But it's not my name."

After dinner—rancid slop Verci wouldn't give to a dog—he managed to get a word with Kennith in the water closet.

"You holding up?" he asked.

"Not at all," Kennith said. "I mean, I'll keep my chin up, but I'm bunked with boys who are keen to bleed me over my skin. And they already beat the hell out of Vellun."

"Pilsen?"

"He's in a different bunkroom, I don't know," Kennith said. "The blazes are we doing? What's the plan?"

"Then we need to let Raych and Jhoqull know where we are, get lawyers—"

"Lawyers, really?" Kennith asked. "Saints, we should have cracked those sheriffs on the skulls the second they came in. Why didn't you?"

"We didn't do anything," Verci said. "Innocent folk don't attack sheriffs."

"We're still in here," Kennith said. "Innocent hardly matters."

"Hey, boys!" someone shouted from outside. "Stop your gabbing and finish up, or we'll come finish for you!"

"Figure it out," Kennith said, and he stalked off.

Verci sighed, and splashed a little bit of water on his face, as much as he could manage from the pathetic trickle of the tap. Figure it out. He hadn't even figured out what he needed to figure out in all this. Why they were here, why with the wrong names? What was going on at all?

"Damn it, Asti," he muttered to himself. "The one time you didn't just fight your way out from the jump, we end up here."

Did anyone even know where they were? Did Raych? Saints above, he hoped she knew more than he did right now.

Yard time the next day was the first time Verci had been able to speak with everyone, or at least his people in Ward Seven.

"Do you even have a plan?" Vellun asked, sporting a nasty fresh bruise over his split lip.

"Not yet," Verci said. "I want to talk to Asti—"

"Asti isn't here," Kennith pressed.

"I know that," Verci said. "But he's on the other side of the wall over there, and we need to—"

"Why not do a rink drop?" Pilsen asked.

"A what?" Verci asked.

Pilsen shook his head. "Children, children I'm here with."

"What's a rink drop?" Julien asked.

"Very simple. Here in the yard. In the meal hall. We're never in those spaces at the same time as Asti, but we are going to be in those spaces, and so is he. So, with a rink drop, we leave something he's gonna find that he knows is a message, and then he does the same back."

It wasn't exactly a terrible idea. "Problem is, we don't have anything to leave, certainly not that he's going to know is from us."

Kennith huffed. "You mean to tell me with all those codes and games and whatever else you two have, you never worked out a thing for something like this?"

"Not exactly?" Verci said. "At least, nothing that's going to be efficient."

"What's not efficient?"

"I could leave a simple message, say, with a piece of limestone on that red brick wall," Verci said. "Like, a symbol and the number 5. If he saw it, if he's in the yard again before it gets wiped away or what, then he could write a return, with a code of where he might drop a longer message. It could take a few days."

"Assuming guards don't find it, or other prisoners, or . . ." Kennith said, shaking his head.

"So do we wait on Asti to figure something out and reach us?" Julien asked.

"Not a chance," Kennith said. "They're already giving Vellun too much business."

"What for?" Julien asked.

"Being too pretty," Vellun said.

"You are too pretty," Pilsen said. "But they're right, we can't sit around waiting for someone to spring us, Kelsi."

"Verci," Verci said softly.

"Right. But if we can get word outside, Josie might send someone."

Saints, of these boys, Pilsen was the only one of them who really knew how to handle himself, the one who might be able to help Verci with a plan. Buried in his skull were a dozen schemes to get to Asti, or trick the guards, or . . . Blazes, Pilsen in his prime probably could have talked his way right out the gates.

But Pilsen was far from his prime now.

"We're not who they say we are," Julien said. "Shouldn't we just demand to talk to a lawyer, or someone from Justice? And maybe since we all were arrested together, they would have to put us together with the lawyer."

"That's pretty good, Jules," Verci said.

"That's what you want to do?" Kennith scoffed.

"Right now, it's the best I've got."

"You could just plan to break us out. Verci Rynax doesn't walk into a room without knowing all the ways out, I thought."

Verci sighed. He had been watching, learning, for what that was worth. "We've got brick walls here, every hallway has a double-gate pass at every junction, and each of those gates are double-keyed and belled. On this level we've got guards with handsticks, and *maybe* a full yard riot can overpower them, but up top, eight more guards with crossbows. Maybe—*maybe*—me, just me, all alone, I could figure out a way to slip through it all and get out. Same with Asti. But a plan that gets you all out, too? That's going to take me some time."

"What do you need?" Vellun asked. "I'm probably only good for seducing a guard, but I can do it."

What would Asti do? "Volunteer for the worst work details. The ones that involve cleaning or other disgusting tasks. The ones no one wants to do."

"Why?" Kennith asked.

"Two reasons. One, those jobs tend to be in different places, and that might give us more access, see more of the prison. Second, rough cleaning work requires things like vinegar and bleach. It's probably stored in only one place—"

"And Asti would have the same idea, to get Almer in with those things!" Julien said.

"There it is," Verci said. "Best I have for now."

"That and the lawyer thing," Kennith said. "We have to presume that Jho and Raych and Helene are probably reaching through Covrane, trying to get lawyers or Justice, and with us with the wrong names, they might not find us."

"Which might be by design," Verci said. "I have to think this is all some kind of trap for us."

"Which raises a lot of who and why questions," Kennith said. "And honestly, I don't care about the answers. I want to get back home."

"So do I."

"Hey, hey," a handful of fellows, all of whom had hashmarks tattooed on their necks came up to them. "Looks like the five of yous are congregating, looks like that indeed."

"We're talking," Verci said. "Doesn't concern you."

"See, there is a concern, there is," the leader of this group said. "Let alone that you've got a chomie and a pirie congregating with these decent folk, and I am not a fan of that sort of thing, no I'm not. But there is also the matter of respect."

"Respect?" Kennith asked.

"Maybe you didn't notice, you folks are all new blood and such, but did you see how folks mostly walk about in this yard, keep their legs moving, while you lot leaned against this wall, all a-whispered."

"It's not your concern," Verci stressed.

"But it is, like. You don't stick to your own, that's a problem, sure, but when you congregate like this, standing in one spot all a-whispering, the guards take note of you. They think you are up to something. And it doesn't suit the Necky-Knock Boys for the guards to start paying closer attention to the whats and whos in this yard."

"The Necky-Knock Boys?" Verci asked. "Is that what you lot call yourself?"

"We run Ward Seven, mate," the leader said. "That's why you need to show some respect."

"Saints, every new thing is the new dumbest thing," Kennith said.

"This is what I mean about lacking respect. Fellows, show the chomie and pirie our regards."

The boys jumped on Verci and Kennith with brutal efficiency. Punches and kicks came in hard, faster than Verci was ready for, and it a few hits he was on the ground, barely getting his arms up enough to project his head.

Then the punches stopped as Julien swung his enormous arms around, sending the Necky-Knock Boys flying in every direction. In moments, he cleared them off of Verci and Kennith.

Then the guards descended on Julien, handsticks out, battering his legs and back.

"Everyone kiss the ground!" a guard yelled. "Faces in the dirt!"

Verci did as ordered—he was nearly in that position already—as did everyone else in the yard. The guards swarmed around Julien, putting irons on his wrist.

"Looks like the big guy wanted to spend some time in the hold box," one of the guards said. "How about the rest of you?"

"Jules—" Verci said, and got a foot on his neck for his trouble.

"Be smart, new boy," another guard said. "He's gonna sit in the box a few days, and you do not want to join him."

Verci didn't have any opportunity to make a stupid choice as they hauled Julien off, he could barely even move. Once Julien was gone, the guard got off Verci.

"Yard time over, every one back to bunks!"

Verci was hauled to his feet, as was Kennith, who was bleeding and holding his arm like it might have been broken. The Necky-Knock Boys dusted themselves off, and with an ugly chuckle, went off.

"You all right?" Verci asked.

"Not at all," Kennith said. "I can't do this, man. I can't."

Verci nodded, helping Kennith make his way. "I'm going to figure this out, I promise you. Even if I have to do it without Asti, I'm going to figure this out."

VERCI SLIPPED OUT OF THE BUNKROOM IN THE NIGHT, MOUSE QUIET. ON his own, he could do that. Even though there were plenty of guards on patrol in the hallways, on the yard walls, Verci could easily move around them without any of them being aware. Saints, he wished he had been alone in here. If he had been alone, even just kept isolated in a ward by himself, he'd have figured out a way to be back on the street in a matter of hours. Even with the guards on high alert, even with the extra measures they were clearly taking now, he saw the holes he could slip through. In some cases, literal holes in the masonry.

But getting the others out, that was so much harder. Especially with them in different bunkrooms, and Jules in the box.

Getting to Jules was the priority. Maybe, just maybe, he could get Julie out of the prison, and he could get back to Helene, tell them what was going on, and they could do something outside. Let Jules do that, and Verci would stay inside, help the others, and get to Asti. That was possible.

Once he didn't have Julien to worry about, he could focus on the others. And he was very worried about Julien. Julien had now been in the hold box for two days. The box was a tiny cell—really just a steel-walled closet—put right off the yard so everyone could hear whoever was inside it. And Julien howled like a broken dog.

Verci tried to get as good a look at it as he could, but the guards would shoo him away if he got too close. The box was small enough that if Verci had been in there, he would have to crouch, but wouldn't be able to sit down either. Spending two days in there would be torturous. For Julien, Verci couldn't even imagine how excruciating it was.

Except he could hear Julien, so he didn't have to imagine.

At night, the guards weren't right by the box. There was a hallway patrol, and while the guards were doing an excellent job with the watch, one place they weren't paying much attention was the hold box.

Julien was just whimpering when Verci got there.

"Jules," Verci whispered. "I'm here."

"You keep saying that," Jules whispered hoarsely. "Why do you keep saying that?"

"I just got here, man," Verci said, looking over the lock. Pretty simple one, he'd have it open in a trice. "I'm sorry it took me so long."

"I keep asking you to get me out, and you keep saying you're here."

Saints, he must be losing it in there.

"Jules," Verci said firmly but quietly as he worked the lock. "I don't know what you must be going through in there, what you're seeing and hearing, but I'm really here right now."

"Verci?" Julien asked. "Get me out of here."

"Almost got it," Verci said as the lock clicked and cracked. The door practically flew open, and Julien fell out on top of Verci. Verci barely had a chance to brace himself to keep the big guy from cracking on the floor, and did his best to gently get Julien onto the floor without collapsing under the weight. "Got you, got you."

Julien looked around, his neck cracking audibly from the movement. "You . . . you're really here. I didn't . . . I wasn't sure."

"Yeah, man," Verci said, caressing the man's head. Julien stunk of sweat, piss and filth, but Verci didn't care. "It's all right, you're all right."

"I couldn't move in there, I couldn't . . ."

"Now you can," Verci said. "Can you get up?"

Julien strained to push his body up so he was sitting. "Give me a minute."

Verci would have loved to tell him to take all the time he needed, but surely guards would come this way soon. "Just a bit. I'm going to get you out of here."

"What about the rest?"

"I can't do that yet," Verci said.

"We can't leave them," Julien said. "No, we're not."

"I'm not," Verci said firmly. "I am getting *you* out. And I'll stay and work with the rest of them."

"That doesn't seem right," Julien said.

Verci got up and helped pull Julien to his feet. "Nothing is right, especially what you went through. I've got an idea to get you out, and then I'll work the rest."

"But what will I do?"

"You get home, you tell Helene where we are, the names we're here under, and that should help."

"Are you sure? Ken would be better . . ."

"But *you* need to get out of this, man," Verci said. "Come on."

"And if you just break me out, the others will get it worse . . ."

"I will take care of it. I'll take care of all of you, we just . . ."

"Well, look here, look here," a guard's voice said. "Looks like someone had a plan."

Verci turned around and saw at least five guards there, all with handsticks. More than he could reasonably handle right now.

"Gentlemen," Verci said calmly. "The poor man was suffering, I had to get him out of that box."

"Well," one guard said. "That's very kind. Guys, isn't that kind?"

"So kind," another guard said. "You don't see much of that in here."

"And the big guy was ready to come out. Weren't you, big guy?"

"Yes?" Julien said meekly.

"Get him out of here and clean him up," the lead guard said. "Send him to his bunk."

Two guards came over and hauled Julien off.

"Now, for this selfless fellow," the guard said, looking at Verci. "You were right, his time in the box was over."

"Just wanted to help," Verci said.

"But now . . . looks like the box needs a new resident. So we're very glad you decided to be helpful and volunteer."

CHAPTER SIXTEEN

It was near the end of the day, Verci could tell that much. The box had tiny cracks that allowed the sunlight in, and he could hear the activity in the yard throughout the day. He didn't cry out or give the guards any sign that he was going to break, though. Whenever he heard folks in the yard, he would start singing folks songs or bar ballads. He didn't know which ward was in the yard at any time, but if it was Ward Seven, his folks would know where he was and that he was all right. And if it was Ward Four, that would be a message to Asti.

He chose the songs as a message. "Get My People Home." "March Back for Me." "My Sweet, She Is Waiting." "Pick a Fight With Me, and My Brother Will Fight You Too," If Asti heard those, he'd know.

If he heard. For all Verci knew, Asti had gotten himself thrown in a box himself. Or worse.

His voice was gone by the end of the day. Nothing to eat the whole time, and water was just a ladleful poured in the hole in the top, only a few swallows actually got in his mouth.

His legs were cramped, he couldn't move them at all, and his arms were no better. Once there were no more yard sessions, then it was just quiet, just him in his thoughts.

This was really where someone would break, he realized. Asti had told him a little—only ever so little—of the torture and abuse he had suffered in the Poasian prison in the Napolics. This was nothing compared to that. Verci would hold it together.

He closed his eyes, shutting out the dark and the pain. If he kept his mind busy, kept it focused, he'd be all right. He'd make it through the night until he fell asleep. They wouldn't keep him in here much longer than tomorrow morning. He just had to get through the night.

He visualized himself sitting in his workroom, in the back of the shop. He made a point of conjuring up the image in his mind in elaborate, painstaking detail. The height of his work chair. The wood grain of his bench. Each tool, on its niche in the wall, he placed them there in his mind's eye, one by one, in the correct place.

Slowly, deliberately, he constructed the entire room in his mind, and held that image. He let himself sit there, fully inhabit the illusion. He was not trapped in a cramped box, he was in his workroom. He was going to build a new gadget. Something to help them all escape.

He opened up the drawer with his supplies. A few choice gears and springs. Yes, that would do quite nicely. He gathered each of them together, ordered them on the table, and got to work.

Yes, he could see it clearly. He just had to focus, and get it done.

VERCI HAD BUILT DEVICE AFTER DEVICE. A TOY GEARBOX, A REPEATING crossbow, a shackle-trap, a climbing rig. Each built with meticulous care, each laid out in their place on his workbench. He was very pleased with all of them, such good work. Perfectly done. Fine additions to his inventory.

The smell hit in the back of his nose first. Acrid, burning.

Smoke.

All of his new devices were smoking. Thin wisps at first, but then thicker and darker. He reached to grab one, but it crumbled into ash.

"No!" he shouted as it fell apart in his fingers. He grabbed the next one, but it also turned to ash. All of them did, and then the whole workbench.

"Stop, no, stop!" he shouted. He couldn't lose it all, not again. He couldn't let it fall apart, he couldn't fail, not again, they'd all . . . Raych was counting on him, Corsi. Asti. All the others. There was so much smoke now, he couldn't see his workroom, couldn't breathe. "I can build it again, I can—"

A hand touched his shoulder. "Verci."

The word, his name, was spoken so gently, filled with such love, that it brought him pure serenity. The smoke cleared away to his empty workroom, and in front of him, a young blond cloistress.

"I know you, don't I?" he asked her.

"Not yet, not really," she said. "I wasn't really me when I came to you, not yet, not the me you're going to know."

"Who are you, and what . . . what is this?"

She took his hand and sat him down. "This is you, locked in a box for too long. You tried very hard to keep your mind together, and you made this delusion for yourself to keep control. But it was starting to collapse, and if it had, you would have completely shattered with it."

"I . . . no . . . I was in my . . . we're in my workshop."

"You're still in the prison, Verci," she said. "You had been falsely arrested, put in the prison, and you got put into the box rescuing your friend. You need to remember."

"Right," he said, pushing through the cloud. "But then, where are we?"

"In your delusion, my dream?" she said with a shrug. "A place where we both can meet, for a moment. A place I could reach you, remind you to survive. Tell you need to get through this, but you *will* get through this, because you have so much more to do."

"You came to the shop, called me Saint Terrent. Sister Myriem, right?"

"I may have done that, but I wasn't myself then. Not who I am now, and certainly not who I will be. But we will meet, and you will get through this test, Verci Rynax."

She said that with such conviction, he couldn't help but believe it. "So just get through this, get out of the prison, and everything will be fine?"

Her eyes welled up with tears. "Oh, Verci. I wish I could tell you that. It's going to be so hard for you, my friend."

"Why can't I just have a normal, quiet life?"

"Because someone has to stand up, Verci. For your family, for your neighbors, for your city."

"Does it have to be me?"

She smiled; a soft, sad smile. "There was a girl in trouble, the daughter of the man who killed your father, and only you could save her. What did you do?"

"You know what I did, I think."

"Because that's who you are. You're never going to just sit there and let things happen. That's why you can't just have a normal, quiet life."

A question weighed down his heart. "But can my son?"

She touched his face, and he could feel her sorrow, but also her faith and certainty. And with all that, a sense of calm filled him, even though there was fear.

"Keep fighting for him, *always* keep fighting for him, and we can hope," she said. She took his hand. "Now, Verci Rynax, stand up."

She pulled him to his feet, but he wasn't in the workshop. He was standing outside the hold box, in the Quarrygate prison yard. Weak, hungry, thirsty as all blazes, but on his feet.

"Gotta say, most folks don't just stand up when they get out of that," a guard said. "You've got some iron, Tacklin."

Verci looked about. Three guards, but no Sister Myriem. Had he really almost cracked in there, and hallucinated her? It seemed so real, though.

"Appreciate the compliment," Verci said. Burying the anger, the fear, the urge to scream, he put on his best smile. "Is it lunchtime? I am rather famished."

THE GUARDS HAD TAKEN VERCI TO THE WATER CLOSET AND STRIPPED him out of his grays, dunked him in the bath for a scrub, and thrown new clothes at him. Verci kept the smart comments going the whole time —*I'm a married man, you know* and *At least buy me a beer, first* and the like—while trying to keep the memory of the dream in his head. What did she say? He needed to stand.

Someone needs to stand up.

Right now, Asti was missing, and surely the others had been lost without him. It had been, what, six days since Helene's party? He had no idea, but he had to get to Jules and the others, and come up with some way to help them. As many ways as he could, try them all.

"Come along, finish getting those on," the guard said as Verci dressed.

"I'm working on it," he said with a bit more edge than he should have dared, and the glare from the guard was definitely a warning. "I do appreciate the fresh grays."

"You're probably going to pull laundering duty next, Tacklin. If you stay out of trouble."

"Why wouldn't I stay out of trouble?"

"Your call, friend. Keep your hands as clean as that outfit."

"It isn't that clean," Verci said. "But if I'm on laundry duty, I'll keep things sharp."

"Just keep your mouth dull, hear?"

"Heard." Verci finished putting on the sandals. "Ready. Where to? Is it meal time? I'm famished but got no sense of time."

The guard handed Verci a canteen, and Verci took a swig. Just water, but it was more than welcome. "Meal isn't for another couple hours. Your ward's on work detail now, but you can get back to your bunk until meal."

"I appreciate that."

"Gotta say," the guard said. "Most boys don't walk out of the box like that." He raised an eyebrow. "Heard you were some kind of insurgent."

"That's what they say."

"Did you serve army or something?" the guard asked, leading Verci down the hallway.

"Nah," Verci said, following his instincts. This guard was oddly chatty, might as well go with it. "Just a tough street kid is all. Can I ask you something?"

"You can ask, but I may not like the question."

"My big friend, the one who was in the box before me, he doing all right?"

"That guy, man," the guard said. "You'd think a guy like that would be a really tough, but he spent a whole day in the infirmary before the doc tossed him out."

"But now?"

"Blazes, I don't know. He hasn't caused me any trouble, I can tell you that."

That wasn't what Verci would call good news, but it could have been worse.

As they went down the hallway, they passed a young man who was clearly not a guard, and not a prisoner. He was wearing a frayed wool suit, patched in several places, and spectacles with a chipped lens, carrying an overstuffed valise. Verci's instinct was lawyer, and an overworked and underpaid one at that, which meant one thing.

"Justice!" Verci called out. "Justice Advocate!"

"Hey, watch it," the guard said, yanking Verci's arm.

"Justice!" Verci called to the young man again.

"You're going to end up back in—"

"Back in where?" the young professional man said, walking over. "This man is calling for justice, you best not be intending to punish him for that."

The guard stammered a bit. "No, but . . . but there's a system to . . ."

"I'm familiar with the system, sir," he said. He looked Verci up and down. "Is there an issue, friend?"

"Quite an issue," Verci said. He glanced at the guard. "Not with him, he's doing his job admirably."

The guard relaxed his grip a bit at that.

"Go on," the young man said. "I don't have much time to waste."

"Sorry, Mister . . ."

"Cheever," he said. "Cheed Cheever."

"Am I correct you are with the Justice Advocate Office?"

"You are," Cheever said. "And I have quite a full load, so . . ."

"Of course," Verci said. "I've been misidentified and held here without trial, without representation, as have several friends of mine."

"No trial?" Cheever asked. "Even a preliminary hearing?"

"There was that, and we were sent here under . . ."

"Presumptive custody," Cheever said with a groan. "If that was done, I'm unable to help until you have trial . . ."

"But the name they arrested me under, it isn't mine, sir," Verci said. "I've not been able to properly identify myself, my family doesn't even know where I am, and there was no legal representation at any stage."

Cheever glared at the guard. "You know that isn't right."

"I had nothing to do with that, chap."

Cheever pulled out a notebook and stylus. "I've got a full docket, but give me the name you were arrested under and your proper name, I'll see what I can be done."

"Verci Rynax is my actual name," Verci said. "My wife is Raychelle Rynax, living on Junk Avenue in North Seleth."

"What name did they charge you under?"

"Tacklin," Verci said. "I forget the given name there. Indick?"

Cheever wrote it down. "I cannot promise anything, Mister Rynax, but I will at least follow up with you." And he pointed a thumb at the guard. "And I expect to continue to hear of the admirability of your work, friend."

The guard made a face, but said, "You can bet a wage on that, chap."

"Capital," Cheever said, putting the notebook back in his pocket.

"Please, try to contact my wife, if nothing else," Verci said.

"I will try, sir, but you must understand . . . I'm already late." He rushed off.

"Feel better, Tacklin?" the guard asked.

"It really is Rynax," Verci said. "And, yes."

"Well, then, maybe we can bring you right to the laundering before supper," the guard said, pulling Verci along. "Since you're feeling so good."

CHAPTER SEVENTEEN

Verci had, out of sheer exhaustion, slept hard on his bunk in Ward Seven, though he was plagued by shapeless nightmares the whole time. When the shrill blasts of the wake-up whistle yanked him out of it, he couldn't remember a single detail of them, just the overwhelming sense of dread he had felt.

"I'm glad you're back," Julien told Verci as they joined the line to the water closets. "I was . . . I was real worried about you in there."

"I managed," Verci said.

"Better than I did, that's for sure," Julien said. "I just . . . thank you, really, for coming for me."

"Had to do it, and it was worth going in to get you out."

"But maybe we should be smart, keep our heads down?" Julien asked.

Verci was surprised to hear that. "We need to get out of here."

"Yeah, but . . . we can make it if we're just smart, I think. The trial will come and we're innocent, so that's going to be fine, right? Because they've got it wrong."

"I don't think we can or should count on that."

"Or Asti will come for us."

Saints, Julien seemed downright broken.

"We're going to play it calm and easy, sure," Verci said. "I did get to talk to a Justice Advocate, and he's looking into our situation."

"See, it'll work out."

"But we also need to keep our options open. That means we stay alert, look for opportunities."

"I dunno," Julien said. "I'm not cut out for that."

"Well, watch my back, and I'll stay alert, deal?"

"Deal," Julien said.

Verci stuck by Julien as they were led along through the washroom, then to the dining hall for breakfast, which was lukewarm porridge with preserves of unidentifiable origins. Verci could not determine what fruit it had ever been, and whatever it was now was barely palatable. Still, Verci ate, as he was ravenous. Like he told Jules, eyes open, look for opportunities. He couldn't do that if he was also fainting.

The fellow next to Verci nudged him. "Looks like the chomie is gonna get knockaround."

"What?" Verci asked, and looked where the guy was pointing to see several fellows—all marked with the same tattoo on their neck—start to move around Kennith at his table. And, notably, the guards weren't doing a damn thing about them being near the wrong table.

"Oh, blazes, no," Verci said, starting to get up.

Julien grabbed him and pulled him back onto the bench.

"No, Verci."

Verci glared at Julie's meaty hand wrapped around his arm. "Ken's going to—"

It started. One of the tattooed boys wailed on the back of Kennith's head with a tray, and when he went down, the others all started kicking.

"Julie, we have to—"

"If we do we'll be just as bad off," he said. "We can't do anything for Kennith."

"That's not—"

"It'll be done in a moment."

And then there were some whistles, and the guards halfheartedly pulled the tattoo boys away. Verci wrenched his way of Julien's grip and jumped over to Ken.

"You all right, can you breathe?" he asked. The poor man's face was a mangled mess, blood pouring out his nose, one eye swollen.

"Ver . . ." Kennith mumbled, but then some folks pulled Verci away as the guards tossed Kennith on a stretcher and took him out.

"How can they—what the blazes," Verci muttered.

"Easy," Vellun said—he was who had pulled Verci away. "We make trouble or noise, it'll be worse for him, and . . ." He nodded over to Pilsen, who looked even more drawn and pale than ever before. He stumbled over to Verci.

"Kelsi, dear boy, this rehearsal is abysmal, and everything about this show is a mess. I have to resign the part."

"It's Verci, Pilsen," he urged. "And this isn't a show."

"I'd say. Those fellows know nothing of how to fake a hit, and I think they really did some damage to the dark fellow. Which is a shame, because there aren't enough of those in the trade. We need a good one to play Cartherat if do *The Sauric Shore* this season."

"Pilsen, we're in Quarrygate."

"Is that one of the new ones? Cobbe or Swanson?"

"Break it up and finish eating, loverboys," a guard said, shoving Pilsen back to the table.

Verci glanced at Vellun. "That bad?"

"Worse," Vellun whispered. "Please, Verci, you have to get us out of here, soon."

The guard grabbed Verci and dragged him over. "And you stay in your place if you don't want the box again." He was shoved back down next to Julien.

"I told you," Julien said. "We gotta be smart, not make trouble. Only way we'll make it."

Verci shook his head. "We can't let anything like that happen again."

If it kept up this way, if he didn't get them all out soon, they weren't going to make it at all.

VERCI HAD BEEN PUT ON LAUNDRY DUTY, AND EITHER THE GUARDS OR his fellow prisoners had plans to punish him, as he was given a pile of clothes encrusted with filth, mold, blood, sewage, and saints even knew what else. He put on the best smile he could force his face to make, and got to work, even whistling while he did it. Soap and water and board, scrubbing like he was happy to do it.

Show no sign they were even close to breaking him.

Which they weren't. Since coming out of the box, his resolve was strong, he knew he could handle whatever they tried here. He was confident he'd find a way. The dream of the cloistress had renewed him, and the encounter with Mister Cheever would hopefully bear fruit.

And if it didn't, he needed to prepare for that as well.

Part of preparing was a matter of determining resources. Who was he in here with, and what could he get his hands on. Fortunately, he was very good at getting his hands on things. He'd been out of practice, but when he was a kid, Pop had made sure he could slide a coin from a man's pocket without any suspicion, and hide it from sight if questioned. Hands never forget those things. He had already managed to slip away a few spoons from the dining hall, a few spring clips from laundry, a couple keys from guards, and a few other bits and bobs from here and there. He had no idea what he was going to do with these treasures, but he was certain it was better to have them and find a use for them later.

And the massive pile of absolutely vile clothing and linens gave him the perfect hiding place that no one would search.

"Hey, Tacklin!" a guard shouted. "Tacklin!"

It took Verci a moment to remember that was him. "Washing as fast as I can, friend."

"Cut out from that. You got a lawyer meeting."

That was very interesting. He had hoped that Cheever would come through, but this was faster than he expected. No complaints about that, then. He might not need his stash of scraps.

He washed off his hands and followed the guard up through the ward, down hallways, and past a set of double-gated portals. Verci kept his eye on the mechanisms as they went through, designed to be impossible to open both gates at once, and opening the outer gate had to be done from the other side. No one could get through—at least in theory—

without someone out letting them out. These seemed to be the only way into the administrative parts of the prison, which is how guards, lawyers, and other visitors came and went each day.

Verci filed the whole route here, the labels on each door, and the details of each gate, in the back of his memory. Hopefully he wouldn't need it, but at this point, he wasn't going to let any opportunity slip away.

He was put in a small room with an actual barred window, so he could see outside. While waiting he walked over and chanced a glance at the street below. Three stories down, and a walled courtyard between the building and the street. Manned guardposts.

"So, Mister Tacklin," Cheever said as he came in the room. "Would you sit?"

Verci sat at the table across from Cheever. "I'm glad you came back so quickly. Can you help?"

"I don't think I'm in a position to, Mister Tacklin—"

"I told you, my name is Verci Rynax, I live in North Seleth . . ."

"Verci Rynax, according to the records I found, died in a fire on Maritan the 28th," Cheever said. "As did his brother and family."

Maritan the 28th. The night of the Holver Alley fire.

"No," Verci said. "That . . . that's not true at all."

"That's what I found when I put in an inquiry."

"Sir, the Rynax Gadgeterium opened two months ago. It's been in the neighborhood. My wife runs the Junk Avenue Bakery."

"I went by there, it looks abandoned and shut down. Papered over, like it hadn't been open in months."

How was that possible? Where was Raych? If she wasn't there, what was happening out there? He needed to get out of this place.

"I'm telling you, you've been tricked. Did you . . . did you read that pamphlet last month? *The Champions of Maradaine* one? Big seller, all over the city?"

"I don't waste time with fanciful fiction."

"Listen to me—"

"Mister Tacklin, I am a rational man. I serve to ensure the best possible justice, I serve to challenge prosecution and judges, to act as watchdog to those institutions. I have seen miscarriage of justice, and I have seen people insist on their innocence despite overwhelming evidence. But I've never seen anything such as this."

"My name is Verci Rynax, my brother Asti, and I most definitely did not die in that fire, nor did my wife and son!"

"Don't shout at me."

Where could she be? Hal and Lian, of course.

"Hal and Lian Elman, my wife's sister and husband, they live on—"

"Listen," Cheever said calmly. "You're either the victim of a very insidious plot, or you are a very charming, dangerous and capable liar. Which would I believe?"

"It's the plot."

"Except," Cheever said, holding up a folder. "Indlen Tacklin, reported to have been behind several incidents of unrest and dissent in Abernar, Kyst, and Maskill. In every case, he uses lies, manipulation, and alternate identities to deceive innocent people to carry out his vicious schemes. He and his brother are among the most dangerous men in Sauriya."

"If you believed that, would you be alone in this room with me?"

"It's not what I believe!" Cheever said. "Saints, Mister Tacklin—"

"Rynax!"

"It's what can be proven! There is nothing on paper to help you. Besides . . ." He shook his head.

"Besides, what?"

"You are charged with High Treason Against the Archduchy. It's not even within the jurisdiction of my office to aide you, even if I was inclined."

"You aren't inclined?"

"With this evidence?"

"You said yourself, Mister Cheever. You serve as watchdog. Allow the possibility this is a plot. If so—"

"It's absurd."

"If so, Mister Cheever, then you would have to admit that allowing me to face those charges would be the grossest miscarriage of justice imaginable."

Cheever bowed his head. "I can't believe I'm saying this, but that is true."

"So help me. Even if I am Indlen Tacklin, I deserve legal counsel, no?"

"I don't have the authority," Cheever said. "But I will write to the right people in Kyst. Because, yes, even if you are the most dangerous man in Sauriya, you deserve a lawyer."

Verci pushed down his rage. The last thing he needed was to further alienate the one possibly ally he had to reach the outside world.

"Thank you," Verci said.

"Now, I must bid you good day," Cheever said. "There's nothing more I can do. My schedule is already overwhelmed, and this . . . but I will write those letters."

"I do appreciate that, Mister Cheever."

Cheever knocked on the door, and the guards came for Verci.

"Wait," Cheever said as they were taking Verci out. "Hal and Lian Elman, where do they live?"

"61 Colt," Verci said.

Cheever nodded, and waved the guards, who dragged Verci out and took him back through the series of hallways and gates to the laundry room.

Verci let himself be taken in silence, keeping his eyes and ears open. Though at the last set of double gates, he noted the infirmary. Kennith was there. So that would be where he'd go tonight.

There was no legal option for them, that was clear. Just like Cheever said, an insidious plot was against them. It would take every ounce of Verci's cunning to find a way out, and by every saint he knew, he'd use it all to do it.

Verci had abandoned caution. At least when it came to his own consequences right now. If the guards caught him threw him in the box again, it didn't matter. Right now he was here in the prison, responsible for four of his friends, and they were all pieces in someone's scheme.

So there was no further consequence to him that mattered, because anything he faced to get out, get home, make things right, they were necessary.

He slipped out of his cell in the night, mouse quiet, moving his way down the hallways to the infirmary. Even though the guards were more alert at night, getting around them was child's play. Truly, he could have done this when he was seven.

Blazes, back then he could have slid between the bars.

The infirmary door was latched, but a simple one that he was easily able to slide open. He found the doctor there asleep on a cot—not alone, it seemed. Someone that Verci presumed was a prisoner from the women's wards was with him, also asleep.

Patients in cots behind flimsy screens. Only a couple of those bunks filled. Finding the one he wanted was easy.

"Ken," he whispered, waking the man up. "You all right?"

"Do I look rutting all right to you?"

"Not remotely," Verci said.

"There's your answer. You best get out before more trouble is visited on you."

"We're already in all the trouble."

"Tell me something I don't know."

"That whatever this scheme is, the player in it is someone way above us. Someone who can make official paperwork that said Asti and I died in the fire."

Ken raised an eyebrow as much as he could with his bruised face. "Like whoever was behind the fire?"

"The thought occurred to me."

"Then we are rutting screwed."

"I'm still going to fight this."

"Fight?" Kennith's voice went a little too loud on that, and Verci glanced around the corner to make sure neither the sew-up or his companion reacted to that. Ken lowered his voice. "What kind of fight are you talking about? You already see what happened to me? To Jules?"

"And what it's doing to Pilsen. Still, we've got to do something."

"Define 'something,' because if it involves any more beatings, I'm going to pass."

"You don't have to do anything," Verci said. "I just came here to make sure you know I'm going to get us all out of here."

Kennith looked at him strangely—in as much as Ken could with one eye swollen up. "I think your time in that box broke your head worse than Asti's."

"Maybe. But I'm telling you right now, Ken," Verci said, taking his friend's hand. "I'm going to get you out of here. I'm going to get all of you out of here, as soon as possible. No matter what it costs me."

"How the blazes you think you're going to do that?" Kennith asked. "Sorry, man, but you don't have your gear, you don't have your tools."

"That's far from all I am," Verci said.

"And you're stuck with the worst of us. I'm just a driver, and look at me. Julien is essentially a child. Pilsen too, at this point, and Vellun certainly isn't cut out for this."

"I will make a plan," Verci said.

"I just don't see how you can do it. This sort of thing, sorry to say, it just isn't a Verci Rynax job."

Verci thought about that, and Kennith had a point. Verci Rynax wasn't the man for this gig, not by any chance. And no one was coming to save them.

"Maybe you're right," he said, getting to his feet. "But as far as this prison is concerned, they don't have Verci Rynax. They're holding Indlen Tacklin."

"What does that even mean?"

"Indlen Tacklin is a revolutionary, a terrorist. One of the most dangerous men in Druthal." Verci noticed some of the sew-up's instruments and chemicals, foolishly left out in the open. A plan formed in his head. "I think I'm going to show them what it's like to have that man locked up in here."

CHAPTER EIGHTEEN

Verci didn't sleep, but he did make sure to get back to his bunk before the sun was up, after spending the night working out a plan to make good on his promise to Kennith. Fortunately, he was able to hole up in the laundry to work out details, draw out a map, and cobble together a couple surprises to put to use.

There might be heightened security in place in the prison, they might be paying more attention, but he was still his father's son. Still able to slip through hallways mouse quiet. Still able to find a shadow or niche when he heard someone coming. If he had the time and the inclination, he could learn every secret in this prison, and be ruling it in a month.

He had neither the time nor the inclination.

What he had was a plan.

It was a crazy plan, one that Asti would never approve of. But Asti wasn't here. Verci couldn't worry about what he'd want or do right now. He had to get his friends out of here, he had to get himself out of here. There was no more waiting.

And it was a plan with an enormous, glaring flaw. The only way he could make it work, he'd have to be in two places at the same time.

He lay in the bunk as the sky started to lighten outside, trying to figure out the way around that problem.

Part of that challenge stemmed from how his plan had to work. One thing had been abundantly clear, as he double-checked all his possible exit routes, went over his options to get everyone out: because there was more security, there was no way he could come up with to sneak his friends out. At least, not without weeks of planning.

Kennith didn't have weeks. Nor did Pilsen. Or Vellun and Julien. And Raych, she couldn't wait weeks.

So his plan was loud and hard and fast. Exactly the sort of ugly plan that Asti hated. He hated it as well, but he didn't see any other way.

Loud and hard and fast. Very fast. He had to light the taper today. He had stolen supplies from the infirmary, the laundry, the cleaning closet. They would be noticed soon.

Today. And he'd have to be two place at once.

No, he'd have to trust one job to someone else.

"Get up, maggots!" a guard shouted. "Stand at doors for counting!"

Verci got in line, as Julien and their other bunkmates did the same.

One job was dangerous, and the other was intricate. He didn't want to ask anyone else to do the dangerous job. But he didn't think anyone else could do the intricate job. He looked at Julien, standing there with the sad, broken look on his face.

Julien could follow instructions, but there were too many for him to handle. He couldn't possibly do the intricate job. And if Julien was given the dangerous job . . .

No, he couldn't ask Julien to do that. He wouldn't get out if he did it.

The guard went by and counted each of them.

"All right, hit the closet, boys. Breakfast in ten, so don't dally!"

Maybe Kennith could do it, but he didn't have a way to get to Kennith in the infirmary to explain it to him. Not before things actually had to get started.

He could write it down for Ken, give that to Jules?

He followed the crowd to the water closets, as they all queued up for their turn.

"All right, all right, I got you," he heard from one of the stalls. Two pairs of legs. Vellun's voice. He must be helping Pilsen in there. Had it come to that? Verci couldn't imagine the indignity Pilsen was feeling. But it was amazing how well Vellun was handling it, considering.

Vellun was handling it.

Verci shoved his way through the queue to their stall.

"Hey, watch it!" someone said to him.

"Watch yourself or I'll feed your tenders to you," Verci snarled back. He went into the stall and wedge the door shut behind him.

Vellun and Pilsen both looked aghast at him. "What are you doing?" Vellun asked.

"Listen very carefully," Verci said. "You all are getting out of here, today."

"What, how?" Vellun asked.

"It's up to you," Verci said, taking Vellun's shoulder. "You do exactly what I tell you, and you two, and Jules and Ken will be breathing free air by sunset."

"Verci, there's no way I can do all that," Vellun said as he helped dress Pilsen.

"It's a lot, I know," Verci said. He had explained what was required as "But once you get to the infirmary, Kennith can help you, you'll have Julien . . ."

"It's too much," Vellun said. "This is what you do, or Asti. Not me."

"I need to get you all out of here," Verci said.

"So where will you be?" Vellun asked.

"In the dining hall, causing the distraction you all need." He had explained it, but now Vellun was sweating.

"Some of us need to piss, potwalkers!" someone shouted from outside the stall.

"How do you get to the rest of us and get yourself out?"

"I'll do my best," Verci said.

"It's too dangerous," Pilsen said quietly.

"Shh, dear, it's—"

"I said what I said," Pilsen said. "And I heard you, boy. There's too much to do, too many moving parts. Vellun's no good at that, if it doesn't stick to the script."

"I can't ask him to cause the distraction," Verci said.

"Of course not, he'll get killed. You'll get killed, dear boy."

Verci didn't care. "I'll manage. The important thing—"

Pilsen shook his head. "The important thing is it all works. That can't happen without you at the lead."

"I can't ask anyone else to—"

"You're not asking," Pilsen said. "I'm doing it."

Verci was stunned quiet, then knocked out of it by the pounding on the stall.

"No, Pilsen, you can't—"

"You're not well, dear," Vellun added, fussing with getting Pilsen's pants fastened.

"Exactly," Pilsen said, pushing Vellun's hands away.

"No, you need to—"

Pilsen grabbed Verci's shoulder. "Verci, my dear, dear boy. I am just holding the last grains of sand in my hand here. I think I have one last performance left in me, so let me . . . please, let me make it count for something."

Verci took Pilsen's hand. "You know how much we love you, old man."

"I know," he said, touching Vellun's face with his other hand. "Get him out of here. And those other boys. You do what you need to do. And you give me my cue, and I'll do what I do best."

The door of the stall kicked open. "Blazes you three doing?" one prisoner asked. He was one of the ones who had beat up Kennith.

"Helping the old man," Verci said, spinning around and lowering his voice. "When I like someone, I help them." He stepped up close to the fellow. "And when I don't like someone . . ."

"What do you do?" he asked. Hand hovering above the seam in his pants. Makeshift weapon likely hidden there.

Verci's hand darted out and snatched that weapon—a jagged blade made from a spoon. He pressed it against the fellow's gut.

"Didn't you know? I'm Indlen Tacklin. Most dangerous man in here. You don't want to know what I can do when I'm upset."

He nodded to Vellun to get Pilsen out of the washroom.

"You're aiming to start some trouble, Tacklin," the fellow said in a growl.

"Oh, friend," Verci said. "I absolutely am."

VERCI SLIPPED INTO THE LUNCH LINE WITH JULIEN. HE EVERYTHING HE needed for the plan now hidden up his sleeves and in his pants, and in a few minutes, it would be the point of no return.

"Where have you been?" Julien asked.

"Busy," Verci asked. "Listen, Jules, you need to trust me and do exactly what I say."

"Of course," Julien said. "What's going on?"

"I'll tell you more when you need to know," Verci said. He palmed a vial he had stolen from the infirmary and slipped it into Julien's hand. "For now, drink that, try not to let anyone see you."

"What's it going to do?"

"Make you really sick," Verci said.

"I don't like the sound of that."

"You'll throw up, a lot, but a few minutes after that you'll be fine. Trust me."

"You're sure?"

"I am."

"All right. But why?"

"Because in about twenty minutes, there's going to be chaos, and I need you in the infirmary at that point."

Jules nodded. "I understand. I . . . I don't like it, but I understand."

Verci looked back up at him. "Trust me. I'll see you there."

"I always trust you," Julien said. He glanced about, and then took a swig from the vial. His face told a whole story, but he pocketed the vial and kept walking along with the line. "How long?"

"Not very," Verci said.

And right on cue, Julien lurched forward, shoving a pair of men in front of him out of his way. He dropped to his knees and erupted the full contents of his stomach, a vile scent hitting the air. Several of the other prisoners blanched and stumbled away, and the guards who approached winced once the smell reached them.

"Blazes happened?" a guard asked.

"He just got sick," Verci said.

"I can see that," the guard said, looking at Julien doubled over on the floor, more surges of sickness coming out of him. "You three, get him up, get him to the sew-up!"

Some other guards struggled to get Julien to his feet without getting hit with more vomit, and took him off.

"We can't eat with that filth right on the floor," Verci said.

The guard sneered at Verci. "Well, I guess you just volunteered to clean it up."

Verci groaned to hide the smile. Exactly what he wanted the guard to say.

"Fine," Verci said. "Where's the mop and such?"

"I'll take you, Tacklin. Come along. The rest of you, go back to what you were doing."

The guard took Verci to one of the supply closets, exactly as Verci had planned. He unlocked the door and gestured for Verci to grab the cart with the mops and bucket.

"That's some nasty stuff back there," Verci said. "Gonna need something strong to clean it up."

"Just mop it. There's vinegar on the cart."

"Come on," Verci said, pointing to the locked cage in the back of the supply room. "It's going to need something like ammonia."

"Fine," the guard said, pulling out his keys. "But only take a little bit, because—"

Whatever he was going to finish that sentence with, it didn't matter, because Verci had already closed the door of the closet and used the mop to knock the guard across the head. Two more hard blows made sure he wasn't about to get up any time soon.

A few moments later, Verci came out of the closet pushing the cart, with several chemicals he shouldn't have loaded up on it, and the guard's uniform worn under his prisoner grays. The guard was tied up naked in the cage in the closet, his skivs shoved into his mouth. Verci locked the closet back up and hid the keys on the cart.

The dice had been thrown now, no turning back. It was just a matter of seeing how they would land.

He hoped he had grabbed the right things from the cage. He had picked up a few bits of basic knowledge about chemicals and reactions from working with Almer, mostly a handful of Almer's admonitions of "never mix these two things together."

Which was exactly what Verci planned to do.

He wheeled the cart back to the dining hall, where folks were making a wide circle around the pool of vomit. Head down, doing his best to look unassuming, he got over to the mess and made like he was about to start cleaning.

Pilsen and Vellun were still in line, with the folks from their cell block in Ward Seven. This was the moment. He glanced up and gave them the nod.

They knew what they had to do, he had laid out the whole plan. As he had originally intended it, Vellun would have been the one with the mop and chemicals right now, and he'd be the one about to draw all the attention to himself before all the chaos was unleashed.

But Vellun and Pilsen were right—too many moving parts, too many things that Verci had to handle himself, if it was going to work at all.

So it had to be Pilsen.

The old man nodded back, and as he did, Verci saw a light in his eyes that he hadn't seen in some time.

Pilsen Gin was ready to give his last performance.

Pilsen held on to Vellun's hand as they waited in line, waiting for the moment for him to go on stage.

He had to think of it as going on stage. The rest was so much fog and smoke, and he knew these fleeting memories and thoughts weren't something he could hold on to much longer. Vellun was here, the dear, beautiful boy, and he was solid and real. Verci was here and real as well. He came in, in costume as a prisoner, working his props like a true professional.

Not props. Not costumes. *You are in Quarrygate prison right now.*

Verci and Vellun are prisoners as well. They are counting on you to escape.

It was so hard to hold on to that. To remember that was Verci, not Kelsi. That the one holding his hand right now was Vellun, not Rendell.

Oh, Rendell, what those monsters did to you. For a moment, he was back in that terrible day fifty years ago.

Stay here, stay in this moment, he reminded himself. He had to hold himself together, if just for a few minutes. But that anger, he could use that. Put that into the work.

Verci looked up and nodded. That was his cue.

"It's time," he told Vellun. He brought Vellun's hand up to his lips and kissed it gently.

"Maybe we can—"

"It's all right," Pilsen said.

"I love you, you know that?"

"I do. Now you go on, find some nice young man your own age to grow old with, all right? You still have so much time."

Vellun squeezed his hand, and for a moment, the last thing Pilsen ever wanted to do was let go.

But he had to. There was a show to do.

He dropped Vellun's hand and walked away, ready to make a scene, one like none other he had ever played. The performance of a lifetime. Over his life on the stage, he'd done all six of Whit's tragedies—always his favorite—and if he was at the end of his tragic life, by every saint, he'd do them one last time.

"Hear me, friends and foes alike, for I will lay down accusations, and when I finish I dare say I will not have a friend left in this room, but so help me, neither will any of you!"

Kendler's last act speech from *The Hawk of Erien* was a good place to start, though he hadn't played that part in decades. Here and now, Pilsen fully understood the tragedy that had often been joked about in playing Kendler: when you were the right age for the role, you weren't seasoned enough an actor to do it justice, and when you were seasoned enough, you were too old. What a Kendler he could be now in the body of a young man.

He glanced back at Vellun, tears on his face. He had a few years in him where he could play Kendler. Maybe now he still would.

"Because I see nothing but villains around me, each one against me, each one against each other!"

"Quiet, old man!" someone shouted. They didn't care what he was saying, but it didn't matter, their eyes were on him. That was the point. He moved to the back wall, away from the doors. Eyes on him, not on Verci or Vellun.

"And do you now stand against me," he called out, switching to Ponic's monologue in *The Sons of Yinro* as he got on the chair. He was doing this show the night they killed Rendell. Surely no one in the audience that night realized that the bloodstain on his shirt was real, but they felt his pain, his anguish. Ponic dies halfway through the play, of course, but it was the best part, damning the two factions who joined in the squabble between brothers, escalating to war. Pilsen kept that energy, that pain as if it was still fresh—it was never gone, no—and aimed it at the others in the dining hall. Petty gang boys, all of them, but they already were factions against each other. This prison was a barrel of boom powder and he would be the taper.

The guards moved slowly toward him as he continued, switching to the Reverend's speech from *Demea*. Oh, he had them now. They knew they had to stop him, they knew they should just grab him and drag him to the box, but he could see it in their eyes. Despite their duty, they were transfixed. This audience was *his* now, he had them. And like any great tragedy, like the dead lovers at the end of *Demea*, where this would end was now inevitable.

Pilsen knew it had to be him to do this, even as he fought his way through the fog of his fading mind when Verci explained everything to Vellun. Vellun couldn't do what Verci needed him to do, but Verci— bless that boy—he couldn't have done this.

"And now look at your hands, and see them empty," he directed at the leaders of one of the gangs. "And how they were kept empty while others were filled." Ossinen from *The Sauric Shore*, the double-tongued manipulator whose wicked, clever words turned friends against each other. Well-placed lies, deliberate half-truths, and soon the rest of the characters were ready to kill each other. The bastards in here were already poised to do that, and it wouldn't take half as much maneuvering to set them off. Yes, with just a gesture at the leader of the Necky-Knock Boys, he reminded everyone else how they were favored by the guards.

Verci had pulled the mopcart near the door, and Vellun was right by them. They were ready to take their moment. Bless those boys, he thought, as he switched to the titular doomed hero of *The Earl of Crestile.* Making that call to arms for would be Crestile's futile last battle, where he knew he wouldn't win the war, but he could buy his sons the time they needed. He called out that now was the time to fight.

Pilsen didn't even see Verci's hand move, but suddenly blood burst from the chests of three of the gang boys, hit with thrown blades. At the perfect spot where his speech had hit its dramatic pitch.

"And see how they kill us, and we will not stand it longer!"

The room erupted into violence, all the prisoners leaping on each other. The guards were buried in the chaos of it, trying desperately to quell a fire that was already in full blaze.

Pilsen looked back toward the doors, but Verci and Vellun—dear, beloved Vellun—were gone. Where they had been standing, plumes of acrid smoke were pouring out of the mop bucket. Everyone else in the dining hall were far too lost in their chaos to even notice that danger.

His performance had worked them into such a frenzy, that none were still minding him as he switched to *The Autumn of Corringshire,* the old man who had lost his fortune, his family, and his mind in his last foolish days. A distinguished role, fitting for his final one.

"And so you fall with me, murderers and traitors, my last breath to spit a curse. I die, and leave you nothing, nothing but rot and ruin."

He got to finish his last line before a guard's baton cracked across his head, and as he dropped to the ground, he felt no pain, no sorrow, and he knew, in his final thoughts, that it had been the best performance of his life.

CHAPTER NINETEEN

Verci was dragging Vellun along down the hall, having stripped off the grays and now in the guard uniform. He was holding a bloody rag to Vellun's head, acting like he was dealing with an injured man as they passed several guards running toward the chaos. Vellun, for his part, was wailing, which certainly sold the bit, but was also not performance.

"Just hold it together for now," Verci whispered once they passed another group of guards. "I know you feel like your heart's been torn from your body—"

"You have *no* idea . . ."

"Hey," Verci said, pulling up Vellun's head so they were eye-to-eye. "I have known that man my entire life, he was family. And we need to get out of here so that all wasn't for nothing. Once we're out, once we're safe, I will wear violet with you and empty glasses in his name. But first we have to get out."

Vellun nodded. "He wanted us to finish this show, so I'll manage. But . . ."

"Yeah," Verci said. He pulled Vellun in close and planted the rag on his head. "Just follow my lead, all right?"

"Got it."

No one questioned them as they made their way to the infirmary, and once there, Verci knew his best weapons were chaos and confusion.

He kicked open the door and dragged Vellun in.

"We've got a total mess in the dining hall, I think there's a fire, we need everybody on it!" he shouted.

There were three guards in the infirmary—the same ones who had brought Julien here. Jules was on a cot, with the sew-up looking him over. Kennith was still in the back room. Perfect.

"Go!" Verci shouted.

One of the guards waved the other two to run off, but he stayed over Julien.

"Sit him down over there, I'll have a look in a moment," the sew-up said.

Verci moved Vellun to the stool, and had him keep the rag on his head. No need to tip them off just yet.

"What are you waiting for," the guard asked. "You hurt or something? Get back out there and knock this business down."

"Yeah, I just need to catch my breath," Verci said. "It's crazy out there. What's with the big guy?"

The sew-up looked up. "He doesn't seem to have a fever. And he's not vomiting anymore. I'm tempted to say he's fine."

"That true, big guy? Are you fine?"

Jules opened his eyes and looked at Verci. They locked eyes, and Julien understood. His giant hands shot out and grabbed the guard and sew-up, and slammed their heads together. They both fell to the ground like fish on the dock.

"We really doing this?" Julien asked.

"We better be," Vellun said, getting up.

Kennith limped over. "Saints, you really are trying to do this madness."

"I told you, Kennith. You're breathing free air before the sun is down. All three of you are."

"Three . . . where's Pilsen?" Julien asked.

"He . . ." Verci faltered.

"He's gone," Vellun said. "He knew . . . he knew he didn't have any time left, and he wanted to use what little he had left to help us. And he . . . he gave quite a show."

"He's dead?" Julien asked, his deep voice quivering.

Verci nodded. "Last thing I saw, a guard had cracked him across the skull, and . . . I don't think . . . there's no way."

"Poor old man," Kennith said. "We should—"

Vellun started stripping the uniform off the unconscious guard. "We should move, and later we mourn. Else it will be for nothing."

Julien and Kennith both winced at the snap in Vellun's voice, but nodded. "What's the play?" Kennith asked.

Verci went into the back room and opened up the linens case, finding the tools he had hidden away there overnight. "Get those two bound and gagged, and then shove them in the water closet, and lock it as best you can."

Julien got on that, while Kennith looked around the room.

"What should Julien and I wear?"

"Keep your grays for now, but getting you out of those is part of the plan."

"So you have a plan?" Kennith asked.

"Damn right I do," Verci said. "And if all goes right, you're going to walk right out."

And we'll get back home to you Raych. Just hold on.

The guard challenged Verci on sight, but it wasn't a challenge of doubt. Verci was in a guard uniform, so was Vellun, and they looked the part enough to pass. But Verci knew, even dressed as guards, their escort of Julien and Kennith right now would be questioned.

"I've got orders from my chief," Verci said plainly.

"I heard it's a bleeding riot in there," the guard said. "What kind of orders?"

"Something about their lawyer screaming all sorts of things of Rights of Man, and produce them right now. He doesn't care what we're dealing with."

"I hear you," the guard said. "Go on."

"Lucky I got this duty," Verci said.

That was the first hurdle, the one that Verci had been less worried about. The double-latch gates to get from the ward into the administrative corridors. There would be cause to escort someone through here, just as he had been yesterday. And with all the chaos, all the better. Folks less apt to press when everything is a mess.

At least, that was the plan, and the plan was working.

The outer gate was opened, and the four of them were through.

"Now what?" Kennith asked. "I can't believe you're going to be able to keep walking us out just because you're in guard uniforms."

"No, that would never work," Verci said. "This plan is audacious, but not quite that audacious."

"So what's next?" Kennith asked.

"Getting you out of those prison grays," Verci said. "When we walk out, only I'll be in the guard uniform."

"How are you doing that?" Julien asked.

Verci pointed to the door they were approaching. "Because I spotted that when they brought me to see the lawyer."

The sign on the door: PRISONER IMPOUND STORAGE.

"What does that mean?" Julien asked.

Verci pulled out the stolen keys and worked the lock. "It means the clothes you all were wearing when you were brought here are kept in there." It came open with his third try. "Pile in, gents."

They all got in and he shut and latched the door, then got the lamps inside lit. Racks of shelves filled the room, each shelf filled with crates.

"We can't waste any time," Verci said. "Get looking."

"Got it," Vellun said, holding up a clipboard. "They've got the inventory here. It's under our arrested names, but . . ." He glanced around. "Julien, this one is yours."

Julien opened it up and started changing into the suit he had been wearing to the party.

"This won't be enough, will it? Even if we get out the door, they'll come arrest us again."

"They try again, we run, we fight. Because now we know it's not some misunderstanding, it was a plot against us."

"Against you and Asti, you mean," Kennith snarled.

"Maybe, I don't know." Verci looked at the clipboard and found his crate. Not that he was going to change, but he got his clothes, and then looked for Asti's. "I know whoever did this was in a position to fake records, claim we were already dead."

"All the more reason not to mess with them!" Kennith said.

"All the more reason not to wait to see how this damned game plays out." He found Kennith's crate. "You're here."

He found Asti's box, and got all of those clothes out as well. More importantly, Asti's knives. Those he put in his uniform pockets.

He searched through a few more crates, hoping to find what he needed. And, yes, exactly as he hoped.

"What's that?" Julien asked.

"Messenger bags," Verci said. "My plan didn't rely on finding them, but oh, they will make it easier."

"What for?" Vellun asked. Verci noticed he had already changed into his suit from the party, but had found Pilsen's crate and put on his rings and pendant.

Verci packed his clothes, Asti's and Almer's—having found that crate as well—into the messenger bags, and handed them to each one of them.

"That'll have to do. Carrying those, in your best suits, well, you might just look the part."

"What part?" Kennith asked.

"Why, lawyers, of course."

HERE WAS THE PART OF THE PLAN WHERE VERCI WAS RELYING ON guesswork and luck.

That was the whole damn plan, Verci admitted to himself as folded up Kennith's grays and hid them inside his uniform coat. *This part is just more so.*

"All right," Verci said getting out two of the cleaning bottles. "In a moment, you all open that door, and I pour these two together. And then we're going to run down that corridor. I'll be right behind you, but in case, take—"

"First right, then fourth door on the left," Vellun said. "I remember."

"Vellun, if anything happens to me . . ."

"Nothing is happening to anyone else," Vellun said.

"What are you going to do with those?" Kennith asked.

"Something Almer once said to *never* do. So this will probably be very bad."

"Why are you doing it, then?" Julien asked.

"Because you all need to be on the run. So we need to make it bad."

"Is that what you did in the dining hall?" Vellun asked. "How bad was it back there?"

"Bad enough to teach a lesson," Verci said. "They wanted to play a game with us, steal our identities and call us the most dangerous men in Druthal. Well, by my sinners, I'm proving them right. Now get ready to run."

He poured the contents of one bottle into the other, and it immediately began to bubble and hiss.

"Go!"

They were out of the storage room like an arrow from its bow, running like mad as the bottle in Verci's hand grew hot, yellow-green smoke coming out the top. Just the hint of the scent of it made him want to retch. Verci ran out of the storage room and spotted one guard running at him.

"Hey, what the blazes—"

Verci threw the bottle at him, and when it hit the guard in the chest, it erupted in the smoke. The man screamed, a horrifying, terrible scream like Verci had never heard before.

Keep your heart hard, Verci thought. *They happily tortured you and Jules, let Ken get almost killed.*

He turned and ran after the others, the smoke filling up the corridor behind him. He got to the room—the same room he had met Cheever in —and slammed the door shut.

"All right, let's get on it," he said. "Now there's more chaos in our wake."

"What's next?" Kennith asked.

Verci thumbed through the keys and found the one to unlock the door that Cheever had come through. It shouldn't be far to the exit gate from here.

"Hey, what's—" a guard on the other side of the door said as Verci opened it.

"We need to get these guys out of here!" Verci shouted. "It's crazy in there!"

"These guys, what?" the guard asked. "Where the blazes did they come from, and—who are you?"

His hand was going for a handstick as the other was bringing a whistle to his mouth. Verci drew a knife and plunged it into the guard's throat.

"Oh my saints!" Vellun cried.

"Come on!" Verci said, wiping off his hand.

No one was going to stop him from getting them out of here. No one.

He pushed through the next set of doors, down some stairs, and along a corridor to another double gate.

Sunlight on the other side of that double gate.

And there was a guard station watching over the double gate. As they came down the corridor, Verci ran ahead and made for the door of the guard station. It was open, of course it was. Only other guards would be coming from here.

"What is going on?" the guard sitting in there asked.

"Total riots inside," Verci said. "Be glad you're in here today."

"Saints, look at you," the guard said. "What happened to you?"

"Those maniacs jumped me, but I knocked them down. I was told to get the lawyers who were in the building out of here. Let them through."

"Them?" the guard asked, pointing at the others through the window.

"Yeah, them," Verci said.

The guard looked at Jules, Vellun, and Kennith, and then he reached for a pull handle at the far side of his station.

Verci grabbed his hand and twisted it, then took out Asti's knife and drove it into the man's palm.

"No," Verci said. "There's not going to be any alarm, any of that.

They're walking out of here."

"You're crazy, you won't get—"

"Hey, friend," Verci said. "What do you get paid for this? Five crowns a week?"

The man's eyes widened for a moment. "Four and ten."

"Four and ten. Now, I'm asking you, do you want to get killed for four and ten?"

"No."

"No," Verci said. "So be smart, friend."

The man nodded.

"Good."

Verci took the man's irons off his belt and shackled his hands behind his back. He then went to the booth controls, opening the first gate and letting the others in. He closed the gate behind them. In a few moments, it would be done. And now he knew what needed to happen next.

"Verci," Kennith said. "What are you doing?" He clearly already knew the answer.

"Gate has to be opened from in here," Verci said. "And both gates can't open together. So I'm going to open it and you walk right out. They can walk right out, right, friend?"

"It's the professional check-in," the guard said. "They'll be outside the wall from here. Right to the street."

"Right to the street," Verci said. "Walk right out."

"What about you?" Vellun asked.

"Listen," Verci said. "You all get home. Go right home. When you get there, tell Raych and Helene and whoever else what's happening. Tell Raych I love her."

"No, Verci," Julien said. "What are you—"

"Asti and Almer are still in here," Verci said. "I promised I'd get you out." He opened the outer gate. "There's out, just walk clear. But I can't leave without them."

"Verci," Kennith said, putting his hand on the glass.

"I'm serious," Verci said. "This isn't your fight, it never should have been. Now go."

"Verci—"

"Go!"

Vellun grabbed the hands of the other two, and giving a solemn nod, pulled the others out. Verci pulled the gate shut.

They were out. Free air. And they could get word to their friends. That was what mattered.

"You're a fool," the guard said. "You don't think you're going to get away with this. That they're going to get far."

"They aren't your problem," Verci said. "But I very much am. Now, I need to get to Ward Four, and you're going to help me. Because like I said, you don't get paid anywhere near enough to choose otherwise."

"COME ALONG, TACKLIN," VERCI SHOUTED AS HE DRAGGED THE PRISON-gray garbed guard along, bound and gagged. The man was putting up a good struggle, not that Verci could blame him. This fellow was probably getting off easier than his compatriots. How many of them got beaten or broken in the riot, or gagged on the toxic cloud? A day or two of mistaken identity was downright kind in comparison.

"What's this?" one of the guards at the entrance to Ward Four asked as they approached the double-lock gate.

"This?" Verci shot back. He kicked his prisoner. "This in Indlen Tacklin. The bastard started a damn riot in the dining hall and nearly escaped. So I was told to get him out of there."

"To Four?" the other guard asked. "We don't want him."

Verci's prisoner thrashed some more.

"I don't blame you," Verci said. "But you've heard we got a blazes of a mess to mop up over there."

"Yeah, we've been locking down every other ward," the first guard said. "See you got out of the worst of it."

"It was a whole donny, let me tell you," Verci said. "Let's bring him in there."

"Really, here? Why?"

Verci scowled, and leaned in. "Truth is, the idea is to bring this bastard in front of his brother, and make him watch while we beat the sinner out of him."

"Who's the brother?"

"Something Tacklin, I suppose."

"We've not had Tacklin in Four for days."

"Huh," Verci said. This was possibly good news, or very bad news. Had Asti already escaped? Were he and Almer already working their own plan? Had Verci rutted everything up? "So where's he at?"

"Down in Twelve, poor bastard."

"Oh," Verci said. He gave his prisoner another kick. "Hear that, Tacklin? Your man is down in Twelve. So let's go see him, yes?"

The two guards gave each other a glance, and opened up the gate. "Yeah, let's get down there."

Verci came through, dragging his man with him, and as they opened up the second gate, one of the guards slammed into Verci as he was coming through, pinning him in the metalwork.

"Go see him in Twelve?" he asked, pummeling Verci's ribs. "You slipped up."

Verci's pulled out a blade and tried to drive it into the guard's neck, but he couldn't get the leverage he needed to reach.

"I'm going to—" he grunted.

"You're going to nothing."

The other guard reached into the gate and ungagged Verci's prisoner.

"He's the damn Tacklin! He already got three of his friends out the door!"

"Did he?" the guard pinning Verci said. "And yet he came back . . . oh, I get it. Looking for your brother to get him out, too."

"That was the plan," Verci said. "Looks like I need a new one."

"He did all that in Seven?"

"I did," Verci said. "So just imagine . . ."

Irons went around his wrist, his arms pulled behind him, as he was yanked out of the double gate.

"I imagine you should join your brother," the guard said. "Yes, I think Ward Twelve will be quite good for you." He nodded to his companion. "Take that fellow—who are you?"

"Pankins! I've worked here for nearly a year!"

"Oh, right. Sorry, Pankins. Take Pankins back to offices and get him cleaned up. I'll deal with Tacklin."

Verci decided not to fight it, not yet, as the guard took him through the corridors to Ward Twelve. If that's where Asti was, that was where he wanted to be. While he was being led, he palmed the makeshift tool he had hidden up his sleeve and worked the lock on the iron. Challenging from this vantage, but doable.

He had it loose by the time he was at the bottom of the stairway and the guard was pounding on a door.

"You might think you're so clever, Tacklin, but like your brother, once you're down here, there is nowhere else to go. You're not going to be in the open air again."

The door opened, not a guard.

"Listen," the man who opened the door said in a rush, barely even looking at them. "Nothing you're doing matters right now, I need you to get Indlen Tack—oh, I see." He grabbed Verci by the front of his coat and dragged him through. "Well done." He slammed the door on the guard's face.

Verci knew exactly who this man was. Major Grieson, Asti's former boss from Druth Intelligence.

"Grieson," Verci said as he whipped off the irons. He immediately used them to clock the spymaster across his perfect jaw.

"Hey!" Grieson said, clutching his face and staggering back. "You've got every reason to clock me, but—"

"You did this?" Verci roared. "When I'm done with you—"

"Asti needs you!" Grieson said, holding up his hands. "He's in deadly danger, and only you can save him!"

"Why should I believe you?" Verci asked.

"If you believe nothing else, believe this," Grieson said. "Possibly the most important thing in this city is Asti, and we have to save him. So let's not waste any more time."

"Fine," Verci said. "Is he down here?"

"No," Grieson said. "He and Cort . . ."

"Almer is with him?"

"They're both . . ." He trailed off, and Verci understood.

"They're both outside these walls," Verci said. Grieson nodded. "Then let's go. And if they're hurt, or already dead, no saint or sinner in the canon will save you."

PART IV
THE WARD TWELVE PROJECT

CHAPTER TWENTY

S *even days ago . . .*
"All right, Tacklin, that lower bunk is yours," the guard said pointing to the one in the dank corner of the cell. The cramped room had four double bunks, and while there was only one other prisoner in here right now, it was clear that with Asti and Almer, it was now a full cell. "And that top one over there is yours, Dale."

"Dale, right," Almer said. He stumbled over to the bunk and gracelessly scrambled to the top.

"What are you doing?" the guard asked, kicking the bed.

"You said this was my bunk."

"It's also daylight, Dale," the guard said. "You think you're getting in it right now? You think it's naptime? You want me to bring you a warm milk, too?"

"Easy," Asti said.

The guard stormed over to Asti, towering over him in a way he probably thought was intimidating. "You got something to say, Tacklin?"

The beast in his skull gave several colorful suggestions, all of which were certain to start a beating. Not that Asti couldn't have this guard, who clearly thought too highly of himself, kissing the floor in two heartbeats. But doing that wouldn't help anyone.

"It's his first time in a place like this," Asti said. "He doesn't know the run of it."

"But you're an old hand, hmm?"

"I've a familiarity," Asti said. This place was a luxury suite compared to the Poasian prison he had been tortured in.

"Then keep your dog in line," the guard said. "Snocker!"

The other resident of the room, who was lying on the bunk over Asti's, made a noncommittal noise.

"I've got better things to do, so take the fresh boys around the ward, make sure they know the rules."

Snocker slinked off the bunk, landing on the ground almost silently. "What's in it for me?"

"Not getting your tenders cracked with a hammer."

"Well, that's a tough choice, then," Snocker said. On the guard's glare, he added, "Joking, man, calm your toes. Scatter to your better things."

The guard stalked off.

"Well, new boys," Snocker said. "Welcome to Ward Four, it's just like the other wards, all terrible. You're Tacklin and Dale?"

"Sure," Asti said. "That's it."

Snocker laughed. "Oh, it's going to be like that? Jolly. Anyhow, here's our bunkroom. The other boys are on their work details."

"Not you, though?" Almer asked, coming down off the bunk.

"I convinced someone else to take my work today," Snocker said. "I can be very convincing when I want to."

"We have that in common," Asti said.

"I bet you can be, hmm," Snocker said. He led them out of the bunkroom. "We're up at five bells, when they do the full bunk check. Here's the water closet, and keeping that clean is one of the work details. The worst, and since your new boys, you'll probably get it."

"Fair," Almer said. Asti was actually surprised how well Almer was taking things right now. Kennith and Julien, from what he saw, were rightly upset, and Vellun seemed on the verge of a complete breakdown. Pilsen, Asti feared, didn't even seem to be fully understanding what was happening. Verci surely had his hands full keeping them together.

Why did they split them up, and why like this? What was the scheme here?

"After count, we're at breakfast with Wards One through Three at seven bells. You sit with the rest of your bunkroom, so you get to see me."

"When does Ward Seven eat?" Asti asked.

"You got a little friend in Seven?" Snocker asked. "You won't see him. Wards Five through Eight eat at eight bells, and then Nine through Eleven—that's the ladies' wards—they're at nine bells. You don't see anyone in other wards unless you get kitchen work detail. And they don't give that to no one new anymore."

Snocker had led them through a meal hall, to an open yard where several prisoners were milling about in various small groups. And around the yard, on upper walls, were a lot of guards with crossbows. And even more in the yard.

"Security here is more intense than I would have guessed," Asti said.

"Yeah, there was a breakout a little ways back," Snocker said.

"Really?" Almer asked. "You know how they managed?"

"They all worked the kitchen, and one of them mixed up something that blew up the wall, and something else to make the guards sick."

Asti glanced at Almer, mouthing, "Could you?"

Almer shrugged. "From stuff in a kitchen? Probably."

"And that's why ain't no one new getting kitchen duty no more. And now the guards are absolute hawks," Snocker said. "Dinner call for us is four bells, and then its full dark and bunk at nine bells."

"Early for my taste," Asti said.

"And mine, but the guards do not take being out of bunk lightly. You gotta drain your whistle in the middle of the night, you're better off just doing it in the corner."

"Is that why it smells that way?" Asti asked.

"You better believe it," Snocker said. "You know those fellas? They look like they know you?"

Asti saw where he was pointing, a half-dozen fellows—kids, really —all giving their full attention to Asti and Almer. Hard glares. Asti didn't quite know why.

"They seem to have us clocked," Asti told Almer. "You know why?"

"Yeah," Almer said. "Three of those boys were in the group you thrashed in my shop the night of the fire."

"I didn't exactly remember their faces," Asti said. He had been in a complete state, the beast had taken over. It's a miracle three of them managed to survive.

"But by the look of them, they remember ours," Almer said. "And hope to settle the score."

ASTI MADE NO ARGUMENT WHEN ALMER VOLUNTEERED THEM FOR THE worst cleaning duties. It was a good way to find an advantage in the prison. The tasks were vile, but brought them to other parts of Quarrygate, and it put them in the supply room, with bleach and vinegar and whatever else what used. Asti marked the wall, hoping Verci would spot it, hoping Verci would have the same idea.

He also hoped Almer could work some miracle with access to chemicals.

"We'll see," Almer said as they were led down one dank corridor. "But they are keeping a real close eye on everything in there. Every jar and bottle was marked or nocked."

"See what you can figure out," Asti said.

"What I figured out was volunteering us for the worst cleaning job they had to do. That's what I told the guard."

"So how bad is the worst one?"

"So here it is, boys," the guard leading them said as he approached a door. "Ward Three. It's been empty for about a month now."

"Why is that?" Asti asked as the guard opened the door. The stench hit them like a brick to the face.

The guard covered his face with a cloth. "So we had a breakout last month, you might have heard."

"There's been rumors."

"Don't get any ideas, friend," the guard said. "But they used some smoke or magic or such that made everyone puke out something harsh. And not, like, normal vomit, no. Nastiest stuff you ever saw. We just evacuated the ward and put people elsewhere. And no one has cleaned it up since, but you boys get to."

"Happy to," Almer said. He didn't even cover his mouth. Asti couldn't even imagine how Almer could stand the stench.

"Now, boys," the guard said. "I'm sure your attention will be drawn to that giant hole in the wall. You might even have a temptation to avail yourself of it. I will tell you, I got five boys with crossbows stationed outside it who will happily use you for target practice if you step a toe too far out."

"Yes, sir," Asti said.

The guard waved them through and stayed on the other side of the doorway.

"You volunteered us for this?" Asti asked. "How are you not retching?"

"This isn't the worst I've smelled," Almer said. "But I wanted us in here because I figured it would so vile the guards wouldn't stick around. Giving us an uninterrupted, unsupervised job."

"Good thinking," Asti said, as he noted the great hole in the wall, with only a tacked-up piece of sailcloth to cover it. He wondered if they actually had the crossbowmen outside or that was just a threat to keep folks in line. Not that Asti wanted to test that theory right now, but if they needed to plan an escape, the hole already blown into a stone wall was a good place to start.

"Also, the nastier the thing to clean, the harsher chemicals they might offer to clean it. It gives me options."

"You really are thinking," Asti said.

"I may not have the streetwise that you and your brother have," Almer said. "But back in school I was quite adept at getting away with things under the nose of institutional scrutiny. And there is the question of, is this Orritan Dale persona I've been assigned also an apothecarial expert, or are our jailers ignorant of what I can do?"

"What they know and don't know is an excellent question," Asti said, keeping his sleeve over his nose. "Honestly, how can you stand it?"

"Get used to these things," Almer said. He put down the buckets and knelt down next to the dried, caked-over mess on the floor and wall.

"I'm impressed, I didn't think they human body made liquids this color."

"I'm going to find a water-closet tap," Asti said. "Certainly not going to get far with this stuff caked over."

Asti went off around the corner, noting that at no point did the smell diminish. It was like it was baked into the walls. Whoever it was that put together this breakout, he'd tip his hat to them, if they didn't burn the whole path for everyone behind them. But perhaps the showmanship was the point.

After going down a few hallways, Asti found a working water closet and started filling the buckets. Hopefully Almer was right, and doing this was the opportunity he thought it could be. They needed to get on top of what was happening, get in touch with Verci and the others, find out why they had been targeted for this. There was no way this was some innocent mistaken identity, but playing along with that idea might be the best way out. Keep every option open for now.

"Well, well, it is the chemist."

"It is him, indeed."

"Fancy seeing you here, man."

The voices echoed down the halls, from however far away he had left Almer.

"You all can't be here," Almer's voice. Asti was already running.

"We can be where we want," one of others said. "That guard does us favors."

"And we've got a score to settle."

"Asti!" Almer screamed.

Asti rounded the corner to see four Scratch Cats surrounding Almer.

"We remember when our boys got killed in your shop," one of them was saying, brandishing a makeshift knife.

"Then you should remember me," Asti snarled, and he leaped on that one, hooking one arm around his neck and grabbing his wrist with the other. He brought down the man's wrist onto his knee while pulling him in a tighter choke, forcing him to drop the knife. "I'm the one who killed your friends that night."

Asti stepped on the knife while spinning the guy to one side, using him to block a blow from one of his friends.

"Run," Asti told Almer, as he delivered a number of punches in the first guy's back, and then pushing him on two of his friends. Then he scooped up the knife—really just a jagged piece of metal with a bit of cloth wrapped around it—and drove it into the belly of the one of them who was still standing.

Almer was running, out of the way of the fight, as Asti put down one of the other boys, then the next. The last one scrambled to his feet and started to run.

Destroy him, the beast said. *Let me kill him.*

Asti held on to the chain keeping the beast at bay. He wasn't about to let it free for a simple fight like this. He grabbed the boy trying to run and slammed him against the wall. "Who are you all? Why are you coming for us?"

"We just wanted the chemist! That was what we wanted!"

"Who sent you?"

"No one, man, no one!"

"Asti!" Almer shouted. Asti looked over and saw two guards had pinned him to the floor, ironing him up.

"On the ground, prisoner!"

Kill them all! Get out of here!

Asti couldn't let himself listen to the beast, not now. He stepped away from the Scratch Cat kid and got down on the ground.

Three more guards swarmed Asti, all of them holding him down and ironing him behind his back. The other guard in the hallway barely paid the Scratch Cats on the ground any mind. Once Asti was secured, they hauled him to his feet and dragged him along, and brought Almer along right behind.

"Looks like the two of you are real trouble," one guard said. "And the ones who are real trouble get sent down to Ward Twelve. Hope you boys like it."

"Welcome to Ward Twelve, boys, you're going to like it down here."

Down was the operative word. Asti hadn't gotten any sense of the full layout of Quarrygate Prison, but they had definitely taken him down several levels underground to bring him to Ward Twelve.

"So what makes Ward Twelve so special?" he asked. It clearly was, since both he and Cort were forced into lockjackets, collared with chains, and led through several portal-lock chambers on the way down. It had taken every ounce of control Asti had to hold the beast in check while they locked him in the jacket, but he knew that as bad as this was, at least right now, lashing out and killing guards would make it worse. Especially with Verci and the others hidden off somewhere else.

He was now certain this whole business was a plot against them. He imagined that if he went too far, it would cause retribution on the rest. That's why Verci was kept separated from him with the others. Five hostages.

"Is this really appropriate?" Asti asked. "I haven't even had a trial yet."

"You're not the only one down here who can say that," the guard said. "But you showed us you're too much of a threat to keep in general population. So Ward Twelve is for you."

"All I did was run away from a fight," Cort said.

"Not how we saw it," the guard said. "Two of you started a fight and nearly killed those boys."

"Started?" Asti asked. "They came at him, and I jumped in there to help him."

"Neither of you has a scratch while those boys are in the infirmary. Some won't make it. So don't tell me they started it."

They came to a hallway that was just a series of iron doors, each one with a guard at it.

"Two new residents!" the guard leading them said. "Which rooms are open?"

"New meat!" a woman's voice called from behind one door.

"Hush up, or you get the pull," the guard in front of that door said.

"Promises, promises."

He grabbed a lever over the door and yanked it down, and the woman inside squealed and choked until he let go and it snapped back into place.

"Three and nine are open," the guard said casually as the woman inside was clearly sputtering and gasping for breath.

"Three and nine it is," their own guard said. He opened up one door to a tiny cell. Moldering cot, pissbucket and, most unusual, a chain hanging from the ceiling. The guard pushed Almer inside and latched the chain to the collar on Almer's neck. Once the chain was on, he got to work removing the lockjacket.

"This is a bit much," Almer said as the jacket was taken off.

"Nothing is too much down here," a guard said. "The likes of all you—"

"There are no likes of me," a deep male voice said behind one door.

"This has to violate the Rights of Man," Asti said.

"Oh, the Rights of Man don't exist down here, son," the guard said, leading him to his cell. He was latched to the chain before they took off his coat. "You've got all the liberty you need in this little box. Walk around as you like, but you cause trouble, you get the pull."

Someone yanked the lever, and the chain tightened, pulling Asti an inch off the ground, dangling by his neck.

KILL THEM ALL, the beast roared while Asti choked. Asti tamped down, keeping a hold on its chain just as much as the chain was holding him. Then Asti was put back on his feet.

"Now, we see you've messed with your chain, Tacklin, well . . . you'll be wishing for the pull then."

"Noted," Asti said.

The guards left and the door slammed shut and latched. On this side, there was nothing even to use to open it. No handle, no lock, nothing to work with at all. Well designed, Asti had to give them credit for that. There was just a slot big enough for a meal tray, and maybe Asti could get his arm through there. But after that, he had no idea. He'd have to work to figure out the next steps to get out of this.

"Sorry to keep you from your little friend," the guard said through the slot.

"That guy?" Asti said. A quick plan formed—if this was a ploy against him, the best thing for Almer would be for Asti to distance himself. "We were just assigned to a cleaning job together. Never saw him before yesterday."

"Well, today's the last day you might see anyone new," the guard said. "That is, until it's time for you to go to Fort Olesson."

Asti had heard of that place: a prison north of Maradaine, high up in cliff country. Only the worst of the worst are sent there, usually for crimes against crown, kingdom, or archduchy. And the folks who go there never come out. Asti had never heard of an escape from there. Not once.

"In the meantime," the guard said. "Enjoy the stay."

CHAPTER TWENTY-ONE

There was no gauging time in the cell on Ward Twelve. No sunlight, no nightfall, not even a lamp-out call to give a sense of nighttime. There were lamps, somehow positioned in a series of niches at the corners of the ceiling, always burning. However the oil was refilled, Asti couldn't see. He was actually impressed by the clever design of it, but he wasn't able to get close enough to sate his curiosity of how it worked. The chain on his collar was loose enough to give him freedom to walk about the room, but he knew eyes were on him through the door slot, and he didn't plan on risking the wrath of the pull until he needed to test something.

So it was him, alone in a small cell, just with dim lamplight, nothing to occupy him but his own thoughts.

The beast would just growl in his mind, but as the uncountable hours passed, it grew louder.

"Looks like you've really misjudged this whole situation."

Liora had manifested from his mind again. She had been, since the whole encounter with the Brotherhood and Saint Bridget's Square, been relatively dormant—just a flash out of the corner of his eye most of the time. Not making herself seen or heard, but a gentle awareness that she was quiet, not gone.

"Hush," he said.

"You wanted to get more information, ride it through to find out what's going on," she said. "And now, here you are. Trapped in more of a cage than he is. You might as well let him free, it wouldn't be any worse." She pointed to the corner of the room, where the beast was also made manifest. Like Asti himself, but red-faced, hair and beard in shambles, chained up in a lockjacket in the corner. Seething.

"Hush," Asti said.

"You really thought you could be on top of the situation, but you didn't even know what the situation was. You thought you were the player when it looks like you and the others were just pieces on the board. Someone else's game of doubleback and you're a sacrifice ploy."

"Why are you even here?"

"You know why," she told him. "You know perfectly well that cells like this? They're designed to break wills. Yours was already broken, and here we are. You're here with me, and with them."

"Door's going to open. Slit all the throats!" the beast howled.

"This is not the time," Asti said.

"You've got nothing but time."

He needed to think things through, decide the next course of action, and thinking with a clear head wasn't going to happen with the two of them being so damn vocal. Still, he had to figure out who did this to all of them, and why, and what he was going to do about it.

Suddenly the chain pulled up, taking Asti onto his toes. He coughed and tried to hold himself up so he wouldn't choke.

The door opened, and one guard came in with a long pole. He stretched out the pole and hooked it onto Asti's collar. "Got him."

"Understood." The chain got release and Asti's feet were back on the floor.

"Come on," the guy with the pole said, and pulled Asti along with it. Once he was out the door, another guard with a pole came along and hooked it onto Asti's collar as well. Both of them were able to move Asti around while keeping him ten feet away.

"Nice and easy, Tacklin," one guard said. "Don't try anything."

A third guard came behind Asti and disconnected the chain.

"So what's this?" Asti asked.

"We're going to go for a walk," the guard in front of him said. "Come on."

Asti was dragged along to a circular chamber with a bit of sunlight. Looking up, it was a high tunnel up to the top, like they were in the bottom of a large well. A large shaft was erected in the center of the room, and another man with a chained collar was attached to the shaft with a pole. He was walking in a circle, one deliberate step at a time. As he passed, the guards connected the end of one pole to the shaft.

"Start walking," the guard ordered. "Stretch your legs."

Asti did as commanded, while the guards stepped clear so they were out of reach for him and the other fellow.

"Keep pace," the guard said. "You two better not get too close." Several guards surrounded them, all with crossbows, to emphasize why they better not.

"Of course," the other prisoner said. "First walk?"

"Just arrived," Asti said. "How long have you been down here?"

"Lost track of the exact time," the man said. Asti watched the way he walked—with precision, with total control over his body. "But I think it's been one hundred forty-five days since I was assigned to this Ward. Is it Alasim the 19th?"

"That's a good count of time for no daylight." Asti said. "I've may have lost a day in the mix but I think you're right."

"I value precision, as best I can," the man said. "Though I am still waiting for my trial. It is apparently taking a long time to organize."

"Six months is quite a long time."

"Don't know why you're eager for the trial, Pell," a guard said. "They'll just ship you up to Olesson for it."

"The trial," Pell—as he was apparently named—said, "will not be about whether I did the acts I am accused of. There is no denial of that. It will be about if I was right."

"Pell," Asti said, memory clicking. He remembered what he had read in the newssheets, even if the westtown sheets didn't cover it too much. "You're the one who assaulted the Parliament floor." Tharek Pell managed to kill a few members of Parliament, hold the whole floor hostage.

"I spoke for the people," Pell said. "Instead of those who had no right to hold them down."

"You two should get along great," the guard said. "Tacklin here is with the Corvian Liberation Front."

Pell looked at Asti, narrowing his eyes. "No, he isn't."

"That's what he's here for," the guard said.

"That's what they say I'm here for," Asti reiterated.

"But it's a lie," Pell said. "And not your lie. Interesting."

"That's enough," a guard said, and a pole hooked Pell's collar. "You'll come quietly."

"I always do," Pell said. "If a day comes when I decide not to, Nisterly, I'll tell you beforehand so you can take Absolution first."

"Such a joker," Nisterly said. Pell was unhooked from the walking shaft and led away.

"Now, he's interesting," Liora said, walking along with Asti. "Makes you wonder why a man like him, and a man like you, are being kept here. There must be a reason, no?"

She was taunting him. But she wasn't wrong.

More time had passed, and Asti only had the fact that he slept and was fed again as an indicator that it was a new day. After he had finished the meal—every meal down here had been oats and bread with fruit preserves, so there was no gauging time but what they fed him— they gave his collar another pull. A sign they were coming in to fetch him again.

He let them proceed without any struggle or trouble, as the guards came in and shackled his arms behind him. Points were clicking together in his head, an idea forming that he did not like the shape of. As the guards took him down the hall, he was focused on the detail that stood out most immediately: each meal down here had been substantial. Oats, bread, and preserves were nothing special, but every other time he had been locked up by someone, he was fed just enough to keep him alive.

Down here, he was fed well enough to stay strong. He was being encouraged to move. To stay active, limber. They had him and the other prisoners under tight control, but there was a purpose to that control.

"What's today's exercise, gentlemen?" he asked.

"Keeping your mouth shut," one guard said.

"Oh, I'm not good at that one," Asti said.

"Learn," the guard said as he opened an iron door. Asti was unceremoniously shoved inside, and the door latched shut.

Another cell, this one with heavy concrete walls, and an ironwork lattice splitting the room in half. Asti got on his feet best he could as the door on the other side of the lattice opened up, and a man walked in. A man who, as soon as Asti saw him, confirmed the suspicion that had been growing in the back of his head. Of course he was behind this.

Major Grieson of Druth Intelligence.

"You're looking hearty, Rynax," he said.

"You're looking like I should shove something sharp in your eye," Asti said.

"You've got every reason to be upset," Grieson said, starting to pace on his side of the room. Asti, with no bidding from the beast in his skull, started working on his shackles. He could get his way out of them, given enough time. After that, getting at Grieson was a challenge. The lattice had enough holes to see through, to talk to each other, but the holes were too small to even get a hand through. And it didn't look like it was designed to be opened at all.

A perfect room to talk to someone who wanted to kill you.

"So you chose your venue wisely," Asti said, trying to work his thumbs to free himself. "It will be quite the challenge to kill you from here."

"You really shouldn't kill me, Asti," Grieson said. "As much as you might want to."

"I really want to."

"I believe it," Grieson said.

"You arranged the arrest. Put me down here. Verci and the others up there in the main prison."

"Correct," Grieson said.

Asti kicked at the iron lattice, really only hurting his foot in the process. Solid metalwork, no obvious weakness to it. "How rutting dare you?"

Grieson sighed, a heavy, weary sigh. "Because I'm absolutely desperate."

That was not what Asti expected. He had expected swagger, gloating. Or at least confidence. There was none of that. Though Grieson was an expert at playing a mark, it's what made him such a notable spy.

"You, desperate?" Asti asked. "How so?"

"How much do you hear from the Office?" Grieson asked.

"Nothing," Asti said. "You made sure of that."

"I had nothing to do with your ouster, Asti," Grieson said. "And months ago I did everything I could to help you and your friends. I pulled strings I didn't even know I had. Do you know what it takes to get an illiterate street girl into U of M?"

"She's not illiterate."

"As far as the college was concerned, she might as well—that doesn't matter. I did you all favors, and I didn't have to. If I had known what was coming, I wouldn't have use my flex that way. I'd have more left for right now."

"Your acting like you don't have flex? You've got me locked up!"

"Let me explain," Grieson said.

"Sure," Asti offered. Time to crack his thumb out of joint, get his hand out of the shackle. What he'd do after that, he had no idea, but one step at a time. "Tell me why you wrecked my life, as well as Verci and the rest."

"If things go well, in a few days, the mistaken identity will be cleared up, and everyone will be set free. No one the worse."

"You don't think even a few days in here is for the worse? For someone like Julien? Pilsen?"

"Believe me that I brought the absolute minimum I felt I needed to insure your cooperation. I could have also dragged the ladies into this."

"My cooperation? That's what you want?"

"That's what I need, Asti," Grieson said.

"Why the blazes do you need me? I'm not in Intelligence anymore."

"Nor am I, really," Grieson said.

That got Asti to stop forcing his thumb.

"Then what the blazes is this?"

"This?" Grieson asked, gesturing to the room. "All of this is the Ward Twelve Project. Not on any books or reports, so when I . . ."

"You've were ousted," Asti said, realizing the truth.

"I smelled the wind and went dark," Grieson said. "Altarn has her grasp over the entire Colonel's Table, nearly all of Intelligence now. And she is tied to something rancid."

"Rancid how?"

"That business with the Brotherhood you unearthed?" Grieson asked. "I'm certain her fingers are in that. And she's had Liora in her pocket all this time."

"Blazes," Asti said. "But that doesn't sound like my problem."

"It very much is, even if you don't realize it. I need to get myself in a position to move against her, or we're all in danger. So my access to this project, the prisoners in Twelve, and the systems in place to put someone I needed in here? Those were the only cards I had to play."

"Then you played them stupidly," Asti said. "I am not here to be your playing piece—"

"I said if all goes well, Verci and the others walk free in a few days. If not, there will be a mountain of evidence against the Corvia Seven."

"You wouldn't," Asti said. Now he popped his thumb out of joint, and used the angry words to cover up his wince.

"If I have to, I don't want to."

"You don't have to," Asti said.

"So you'll cooperate," Grieson said.

"Why the blazes are you doing this to me?"

"For one, because you've already tangled with the fellow I'm sending you after. I need your experience."

"I'm sure you have plenty of people who have that experience."

"I don't, not that I can trust."

Asti wished he didn't understand what that meant. "You can't trust anyone in the Office right now. So, because I'm out . . ."

"I know where you stand. And . . ." Grieson moved a bit closer to the lattice work and tapped his skull. "Because of what's up here."

"You mean . . . what the blazes do you mean?"

"I mean, Asti, there are other things that aren't on any books or reports. And one of the most important ones, one of the most dangerous ones . . . it's in your head. And I only know that you have it in there, I don't even know exactly what it is."

"Why . . ." Asti didn't even know what to say to that. "How can you stand there and know that?"

"Secrets are the job."

"I left that job. I have a normal life, and a plan to—"

"I know about your plans. I gave you your normal life. Same with all your friends. You get me through this, everyone walks out back to them."

Asti pulled his hands free, and in a quick, fluid move, jumped forward while he painfully snapped his thumb back into place.

"When I get my hands on you, Grieson, I will—" He grabbed the lattice, and when he did, felt a jolt course through his body.

"I know you will, which is why you never can, Asti," Grieson said. "Instead you're going to be part of the Ward Twelve Project. You'll take your team on this mission, and do it clean and quiet, and when it's done, everyone goes home."

"And then I tear out your throat," Asti said, pulling himself to his feet. Saints above, that hurt.

"If you still want to then, I'll understand. But you are going to do this for me." He went back to his door and knocked it twice. "For what it's worth, while I need you for this mission, and will use your brother and your friends as leverage until it's done . . . I truly am sorry about this."

The door opened and Grieson walked out. Asti, left alone in his side of the cell, howled in futile rage.

ASTI WOKE UP, BOUND TO A CHAIR. HE DIDN'T EVEN RECALL FALLING asleep, or where he was when he did so. When had he left that meeting cell with Grieson? He didn't even recall. He had lost time in there, and that unsettled him even more.

Which, given that he was bound to a chair, alone in a large circular room, was saying something.

Another chair was rolled in by a pair of guards, this one with Tharek Pell bound to it.

"Is this typical?" Asti asked him. "A usual evening in Ward Twelve?"

"I'm not certain of the time," Tharek said. "But this is a new experience for me."

"Not for me." This came from the next person being wheeled in, a Lyranan woman of indeterminate age. "Third time for this particular arrangement."

"Arrangement?" Asti asked.

"It's so much fun," the Lyranan woman said. She looked to Tharek. "You know him?"

"They say his name is Tacklin," Tharek said. "I doubt that's true."

"What do they have you for?" Asti asked her.

"Espionage against the crown, murder, attempted murder, and executing a jailbreak."

"Could use that last one right now," Asti said.

The next man was wheeled in—singing an old wartime tune—and when he was placed in the room, it was clear they were setting them in a circle. Then a man bound in mage shackles, twitching and ticking. Then Almer. Then an incredibly muscular Ch'omik woman.

"Jackdaw!" the singing man called out. "Good to see you're alive. They put you down here as well?"

"Shut your face, Erno," Jackdaw said.

"My face is never shut, though your words fiercely cut, we find ourselves in another rut . . ."

"I will cut your heart out."

"I just think we should be happy we're alive, old girl, to laugh and sing another day."

"Quiet, quiet," the twitchy man said.

"She's just mad because we worked a beautiful escape, only to be dragged back to Quarry."

"That was you?" Almer asked. "The chemical work in the kitchen?"

"That was Jensett, gone to the sinners," Erno said.

"Going to send you to the sinners," Jackdaw said.

"I did nothing to you, ma'am. We all failed."

"Hush hush hush!" the twitchy man said. "All of your chattering."

Almer looked across the circle at Asti, "So they dragged you into this, too, Tacklin?"

"You know him?" the Lyranan woman asked.

"We've met," Asti said, hoping he was covering all his tells. "Decent carriage-man in a pinch."

The Lyranan woman glanced back at Almer. "Must be quite the driver to end up in this mix."

Another man walked in, not a guard, but he had an official bearing to him, despite no uniform. "All right," he said in a rolling Waish accent. "Looks like we have seven of you here today." He took a pouch off his belt, and emptied a number of colored crystals into his hand.

"What's all this?" Tharek asked.

"Unpleasant," the Lyranan woman said.

"So," the Waish man said. "The name is Yendick, we're all going to get to know each other very well in a moment."

"How well?" Asti asked.

"Well enough," Yendick said, coming up to Asti. He pressed one crystal into Asti's sternum, and with a searing moment of heat, it stayed in place. "So welcome to the team, Marin Tacklin."

Whatever this was, they were still using the arrested alias. Was this what Grieson wanted him to do? What was this?

Yendick then went to Tharek, attaching another crystal to him. "Tharek Pell, welcome." Then further around the room to each one. The Lyranan woman was Pra Yikenj. Then Erno Don, the happy singer, and Kat'rick-Ra, the Ch'omik woman called Jackdaw. And the twitchy fellow was just called "Hoskins."

Almer was still called "Orritan Dale." Asti wasn't sure why this whole business still maintained the fiction of their identities, or if Yendick was aware of them being fictions. For the moment, he might as well use the name Marin Tacklin.

Almer winced as Yendick attached the crystal to him. "That wasn't that bad," he said.

"That wasn't the real thing," Yikenj said.

"No, it wasn't," Yendick said. "That was just the priming. Now for the attuning."

"The what?" Asti asked.

"Brace yourselves," Yikenj said.

Yendick took the last crystal and pressed it to his own bare chest, and Asti felt the one on his chest grow hot once again. Then that searing heat spread throughout his body, every ounce of him on fire. The fire grew hotter, stronger, and it wasn't just his body on fire anymore. It was also Yendick, shouting out in agony.

No, that agony was Asti's. The shout was his, erupting from his own throat. Most of them were screaming, save Tharek and Yikenj, holding in their pain.

But Asti could feel it, feel how much it hurt them, just as it hurt him.

And it hurt the beast and Liora as well, as they joined in the chorus of torment.

CHAPTER TWENTY-TWO

When the searing pain subsided, Asti was in another room, unshackled from the chair, now finding himself on the floor. Had it been that long? Had he blacked out from the pain?

There was still pain, but it was now a dull ache, both coming from the crystal in his chest, and a throbbing in the back of his head.

"Everyone make it through that?" Yendick asked. He was still standing in the center of the room, and the rest of the folks—the other prisoners, Asti reminded himself—were all on the floor like Asti.

"You're a right bastard," Jackdaw said. She jumped to her feet and leaped at Yendick.

"Don't bother," Yikenj said dismissively.

Jackdaw threw a heavy punch, the muscles on her massive arm bulging. But with her fist inches from Yendick's face, she was frozen. She looked at her fist in disbelief.

"The blazes?" she asked.

"Good, that shows you are properly attuned," Yendick said. He tapped at the crystal on his chest. "You are connected to me, me to you, and thus, all of us to each other."

"What have you done?" Asti asked.

"As I said, I've attuned you. You're about to go out of here on a mission, and we couldn't exactly have you walking lose with no restriction. This keeps you in line."

"How so?" Hoskins asked, though his attention was more on the ceiling.

"I can show you," Yikenj said. She looked Tharek up and down. "I heard about you. You killed a marshal with a button off your coat. In my country we call that novice work."

"Do not test me," Tharek said.

"It's not really a test if you aren't going to pass," she said. "Go on, show me how easily you could kill me."

"You think I cannot?"

"What is this, exactly?" Almer asked.

"Go on," Yikenj taunted.

Tharek drew back his fist for a punch, but then stopped still.

"It doesn't work," Yikenj said. "We cannot hurt him. We cannot hurt each other."

"Very simple," Yendick said.

"Magic?" Erno asked.

"That is not magic," Hoskins said. "That is something else."

"How do you know?" Jackdaw asked.

"Because I'm a mage, at least of sorts," Hoskins said. Then a smile crossed his lips. "And now my friends are here."

There was a skittering noise above them, and then three flashes of fur came out of a crack in the masonry. They dropped down and landed on Hoskins's shoulders.

"Squirrels?" Almer asked.

"Better friends than any person I've met," Hoskins said. One of the squirrels fed him a nut. "Yes, thank you, Jandie."

"You just let that go in your mouth, then," Erno said. "Squirrel put a nut in your mouth, and you're all right with it."

Asti turned his attention back to Tharek, who was trying to force himself to strike Yikenj, but couldn't.

"My arm will obey! I am its master!"

"Not anymore," Yikenj said. She wandered to the wall and pulled a loose stone out of the mortar. "Until he releases us, we cannot intentionally harm him or each other."

She threw the stone hard, and it bounced off three walls, back to her hand. She did it again, and again, and again, and then her arm locked as she attempted a fifth throw.

"You see?" she asked. "That time I wanted to bounce it right to his head. We can't even *want* to."

Asti was impressed with her skill. She was trained in the *aiken-taz*, the Lyranan throwing art. The legend was that an expert could throw almost anything with deadly accuracy, make anything into a weapon, and for the very best, not even be seen throwing it. It also meant she was Lyranan Intelligence. How did she end up here?

"I refuse to accept it," Tharek said.

"I'm with him," Erno said.

"The door is right there," Yendick said as he pulled a trunk to the middle of the room. "You don't like it, leave."

Erno went right for the door, and as soon as he was in the hallway, the dull ache in the back of Asti's head became noticeably sharper. He winced, and tried to bear it, but it grew stronger and sharper, like a knife being driven into the base of his skull.

"The blazes?" he shouted. Everyone else—save Yendick—was reacting the same way. Even one of the squirrels had fallen to the ground grasping its head.

Yikenj stumbled to the doorway, one hand pressed to her temple. "You better get back here!" she shouted.

"Right," Yendick said. "In addition to not being able to harm me or each other, you cannot move too far away from me, or each other." He casually opened up the trunk and pulled out sacks.

"Erno!" Jackdaw bellowed. "Get back here!"

The pain suddenly eased a little, and then subsided back to that dull ache. Erno stumbled back into the room.

"That is some dirty cards, old boy," he said weakly.

"So, you're the control," Almer said to Yendick. "You're in charge of whatever it is we need to do?"

"I am just the leash to hold you very dangerous folks in check. I am not in charge at all." Yendick handed a sack to each of them. "But you do have a mission to complete before I can release any of you, so please get yourself ready."

Asti opened his sack to find a set of clothes—not his clothes, exactly, but the sort of clothes he would wear on a dangerous job. Boots that were strong enough to run in, but soft enough to move quietly when needed. Dark blue slacks and pullover, the sort that were easy to move in. Heavy leather vest with metal plating sewn in. Belt with pouches and pockets.

And many knives.

"You want us all to get dressed?" Asti asked. Yikenj had already stripped off her prisoner grays and was putting on her provided outfit, which looked like the Lyranan equivalent of the outfit provided to Asti, with a top that more like a padded caftan.

"This is a mockery," Tharek said, pulling out his tunic. "Are you trying to insult me?"

"Never," Yendick said.

"Then why given me a Spathian uniform?" he said, holding it up.

"You're a Spathian?" Erno asked. He had happily stripped down to his skivs.

"I should be, but I am not. I was denied advancement."

"Well, if you should be, looks like they're saying so," Erno said, taking a bow out of his sack. "You all got Callie back, I thought she was gone for good!"

"I should have guessed you named your bow," Jackdaw said.

"And they've given you your delightful weapon, I see," he retorted.

Tharek raised an appreciative eyebrow looking at Jackdaw as she drew it out of her sack. "Is that a *n'disro*?"

"You know what it's called," she said, holding the Ch'omik weapon resembling a barbed rowing oar. "Impressive."

Tharek's voice took on a slight softness. "May I?"

Jackdaw looked apprehensive, and then flipped the weapon over, offering the handle to him. Tharek gingerly took it from her, and held it reverently.

"The craftsmanship, the balance," he said quietly. He spun it over in his hand, taking a few practice swings. Then he presented it handle-first back to her. "Thank you, an honor."

"So, we've got me, the singing archer," Erno said. "The ex-Spathian, the squirrel mage, a Lyranan throwing master, the Ch'omik head cleaver, mister I-have-all-the-knives." He pointed to Asti. He then spun to Almer. "But you remain a mystery. All you have in your sack are some ordinary clothes."

"Tacklin already told you what I do," Almer said. "Carriage-man."

"So this is a job with carriage?" Yikenj asked Yendick.

"I've not been briefed on that," Yendick said.

"So what is the mission?" Hoskins asked. "And why would we do it?"

"You'll do it, because if you don't, that crystal never comes out, and you will be very unhappy when I go home."

"And what if I figure out how to kill you?" Tharek asked.

"You'll all have a very painful death. Please don't. Please keep me alive as you do the job."

"So what is the job?" Asti asked.

"I wasn't briefed," Yendick said. "I was just told, in terms of actually running it, you're in charge, Tacklin."

"Why is he in charge?" Yikenj asked.

"Because," Grieson said as he came in the door. "He's the one who's tangled with the target before."

Asti's hand froze in place, stuck by his primal instinct to drive a blade into Grieson's neck.

"You've tangled with him before?" Tharek asked Asti. "So who is it?"

"I'd like to know that myself," Asti said. He looked pointedly at Grieson. "There's quite a few things here that I would like to know."

Grieson nodded and stepped to the center of the room. Asti kept trying to make his hand throw a knife into his throat, but it was clear whatever magical or mystical control these crystals had over him, that protection extended to Grieson.

"So, this city has suffered something of an infestation," Grieson said. "A cult, known as the Brotherhood of the Nine, has infiltrated various levels of government and infrastructure. This has proven to be possibly the most dangerous threat to crown and throne."

"Oh no," Tharek said flatly. "A threat to the crown."

"In fact," Grieson said. "Their reach was able to manipulate organizations beyond the official. Who do you think was giving your man Lannic his orders, Tharek?"

"I was no one's puppet," Tharek said.

"Go on," Asti said, trying not to show anything on his face of what he already knew.

Grieson took the cue. "The full extent of the Brotherhood's influence is still unknown. We know some of the things they've had their fingers in. The Strephen Affair, the Dentonhill Children, the Andrendon, the Haltom's Patriots, just to name a few."

He had named the one that had Asti's attention.

"But they were broken up," Asti said.

Now everyone in the room looked at him.

"So you have dealt with this before," Yikenj said.

"I dealt with an incident," Asti said. "And I thought the leader was killed."

"You do this with him?" Jackdaw asked, pointing to Almer.

"Oh, no, I wasn't part of that," Almer said.

Grieson coughed. "While the Brotherhood seems to have been partially crippled when their plans were routed a few months ago, it's clear they still have gears moving throughout the city. We strongly suspect that their leader is active in the southwestern part of the city, building new members of his cult."

Asti stepped forward. "Their leader? The Dragon?"

"The what?" Erno asked. "I . . . that's a . . . what?"

"I agree with him," Hoskins said, pointing to Erno. "And following that up with, *I beg your pardon?*"

"Do you want to explain who we're talking about, Mister Tacklin?" Grieson asked.

"I'll leave it to you," Asti replied.

"We don't know a lot about the man called Crenaxin. He was a complete mystery until recently, but the information we have indicates a man of refined knowledge and education, though we have not identified where he was educated."

"That name is Kellirac," Yikenj said.

"I wouldn't swear that he is," Asti said. "At least not by look or accent. He's more like a North Maradaine dandy."

"So you did encounter him," Tharek said.

"And I thought he was dead," Asti said.

"You didn't make sure?" Yikenj asked.

"There really wasn't a body," Asti said.

"Leave him be," Almer stressed. "He doesn't need to explain himself here."

Grieson coughed. "The point is, we're seeing signs of him building a new cult, and we need him ferreted out and caught. Alive."

"He is dangerous alive," Asti said.

"Dangerous how?" Tharek asked.

"He can . . ." Asti wasn't sure how to describe it. "He can speak to you, and it burrows right into your skull. And then you stop being you, but instead his puppet."

"He did this to you?" It was Yendick who asked, looking slightly spooked.

"He tried," Asti said. "The only reason it didn't work was because my brain is already broken."

"Broken?" Yikenj asked.

"Tacklin here has experience leading folks in . . . independent covert operations," Grieson said.

"Is that a polite way of saying he's a terrorist?" Hoskins asked. He looked over to Asti. "I mean, if so . . . respect to you."

"Terrorist is just what they call those who fight for their truth," Tharek said. "A truth that they are afraid of."

"I've done some things under the nose," Asti said.

"This sounds like a delight," Erno said. "Nothing like a chance to step outside, stretch our legs, and capture an extremely dangerous man alive."

"Besides," Yikenj said. "We don't have a choice."

"You don't," Grieson said pointedly. "But believe me when I said, it's what's best for the country, for the city, and for you." That last line was aimed at Asti.

"Follow me," Yendick said, walking toward the door. "If you don't, well, your head will explode."

YENDICK LED THEM ALL OUT OF THE CHAMBER, AND IT BECAME CLEAR to Asti they were no longer even in Quarrygate Prison. That chamber was a singular room built in a large, open floor.

"Did you move us once Yendick put that whammy on us?" Asti called out to Grieson.

"You were all out," Yendick said. "It was the easiest time to get you here."

"You wouldn't think they'd give me this back while still inside the prison?" Jackdaw asked, holding up her weapon.

"So where are we?" Asti asked. His sense of direction and location had been upended. They were in some sort of industrial building, like an abandoned factory or warehouse.

Grieson answered. "In Carrol Creek. In what was one of the war shops on Quarry Road." The war shops were the several factories built in the last century, to churn out uniforms, weapons, tinned food, and anything else that was needed in the Island Wars. Once the war ended, though, all those places weren't needed anymore, and they were shut down. Some of the buildings had become new factories or refineries, but there were plenty of empty ones still littering the western neighborhoods.

"And this is a useful place for us to be?"

Grieson walked over to a table—just a worktable with a chair sitting in the middle of the factory floor—and picked up a folder. "This is the neighborhood where we think Crenaxin is rebuilding his cult." He handed the folder to Asti. "Remember, Tacklin here is in charge."

Asti glanced around the others, who seemed to be more interested in looking around the place, as well as testing the limits of their mobility.

He lowered his voice, turning to Grieson. "Why go through this to get Crenaxin, if it is him?"

"The Brotherhood has its fingers in Intelligence, but I need proof," Grieson said. "The country is in grave danger, and—"

"Save it," Asti snapped quietly. "So all these bastards have to answer to me, right?" he asked louder.

"Well, they *should* cooperate," Yendick said. "Especially since—"

Asti got a stab of pain in the back of his head, and Yendick scowled. "Erno, stop it."

Erno was near a door, taking slow steps forward. "Just testing the range."

"Cut that out," Asti said, going up to Yendick. "Go on, especially since what?"

"Since the longer you're all attuned, the more you'll gain sympathy with each other."

"What does that mean?" Hoskins asked.

"Right now you feel pain when you're too far from the center. Me. And from each other. And you can't harm each other. But soon you'll also feel each other's pain, and other sensations. Read each other's emotions. Sometimes even deeper."

"That sounds terrible," Almer said.

"We stay like this for too long, and you'll all lose your sense of yourselves to the collective thought." Yendick chuckled. "And since I'm the anchor of this unity, that means you'll become extensions of my will. At least, that's my understanding. I've never tested that theory to its final point."

"All right, this isn't typical magic," Asti said. "Tell me what you are, what you do."

"I don't answer to you," Yendick said.

"You do, because I'm in charge, he said. And this team can't move away from you, so the team includes you. I need to know what I'm working with here."

"Answer him," Grieson said.

"I'm not a mage," Yendick said. "There isn't a Druth word for what I am. In Waisholm, I'm what's known as a *gwynud.* Sort of mage and priest and stonecaster, all swirled together."

"I said he wasn't a mage," Hoskins said.

Asti wasn't familiar with the term at all. "And you, Hoskins. You are a mage, but . . . with squirrels?"

"As accurate a description as any," Hoskins said. "The folks at the University Magic Department would certainly quibble with the terms, but mage is serviceable enough. The squirrels are my friends, and I've learned to shape magic to commune with them."

"All right," Asti said. "So you can talk to them, control them, what?"

"I can't control them, they're their own people," Hoskins said, stroking the head of one of them. "But I can tell them what I need, and they are very cooperative."

"So, you can ask them to do things?" Asti asked. "Can you tell what they see, or can they . . . look I don't want to pretend I get it, so . . ."

"I can't see through their eyes, exactly," Hoskins said. "But they can convey what they've seen to me."

"And it's just these three, or . . ."

"These three are my close friends," Hoskins said. "Jandie, Yandie, and Venn. But I can communicate with others."

"All right, so that's scouting," Asti said. He nodded to Almer, "Transport is covered, right?"

"If we've got a carriage here I can use," Almer said. "I don't suppose they brought one of mine." He stressed *mine*, though Asti wasn't sure if he meant one of Kennith's carriages, or his own supplies from his shop. Still, Asti thought it was wise to keep the degree of his connection to Almer hidden for now, as well as who they really were. He knew what Almer's real skills were, no need to share that with the rest of the group.

"And the rest of you are muscle," Asti said. "Though clearly highly skilled muscle."

Pra Yikenj strolled over to him. She pointed at Erno, Kat'rick, and Tharek, "Not exactly subtle, those three, are they?"

"If we have to stop the fellow I tangled with before, the last thing we need is subtle," Asti said. "You don't exactly blend in, either."

"You would be surprised, Mister Tacklin," she said with a chuckle.

"You would be amazed how invisible a foreign woman can be in this city."

"I believe it," Asti said.

She gave him an odd regard. "You're woven from the same thread as him, yes?" She nodded over to Grieson, conferring with Yendick. "A disgraced agent?"

"Let's not talk about it."

"I've been in this business a long while, Mister Tacklin," she said, and this time she said his alias like it was an amusing joke they had shared. "And I've done this little game before. Once they even put me in your boots, being 'in charge' of the mission."

"How'd that go for you?"

"Well, I'm still alive, aren't I?"

He lowered his voice. "So, everything they said about these crystals in us, that the truth?"

"I've not found it to be otherwise."

Asti took that in. Surely there was a way to work around these crystals and Yendick, but Asti didn't have the knowledge—or the time, frankly—to focus on that.

Focus on the job, get it done. Grieson was a bastard, but he was a bastard with enough of a decent streak that he wouldn't make Asti an offer he wouldn't honor. Get the job done, find Crenaxin, get him gone, get Verci and everyone else home.

And do that with a team forced upon him that he didn't know or trust.

Simplicity itself.

Still, he had some assets here. With Yendick and Hoskins, he had magic, and the sort that could be useful for scouting or surveillance. Yikenj was a spy with a good eye. Erno seemed deeply annoying, but his body language showed a man who knew how to hold himself, how to use that bow, and the singing and attitude was clearly a ruse to throw people off their guard. Kat'rick seemed very competent. And Tharek? That man could probably kill everyone in the room before Asti could whisper his name, were he not leashed.

And Almer, hopefully Asti's secret in the hole. He didn't know if keeping their connection secret was a good idea, or if hiding Almer's real skills was at all helpful, but he'd take whatever advantage over the situation he could.

Asti thumbed through the briefing folder. A few reports, all about folks who lived within a few blocks of here. The same story, again and again. People went missing, their families filed reports with Constabulary. Then the missing person turned up, but their loved ones barely recognized them. Completely changed, in mind, in spirit, the term "as if touched by God" came up a few times.

They also often spoke about being part of the "symphony."

Asti hadn't crossed that term the last time with Crenaxin, but the rest of it all tracked. This looked like the man was building up a new cult.

A new Brotherhood.

Blazes.

As much as Asti hated agreeing with Grieson, it had to be shut down, and who else could rutting do it? Asti didn't want the job, but he understood why Grieson had come to him, that he felt only Asti could get it done.

"I could get this done a lot better with my brother," Asti called out to Grieson. "If the important part is getting it done."

"Maybe you could," Grieson called back. "But I need you as desperate as the rest of these folks."

"I'm not desperate," Erno said.

"You're not?" Grieson asked. "Maybe this will inspire you."

He held out his hand and squeezed his fist, and Asti realized he wore a bracelet covered in tiny crystals, and one started glowing. Erno screamed and dropped to his knees.

"Like I'm holding your heart in my hand, Don. I can squeeze until it bursts, so do *not push me*."

He released his fist, and Erno stopped screaming, but still fell to the floor, gasping for breath.

"Does anyone else want a demonstration?" Grieson asked.

"No, they don't," Asti said firmly. "We're on it, aren't we, folks?"

There was a murmur of assent from everyone, who all stared shocked at Erno. All but Yikenj, who just watched with dark, knowing eyes, and a passive expression on her face.

"Come together, then," Asti said, waving them all in. "We've got a job to do."

CHAPTER TWENTY-THREE

If Asti really had his way, he would have split this team up into three groups, to fully scout the folks in this neighborhood who had returned home but were believed to still be in Crenaxin's thrall. But the unbreakable rule in this mess was that none of them could get more than a couple hundred feet from Yendick. Grieson was not tied to them in such a way, as he left the factory safehouse without any issue. The rest of them were all tethered to each other, which made what had to happen next, if nothing else, extremely awkward.

They needed to do subtle work right now, watching and observing these targets that, hopefully, would lead them to Crenaxin. And this team was not subtle.

Asti enlisted Tharek and Almer to help him dress the wagon, putting a cover over the back of it, so the crew could pile up in the back and not be noticed. It wasn't ideal, but nothing about this was.

The wagon was parked, horses hitched to it, at a relatively busy, if threadbare, market square a few blocks into Carrol Creek. It was the sort of place where everything was being sold on rickety tables, the pickings were meager, and everyone was desperate to sell. Asti was very familiar with this sort of thing, but in this neighborhood it was even more pathetic than the ones in Seleth.

"Should have gotten us set up as a seller," Asti muttered. "A table, a few useless things to sell, and we wouldn't stand out at all."

"We're going to stand out regardless," Tharek said. The two of them were strolling through the square, essentially making a circle around their wagon, where most of the rest of the group was huddled under the canopy cover. Only Almer sat at the driver's seat, looking very conspicuous, but that couldn't be helped. Though folks here were probably too involved in their own troubles to honestly care that much about a strange wagon that stood out.

"As long as the constables don't make a scene, I suppose it's fine," Asti said, looking back. "It looks like he's setting up to sell drugs there, or to pick up something contraband."

"As do half the people in this square," Tharek said. "Do you see Yikenj?"

Pra was the only other one not in the wagon, as she insisted she could find and track their target while being unnoticed. Asti was skeptical, but he had to admit, even though he could feel her in the back of his head, clearly near the edge of the safe distance, he couldn't spot her.

"Not at all," he said.

"She is a capable spy," Tharek said.

"That is what we need right now," Asti said, looking up to the trees lining the walkway. Half-dead, leafless things with twisted branches. The hot dry summer followed by a bitter autumn had not been kind to them, and Asti doubted that anyone was making a point of taking care of them out here. Still, two of the squirrels were moving along the branches, following along the path Asti and Tharek were walking.

As strange as it was, if the squirrels were as reliable as Hoskins claimed, they would be excellent resources for this gig.

"Is that our man?" Tharek asked, nodding toward the people at one of the shop tables. An older man, maybe in his fifties, selling trinkets at one table in the middle of the square, with a young woman selling by his side. Her expression was dour, miserable, while he was beaming with a near maniacal glee.

They were looking for a man named Victor Scander, who had apparently disappeared two weeks ago, reported missing by his daughter Irena, and returned home a week later. Of all the reports Asti had dug through, he had flagged Scander as the best candidate for them to scout. There were eight people whose disappearance had been reported and were found again, and while each of those eight had been in some form of rapture—that's how it was described in the reports—only Scander returned to his family life afterward.

The rest of those folks, they simply told their loved ones they were now part of the symphony, that they understood their place in the world, and to leave them alone forever.

Gone to rejoin the cult, clearly, serving the Brotherhood.

According to the report, Scander had agreed to return home with his daughter, saying he would help her understand.

That was two days ago. Asti's theory was that sooner or later, Scander would either bring his daughter to the Brotherhood, or bring the Brotherhood to his daughter. If they could find him in time, he could lead them all to Crenaxin.

"Might be," Asti said. This was why he wanted to split things up. Three places he wanted to watch: here in the square, where the Scanders were known to set up their table, the pub two blocks from here where they would also occasionally sell from while Irena waited tables, and the flop they lived in, a block in the other direction.

Asti had to settle for having a squirrel keep watch at the apartment window, a concept he couldn't even conceive of yesterday, while the team all came here. The apartment had been empty when they first went there, and Asti hoped that meant they had gone to work.

He still was unsure of what Scander and his daughter looked like, but the pair at the table were good candidates.

"What do you see as my role right now?" Tharek asked.

"Hang back," Asti said. "If they are the Scanders, I'll want you to stay walking around the square as unobtrusively as possible, be ready to follow him if he goes somewhere, while I go back to the wagon."

"Why did you choose me for this task?"

"Flatly, I find you a bit more trustworthy than the rest," Asti said.

"Interesting," Tharek said.

"I mean, you are clearly incredibly dangerous, but you're also . . ." Asti thought about the best way to phrase it to not upset the man. "Uninterested in deception. And unlikely to try anything stupid."

"I can appreciate that assessment," Tharek said.

"Hang back," Asti said, approaching the table. He noticed one of the squirrels following along over his head, while the other came down from a tree and was scurrying about near Tharek. Asti wasn't sure how well Hoskins actually controlled the creatures, but they were certainly doing the job Asti had assigned them.

Blazes, the squirrels might be the most reliable part of this team.

He went up to the table, putting on an air of disinterest. He ran a finger across the table, with a show of assessing the items for sale, as if he didn't care a whit about the folks working behind it.

"Is there something you're looking for, friend?" the young woman asked, her voice like a branch that was strained to the point of breaking.

"Perhaps, perhaps," Asti said, drumming his fingers. The items for sale were largely kitchen tools: cheap tin pans, egg whiskers with hints of rust, dented teakettles, and a variety of utensils. He looked up, making eye contact with the young woman. "My mother, she sent me out here to get her a boilpot. I mean, I think she has a perfectly good boilpot, you know, but she wants another. Not big enough, she says. Drives me a bit up the stairs, if you get me."

The girl sighed, her eyes darting over to the man next to her for moment. The sort of glance that said, *yes, I get you, this one is the same.*

"How big are you looking for, friend?" the man said, his voice almost a song.

"This woman," Asti said, laying it on hard. "She claims she's got a friend whose coming in on a fishing boat from around the gulf. Bringing lobsters, bringing them alive, if you've heard of such a thing."

"Not ever," the girl said.

"My mother, she's from up in the north country, from the gulf shore, where this is a thing they do, and she's very excited," Asti said. "Won't stop going on, even singing the songs from up there. Blazes, it's in my head now. *Oh the waves crack down, across the shores of Erien.*"

"How big of a pot is that, friend?" the girl asked.

Asti made some gestures to indicate the size of a pot. "She keeps going on about this lobster thing, says it will be part of the greater symphony."

The girl made a noise of utter exasperation.

"Has she experienced the symphony friend?" the old man asked, his eyes lighting up. "Is she one of the blessed ones?"

"She's always been a blessing to me, friend," Asti said.

"Hold on to that," the girl said. "We don't have the sort of pot you need. Might be best if you moved along."

"But if the blessing—" the old man said.

"Best if you moved," the girl said sharply. Her eyes screamed of danger.

"Good day to you both," Asti said, walking away. This had to be the Scanders, no doubt. He glanced up to the squirrel above him, and gave a signal to it. Then he muttered to himself how ridiculous this was.

Ridiculous doesn't matter, he thought as he walked away. *Just get the job done.*

"ALL RIGHT, WE NEED TO MOVE," ASTI SAID AS HE GOT BACK TO THE wagon. "I'm pretty sure Scander is our man here, so we want to keep an eye on him."

"Jandie's watching him," Hoskins said. "Yandie is over Tharek, and Venn on the Lyranan woman."

"That's good for tracking things," Asti said. "And—listen, I'm not being disrespectful, but—how much can they really watch what's going on?"

"They're good observers," Hoskins said. "But they're going to see what they think is important, not what you would. I get it."

"So we need to keep our eyes out there." Asti handed a cheap fiddle he found in the market to Erno. "How's your corner crooner game?"

"That's just degrading, friend," Erno said.

"Right now, that's the kind of bow work I need," Asti said.

"I can do it, but I am much better than this," Erno said.

"He's not," Kat'rick said.

"What are you on about?" Erno asked. "I was making more money doing the wandering songster bit than I did as an archer for hire."

Asti grabbed the cap off Almer's head and handed it to Erno. "You'll place yourself in sight of the Scanders' stall, lay out the cap, and watch for anything strange."

"Fine," Erno said. "But I choose my own songs."

"I honestly don't care," Asti said. He leaned over to Almer. "Hey, Dale, I want you to move the wagon to the western corner. Kat'rick—"

"Stay in the wagon, yes," she said. "For I am conspicuous."

"And if anything goes bad, protect Dale and Hoskins."

"I can protect myself," Hoskins said.

"Not me?" Yendick asked.

"You're with me," Asti said, gently taking Yendick's arm. He wanted to yank the man out of the wagon, but Asti had a sense that the magicks that kept him from enacting violence on Yendick extended to even that. Instead he just eased him out and started to walk toward the Scanders' stall.

Almer started moving the wagon as Erno hopped out and went to his corner spot. Asti noted Tharek circling on the perimeter of the shopping bazaar, and Yikenj—Asti couldn't see her, but he could vaguely feel her presence through the crystal. That was a somewhat disquieting sensation.

"Why am I with you?" Yendick asked.

"First off, I need you in a central spot, and nimble. I need to move the wagon without forcing Tharek and Yikenj to be towed along."

"Fair enough. And second?"

"Are you Intelligence, or just one of Grieson's contracted talents?"

"Closer to the latter."

Not quite an answer. "I need to know if you're only useful as a leash, or have other skills."

"Like what?"

Asti sighed. "So this Crenaxin fellow, he's able to exert mystical control over folks. It didn't quite work on me, but his voice holds power, and they don't just do what he says, they *want* to do it."

"Interesting. But it didn't work on you?"

"My brain's already broken," Asti said.

Yendick looked at Asti, his eyes narrowing. "Yes, I can see. That's interesting."

"And that's what I need to know. You can *see* mystical and magical things that most of us can't."

"To a degree," Yendick said.

"Yeah, which is why I want you to get a look at Scander, see if you can see that influence on him, and maybe to who and where it's tethered."

"Presuming it works that way," Yendick said. He frowned, but nodded. "It's not a terrible idea."

"Glad you approve," Asti said. "This way."

Erno was now making a spectacle of himself, which was what Asti was hoping for. He wanted anyone who was walking through the bazaar —including the Scanders—to have their full attention elsewhere, instead of looking at Asti and the wild bearded man.

"My song'll make you shout,

My song'll knock you out."

Erno was actually pretty good, Asti had to admit. Yikenj even stepped out of whatever shadow she was hiding in to watch him.

Asti's attention was too much on Erno and the Scanders, that he didn't even notice the pedalcart until it crashed into Yendick and knocked him down. Asti felt a rush of pain as if he had been hit, and the sudden surprise of it forced him to drop to one knee. He stifled the urge to scream, and then as quickly as the pain had struck him, it vanished. All the sensation from the crystal vanished: the pain from Yendick, the connection to the others, everything.

Asti looked up at Erno, and the grin on the man's face told a whole story. Erno jumped to his feet and started to run.

"That rutting idiot," Asti muttered. Erno was already tearing his way down the lane through the park. Yikenj seemed to be still recovering, and Tharek was moving to Yendick.

Asti shouted to Yikenj, as he started running after Erno. "Stop him!"

Yikenj threw one of her darts, but it missed the mark. Blazes, that man was fast. Asti struggled to keep pace, let alone catch up.

"Get back here!" he shouted as Erno pulled someone off their horse and jumped on.

"I think I've sung my last song for you all!" Erno called back as he spurred the horse on. "I hope you enjoyed the sh—"

Asti felt it through his whole body, like hitting a wall, as the sudden pain nearly stopped him dead. He dropped to his knees, and he was fully aware of every sensation through the crystal, the rest of the team feeling the same, and the power rippling off Yendick.

And Erno, a hundred yards away, dropped off the horse as blood gushed from his eyes, ears, and nose. His whole body shuddered and collapsed in a pool of that blood.

Hands were on Asti's shoulders, pulling him to his feet. Yikenj.

"Come on," she said, pulling him back toward the safe radius of Yendick's influence. "We need to get out of here. We have made quite enough spectacle for today."

CHAPTER TWENTY-FOUR

Asti and the rest returned to the factory, which was the last thing Asti wanted to do, but after what happened to Erno and what they all went through—physically and mentally—there was no way they could keep up the scout in the bazaar. They all needed to rest, but also they couldn't stick around after that. Asti wondered what would happen when Constabulary found Erno's body, but he also felt that wasn't his problem. If that created some minor difficulty for Grieson, he certainly didn't care. Grieson wasn't even here.

Almer had taken it upon himself to make a meal for everyone with the supplies on hand in the factory. Almer seemed the least affected, at least outwardly, by the incident. In Asti's time on the streets and in Intelligence, he had met very few folks who seemed as imperturbable as Almer. The man had been scared or angry at times, but even in those moments, he was as solid as an oak. When the mages took their fingers, Ken and Helene had cracked, and Asti couldn't blame them. But Almer acted like it was just a mere inconvenience.

Asti hated being in the middle of this right now, and hated that any of his friends had been swept into it, but he was grateful to have Almer at his side right now. Almer could be depended upon.

The food he made was perfectly palatable. Nothing especially interesting, but the ingredients he was working with weren't giving him anything to start with. Root vegetable soup with barley, a meal no one would complain about, and no one did. Each of them took their bowl and went to as separate of a corner as they could manage, sitting and eating in silence.

Hoskins did come up to Asti after he ate. "I've got the fellows on the Scanders, they'll keep an eye on things, let me know if something odd happens."

"Thanks," Asti said. "It's good, at least, they're not restricted in where they can go."

"Oh, they wouldn't be able to stand it," Hoskins said. "Venn was very troubled by what he saw with Erno."

"Really?" Asti asked. "Sorry, that just surprised me. I figured, you know, for an animal, that sort of thing is normal."

Hoskins scratched at his scraggly beard. "Near as I understand it, death, even violent death, that's part of what they see as the cycle. Hawk gets a mate of yours, it's a thing that happens."

"Right," Asti said, doing his best to embrace this conversation about the philosophical outlook of squirrels.

"But this was different, as . . ." Hoskins looked like he was struggling to explain it, even understand it himself. "There wasn't a hawk, if that makes sense?"

Oddly it did. "Well, I hope they have a better night watching the Scanders."

"That's very thoughtful of you, Marin," Hoskins said, and he went off to one of the cots. "I'm glad you have shown them some respect."

The cots had been set up behind a few blinds, to give some small modicum of quiet and privacy. Very little, but some.

"Almer," Asti said quietly as he came back to the stove. "Everything all right with you?"

"Kat'rick is at least interesting company in the wagon," Almer said. "For what this all is, it's fine."

"I think you'd say that if you were on fire."

Almer shrugged to consider that. "Depends on the cause of the fire."

"Listen," Asti said. "As far as we know, Verci and the others are still locked up, and no one outside knows where we are. Tomorrow, if you find a chance, get a moment—"

"To send word to Kimber or your families?" Almer asked. "I've been thinking on that, but I've not had a moment."

"Good," Asti said, then noticing Yikenj was approaching. "Get some rest, Dale, I'll take care of cleaning this up."

"Such an egalitarian leader," Yikenj said. "Taking his appropriate share of the work. Very Lyranan."

"I was under the impression your people were all about hierarchies and rank."

"With that comes responsibility," she said. "And it is considered deeply improper to shirk that, even at high station."

"So, you've done all this before," Asti said. "Has anything like . . . that happened to you before?"

"That moment where the connection was lost because something distracted Yendick?" she asked. "Yes. But this is the first time someone took advantage of it, that I know of. Or rather, that they got far enough away and it did that to them. Which was intriguing to see."

"That's gruesome," Asti said.

"Certainly, but it did answer my curiosity. I did wonder what happened when they went too far. One could test the boundary of control that Yendick has, push the edges of the pain, but one would surely simply pass out before they could push so far as to be killed by it. And even the sternest of souls would feel compelled to move closer instead of enduring that, I would think. So now we know."

"It is troubling," Asti said. "Also, we're prevented from trying, but is Yendick?"

"What would happen if he decides to just run off?" she asked. "Not a question I wish to learn the answer to, thank you."

Asti kept cleaning as the others made their way to the cots, and lamps went out. Soon he found himself sitting alone in the light of a single lamp.

"Not planning on sleeping?" Liora manifested in front of him.

"Not going to pretend I'll be able to," he said quietly.

"Come on, was seeing Erno get his just deserts there that troubling?" she asked. "I mean, you did not like him, don't pretend you did."

"Didn't like the man, didn't make it less disturbing," he said.

"Saints, I must really be losing it if I'm willing to have an actual conversation with you."

"What other options do you even have?" she asked. "Your choices continue to constrict and constrict, soon it's going to choke you. You know, even if you manage to get through this—catch Crenaxin, saints preserve you—and even *maybe* if in doing so, Grieson keeps his word, and then you and Verci and all the others get to go home, well . . . then what? Are you still going to sabotage the Andrendon? Or have your revenge on the folks behind it? And where is that going to leave you, hmm? No better off that Erno Don, I would bet."

"You hush up now," Asti said.

"But more likely is there will just be more dead bodies in your wake. Maybe Almer is next. Or Verci. Or Raych or the baby, or even your precious Mila."

"I said hush up," Asti hissed.

"I hadn't even said anything yet."

Asti turned around, and Tharek had come out to the kitchen, stripped down to just his skivs. His body, despite the handful of scars marking his chest and arms, was an impressive display of human perfection. Like he had been carved out of marble.

"Now this is impressive," Liora said.

"Sorry," Asti said. "Just . . . talking to myself."

Tharek came closer, filling up a cup at the water spigot. "You tell yourself to hush up when you talk to yourself?"

"Other parts of my head tend to say stupid things," Asti said.

Tharek leaned against the counter and took a sip. "I've learned that when I really listened to the supposed stupid thoughts in my head, they turned out to be hard truths I needed to hear."

"A bit of that as well," Asti said. "Including the things I don't want to hear."

"Like this is a doomed mission and we'll all be killed?" Tharek asked. He shook his head, and Asti was very aware of how close the man was standing to him. A dozen conflicting impulses ran through his skull. "If someone takes me out in a fair fight, that's a fine enough way to die. I've lived and fought by my skills, so if someone has the skill to kill me, that's something I can honor. But to die because of some . . .

petty trickery like this." He tapped at the crystal in his well-muscled chest.

"I feel you," Asti said.

"Erno was a nattering fool, but no one deserved to die like that."

"All the more reason to finish this and get out of here."

"Out." Tharek scoffed. "I think for both of us that just means back to the prison, where a sham trial awaits us."

"A sham?" Asti raised an eyebrow. "You did actually kill four members of Parliament, right? And something like a dozen marshals?"

"My actions don't mean my trial won't be a sham," Tharek said, turning to face Asti directly, his dark eyes piercing. "If anything, they guarantee it. This is probably the closest to freedom I'll have."

"Now where is this going to go?" Liora asked.

Intelligence had trained Asti in techniques of seduction, and he'd used those skills on several men and women to serve his missions. Tharek was doing exactly what Asti would do if he needed to seduce a mark, but Asti wasn't sure if it was a ploy or Tharek genuinely trying out of his own interest.

"We should enjoy what little freedoms we can, then," Asti said.

"Exactly my thoughts," Tharek said, and he closed the distance in a snap, kissing Asti hard and rough.

Asti pushed away, even though his heart was pounding. "Listen," he said as he got control of his breath. "I don't really do this, or at least haven't . . ."

"Not for a while," Tharek said.

"It's just that—I'm not right in the head," Asti said.

"I got that with the talking to yourself," Tharek said, putting a hand gently on Asti's chest.

"It's that my head is very dangerous. I don't let people get close, people who I care about, because . . ."

"That's fine," Tharek said. "I'm not going to pretend that I'm someone you care about."

"My guard needs to always be up."

"Mine is never down," Tharek countered.

"If I slip up, if I let myself let go . . . people get hurt," Asti said. He reached up and tapped the crystal on Tharek's chest, even as he kept his hand there. "Even this might not stop me."

"Don't worry," Tharek said, a sly smile crossing his lips. "However bad it is, I'm sturdy enough to take it."

Tharek kissed him again, and for once—saints, just for once—Asti allowed himself the indulgence of accepting the comfort and pleasure that came with it, and all that followed.

ASTI HAD GOTTEN THE CREW OUT IN THE CARRIAGE BY DAWN, WHICH was the source of some muted grumbling from Yendick, but everyone else took it with as much grace as they were able. As horrific as it was, Erno's death made everyone a little more cooperative. That was more than useful for Asti.

On the intelligence from the squirrel's recon—a concept that Asti had now fully embraced as delightful—Scander was still in his apartment with his daughter. The Scanders, according to Jandie, "had a man beast in their nest for nibblings"—which Asti presumed was a man who came for dinner. Jandie was not a useful witness for further details on this man, but he left "before the moons were highest," which was at least a time frame.

None of the squirrels took any initiative to follow said man to wherever he came from. Disappointing, but Asti knew he couldn't have expected more from them. Most people didn't think like he did, he couldn't expect squirrels to.

As they rode together to the Scanders apartment, Asti gave out the orders for the day, starting with Hoskins. "If you can't get any more details out of Jandie, then at least see if he—"

"She," Hoskins said, scratching the ears of the squirrel in his lap, which might have been Jandie, for all Asti knew. They looked the same to him. Another squirrel was perched on Hoskins's shoulder, and the third was still watching the apartment.

"She can scout around the neighborhood, maybe get all the other squirrels they can, see if they can find that guy again, where he is."

"I'll see what I can do."

"Only you can do it. You're the only one who has mobility of any sort outside the circle."

"I will try," Hoskins said, rubbing the sweat off his brow. He started mumbling while looking back and forth between the two squirrels.

"Dale, park the wagon on the corner in front of the boarded-up shop, put up a show like you're waiting for someone else. Kat'rick—"

"I know," she snarled. "Stay out of sight in the wagon, protect the magic men if there is trouble. Of course that is what it is."

"Right," Asti said. He didn't have time or inclination to dig any deeper into that. She accepted her current assignment, however grudgingly. If and when this mission got to the point where he needed someone to kick open a door and cut through fools like they were water, he'd be glad to have her. But they were not at that point. "Tharek, take point across the street, watch the front door of the tenement, and be on hand if Dale gets any trouble for parking the wagon."

"If that's what you need," Tharek said, his voice almost a purr that sent a charge up Asti's spine.

Yikenj clearly noticed and raised her eyebrow at that. "I'll circuit the perimeter from rooftops, out of sight," she said.

Not exactly what Asti wanted from her, but good enough. "Fine," he said. "You and I hop out before we stop, and Tharek, wait until they park."

"On it."

He looked out the back of the wagon, and seeing they were near the apartment, signaled Yikenj and jumped out. They both ducked into the alley behind Scander's tenement.

"It isn't like I am any more inconspicuous than Kat'rick," Yikenj said.

"I need a spy more than an assassin right now," Asti said.

"I think the last thing you want is a spy," she said. "I should remind you that Tharek is still a revolutionary who tried to overthrow the government, and a brutal killer to match. No amount of romance will soften him."

"I'll remind you that I am as well."

She grinned. "No, you are not a revolutionary. You are certainly not

Marin Tacklin, nor is the driver named Dale. I don't know who you are or why you are here—not yet—but you are definitely not what you are pretending to be."

"I am definitely a killer."

"Yes," she said coolly. "Yes, you, like me, were a servant of the state. I can see that in you. Abandoned by those we serve."

Too rutting insightful, she was.

"So they abandoned you?"

"I'm in a Druth prison, yes? Forced to serve a different master." She chuckled ruefully.

"Right," Asti said, something in what she said starting to stir in his head. "Get up top, make a circuit."

She glanced down the alley. "Actually, I'm going to stay on the ground. There might be . . ." She went off before finishing her thought.

On some level, Asti didn't care as long as she didn't push the perimeter. She was capable and had good instincts, and if she found a lead that ended this all sooner, all the better.

He climbed up the wrought iron backstair on the opposite building, to a spot where he could see into the Scanders' window. The daughter was in the main room, preparing breakfast, while the old man was in the bedroom.

Forced to serve a different master ran through his head. That was what Crenaxin did to people, right? His words had a power behind them, and folks would just serve him, a total subservience to him. But Victor Scander, from the conversation in the park, didn't quite seem like that. He was more like someone who had *found* something, rather than being forced into it.

Maybe with faith—or whatever the power Crenaxin wielded was—there wasn't much difference.

A squirrel dropped down next to Asti, looking at him expectantly.

"What?" Asti asked, having abandoned any sense of feeling foolish about this.

The squirrel gestured to the bedroom window.

Asti looked back, seeing the old man had stripped completely naked. This was not something Asti was particularly needing to see, but the squirrel kept nudging him. He looked closer.

Victor Scander was covered in welts. They would be serious scars soon, but right now they were still fresh, still healing, angry and deep red. There was even a section in his side that looked like an animal had taken a bite out of him.

Asti watched as Victor ran his fingers along each wound, tracing along while a look of pure bliss crossed his face. Reverence for each injury.

That was something new.

"Crenaxin was a freak, but not *that kind* of freak," Liora said, manifesting next to him.

"Really don't know everything about him," Asti said.

"You're already thinking it," she said.

"I'm thinking that's important for reasons we don't understand."

But she was right, something felt off about this.

"Hey," Asti said to the squirrel. "Get Hoskins over here." It seemed to understand as it scampered away. Asti climbed back down, and Hoskins was coming over by the time Asti reached the mouth of the alley.

"What's going on? Something about the old man being bit up?"

"He's got fresh wounds that he's treating . . ." Asti looked for the right word. "Like they're sacred."

"That's strange."

"Spread word among your friends," Asti told him. "See if they can see anyone else who has those kind of injuries. You remember those other names from the other files?"

"Somewhat."

"Well, try and have the squirrels check those folks out."

"Marin, they're very smart, but they don't tell humans apart very well. Or understand names and addresses."

"It's pitiful this is the best resource available," Liora said.

"Well, I am, so show some respect," Hoskins said, and huffed off.

Liora raised an eyebrow. "That was interesting."

"You shut your face," Asti told her, as useless a thing as that was. He was about to say more when he noticed some movement from the alley across the street. Someone being pulled into the shadow.

Asti carefully crossed the street, pulling a knife as he approached.

Once he was in the alley, he saw exactly what he expected and feared: Yikenj over a body, her cord still wrapped around the fellow's neck.

"The blazes are you doing?"

"He was sniffing around the wagon. And your loverboys didn't even notice."

Asti swore in a few languages. "Now what are you going to do with him?"

"Rifle his pockets and leave him with the rubbish bin. No one would think it was anything but a bad robbery."

Asti shook his head. "Wait, lift up his shirt."

"Your perversions continue."

"Just do it."

She obliged, and the man had a pair of barely healed injuries on his chest, two circles on either side, like he had been held in place by some kind of sharp clamp.

"That is curious," she said. "You think he's connected to this cult?"

"I do, but I wonder if the cult isn't what we think."

"You might be right," she said. "I noticed him coming from another abandoned factory around the corner. There might be more activity there. I wanted to check it, but it was out of our range."

Asti nodded. "Then that's worth checking out later. For now, let's move him and get us all out of here."

CHAPTER TWENTY-FIVE

"Why are we back here?" Yendick asked. They had returned to the safehouse, partly to regroup and gear up before making a move on the abandoned factory, and partly because Asti didn't want any of them about when the man Yikenj killed was found. "You still have plenty of daylight, you should be—"

"You need to hush up," Asti told him. "We don't want daylight when we make our move. And if I am forced to have you as an anchor around my neck, the least you can do is be quiet."

"Don't push me," Yendick said. "You don't want to know what else I can do to you. To any of you!" He pointed an accusing finger at each member of the crew. "I was merciful to Erno, frankly."

"Let me tear him up," the beast growled in the back of Asti's head. "No crystal will hold me back."

Asti wasn't sure if the broken parts of his head could somehow work around Yendick's power that prevented violence against him. It had protected him from Crenaxin's power, after all—

"My bindings can and will," Yendick snapped back at Asti.

"Can and will what?" Almer asked.

"That's a second time," Liora said, appearing next to Asti. "This is very interesting."

"Listen," Asti said, talking over her. "All of you, rest a bit, get a bite, check your gear. We go right after sunset."

"Trying so hard to be in control, Asti," Liora said.

"He's right," Tharek said. "If this target is the real thing, we want some cover of darkness, and to be fresh."

"Fine by me," Kat'rick said.

Folks all went off in separate directions, Yendick grumbling the most as he went. Asti went to his cot and lay down, hoping to push the other voices in his head away.

After what felt like two minutes with his eyes closed, there was a tap on his shoulder. Asti's hand shot out, but he stopped before he grabbed Almer by the throat. Or, he was stopped by the force of Yendick's power.

"What is it?" he whispered.

"There was a surprise under my cot," Almer said. "Your friend Grieson must have had my shop raided, he brought a few supplies for me."

"Anything you can make use of quietly?"

Almer shrugged. "A bit. Whoever actually gathered things had some sense, at least. I've mixed up a few things already. And here." He handed a vial over.

"What's this?"

"Drink it. It'll quiet some of the things in your skull."

"I'm fine."

"Asti," Almer said. "I heard a woman's voice. She called you Asti. Which means that this thing?" He tapped the crystal on his chest. "It's doing something more to you, and sharing that with me. Probably not just me."

"No, not just you, I think," Asti said.

"So take that, calm down, and let's get moving. Folks are nearly ready."

"Ready?" Asti asked. "It's only been a moment."

"You lay down two hours ago," Almer said. "Sun's nearly down."

"Saints," Asti said. "All right, be right on it."

Asti waited a moment for Almer to leave, and looked at the vial.

"Oh, you want to silence us," Liora said. "That's just a patch, you'll never be rid of me."

"It's a start," Asti said, opening the vial and downing the bitter contents. He hid the vial under his cot and came out, heading to the kitchen.

"You good?" Tharek asked him as he came over.

"Fresh and ready," Asti said. "When we get there, we'll first scout the perimeter, and if it looks good, you and Yikenj take point going in."

"That's a plan," Tharek said. He handed Asti a hunk of bread with soft northern cheese slathered over it. "I'll rally them, and we'll go when you're good."

"Thanks," Asti said, taking a bite.

"All right, let's load up!" Tharek said. "We're looking at a long night, hopefully no trouble, but this is no time to go soft!"

Asti chuckled as he ate. That was not going to be a problem Tharek Pell would have.

THE WAREHOUSE WAS DEFINITELY NOT ABANDONED, DESPITE ATTEMPTS to make it look that way. Asti had first cautiously scouted around the building, and had both Tharek and Yikenj work the perimeter, as well as the squirrels. Most of the windows had been completely blacked over, but there were several signs of current occupation. Some footprints in the muddier parts of the ground around it, a bit of flicker of light in the windows despite the blacking, light tufts of smoke from the chimneys.

Someone was in there.

"So let's make our move," Tharek said when they reconvened at the wagon. "There's a loading door on the west side, a sky window on the roof. We could crash through both at once, take down anyone inside."

"We don't know what we'll find inside yet," Asti said. "It could be a maze inside, let alone how many people."

"I don't think it's too populated," Yikenj said. "There'd be more signs if there were a lot of people inside."

"It's very possible this is not our final target," Kat'rick said. "This may be connected to this Crenaxin fellow, but he is not here. Too bold a strike, too loud, and we may spook the people we are trying to catch. They'll go to ground."

"Are we supposed to kill him or catch him?" Almer asked.

"Catch is ideal," Yendick said.

"Ideal," Asti said. "And what are the consequences for a less than ideal outcome?"

Yendick shrugged. "I have not been given specific orders about that."

"And you wouldn't tell us if you had," Yikenj added.

"I think we should have the squirrels go in first," Asti said. "See if they can give us a better sense of what's going on in there."

"Yandie doesn't want to," Hoskins said, stroking the head of the squirrel on his knee. "She says this place smells ugly."

"I don't care what it thinks this place smells like," Tharek said.

"Wait," Asti said. "Can she expand on that? Ugly how?"

Hoskins conferred with the creature, and then with the other one on his shoulder, then looked up. "It's not clear, but they are both spooked. Like this is a graveyard."

Asti wasn't sure how to phrase the question he wanted to ask. "Did they say graveyard, or is it just like one?"

"It doesn't directly translate like that," Hoskins said.

"If Yandie doesn't want to go in, what about the others?" Yikenj asked.

More conferring. "They are willing, but not happy."

"Willing is all I need," Asti said. "Send Jandie and Venn inside."

Hoskins nodded solemnly, and the two squirrels scampered off. Yandie, having stayed on his knee, scurried up into his chest, and he held the little animal closely.

"How long will we be waiting?" Tharek asked. "I'll take another pass." He jumped out of the wagon.

"Same," Yikenj said, and slipped out.

Kat'rick sighed. "This is where Erno would have had an annoying song."

"Thought you hated him," Almer said.

"I did, but . . . I did like the songs."

Several quiet minutes passed, and Asti noticed Yendick, curled up in the corner of the wagon, starting to snore. Asti was a little jealous, but also annoyed with how little the man cared about any of this. Their lives were in Yendick's hands, and the bastard couldn't even bother to pay attention or give a damn.

Suddenly Yandie perked up and ran out of the wagon.

"What was that?" he asked Hoskins.

"Something is wrong," Hoskins said, getting out. Asti clambered after him, Almer and Kat'rick behind him.

"What is it?"

Yandie was running across the lot in the dark, and he could see it came across another squirrel. Then Hoskins cried out, covering his mouth as he dropped to his knees.

"What?" Asti asked.

"Jan . . . Jandie is dead," he cried. "And Tharek is in trouble."

"Blazes," Asti muttered. Pointing to Kat'rick, he said, "Find Yikenj. Al—Dale, stay with him." He ran off, around to the back entrance of the warehouse. As he feared, the door was now cracked open. Stupid Tharek, acting on his own. The man knew better, damn it.

A wave of pain filled Asti. Not his own, but Tharek's. He could feel it, a crunching tear through his body.

Asti risked going through the door, and there was Tharek, caught in some monstrous contraption. Verci's work had made him familiar enough with gear and springwork to see what it was—some sort of spring-powered torture device, in which Tharek's arm was caught on one end, and his leg in the other, while something else had wrapped around his face. It was clear the man could barely breathe, let alone cry out, and it was taking every bit of strength he had to keep the manacles from twisting his limbs clean off.

"Tharek!" Asti shouted, keeping himself from dashing over. He could see the tangled spiderwire coiled around Tharek's other foot, and several more lines of it stretched out over the ground. And then, on the far end of the room, the remains of a squirrel's body, having been torn into several parts.

"Give me a moment," Asti said, trying to keep himself calm, even as

Tharek's agony twisted in his own limbs. "I'm going to get you out of this."

First he had to just get over to the man without triggering anything else. That would be hard enough. Carefully, he stepped over one line of spiderwire, then ducked under another, while he prayed to whichever saint would listen that he not set anything else off. If this entrance was so elaborately trapped, what else could there be here?

Tharek kept thrashing, his powerful arm bulging red, veins popped out, blood trickling down to the floor. Asti pulled out a knife and cut the tangle of spiderwire free, the first and easiest thing to do.

"Hold on, hold on," Asti said, touching Tharek's chest. "I'm here."

Tharek seemed to calm a little, his breathing slowing down. Asti reached up and cut at the cloth bound around Tharek's face. It was held taut and hard to cut through, but once he got some purchase on it, it started to tear. In a moment, Asti had it off, and Tharek took a desperate gasp of air.

"Keep it together, I'm on it," Asti said. "I'm getting you out."

"Can't . . . much . . ." was all Tharek could manage.

"Asti!" Almer was in the doorway.

"Stay back!" Asti said. "There's still more traps in here! I need to cut him out."

"Those binds are steel," Almer said. "You can't cut it."

Blazes, he was right. He couldn't cut through, and there wasn't an obvious latch to spring it. Still it had to open somehow. Verci would know how.

"Cut at the joint," Tharek said. "Take the thumb."

"Better," Almer said. "Catch." He tossed a vial to Asti.

"Acid?" Asti asked, opening the vial. The scent was familiar, like most of the things from Almer's workshop. "Hold still, Tharek."

"Really can't." His arm buckled, and then shot up with a horrifying snap from his shoulder. It was stretched too high for Asti to easily reach the manacle. He knelt down and poured the acid on the one around Tharek's ankle, all the while using his blade to try to gain some leverage and spring it open.

Then, as both lines were about to tear the man apart, the manacle gave. It flew off, retracting in the wall, while Tharek went hurtling up with the other one, toward the ceiling.

Asti moved on instinct, throwing the vial at the manacle on Tharek's wrist. Tharek screamed, and several forms of pain coursed through Asti's body from him. Then the manacle cracked, and Tharek dropped to the ground, still screaming.

"Here!" Almer said, throwing another vial. Asti caught it and emptied its contents on Tharek's wrist, guessing that it must be something to counter the acid that was burning the man's flesh. The pain Asti felt through the crystal connection subsided, but wasn't gone.

"You all right?" Asti asked.

"Careless," Tharek said. He got to his feet, cradling his arm. "I can walk."

"We should get out," Asti said. "I don't know what else there could—"

"Trouble!" Kat'rick's voice echoed from outside.

"Help him," Asti ordered Almer, and he ran out, to see over by the wagon several figures attacking, while Kat'rick fought like mad to hold them off.

ASTI HAD HIS KNIVES OUT AS HE JUMPED INTO THE FRAY, WHILE Kat'rick was magnificent holding her own against her attackers. She was sweeping her powerful blade around her body with such speed and ferocity that none of them could get too close. There was one man on the ground already, his arm separated cleanly from his body, to show the others what they risked in a fight with her.

He went right for one. All of the attackers were dressed in the same dark clothes with hooded coats, all looked the same. New cultists in the Brotherhood? No time to think on it, he sank his blade into the fellow's shoulder.

"Where's Yikenj?" he shouted at Kat'rick while he pulled one man down.

"I didn't find her!" Kat'rick kept fighting, but these folks were too nimble, too well trained, and managed to stay clear of her.

Almer and Tharek were coming up, and Tharek, despite his right arm hanging limp, drew out his blade with his left hand.

"Get to the wagon, we need to get out of here!" Asti called.

A few of the attackers turned their focus on Almer and Tharek, while the others kept their focus on Asti and Kat'rick, pushing them back.

Keeping them all away from the wagon.

"Wait," Asti said. "Don't let them—"

Two more men dashed out of an alley, through the opening their compatriots had made, and going right for the wagon. They went right in and grabbed Yendick, pulling him out into the street.

"How dare you—" he started, his body crackling with energy. But as soon as he did, one of the men reached out with his ashy hand, similar energy coming off of him.

"What is he—" was all Asti could say before the man touched Yendick on the chest, and suddenly there was power channeling through Asti's body. He couldn't move, and it was clear none of the others could as well.

"Tojaom gao pillaol!" he shouted, and two of the attackers ran into the alley and came back out carrying the paralyzed body of Pra Yikenj.

Asti understood, so clearly, but too damn late. He couldn't do anything as they brought Yikenj to the other man, and he placed his hand on the crystal on her chest.

Pain surged through Asti's body as Yikenj's crystal shattered, and she gasped, clutching to her chest.

A grand smile crossed her face.

She walked over to Yendick, still held firm, and pulling a blade from her belt, tore open his shirt and sliced his belly open.

Casually, calmly, she turned and walked over to Asti. She leaned in close, like she was about to kiss him on the cheek. With a throaty whisper she said, "Sorry, friend, but it's just business. I know you understand."

She slapped his face lightly, chuckled, and walked off, the rest of the attackers going with her. The one holding Yendick in place went last, and when he let go, they all collapsed to the ground.

Asti pushed himself over to Yendick, bleeding on the ground.

"Help me!" he shouted, ripping off Yendick's shirt and using it to stop the bleeding. "Get him in the wagon!"

"What just happened?" Kat'rick asked.

"Yikenj had a damn plan," Asti said, kicking over the man he had killed. Lyranan. "Her people showed up to free her."

"So why are you saving him?" Hoskins asked.

"Do you know what happens if he dies?" Asti asked. "I bet it isn't good for us."

"Dhotou," Kat'rick whispered. *"Wep kwimjhu dhotou."*

Tharek pulled himself up in the wagon, and then dragged Yendick, still bleeding and muttering, up with him. Asti and the others climbed in, and Almer snapped the horses to a sharp pace, sparing no time.

"What will happen to him?" Hoskins asked.

"She knew exactly what she was doing," Asti said, looking at the wound he was attempting to bandage. "She wanted to put him out of commission without killing him. This could bleed out for hours."

"How did she even do all that?" Kat'rick asked.

"She's a spy," Tharek said. "She managed to reach out to her people, and they knew how to free her."

"Least of our concerns now," Asti said. "We need to get back to the warehouse. Between Yendick and your arm, we're in no shape to continue."

In a few moments, they were back in their safehouse, and Almer was getting to work closing the barn doors and locking things down. At least he was in his right head.

"Was that even the right place?" Hoskins asked. "Or did we lose Jandie for nothing?"

"It was right for something," Tharek said.

"It may have been the right place, but don't think it was what we were looking for," Asti said.

"What does that mean?" Kat'rick asked.

"It means I think Grieson has this all wrong. It's not Crenaxin or the

Brotherhood in there. I don't know who is doing this, but this isn't who Crenaxin is at all."

Tharek signaled Asti closer, and nodded to his arm. "Grab hold."

Asti took the man's hand and held it firm. Tharek braced himself, and Asti gave them arm a yank, and with a sickening pop it went back into place.

"Now what?" Kat'rick asked. "If this isn't who we're supposed to find, what are we doing?"

"There is a more important question," Tharek said, flexing his fingers.

"Which is?" Asti asked.

Tharek growled, and grabbed Asti by the front of his shirt. "Is your name Asti Rynax?"

CHAPTER TWENTY-SIX

Asti's instinct was to shove Tharek away, but apparently that thought was too violent for the crystal connection. His arm was frozen in place, refusing to obey his thoughts. It was obvious that Tharek had no intention beyond holding his shirt, as threatening as it felt. He was still just as bound, despite whatever damage the Lyranans had done to free Yikenj.

"What makes you think that?" Asti asked, as if there was any merit to maintaining the ruse.

"He called you Asti," Tharek said, pointing to Almer. "And there had been other things as well."

"Venn thought something was up with the two of them," Hoskins said. "He saw some things with them."

"What sort of things?" Tharek asked.

The squirrel scampered off.

"Asti Rynax?" Kat'rick asked. "Does that name have significance?"

"Oh, it does," Tharek said.

The squirrel came running back with the empty vial from Asti's bunk.

"He says the badger man gave it to Asti," Hoskins offered.

"I'm the badger man now?" Almer asked. His attention was on bandaging Yendick, which was actually the most important task right now. Asti was still frozen with his desire to strike hard at Tharek, and having him, Kat'rick, and Hoskins all focused on him did nothing to ease that instinct. They couldn't hurt him, but his need to hurt anyone, to let the beast out, was paralyzing him.

"What was this?" Tharek snapped back.

"Something to calm his nerves, so he could do the job."

"And where did you get this nerve calmer?" Kat'rick asked, moving to loom threateningly over Almer.

"I made it," Almer said. "My name isn't Dale, he isn't Tacklin. You know this, clearly. And I'm not a carriage-man, I'm a chemist."

"And you two know each other quite well?" Hoskins asked.

"Yes," Asti said. "His name is Almer Cort."

"And you're Asti Rynax," Tharek said.

"Yes," Asti said. "What does that matter?"

Tharek let him go and stormed away. "Do you know about him? You lot, did you? Who he is?"

"Should we?" Hoskins asked. He conferred with Venn. "No, I don't get it either," he muttered to the animal.

"The guards let me know. Gave me that pamphlet to read."

Asti groaned. "*The Champions of Maradaine*?"

"An actual hero!" Tharek shouted. "Saved the city!"

"What is this?" Kat'rick asked.

"This upstanding fellow, this pillar of the community," Tharek said. "When some trouble with monsters or some other sewage spilled out into the streets, he was there, saving the people!"

"This upsets you?" Asti asked.

"Fighting shoulder to shoulder with two constables, the Thorn, and best of all, Dayne Heldrin and Jerinne Fendall!"

Tharek said those last two names with such venom, it was clear it was personal.

"You fought with the Thorn?" Kat'rick asked. "He's your friend?"

"Friend is a strong word."

"And those Tarian puppets!" Tharek snarled.

"So, why the blazes are you in this with us?" Hoskins asked.

"I wish I rutting knew," Asti said. "Because Grieson wanted me here, because he thought we needed to catch the same guy we fought in that damn pamphlet."

Tharek spun on Asti. "The Dragon? The Brotherhood? That's who these bastards are?"

"That's what Grieson thought," Asti said. "But—"

"Enough!" Yendick shouted. He pulled himself up off the cot. "You aren't even Tacklin? This is intolerable!"

"You didn't know?" Kat'rick asked.

"No!" Yendick said. "And so I've been saddled with you inept morons! Not told anything I needed to know, Grieson lying to me! And then this happens!" He pointed at his gut, the bandages still seeping with blood.

Asti tried to talk some sense. "Yendick, you need to stay down, that injury—"

"Shut your lying face!" Yendick shouted. "I've had it with all of you! I should walk away and let you all die! I should snap my fingers and burst your rutting skulls!"

"Easy, easy," Almer said. "No need for that."

"Right," Yendick said. "This has been disaster enough. But for now, I just need some peace."

He snapped his fingers, and as soon as he did, Asti dropped into a black void, into the hardest, deepest sleep he'd ever had.

ASTI WOKE, HIS FACE ON THE CONCRETE FLOOR, HIS HEAD POUNDING. The blackout drapes had been pulled in the windows in the safehouse, but Asti could see that outlines of strong sunlight around the edges. It must already be midmorning.

Everyone else was still exactly where they fell, save Yendick, who was sitting a chair shirtless, fresh bandages around his wound, mug of tea in one hand and a pipe in the other.

"Well, we've decided you get to wake up," Yendick said, taking a puff. "Though there's still some debate over the next steps."

"Hush up, Yendick," Grieson said, walking into Asti's field of vision. "But it does seem like everything is messed up, doesn't it?"

"You're not wrong there," Asti said, pushing up to his hands and knees. Almer and the others were all doing the same, all moving slowly.

"What the blazes went wrong, Tacklin?" Grieson asked.

"You can drop that Tacklin sewage," Asti said. "They all know who I am."

"Why the blazes is that?" Grieson snapped.

"Besides the fact it was a stupid idea?" Asti shot back. "I mean, sure, I get it in terms of your whole ploy to throw me and the others in the prison. But once I was here, there was no rutting point to it."

"The point was to keep your identity—"

"And you put me in here with Almer?" Asti said, gesturing to him. "Let alone the way my broken skull is played by this stupid crystal!"

"So I gather you two know each other," Tharek said.

"He was my oversight when I was Druth Intelligence," Asti said.

"Just tell them everything, why don't you?"

"Why don't I?" Asti said. "I mean, what's the harm? Either they'll be dead or locked back in Ward Twelve."

"Yikenj got away," Hoskins said quietly.

"And how the blazes did that happen?" Grieson asked.

Asti shrugged. "This wasn't her first time on one of these missions. My guess, she managed a dead drop to her own people, who had worked out a way to separate her from the attuning."

"And the rest of the bond is secure?" Grieson asked Yendick.

"Why do you think I put them to sleep and kept them there?" he asked. "Partly just to make sure I was still in control."

"Good."

"Something is off with Tacklin. Or Rynax. Whoever he is."

"Off how?"

"More voices from him."

"You heard that as well?" Kat'rick asked. "Thought I was losing it."

"He's been touched by something," Tharek said. "That's why he was immune from Crenaxin's power. Why you thought he was useful for this."

Blazes, Tharek was an absolute razor, cutting right to the skin.

"That's definitely part of the trouble here, Grieson," Asti said. "This isn't Crenaxin."

"What are you talking about?" Grieson asked. "Everything points to his cult starting up again here."

"There's a cult, I think," Asti said. "But I don't think it's Crenaxin."

Grieson rubbed his face in annoyance. "Where is this coming from?" He looked to Yendick. "What do you think?"

"What do I know? That's not my job. My job is just to keep a leash on them, that's what I do."

"You did it terribly."

"How was I supposed to know Yikenj could get a Lyranan mystic to disconnect her?"

"Yikenj doesn't matter!" Asti shouted. "I'm telling you, what's happening in this neighborhood, it doesn't seem like the Brotherhood at all."

"No, no, it fits," Grieson said. "The change in behavior, the people leaving their families . . ."

"Talking about being part of the symphony?" Asti asked. "I mean, I don't remember hearing any of that the last time."

"No, it was mentioned before," Grieson said. "I have a record of an interrogation, where someone says the Brotherhood hired him to create a symphony."

"Well, I can tell you, the gear trap I cut Tharek out of, I didn't see that with the Brotherhood at all."

"Gear trap?" Grieson asked.

"Nearly tore me in half," Tharek said.

"And another killed Jandie!" Hoskins cried.

"Wait, wait, gear traps, multiple?"

"If anything it sounds like that other business you grabbed Verci for," Asti said.

"Rutting blazes!" Grieson said, turning Poasian pale. "Yendick, we need to scrub this, get the blazes out of here, get them back to the prison."

"Wait, what is this?" Almer asked.

"Something we don't want any part of," Grieson said. "If it isn't Crenaxin, if it's *him*, there's no point to any of this."

"This must be bad if it spooked him like this," Kat'rick said. "What is this about?"

"The gear trap, the machines," Asti said. "It's something my brother was brought in to disarm, and—"

Tharek looked up, his hand going to his sword. "Someone just came in here."

"I didn't hear anything," Almer said.

"No, he's right," Hoskins said. "Venn just—oh!"

"Blazes, he's here, isn't he?" Grieson said. "We need to get out now!"

"Who?" Kat'rick asked, holding her weapon in a defensive pose.

"He was called the Gearbox Killer," Asti said.

Suddenly all the lamps in the warehouse went out, leaving them in near darkness, save the thin outlines of sunlight seeping around the blackout shades. Asti couldn't see a damn thing.

"A descriptive sobriquet that lacks poetry," a voice echoed from several directions. "Not one I chose for myself."

"The blazes is that?" Yendick cried.

"Everyone run!" Grieson shouted.

"Too late!" the voice cackled. "Time for you all to learn, as those that truly fear me do. My name is Sholiar!"

ASTI HAD HIS KNIVES OUT, BUT SOUNDS WERE ECHOING FROM EVERY direction. He couldn't see a blazing thing, and had no idea where anyone might be coming from.

"Blazes, blazes, blazes!" Grieson shouted. "We need to get out of here."

"What is this?" Tharek asked. "Face me, you soft coward!"

"And what is your face to you?" Sholiar's voice called out. "What would you sacrifice to keep it?"

"I would—" was all Tharek said before he made a grunting noise, and Asti heard springs and snaps like one of Verci's windup boxes. Asti jumped to Tharek, finding the man on the floor, trying to keep a spring-loaded jaw trap from clamping down on his face.

"I need some rutting light!" he called out.

"Will your song be filled with less fear if you can see your fate?" Sholiar's mocking voice continued.

A bright glow came from Yendick's hands, letting Asti see what he was dealing with. The thing was trying to snap shut on Tharek, who was barely able to keep it from doing that. Asti wasn't the mechanical genius Verci was, but he had enough sense from being around him have a hint of how things like this worked. He found the joint that looked most vulnerable, jammed his knife in it and twisted. The blade snapped, but so did the spring, making the jaw trap go flying off, away from Tharek.

"We need to—"

"You need to stay out of my business," Sholiar said from the shadows. "But since you've decided to involve yourselves, I will make you my business."

A whistling noise cut through the air, and as quick as Asti could see, Almer and Hoskins had become ensnared in cables. Kat'rick had only avoided that fate by a quick slice of her blade.

"Come on," Asti said, pulling Tharek to his feet. The man was actually trembling. "Get them out."

"Run!" Grieson said. "Just all of you—"

"Oh, they'll run," Sholiar said. "I'm very interested to see how motivated they can be. Very interested indeed."

Another whistle cut, and a net whipped over Grieson, pinning him to the ground.

Each of those attacks had come from a different place. Sholiar moving through the darkness, in an arc around the room. Asti drew another knife and threw nearly blindly.

"So let's—ah!"

Struck true, thank Saint Senea.

"Now I have you," Asti said, and he spotted the silhouette of the man near the warehouse doors.

"Do you?" That came from Sholiar and Liora at once, and her sudden appearance made Asti stumble when he had intended to charge.

That stumble cost him a second, and in that second, something else wrapped around Yendick, and extinguishing his light. The darkness only lasted for a moment, as the warehouse doors flew open, sunlight pouring in.

A team of horses were right outside, and the man by the door—Sholiar, surely—stood in shadow with a manic grin across his pale, wild face.

A rope was tied to the horses' yoke, the other end of which was wrapped around Yendick.

"Now I'm afraid I must run," Sholiar said. "But I suspect, so do you."

He leaped from his spot on the ground onto one horse, and that was all it needed to take off like a shot. The horses raced down the road, and Yendick was yanked away and dragged along with them.

Immediately, Asti felt the distance between him and Yendick burn in his skull.

"Go, run!" he told the others. They needed no prodding. Kat'rick had cut Almer and Hoskins free, and Tharek was already charging down after Yendick like a mad bull. The others were right behind.

The pounding in Asti's skull was becoming more than he could bear. He tossed a knife to Grieson, still struggling under the net. He didn't have much time, but he had to make one thing clear as he started to run.

"Get me Verci!" he shouted to Grieson as he chased after the rest. "I can't do this without him!"

His head pounding, burning, Asti ran like all the sinners in the canon were at his heels. Maybe they were, that was how it felt.

Asti couldn't see Yendick, but he could feel him, in the back of his skull, he knew where the man was, being dragged by horses at a near gallop. His body getting knocked and cut and bruised.

He could see the group, running as hard as they could to keep up. Tharek at the front, muscles pounding like a race horse. If anyone could catch the ones pulling Yendick, it was him. Kat'rick was right on his heels, endurance making up what she lacked in speed. He could feel

Tharek forcing his way through the pain, but Kat'rick wasn't even close to buckling.

Almer and Hoskins, though, their lungs were on fire. They were losing ground as they stumbled in their run. Asti caught up just as Almer was about to drop.

"Got you," he said as he grabbed him, keeping him on his feet.

"I can't . . ." Almer wheezed.

"You're not dying on me today," Asti said. He couldn't carry the man, not and still keep pace, but he could keep him from falling over as he found his feet.

"Come on!" Hoskins yelled, his face red as he gasped for breath. He tripped and started to fall, but Kat'rick was right there, catching him before he did. She scooped him over her shoulder and spun around, reclaiming her pace without losing a beat.

Then there was a shift in the sensation, an easing of the throbbing pain in the back of Asti's skull. Pain still radiated from Yendick, but he was alive, Asti could feel it.

Tharek was stopped a bit ahead, leaning against the wall in an alley and catching his breath, and Asti forced himself to push ahead to get up to him, letting the others come at their own pace. The immediate danger had passed, now they needed to assess the situation.

"Where?" he asked Tharek as he approached.

"That one," Tharek said, pointing out of the alley down the street to the near-empty square. Across the other side of the square, another old factory, one that looked like it had been shut down for some time, but definitely not abandoned or unoccupied. Even in the daylight, they could see lamplight in the window, flickers of movement. Plus four or five bruisers standing around the front door.

"So that's the trap," Asti said.

"We need to strike," Tharek said. "We can carve though those fellows at the door."

"Ones at the door, sure," Asti said. "But what's beyond the door?"

"Yendick," Tharek said. "As much as I loathe to say it, liberating him is our paramount concern."

"He's definitely in there?" Almer asked, as the rest caught up.

"Since the horses went in the front door, he doesn't seem to have moved too far," Tharek said. "You can feel that?"

"I can," Asti said. Not that he could sense exactly where Yendick was, but if he had kept moving, that burning, pounding sense of imminent death would be in the back of his skull.

Yendick was in pain, though, and terrified. Asti realized the man must have been shielding his own feelings from the rest of them all this time, because now those emotions and sensations were coming in strong.

"That is definitely a problem," Liora said, manifesting next to Asti.

"Who is she, now?" Kat'rick asked, pointing right to her.

"A symptom of my broken mind," Asti said. "Try to ignore her."

"Oh, I finally get to be heard, there will be no ignoring," Liora said. "And you all have a serious problem here, you need to listen to anyone with a good idea."

"Is she real?" Hoskins asked, trying to touch her form.

"There is a real woman, his old partner," Almer said. "A right miserable woman who betrayed him."

"Did I betray him?" Liora asked. "Or did I sacrifice him for a greater cause?"

"Shut it, we don't need you."

"We need to tear through those guards, kick the doors open and get our man out of there," Tharek said.

"Not the best plan," Asti said. "And you know that."

"That Sholiar fellow is going to do saints-only-know to Yendick," Tharek said. "We don't have time to waste."

"That's Sholiar's place. We already fell right into his trap."

"No, we—"

"He came at us, chose a fight, and was ready to take Yendick and drag him to precisely here," Asti said. "And we saw what he had set up at the temple. Don't doubt, this place is ready for us. We need to scout it, and wait."

"Wait for what?" Kat'rick asked.

Liora gave a sly smile. "His brother."

"Your brother?" Tharek asked. "Why would we—"

"Grieson has him at the prison," Asti said. "He put me on this mission because he thought it was Crenaxin he was trying to catch, he thought my mind would be able to handle it. For this Sholiar fellow, we need my brother."

"Why?" Hoskins asked.

"Sholiar makes machines, traps, and death devices. Put one in the Parliament floor—"

"Really?" Tharek asked. "Have to respect that."

"Which Verci was able to disarm. Same with another trap—a death jacket—that Sholiar had put a young woman into. If anyone can get us in there safely, get us through Sholiar's genius, it's Verci."

Tharek, Kat'rick, and Hoskins all scowled, and looked to Almer. "You know this brother?" Tharek asked.

"I do," Almer said. "And Asti's right about him. But we may not have that kind of time."

"Why do you—oh"

Asti could feel it—they all did. Something had shifted in the sensations from Yendick. Not quite pain, but discomfort, building pressure.

"Sholiar's put him in one of his machines," Asti said.

"It's going to kill him," Kat'rick said. "We have to move."

"Wait," Asti said, having a revelation. "Scander, the other fellow. They had fresh wounds. Is it . . . is it possible?"

Tharek caught on. "This Sholiar caught them, put them in a machine, and the experience was somehow . . . revelatory?"

"A religious experience even," Asti said. "Being part of . . ."

"Sholiar's symphony," Liora finished.

"So maybe Yendick will survive this," Hoskins said.

"Survive but converted to that zealotry is very bad," Kat'rick said. "Especially with all our fates so tied to his."

"We need to go in there," Tharek said. "Pull him out, and be done with this madness."

"I agree," Asti said. "But we can't be foolish. We need to do this smart, and do it together."

"I don't need to listen to you," Tharek said. "Or that lady in your head."

"No," Asti said. "But I need you, Tharek. We're all stuck together, and we can't do this without each other."

"He's right," Kat'rick said.

Tharek growled and said, "Fine. What do you suggest?"

"Hoskins?" Asti asked. "Can you get your friends inside to scout?"

"I'll see if I can get any squirrels to listen to me," he said as he closed his eyes. "But I don't know if they will."

"Whatever you can do," Asti said. "We need to know what's going on in there, and then have a plan to strike hard and quick, pull Yendick out, and get back to Grieson."

"Grieson?" Tharek asked.

"We need to be disconnected, and Yendick will only do that for Grieson. It's our only chance to be free of each other."

"All the sooner, all the better," Tharek said. "Where are your squirrels, man?"

"On it," Hoskins said, as a pair of gray squirrels went chittering past the alley. "Let's see what we can do in there."

Asti nodded, giving a little prayer that he hoped whatever they could do, it would be enough.

CHAPTER TWENTY-SEVEN

The five of them huddling in the alley should have drawn all of the wrong kind of attention, but this part of town seemed to have no Constabulary presence. Nothing worth policing here, most likely. The heavies outside the factory door were clearly there as bait—no one was patrolling or even making an attempt to do anything beyond stand at the door and look intimidating.

Sholiar knew they were watching. He wanted them to come.

And they blazing well had to, which was the last thing Asti wanted to do.

The circumstances were terrible, so at the very least they could scout the mission, determine their assets, have a plan. Thank whatever saint was watching over them that they had still been dressed and ready for action when they woke up, and didn't have to chase after Sholiar unarmed.

Assets: Asti had several blades, and no injury that was limiting or debilitating. He was as close to fighting peak as he could hope to be. His head was as clear as he could hope, though Liora had made herself an active presence that he couldn't shut down. The beast stayed on its chain. It wasn't even fighting right now. Perhaps Almer's concoction held it at bay better than Liora.

Almer wasn't in good shape, certainly not ready to fight. No weapons, but he did have several chemicals in the pouches on his belt. A few smoke shots, one explosive boom, and a few vials of acid.

Tharek was hurt, even if he wouldn't admit it. But an injured Tharek was likely worth more than almost any other warrior. He had his sword and a few knives.

Kat'rick had her blade, which could deal some serious damage. Any plan Asti came up with would need to involve Tharek and Kat'rick as pure force, which they could definitely deliver.

Hoskins was an asset Asti couldn't fully figure out. His thing with the squirrels, Asti couldn't deny that was useful. He was counting on learning of what was going on inside from the man. But his instinct told him Hoskins wasn't reliable, something was off there. Asti couldn't put his finger on why he felt it, but he suspected the man was holding back.

Asti had climbed up to the top of the building they had been hiding behind, to get a better look at the factory. Wide open area all around it, no easy way to sneak up. And other than the front doors and window, everything else boarded up.

This was very much a trap, and they were going to have to walk in.

He came back down to the group, who were all looking impatient.

"Can you feel it?" Kat'rick asked. "Yendick is about to crack. Either his will, or just plain in half. I don't want to know what'll happen to us if he does."

"We can't wait," Tharek said.

"They're right," Liora said slyly. "You know you can't hold out for Verci to come rescue you."

"I don't think they're coming," Almer said. "Could Grieson even find us?"

"Grieson can definitely find us," Asti said. "If nothing else, believe that."

"But he might have just written us off," Tharek said. "He looked terrified when he realized it was this Sholiar fellow."

"With good reason," Asti said. "Fine, Hoskins, what do we know?"

"There's a large work floor with a lot of . . . I'm presuming torture devices. Squirrels said 'metal beasts.' But there's not a clear route to that work floor."

"How did the squirrels get there?"

"Crawlspaces and rafters, nothing we could move through. They say there's a lot of doors, and lot of walls."

"Can they lead us there once inside?"

Hoskins shrugged. "They can try."

"No time to waste, Asti," Liora said.

"Must she?" Tharek asked.

"Not my choice."

"Keep her in check," Tharek said. "We need to strike."

"Right," Asti said. "All right, we're going to move in hard and clean. I'll take center, Tharek on my left, Kat'rick on my right. You two neutralize those guards quick and hard. I get the door open, deal with any immediate threat from inside. Almer and Hoskins, you get inside the wedge the three of us make, try to avoid a direct fight if you can. Hoskins, have the squirrels then take point and lead us in to where Yendick is. We move quick and hard."

"No mercy?" Kat'rick asked.

"We can't spare mercy right now," Hoskins said.

"When we get to Yendick, cover Almer and me, and we'll try to get him free."

"Are we going to be able to do that?" Almer asked.

"I would prefer Verci be here with his toolkit, and he could dismantle whatever traps we find, but . . ."

"There's no time," Liora said.

She was right, damn it.

"We set?" Asti asked. "Any questions?"

"What are we waiting for?" Tharek asked.

Asti tapped Tharek on his chest. "All five of us walk in, six walk out. Make sure of that."

"If I must be a Tarian today and keep them safe, so be it."

"All right," Asti said. "No time to waste."

Knives out, he charged in. He could feel Kat'rick and Tharek at his sides, rushing at the heavies at the door. No mercy was exactly right—they were brutal as they carved into these fellows.

Asti hit the door. Barn door, big enough load a whole carriage in. He grabbed hold of the handle and pulled it open, the thing swinging wide. Lighter than he expected.

Glance to either side. Heavies dispatched with ease. "We ready?"

"Let's go," Tharek said.

A trio of squirrels ran ahead of Asti as he pushed inside. It was a surprisingly small room, with great steel panels surrounding them on all sides. Nowhere to go.

"So what do we—" Almer started, as the main door slammed shut behind them all.

"Wait a damned—" Tharek said, and as he did, the steel panels all spun, sweeping Tharek, Kat'rick, and Hoskins in separate directions. Almer would have been swept up by a panel if Asti hadn't grabbed him and yanked him close. Even still, Almer was clipped by the wall as they were knocked down a chute and slid into darkness.

"Asti!" Almer shouted, and just as they were about to be ejected into another room, Asti braced himself against the chute wall and held on to Almer, stopping them both.

"You all right?" Asti asked.

"Arm bleeding, something might be broken," Almer said. In the position they were in, stuck in the chute, Asti couldn't see what they would have dropped into.

"What do you see?" Asti asked.

"Something with cuffs and locks and gears," Almer said. "This chute is pretty narrow, so it's only because we're together that we were able to stop ourselves and not get caught in that."

"Can you get down without getting caught in that device?"

"Maybe if we reposition, you can lower me by my good arm."

Asti twisted around a bit, got himself to where he could manage such a thing, and lowered Almer down as far as he could.

"Let go, I think I can drop safely."

Asti did so, and then crawled out to look. Definitely some device to ensnare a man, and then take him off along a railtrack. He hopped down to the side of it.

"Let's not set this off," Asti said.

"But do we follow the track?"

"Not much choice," Asti said, drawing a knife out. Then there was a clicking sound, which startled him enough that he almost threw it toward the source.

A squirrel on the floor, chittering at him.

"I guess Hoskins' friends are still leading us."

"Right," Asti said. "Maybe he and the others are all right." He couldn't feel anything in the crystal that told him otherwise, beyond fear and anger from everyone. And that was strong, so strong that's all he could feel.

"Is your connection to the crystal getting more intense?" Almer asked. "Like too much noise to hear anything else through?"

"Now that you mention it, yes," Asti said. "Everything's too loud to make sense of it all. So ignore it."

"Easier said than done," Almer said. "But I wasn't sure if it was the crystal or my arm."

Asti got Almer's coat off of him and checked his injury. The arm was definitely broken, twisted in an unnatural way. Asti tied his coat into a sling as best he could. "That'll have to do for now."

"Only way out is through," Almer said.

Asti helped Almer as they followed the squirrel up the passage along the railtrack. "Not seeing any further tripwires. They probably assumed whoever fell in would be trapped in the device."

"Small comfort," Almer said. "How does someone build this?"

"Are you talking about what kind of sick mind it would take?"

"That's easy to understand," Almer said. "I'm talking about money, resources. Getting the space here to build it, the equipment. Smithing specific parts. Manpower."

"Verci does a lot of scrounging and creative use of found material."

"But nothing like this," Almer said. "I wonder who this Sholiar is, exactly."

"Well, if you want to spend time asking him, that's your business. Do you think we're closer to Yendick?"

"Only because the squirrel is jumping." Which it was, excitedly, as they approached what appeared to be the end of the passage. There were a set of double doors here, designed to swing out.

"I've got an idea," Asti said. "Stay with the squirrel. When the doors are open, slip out, and then try to get to Yendick."

"What will you be doing?"

"Hopefully driving a blade into Sholiar's neck, but I've learned not to hope too much."

Asti went back down to the bottom of the passage, to the trap designed to catch a man falling out of the chute, and then likely send him careening along the track and through the doors into Sholiar's waiting arms.

"Just a matter of triggering it without getting trapped," Asti muttered.

"You aren't as clever as all that," Liora said. "Verci could do it, but he isn't here. Without him what even are you?"

"Stubborn enough to get this done, that's what," Asti said, looking under the device. A modified minecart, with what looked like a pressure switch underneath that would make everything on top snap shut, and release the spring to send it flying along the track. He could never build it, or safely dismantle it, but he didn't need to do either right now. He hung unto the edge of it, swung his foot over and kicked hard where the center of his body should land, pulling his leg back as quick as he could.

His foot almost got snared as it all snapped shut, but it missed him, thank every saint.

The cart flew off, giving him no time to think further on it. He buzzed right past Almer, through the doors that swung out, sending him into a well-lit chamber.

"And finally, I was wondering—well!"

Asti leaped from the cart onto the first person he saw who wasn't trapped in a device, but it turned out not to be a person, just a life-size doll standing in the middle of the room. He had already tackled it to the ground and stabbed it before he even realized.

"You are something of a clever one, aren't you?" Sholiar's voice echoed from around him. "I'm always interested by the clever ones. They always think they're a step ahead."

A beam of light swung across the room, landing on Yendick, stuck in some elaborate torture device, pressing slow weight on him. Asti started toward him, but the beam swung again—Kat'rick, in the same situation. Then again, Tharek. Then again: Almer, held by two muscled mooks.

"Is this your game?" Asti shouted. "When I find you—"

"When you find me, yes," Sholiar said. "I'm sure you will deal such elaborate violence on me, I can see that. But you can't do that if they all don't survive."

From an unseen point in the ceiling, a group of chains dropped and dangled near Asti. In the same moment, something clicked in the devices holding Yendick, Kat'rick, and Tharek, and that slow press accelerated.

"Better grab those chains to save them, friend."

Asti swore and leaped at the chains, grabbing all four and pulling them down. Some of the weight released, but he could feel that he was the only thing keeping it from dropping.

Then a trap clamped over his foot.

"I am always a step ahead," Sholiar said, stepping out of the shadows. "Now I have you just as trapped."

"I can get this clamp off," Asti said.

"I'm sure, but your hands are pretty full right now. You're very busy keeping your associates alive." He came up and ran a finger over the crystal in Asti's chest. "And you are definitely invested in that. Very intriguing, this. I can't wait to learn all about it."

Asti tried to grab him, but even letting go of the chains with one hand for a second caused them to slip. He clutched them harder as Yendick screamed out. From the corner of his eye, he saw Almer being shoved into the minecart trap, he was in no condition to resist.

"Yes, you are rather stuck, indeed. Now, I have much work to do."

"I will make sure you—"

"Yes, yes," Sholiar said. "But for now, you're their only hope. You're your only hope."

Liora appeared in front of Asti. "You're familiar with this game, Asti. This is what you do every day to keep your friends and loved ones safe."

"All you have to do," Sholiar said, an absurd grin spreading across his face, "Is not let go of that chain."

Asti held on to all the chains, the ones keeping the others from getting killed, the ones in his head.

Tharek, Kat'rick, Almer, Yendick, each of them were in pain. Each of them were afraid, in their own way, and he could feel all of that. Plus his own pain, his own fear.

"That's it," Sholiar said, looking at Asti. "Yes, I see you're starting to understand. You've been down this road before, haven't you? You've faced fear like this before. You've felt pain like this before. The others, they're tough, they've been through trouble, but you . . . oh, you, yes. You really know."

"When I get my hands on you—"

"Yes, those hands are very busy, though," Sholiar said. "Holding that chain is hard, it's taking quite a bit of your strength, but you . . . you'll bear it. You'll hold it. For hours, I see that in your eyes already."

Sholiar stood face to face with Asti. So close Asti could choke the life out of him if he could just let go, just for a moment.

"You know, I was excited to get your friend there. He's the source of the power, and I wanted to know more about that, understand what he does. Because you're feeling him, and he you. And that bond between you, you had to follow. Amazing. That kind of power. That's what I want to understand."

"Understand what?" Asti asked through grit teeth.

"What is pain, exactly? What is fear, what is terror? Can I pour it out and measure it? Can I know, empirically, objectively, how much pain you each are in, how much fear? And if I can pour it out and measure it, then there are so many questions that follow." He reached into his pocket and pulled out a glass bottle with a spritzer on the top. "Can I extract that fear, that pain, capture its essence, like one can pull out the base notes of a scent from a flower. Where do I cut you, sir, to drain you of your fear? What oils draw the terror out of your body? How do I make a perfume from your soul?"

He spritzed into Asti's face. Asti sputtered and swore as Sholiar laughed and walked away.

"Now, you," he said to Yendick. "You've got something truly special in you. Beyond magic, beyond science, and I think it might be just what I want. You can capture their fear, their pain, and send it to the others. Fascinating. And it's clearly something with these crystals." He tapped the one in Yendick's chest. "It's very exciting!"

"You . . . you . . ." was all Asti could say. He still couldn't quite breathe, the perfume still sticky-sweet on his face.

"Yes, I know," Sholiar said. "Since you can feel everything from each other, it's time to really see what that means. And have each of you truly face your terror, your pain."

"I'll show you terror and pain!" Tharek said.

"Look at you," Sholiar said. "So many scars on you, so many more inside. I'm really going to enjoy this experiment."

"What do you want?" Yendick asked, his voice hoarse.

"I was told to conduct a symphony of fear and pain," Sholiar said. He laughed and stepped into the center of them. "And I can hardly conduct a symphony without musicians! And each of you, each of you, must learn how to truly be masters of your instruments."

He walked over to Asti.

"Yes, but I think you do know how to play yours. Which is good, because I am in need of a virtuoso for this particular score we're about to play."

"You forgot . . ." Asti said.

"I what?" Sholiar asked.

"You forgot . . . there was one more of us."

"Oh no, is someone else still here? Be assured, whatever other friends you have, they are also rats in my traps."

"Not rats," Asti said.

He could hear the chittering all around.

Dozens and dozens of squirrels swarmed into the chamber from every direction.

"Oh, this is new!" Sholiar exclaimed.

The squirrels poured in, all of them going right for Yendick. They clawed and bit and chewed, scratching at the machine parts binding him. A couple got caught in a gear, and there was a terrible burst of blood and a squeal. But there were so many squirrels, it didn't slow them down. They just kept coming.

"Now you're going to get it," Asti said, tensing his shoulders so he could leap on Sholiar as soon as he was free.

"So it might seem," Sholiar said. "Well, this truly would be a frightening moment for me, wouldn't it? Wish I could feel it."

The squirrels pulled Yendick out of his device, and he almost collapsed to the ground, but they caught him. Dozens of them lifted him up on their backs and scurried away, taking Yendick with them.

"Good work, Hoskins!" Asti shouted. "Now get him!"

The squirrels all ran out, following with Yendick.

"Hoskins!" Asti shouted. "Get us out of here!"

The squirrels all retreated from the chamber. All gone, so was Yendick.

"Hoskins!" Asti screamed.

"Is this where I'm going to get it?" Sholiar asked in a faux whisper. "Or do I need to keep waiting?"

ASTI COULD FEEL EVERY TIME HIS GRIP ON THE CHAINS SLIPPED EVEN AN inch—a blade pressed ever so slightly deeper into Kat'rick's flesh, the weight on Almer's chest pushed a little harder, Tharek's limbs were stretched a little further. Asti felt every bit of that, as well as his shoulders being wrenched, his hands tearing raw.

But he couldn't let go. He wouldn't let go.

"Now," Sholiar said, strolling up to Asti. "You are doing a remarkable job, so far. The determination on your face is quite something."

"He doesn't even know how ready you are to hold on, does he, Asti?" Liora said.

"While I wish I still had that bearded fellow to play with, I did learn enough about this," Sholiar said, tapping on the crystal in Asti's chest. Asti wanted to grab his hand, to break his fingers, but he couldn't risk letting go, even for a moment. He tried to bend his head and bite Sholiar's hand, but Sholiar was quick enough to pull away.

"Oh, interesting. You're still present enough, intent enough to do that. That'll change." He chuckled and walked around Asti. "Now, like I said, I've learned enough about this crystal do know how the four of you are bound to each other. Joined in pain, joined in death.

Which is incredible, let me tell you. What I could do with that power."

"What I could do . . ." Asti muttered.

"Yes, I know, you're very dangerous," Sholiar said. "But stay with me here, sir, while I ruminate. You each feel each other's pain, and the crystal is a conduit that captures that. What else can I capture with that crystal, if I crack into its secrets? Into yours? Your joy? Your sorrow? Your very soul? What can I pour into a crystal and make my own possession?"

"Do something," the beast urged. It was now in the corner of the room. Not a room, a cell.

"He's right," Liora said. "Right now, everyone is going to die, sooner or later. You'll give in and drop that chain. But if you do it when your body breaks, you'll be too weak to do anything about this."

"Set me free!" the beast shouted. It was being held by a chain, the chain Asti held.

The chain was getting hotter.

Sweat dripped into Asti's eyes—he couldn't quite see clearly anymore. Where was he? Where did Tharek and Kat'rick go? He could feel them—their pain, their anger, their fear—but he couldn't see them or hear them anymore. He wasn't on the factory floor anymore, but in a cell.

That cell.

"You've brought yourself back to Levtha," Liora said. "Back to where you and he first met?"

"No," Asti said. "Almer, are you there? Where are you?"

"I don't think he can hear you," Liora said. "Maybe he's already dead."

"No, I would know, I would feel it."

"Asti," she said. "You can't save him. You can't save any of them. You can't even save yourself. But maybe you can just drop the chain . . . and you'd be free."

"Just be free!" the beast shouted.

"Imagine," she said. "Not having to worry about anything anymore. Not about Tharek or Almer or the others. Not about the Andrendon, or the fire. Not about all those people who want so much from you back in

North Seleth. Not simpering Kimber and her cow eyes mooning over you. Not Verci, Raych, and the baby, who would all be better off without you."

"No," Asti said.

"Right, you can't let it go," Liora said. "You can't let anything go? Asti Rynax has to be so responsible for everyone."

"No," Asti said again.

"There you go. Now we're getting into something interesting." Sholiar's voice, somewhere in the distance. Asti couldn't see anything but the cell, the beast, and Liora. "Soon you'll be part of the symphony."

"No!" Asti said. "I won't let go!" He could still feel the chain in his hand, hot and hard. Still solid his hands. That was real. The rest of this was his broken mind, trying to trick him. Sholiar trying to trick him. Liora trying to trick him.

"You will," she whispered. "Sooner or later, you will be broken."

"Sooner or later," Sholiar's voice said. "You'll be mine."

"Sooner or later," Liora said. "You'll let go."

"No," Asti whispered. He'd hold that chain. No matter how much it hurt. No matter what it would take. He wouldn't let go.

PART V
THE RYNAX FAMILY

CHAPTER TWENTY-EIGHT

Verci was well aware of the amount of spectacle he was making by taking Grieson's horses and pounding them at full gallop from his safehouse in Carrol Creek to the Gadgeterium, Grieson riding hot on his heels the whole way. He didn't care what Grieson thought, or any of the people who saw the commotion they were making. He did feel bad for the horses, though.

Grieson had told Verci everything as they went through the secret passage from Ward Twelve to the safehouse—more of Maradaine's infamous tunnels—and it had taken every ounce of self-control Verci had to not slit the man's throat then and there.

Everything they had gone through: the arrest, the time in the prison, Verci and Julien in the box, Kennith's attacks, Pilsen . . . damn it, Pilsen. All that had been Grieson and his stupid scheme to manipulate Asti.

And now Asti was dealing with that maniac who had built those horrifying machines in the Parliament, made that evil murder jacket that Verci had barely been able to disarm.

"We don't have any time for this!" Grieson urged Verci as they arrived at the Gadgeterium. "Sholiar could have already . . ."

"And if so, you're going to pay for it," Verci said as he went inside. "But if you expect me to be able to deal with this madman, deal with whatever sadistic inventions he's got, I'm not going to have a chance unless I have my gear. You should have thought of that from the beginning."

Grieson stood in the apartment door. "We didn't know it was Sholiar from the beginning."

"Even stupider of you," Verci said. "Raych! Raych!" There was no sign she was here. Verci glanced at the dishes by the washtap. Dirty and crusted. She hadn't been here for at least a day.

Things on the table: dirty wineglasses and teacups, but also street plans, a building blueprint. Some of his inventions laid out on the floor.

"The blazes was happening here? Where is Raych?"

"We . . . I'm not sure," Grieson said. "She was being watched—her and Kesser and the Ch'omik woman—but they managed to ditch their shadows two days ago. They're doing something for Missus Holt, but we—"

"They're what?" Verci couldn't believe it. "When I have time for this reckoning, you will receive it. But first Asti."

Verci tore off his prison guard uniform and grabbed his own clothes, the ones he'd wear for a gig. Not that he had time to really prepare. Had to be quick and simple. Bandolier of darts. Asti's knife belt. Simple tool-kit, a few more specific tools from his larger box, put them in his vest pockets and—where was it?

"What do you need?"

"I've don't see the chaincracker here. Everything's in chaos."

"Maybe Raych is using it."

"Shut it." He could take his gauntlet, but he'd have to prepare the shots, and he didn't have time to load the chemicals safely. Plus his collection of Almer's chemicals looked like it had been ransacked. Two putty balls and one acid ball were all that was left. Verci pocketed those. Also one of the grapplers, springs already wound, had been carelessly left on the floor. He checked the safety latch, put it in his knapsack with a rope and few springsnaps—little more than fancy mousetraps. Little else was left.

Hopefully, whatever reason Raych had to take all his equipment, it was serving her well. Any help he could give her.

"We need to go—" Grieson grabbed Verci's shoulder.

Verci took the man's wrist and twisted it behind his back, snapping his thumb in the motion. Grieson cried out in agony.

"Let me make one thing very clear, Grieson. You are not touching me or anyone in my family ever again. You test me, you will find I am capable of just as much brutality as my brother. We were raised together."

"All right," Grieson whimpered.

"And if you doubt, look back at the prison right now. Look at what I did when I decided to be Indlen Tacklin."

"You've made your point," Grieson said. "I need you, so does Asti."

Verci pushed him away and looked down at the notes on the table. The Druth History Museum? And notes about a gala . . .

"Is today the twenty-third of Alasim?"

"Yes."

"Blazes, that means this—" he gestured at Raych's notes. "It's happening right now. Damn it."

"We have to go."

"Fine," Verci said. *Raych, whatever madness you've fallen into be safe, be smart.* He grabbed a stylus and wrote a quick note on the table.

My love—

I'm free, but Asti needs to be saved. See you very soon.

All my heart

—Verci

That would have to do.

"Let's go," Verci said, brushing past Grieson. "And you better pray Asti is still alive."

Let alone what Raych was doing, and whoever she was doing it with.

"And that Asti is still alive?"

"I think so. I'm not tuned into them quite the same way as they're all tuned to each other, but I can sense them," Grieson said. Verci didn't understand a damned thing about this business with magic and crystals, and he didn't want to listen to Grieson any more than necessary.

Not to mention he barely trusted Grieson to be telling him a whit of truth about all this. This could all be some elaborate trap.

But no, if anything, Grieson seemed legitimately terrified in all this.

"So how can you be sure?"

"The sensation is getting stronger here," Grieson said as they rode into an open square—though one that looked neglected and abandoned. Not entirely abandoned, Verci realized—there were several bloody bodies outside the main doors of one factory.

"That looks like Asti's been here," Verci said, getting off the horse.

"Any of these bastards, honestly."

"Hey," Verci said, grabbing Grieson by the front of his shirt as he was dismounting. "These people are the ones you used as weapons."

"They were all I had left," Grieson said.

"You had enough to take us in, to change records so that we were dead . . ."

"Imbedded systems, orders done blindly with code words and dead drops. Not real power . . ."

"You will fix that, or so help me . . ."

"It's done, I swear," Grieson said. "Everything is undone with a simple signal, which is already handled."

So, if nothing else, Kennith, Vellun, and Julien were fine. No risk of getting arrested again. Now it was just a matter of saving Asti and Almer from this madman.

"Can you sense them in there? Still alive?"

"Yes," Grieson said.

"Then let's get in there." Verci said. He drew out a knife and approached the door. Several bodies, hacked in many ways. Brutally and efficiently.

Wait, no. Two men on the ground were still breathing.

"Yendick," Grieson said, kneeling next to one of them. "What happened?"

The man briefly opened his eyes, but he didn't seem to be able to focus them anywhere. "What did . . . who?"

"It's Grieson. Where are they others?"

"Others?" Yendick's hand weakly went up to his head. "I can't . . . I'm not . . ."

"He's your crystal man?" Verci asked. "And who's this one?"

"That's Hoskins, the squirrel mage."

"Saints, why do I even . . ." Verci squatted down next to Hoskins, who seemed out cold, and slapped him. "Hoskins. Wake up."

"Wha—?" Hoskins looked around. "Have to get out!"

"You are out," Verci said. "Where's Asti? And the others?"

"I . . . still in there. It took . . . it took all I had . . . to get Yendick out. Had to get him. We need to go."

"They're exhausted," Grieson said.

"Sounds like that's the only reason they didn't run away," Verci said. "Sounds like they were ready to abandon the rest in there."

"It'd be a mercy," Yendick said. "Let them die quickly instead of what . . . what's happening to them."

"Asti and the others are in there? Where? Let's move."

"They can't even stand," Grieson said.

"Fine, stay with them. I'll move faster on my own."

"Verci, wait," Grieson said. "If you . . . if you *can*, take Sholiar alive."

"Why would I do a thing like that?"

"Listen," Grieson said, moving to grab Verci by the front of his shirt, but stopping short before he touched him. The makeshift splint on his thumb surely served as a reminder. "There are forces in play in this city, and the Brotherhood was . . . *is* a part of that. I need evidence, intelligence, to stop it before it goes too far."

"And Asti is a part of that?"

"Asti has secrets in his mind that he doesn't even know about. All of it is connected back to the same source of rot, the rot that put me on the run, the rot that broke him. I've been cut off everywhere, and the only thing I have left, the only chance I have is that man. I understand, you do what you have to do to save your brother, that's the most important thing—"

"It is," Verci said.

"No, *the most important thing*. If the Brotherhood, if Altarn start what I think they have planned, what's in Asti's head might be our only defense."

"And you need Sholiar to stop it before it comes to that." Verci swore, but nodded. "That man is too dangerous, I can't swear I can take him alive. But I won't make a point of killing him just for the sake of it."

"Fine," Grieson said.

"Now," Verci said, walking up to the door. "Time to crack your secrets."

"Wait," Hoskins whispered hoarsely. Verci looked back at him; he now had a squirrel perched on his chest, feeding him nuts. "This is Kolo. He's going to show you a way into the chamber Asti and the others are in. You'll be able to avoid most of the traps, I think."

The squirrel hopped off of him and ran up Verci's leg, perching on his shoulder.

"All right," Verci said. "Then let's go see what we can do."

I'm coming, brother. Just hold on.

Moving through the crawlspaces behind the walls of Sholiar's trap-filled maze was slow going, but Verci had to admit, since he was taking this route, the best way to do it was with a squirrel to guide him. This little fellow was clever, and pointed out several dangers that Verci might not have spotted in time.

Blazes, Verci might not have even spotted the access panel that led him behind the walls like this, and instead gone through the heavily trapped route that Sholiar would have wanted visitors to take.

Plus taking this route let Verci see the machinery of the traps, insight into how Sholiar's mind worked. One pattern he started to see: Sholiar loved designed excess. His builds worked with multiple redundancies. A trap never had a single trigger, but four or five, each one different. The way the trap engaged would activate several different parts of machinery, create multiple actions at once. And there was something chaotic, convoluted to the designs, making it challenging to see how it all worked.

The results were traps and machines that probably did too much—in many cases not merely killing the victims but leaving them completely mutilated—but also ones that were exceedingly difficult to disarm.

But seeing them from the inside, Verci realized that disarming would be hard, but outright sabotage, less so. Too complicated, Verci had long since learned, often also meant too delicate.

That said, Verci had to appreciate the craftsmanship on display. So many of the parts were made with fine detail, absolutely intricate work. Verci had to envy the resources Sholiar must have had to make all this.

At points in the journey, Verci knew he was right outside the chamber where Sholiar had Asti and the others captured. Where they were being tortured. He could hear their cries of anguish, including at one point where it was definitely Almer.

And he could hear someone, who he assumed was Sholiar, raving about pain and fear and capturing the soul.

Saints, what a pretentious ponce he was.

The squirrel led Verci up a ladder to another access panel, and that opened into a small room—a room with a glass window overlooking the chamber with Asti and the others.

He could see them all—three people in devices designed to mangle their bodies, and Asti's feet clamped to the floor, holding on to chains that went up to the ceiling. Verci followed the chains to series of pulleys and counterweights and quickly realized what was happening: Asti's was pulling on the chains to prevent further injury of the other three. If he let go, they would be maimed, if not killed. Plus what looked like a forge or oven of some sort, heating up the chain Asti was holding.

And Sholiar was walking around Asti, taunting him.

Verci looked around the rest of the room—several panels with levers, handles, pullcords, all manner of controls. Sholiar probably designed it so that he could control every element of his torture chamber from here.

There was no way to determine which control did what, not without just experimenting or opening up the panel, no time to do that. Not to mention doing that could kill Asti and the others.

But two things jumped out to him.

First, there was a valve that connected to a pipe that led up the wall, to a network of pipes Verci could see along the ceiling of the chamber—pipes that had oil lamps connected to them. And then a lever that was connected to a similar system. Lamp shutters? Close the valve, pull the lever, and it goes dark in there.

Second, an earhorn on an echo pipe. At least, that seemed the obvious use. It was shuttered as well, but it was obviously connected to the copper pipes that went around the chamber. Open the shutter, whisper into the horn, and your voice went out to a pipe somewhere in the chamber.

A dial on the box. Move the voice.

That was something he could use.

He looked back up to the gearworks on the ceiling. If he got up there, he could dismantle the counterweights—nothing for Asti to hold up, nothing to further torture the others. And there was a trapdoor in the ceiling of this room, a ladder leading up to them. Getting up there would be easy, but Sholiar would spot him. And he surely had weapons on him, and Verci would be a simple target to hit in the rafters. Unless Sholiar was distracted.

Pieces clicked together, as Verci got to work with the tools and devices he had on him. A bit of spiderwire across the doorway. A few springsnaps in the right places, careful placement of darts and one of the putty balls. It would have to do.

"The question is, sir," Sholiar was saying on the floor, "not how long you're able to endure this, but what will you become when you no longer are able to? When that moment comes, I can't wait to meet who you'll be."

Here was the moment. Verci opened the earhorn shutter and then pulled the lever for the lamps. Darkness fell over the whole chamber.

"Oh, look at that," Verci said in the earhorn, his voice then echoing all over the chamber. "Isn't that a clever design. You really do have some cute ideas."

"What the blazes?" Sholiar called out. "Who dares?"

"Who dares?" Verci whispered back. "You really talk like that?"

"Oh, someone thinks they're clever," Sholiar said.

"Not that clever," Verci said. "It didn't take much to slip past your terrible traps and get into here."

"Terrible?" Sholiar asked. Verci could hear him moving, heading up to this booth. Perfect. Mouse taking the bait.

"I mean, to the untrained eye, I'm sure they're impressive, son," Verci said. "But honestly, overdone. You mistake complexity for quality. You really overthink these things."

"You have some notes for me? Maybe I'll crack your head open and read them."

"You really made so many mistakes. But one in particular."

"Illuminate me." Right outside the booth. Time to move. Verci went up the ladder, through the trapdoor to the ceiling grid. It was completely dark, of course. Verci had to go by touch and memory. But those nights where Pop had him practice while wearing a blindfold would pay off. He could find his way up to rafters, crawl out to those gearworks, and disconnect the weights with his eyes closed. He'd have to.

Verci heard the door to the booth open, a snap of spiderwire, the clack of springsnaps.

"Really?" Sholiar shouted. "You think a couple dart traps and spider-wire would trick me? Amateur."

Perfect, Verci thought as he made his was across the rafter. There was one bit of light up here, the glow of that furnace heating Asti's chain. Point of reference. Help him find his way to the gearworks. He was almost there. And Sholiar was mad, and proud, and hopefully just cocky enough to underestimate him.

Verci pulled the grappler and clamped it to the rafter, turning back to the booth. *Please, Saint Senea, let him fall for it.*

"Now you're going to see."

"You're going to see," Verci shouted. "You made one very big mistake with your traps, Sholiar,"

The lamp shutters lifted.

And another springsnap went off.

Sholiar screamed.

The springsnap on the lamp shutter control, with the acid ball wedged into it. Sholiar was holding up his smoking, bloody hand, the flesh searing.

"You put my brother in them."

He aimed the grappler at Sholiar, and released the spring. Its hook launched out and grabbed Sholiar's chest, and Verci cranked the cord back in, pulling Sholiar out of the booth and dangling him from the rafter. Verci pulled out the putty balls and threw them at him. In moments, Sholiar was covered in the sticky mess, unable to move as he dangled on the wire.

Sholiar looked up at him, and smiled. Weakly, he rasped, "I won't make that mistake again, then."

Verci didn't pay attention, he got to work. First he closed the vents on the furnace, and pulled a lever taking the chain out of them. Disconnected the weights, and they dropped to the ground. No more pressure on the folks in their traps, but Asti was still holding on to the chains, like they were still keeping the others alive.

Verci made his way to the ground. Two muscle-bound mooks came at him, and Verci wasted no time putting darts in their necks before they could close the distance.

He looked back to Asti, still not letting go. Maybe there was still something else connecting him and the others, and he knew he couldn't let go yet. Sholiar and his redundancies. So get the others free.

"Almer," Verci said, running up to him. "Let's get you out of this."

"Verci," Almer said weakly. "I thought that was you."

"I wasn't going to leave you all behind," he said. "Already got the others out of the prison."

"That's good."

This trap was designed to let the person in it be released. Like Sholiar wanted folks to be able to get out when he was done. A few latches and levers, and Almer was out.

"The others," Almer said. "Get them."

"You all right?"

"Arm's no good," Almer said, holding it up to show a nasty break. "Go."

The Ch'omik woman and the big guy were both dazed, like they had passed out from the pain, and were only coming to just now.

"Easy, easy," Verci said as he let the woman out.

"Who are you?" she asked.

"The guy getting you out."

She looked up at Sholiar, stuck like a bug in the putty. "Is that him?"

"That's him."

"Can I kill him?"

"Grieson would prefer he wasn't killed, apparently."

"Bastard."

The big guy just fell out of his device and slumped to the ground.

"You all right?" Verci asked.

"I've failed," he said. "It will not happen again."

The squirrel scampered over to Verci.

"Yes, I see you," Verci said. "Get Grieson, hmm? So he can help get these folks out."

The squirrel went off. Verci had to focus on Asti.

"I'm here, brother," Verci said. He unclamped the latches on Asti's feet. "You're out now, and they're safe. You can let go."

But Asti's eyes were focused on the chains, his expression didn't change.

"Asti!" Verci said. "You're free, let go."

"He's not listening to you," Almer said. "She's got all his attention."

"She?" Verci asked.

"Liora," Almer said. "But he's so deep in his head, I can't even hear him anymore, just her."

"Can't let go," Asti whispered. He held still, nearly like a statue.

Verci tried shaking him. "Asti! Listen to me!"

"Can't let go."

"Asti!"

"ASTI, YOU CAN LET GO. IT'S FINE, JUST LET GO."

Asti heard the voice, Verci's voice, but he knew it was a trick. He couldn't trust any of it. Here in this cell again, nothing was real, nothing but the chain.

And Liora and the beast. They were real.

But Verci couldn't be there, he couldn't be. And he couldn't let go of the chain.

"Like Verci would be here to save you. Like he could." Liora was right in Asti's face. "He knows you're a failure. He knows he's safer without you. His wife and child are safer without you."

Asti had no response to that. She was right.

"You put him in danger. He was stuck in that prison because of you, and your stupid plan, your stupid revenge. And against who? Me? The people who burned your house?"

"They . . . they . . ." Asti could barely find breath, let alone words.

"They're building something, something to help the whole city. And what have you done?"

"I've . . . I've tried . . ."

"You've done nothing but ruin everything you touch. A broken man, a killer."

"I killed with you, I killed for you."

"And you will again," Liora said. "All I need is you to let it take over. And then you'll really serve as you were meant to. You'll be the weapon you were supposed to be."

"No."

"Come on, Asti," Verci's voice echoed in the distance. "By every saint, it's done, just let go. We walk right out."

"There's no way I walk out," Asti said. "I'm not getting out this time."

"You never got out," Liora said, gesturing around the cell they were in, the cell in Levtha where the Poasians tore his mind to pieces. "This is where Asti Rynax died. What escaped, that was just a broken shard. A shattered waste, not even worthy of being called a man."

"I am . . ." Asti tried to say, but the words were too hard. He couldn't even make himself believe them, couldn't get his mouth to say them. Maybe they weren't true at all. Maybe Liora was right.

"You know I am. Because I live in this broken head of yours, and nothing, nothing you can do will get rid of me. I am the truth you need to admit, Asti. I am the part of you that you hate, and you hate yourself. There's no absolution, no amount of penance, that will clean the blood on your hands, the sin on your soul."

"I . . . I saved . . ."

"Burn for your sins, Asti," Liora said. "And when the fire consumes you, all that will be left is me, and that." She pointed to the beast. "And then you will be what the Brotherhood meant you to be. Then you will—"

Liora was interrupted by a crack of metal and flesh, and she dropped to the floor of the cell. Standing, bright and luminous where she had been, was a young woman in old armor, painted blue. Her cloistress cowl barely contained the wild blond hair underneath. And in her hand, she held the mighty mace that she had felled Liora with.

"Kindly be quiet, you vicious miscreant," she hissed.

"I . . . I . . ." Asti said, barely able to speak. "I know you."

The blond holy woman smiled. "Of course you do." She came up to him and gently placed a hand on his face, touching him like a cool breeze. "Oh, Asti, you know she's a liar, right?"

"No, no, she's telling the truth."

"No," she said. "We've not yet gotten to the point where you trust me, or believe me, and . . . when you really see me again, when we truly meet, we won't understand each other, but . . . I need you to have faith in me right now."

"My faith . . . my faith is as shattered as the rest of me."

"I know it is, dear friend. I know it is. But listen to me, she was lying to you, Asti."

"No, she wasn't," Asti said.

Liora moaned and started to rise. "Who the blazes are you, kitten? This head is my place to play."

Sister Myriem—Asti realized who she was—knocked Liora back with another blow of her mace.

"No more," she bellowed, a voice that shook Asti to the center of his being, "I abjure you, in the name of Saint Alexis." She knocked Liora back again. "I abjure you in the name of Saint Bridget." Another blow sent Liora into the wall. "With every bit of power God has granted me, I abjure you."

Then she grabbed a piece of the wall, which became a great iron door, and slammed it closed over Liora.

And there was silence.

"Asti," Sister Myriem said, limping back to him. "I don't have a lot of strength left."

"Neither do I," Asti said.

"I know you don't, that's why you need to let go now."

"I can't let go of the chain," Asti said. "I can't let it loose. Like Liora, I can't . . ."

"Liora is gone," Sister Myriem said. She pointed to the iron door. "There is nothing behind that door you need, do you understand?"

Asti looked to the beast, still on its chain. "But it's still here. If I let it loose, if I let go."

Myriem struggled to walk to the beast, and took its hand. "He's nothing to be afraid of. All he is, is a piece of you. You think he's a danger, but, he's just like you." She guided the beast closer to Asti.

"He'll . . . he'll kill you."

"No," she said. "He and I, like you and I, we're old friends. You have your own journey still, but it starts here, with you accepting the truth about him, and the truth about yourself."

"What truth is that?" Asti asked.

One hand holding the beast's, she cupped Asti's face with the other, and the warmth that came from her, the love, the faith, was more intense than anything Asti had ever felt.

"That you, Asti Rynax, are a worthy soul."

She kissed him on the forehead, and Asti's fear, his pain, it all faded away as she whispered, "Now let go, and take his hand."

Asti let go of the chain and reached out, and a hand grabbed his, and then both hands.

Asti looked up, and the cell was gone, the beast was gone—back in Sholiar's lair.

And clutching both his hands was Verci.

"Are you with me, brother?" Verci asked.

"Here," Asti rasped. "You came."

"Of course I came," Verci said. "When it's you, I'll always come."

Asti grabbed his brother in a tight embrace.

"Are we all right?"

"I have Sholiar wrapped up like a Terrentin gift for Grieson, Almer and the others are out of their traps. We can walk right out."

Asti pulled back and looked at Verci's face, seeing how tired his eyes were, how much anger and pain they held. "Everyone else?"

"Ken, Julie, and Vellun are out, they're safe. Pilsen . . . we need to raise several glasses for Pilsen."

"No . . ." The last bits of strength that kept Asti standing failed him, his knees turning to water.

"He saved us, he did," Verci said. "A great last performance."

"I've definitely been saved," Asti said. The memory of the vision in the cell—the nightmare—was hazy and fading. But Liora was completely silent now. Gone from his mind. And the beast, not gone, but . . . content.

"Can you walk?" Verci asked.

"If you help me," Asti said.

"Every time."

CHAPTER TWENTY-NINE

A wagon had arrived quietly, and the immobilized body of Sholiar was loaded into it. Asti sat on the curb of the walkway as the pair of Intelligence cleaners dealt with that and the dead bodies with simple efficiency.

"I thought you had no power," he said to Grieson.

"I have no personal power," Grieson said. "I have drop codes for putting in directives to embedded and isolated operatives. You know how it goes, orders come and you don't know who made them. I had access to just enough systems that aren't corrupted, *can't* be corrupted, because there are blinds in place to prevent that."

"And that's how you cleared our names again?" Verci stressed, looming over Grieson. "That's done?"

"It's done, orders in. By now, on paper, everything connecting you to the Tacklins is gone, the documents claiming you were dead are corrected. It's like it never happened."

"One of our friends is dead," Asti said. "It happened, and I will—"

"Easy, Asti," Verci said. "You're in no shape to kill him right now."

"So we're going back to Quarrygate?" Tharek asked as Yendick disconnected Almer from the crystal. "You let them go, but I have to return? This is injustice."

"I wasn't supposed to be in prison in the first place," Asti told him.

"The whole Tacklin thing was a cock-up. Like I told you."

"And Grieson knows if he doesn't let Almer and Asti go, I'll kill him," Verci said. He gestured to Kat'rick, Tharek, and Hoskins. "Though I might be inclined to insist the same for these three. Especially the squirrel guy."

Grieson moved in closer to Verci and Asti and whispered. "I cannot let them go. Tharek still has a very public trial pending. Kat'rick is earmarked for other missions like this, and Hoskins . . ." He glanced over at the man, sitting weakly on the wagon with a squirrel on his knee. "He's an actual monster. He massacred an entire village to make it a haven for himself and the squirrels."

"Really?" Asti said. "He seems harmless."

"An entire village," Grieson stressed.

Asti shrugged. "I guess they should go back." He pulled himself to his feet and came up to Tharek. "Listen, I . . . this all has been a mess, but . . ."

"Silence, Rynax," Tharek said. "We had a moment of connection, do not think it was more than that. We both needed a sliver of joy, and we took it."

"Right," Asti said. "I wasn't going to make a romantic declaration or anything."

"I have already had my heart torn out in front of me," Tharek said. "I wouldn't have had anything to give you in return."

"All right," Asti said. "Good luck with the trial."

"Luck will not serve me," Tharek said. "May you find some peace in what's to come for you, and I will strive for the same."

Yendick sighed, and made a gesture, and Tharek, Hoskins, and Kat'rick all dropped out cold. "I don't need all these goodbyes from you all. Let's get them back, Grieson."

"Get Asti out," Grieson said.

Yendick walked over to Asti and put his hand over the crystal. "If you don't mind, I'm going to fade the tether instead of break it."

"What does that mean?" Verci asked.

"It means it will take about a half a bell for the connection to truly end, but it will go slowly. He won't be bound to us by proximity, though."

Asti understood. "It's so he and Grieson can get away without me killing them."

"I could kill them," Almer said.

"Don't push yourself," Verci said. "It's fine, we don't want to kill them today."

"We don't?" Asti asked him.

"Not quite."

Asti felt a warmth pull out of his body through the crystal into Yendick's hand, and then Yendick walked away.

"That it?"

"The crystal will crumble to dust as it fades," Yendick said, getting in the wagon. Grieson gave the Intelligence officers a signal, and they drove off.

"You're not going yet?" Asti asked. "You want to wait until it fades?"

"No," Verci said. "He's going to answer some questions. Like why he said you're the most important person in the city."

"Me?" Asti asked.

"There's too much going on to explain here in the middle of the square," Grieson said. "Let's start walking you home."

"We walk, you talk," Asti said. Grieson nodded, and they made their way toward North Seleth.

"Everything I told you before is the truth. Intelligence is almost completely corrupted, and Colonel Altarn is at the center of it."

"That name is familiar," Asti said.

"She was in charge of magic projects a few years back, but she's gathered power, and is now at the colonel's table, and has the chief in her palm. She's got her fingers everywhere. And I'm certain she's tied to the Brotherhood, and she's who was controlling Liora during that Henterman affair."

"Do you know where Liora is now?"

"I think she's out of Maradaine, but I can't be certain. I have so few resources, but what I do know is the Brotherhood is not gone. You might have cut out some of the roots a few months ago, but there's still tendrils everywhere in the city, and I fear they are looking for the very things I've been trying to keep hidden."

"Such as?"

"It's better if you just try to keep it safe without knowing what it is."

"Even assuming I'm inclined, how am I supposed to keep it safe?" Asti asked.

"Where is it?" Verci asked.

"A couple places, but most notably," Grieson said, stopping at the mouth of an alley to look at Asti. "It's inside your skull."

"What they did to me at Levtha?" Asti asked.

"What we did together before that," Grieson said. "Levtha was about getting that from you. You don't remember, but—"

Whatever words were to follow, Grieson didn't get to say them. His throat burst open with blood, and he dropped to his knees, clutching at his neck. Asti dropped down, tried to hold on to him, stop the bleeding.

"What happened?" Verci asked, looking around with knives drawn. "I don't see anyone."

Grieson's hands dropped away, limp, and Asti saw what killed him.

"You won't see anyone," Asti said. "It's a Lyranan throwing dart."

"Lyranan?" Verci asked. "Why?"

Asti looked up to the rooftop across the street, then to the darkness of the alley below. Not that it mattered. Pra Yikenj could be anywhere. And as inconvenient as this was, he couldn't blame her. He only hoped her desire for revenge ended with Grieson.

"I'll explain, but we need to get off the street. Let's get home."

RAYCH RAN HOME LIKE DEMONS AND SINNERS WERE AT HER HEELS. SHE had no sense of the spectacle she was making, clearly anyone who saw her must have thought she had lost her mind, but she didn't care. didn't feel anything in her legs or lungs or heart, she didn't feel anything in her body at all, she just ran.

Verci had gotten the others out, and he went back for Asti. He must have succeeded. He had to be home already, waiting for her. She had to believe that or she would fall apart.

She nearly crashed through the back door of the Gadgeterium, pounding up the stairs into the apartments.

"Verci! Verci!" she called out as she burst into their apartment. Everything was still a mess from the last time she had been here two days ago. She had been so focused on pulling this job, it had been the only way to get Verci back, and . . .

There was a note on the table. She grabbed it.

My love—

I'm free, but Asti needs to be saved. See you very soon.

All my heart

—Verci

Finally the exertion of running caught up with her, her heart slamming in her chest, her breath short, and all the tears of the last week finally pouring out of her. She dropped to her knees, her lungs burning, her face wet, as she made the dry heaving sound of sobs that had no breath to support them.

Then hands touched her shoulders.

"Raych?"

His hands. His voice.

She spun round as she got off her knees, to see his face. His face was scraped up, his chin patchy and scraggly—he never could grow a beard —and he smelled absolutely awful. She didn't care.

She grabbed his face and kissed him, kissed him like she wanted to consume him completely, as if in the act of kissing him she could make him so completely a part of her that he could never leave her side again.

When her need for air finally won over her need to kiss him, she pulled back and looked deep into his very tired eyes.

He smiled that infuriating smile of his. "So did you rob a museum for me?"

She burst out laughing, more tears with it. "Not the whole museum, just five paintings."

"Were they good paintings?"

"Extraordinary, actually," she said. "You . . . you look like you had a busy day."

"Well, I didn't get a lot of sleep, and then I unleashed unholy terror on Quarrygate Prison to get our friends out, then went back, and had to save these boys from the Gearbox Killer." He gestured to the door, where Asti and Almer were both holding each other up, both of them looking absolutely wretched. Almer's arm was twisted in ways no person's limbs were supposed to go.

"Sweet prophets, look at you!" she said, going over to them. She kissed each of them on the cheek, and took a moment to take in Asti's face. His eyes, for once, didn't seem anywhere near as troubled as usual. "Are you all right?"

"I'm in considerable pain, but . . . oddly, yes."

"We should get you to Doc Gelson's, or better yet, get him here," Verci said.

"What's this about you stealing paintings?" Asti asked.

"From the Druth History Museum, yes," she said.

He chuckled. "I don't know if I would ever try that."

"You would, if you needed to," she said. She looked back to Verci. "I was ready to do whatever I needed to for you all."

"I know the feeling," Verci said.

Helene came up the stairs, and immediately embraced Almer and Asti, though Almer yelped when she did.

"Oh, sorry," she said. "Saints, what happened to your arm?"

"A number of unpleasantries happened," Almer said. "I hate to further burden, but getting to the doctor would be ideal."

"Jhoqull and the others are outside," Helene said. "We weren't able to run as fast as you."

"Doc Gelson is at Kimber's," Raych said. "Also Lian and Mila are probably there as well."

"Mila helped you with this?" Asti asked.

"How else do you think we pulled it off?" Helene shot back.

"Wait, Lian?" Verci asked. "You dragged her into it?"

"It was a family problem, family solutions," Raych said.

"So where is Corsi right now?" he asked.

"He's with Hal at their house," Raych said. "Should we first . . ."

"No, let's get Asti and Almer to Kimber's so Gelson can see them. Plus I suddenly realized I'm absolutely ravenous."

"Same," Asti said.

"Also," Verci said, his tone shifting a little. "It's probably best we have everyone together right now. We've got glasses to raise tonight."

Kimber's Pub was filled with many of the same folk it had several nights ago, before the Sheriffs had come in and dragged seven of them out in irons. Verci's eye stayed on the door the whole time—even with the promise that their papers were clean, all forgotten, he couldn't shake the feeling that something, anything could knock the ground out from under them.

Doc Gelson had taken a look at Asti and bandaged his hands—far more torn up than Asti would have wanted to admit—and gave him two doses of *doph* for the pain. "Might want to stay away from the bottles tonight on that," he added.

Almer's arm was set and bound, but Gelson said, "I can't promise you aren't going to have to lose a couple fingers in a few days."

Almer shrugged at that. "Other hand is still all five."

Verci was amazed how unaffected Almer seemed by everything.

The atmosphere in the room was subdued, as folks were engaged in quiet conversations at various tables. Mila sat with Lian and Kaiana, Jhoqull and Kennith were in a corner in the back, Helene and Julien by the bar. Asti sat at the bar as well, alone at the end, though Kimber stayed close, her eyes never leaving him.

Verci and Raych sat at the table closest to the bar, and even though his alert was up, he was just happy to get some real food in his stomach.

"I've not eaten anything decent in days," he said.

"Please eat all the pastries tonight," Kimber said. "I don't want anyone not already in here to even see them."

Verci took another one, happy to eat it. "This is your work, my love, isn't it?"

"It is," Raych said. "But Kimber's right, we should probably make sure we eat all of them, they're technically evidence that could link us back to the museum."

"I really want to hear this entire story," Verci said.

"If you tell me both of yours," she said, looking up to Asti.

"You really don't want to hear mine," Asti said quietly.

"Mine has its harrowing moments as well," Verci said. "It was . . ."

Before he finished that thought, Vellun came back from the water closet, took his glass off the bar, and got on the stage.

"So," Vellun said, his voice choking just a bit as he held up his glass. "Today we . . . we lost the dearest man I've known. I'm not going to pretend this hasn't been coming for months. I . . . I've been with him, I've taken care of him through the bad days, and there were some *bad* days. Especially the last few."

"That's the truth," Almer said.

"But on the good days . . ." Vellun took a moment, too worked up to continue. "I'd known him for a few years now, when he was at his lowest, really. Living on pence grifts, trying to put together plays in the most broken dives of the west side, working in rut-shows just so he could perform. But all that time, he never lost his spark. He saw something in me—"

"Your extremely pretty face!" Helene said, and Vellun laughed.

"That was probably it, yes," Vellun said. "But with that, he took me —a stupid kid who surely would have ended up arrested or dead for doing doxy work—and he taught me every grift and trick he knew. He told me stories about the days—about your father, Rynaxes. And yours, Hel. So many stories. And he taught me to love words. Made me read every damn Whit play, as well as Neville and Bonfi and Agosti and I don't even know what. And he . . ." Vellun stepped down and sat on the stage, crying too hard to finish the sentence.

"And he loved you," Verci said. "Right to the very end."

Vellun nodded, and buried his face in his hand.

Verci stood up, raising his glass. "I'd been seeing Pilsen perform since I was a kid. Back when he still had shows in Seleth, Dad would take Asti and me out to watch from the pits. I must have seen him in twenty plays. And when he was preparing a grift, the way he could switch up his game at the snap of his finger."

"He could become a whole different person with a word," Mila said. Switching her own accent and bearing to something far more regal, she said, "I learned so much from him, and still had so much to learn."

More laughter filled the room.

"And his final performance," Verci said. "When I tell you—he could have done anything, *anything*, to make enough distraction for Vellun and me to do what we needed to do—but instead he made his final performance matter. He was . . ."

"Towering," Vellun said. "He was beyond anything. And he was a beautiful man who . . ."

There was an uneasy silence, and Raych touched Verci's arm. "All those songs your father taught you, which one was Pilsen's favorite?"

Verci had to think about that. There was something, a wisp of a memory Verci couldn't quite find, the tune just on the edge of his thoughts.

Then Asti started to sing, first slow and quiet.

"Bo a egnot

Rel crost haue

Fru sentad, fru sentad, fru sentad oe qui

Prei doat crost asi

Vae vul gespu

Fru sentad, fru sentad, fru sentad oe qui. "

It was an old song, in the vulgar dialect of the Luciex province of the Kieran Empire where Pop was born. It told a story of rebels leaving their village to hide in the mountains, saying goodbye to their loved ones, and then realizing too late that leaving did not keep the soldiers from tearing apart their village searching for them. They return and vow vengeance, and go off to fight, once again saying goodbye.

"Fru sentad, fru sentad, fru sentad oe qui. "

Pilsen had loved it when Pop sang that song—one of the few bits of sentiment of his old homeland—and even though he didn't understand the words, he would always join in with the chorus, belting it out with such joy and energy. Which Verci found himself doing with Asti.

"Fru sentad, fru sentad, fru sentad oe qui."

Asti was on his feet now, taking Verci by the arm, as they both sang this song to each other, to the room, like singing it was a victory. Like it was a promise.

"Fru sentad, fru sentad, fru sentad oe qui."

Everyone else in the room—none of them knew the lyrics, and Verci knew them only as words in the song, not their real meaning—but everyone quickly caught on to the rhythm of the verses and joined in with the chorus each time it came up.

"Fru sentad, fru sentad, fru sentad oe qui."

Verci realized, looking into Asti's eyes, that this was a promise he was making, as they said goodbye to Pilsen. A promise that this would *never* happen again. That he would stop anyone who tried to hurt the family in this room.

That they would all do it together.

"Fru sentad, fru sentad, fru sentad oe qui!"

The last round was raucous, spirited, as all of them were shouting the chorus together, and as they ended the song, everyone was laughing and crying together.

"Well now," Lieutenant Covrane said from the entryway of the taproom. "Looks like I came to the right place."

HELENE STOOD STUNNED FOR A MOMENT, AS DID EVERYONE ELSE IN THE room, and she realized it was on her to break the tension. She went over to Covrane and kissed him.

"Jarret," she said. "I'm so glad you're here. As you can see we've had some good news."

"Indeed," Covrane said, walking over to Julien and embracing the big man. "Glad to see you are all right."

"Mostly," Julien said.

"Good, good," he said. "And the Rynax brothers. Glad to see you are back here, right where I last saw you."

"It's good to be seen, Lieutenant," Verci said.

"I'm sure," Covrane. "Because I can tell you, I have had the strangest day. I have been trying to find out what happened to you boys—"

"Jarret was livid about the lack of proper procedure or courtesy when those Sheriffs arrested you," Helene said. She wasn't entirely sure what to say, or what Covrane even knew about what the boys had all been through. Or what she had.

"It was intolerable," Covrane said. "And as much as my apology on behalf of . . . well, as much as I can speak for law enforcement in this city . . . I guess it doesn't mean much."

"Understood," Asti said. "And the sentiment is noted."

"But this is fascinating. I had been trying to get any information, putting out inquiries, so these ladies could at least work the proper legal channels to help you all, even just to find you. We had no idea where you even were."

"Terrifying," Raych said.

"And this is where it gets fascinating. All my queries were met with silence. And then this morning a report landed on my desk, and do you know what it said?"

"I can't even guess," Asti said drily.

"That you two were dead. Not that you died in custody or such, no. That you have been dead for months."

"Absurd," Helene said.

"Which is what I said, and I went and tried to track down where this report came from. I'm digging through archives, asking folks, and then I get another report. Guess what it said?"

"That the report on our death was incorrect?" Verci offered.

"On the very nose," Covrane said. "Despite this, on its face, convincing report of your deaths, this file I received noted that the first was a deplorable error, an error that led to a series of mistaken identities and mixed-up documents, which resulted in the accidental arrest of you all, the false death reports being put out, and that you were all now released on your own liberty, and I should consider the matter closed."

"We're just very grateful it was sorted," Verci said.

"Sorted and closed," Covrane said. "I'm very glad for you all. But I must ask you to excuse me for a few private words with my intended."

He took Helene's hand and led her out of the taproom, to a quiet niche near the stairs.

"Sorry I didn't let you know sooner," Helene said. "It's been—"

"A busy day?" he asked. "I'm sure it was."

There was danger in his tone.

"The important thing," she said firmly, "is that all this trouble is behind us now. Julien is home, it was all a misunderstanding."

"It's quite a strange misunderstanding," Covrane said. "The idea that seven men who all know each other could get arrested under the wrong names, while their correct names are listed as declared dead months ago, and then to be suddenly sorted out? It's patently absurd, Hel."

"It is, I agree," Helene said. "But you're the one who said that's what happened."

"That's what I was told," he said. "But something deeply odd was afoot, and I'm worried how much you are a part of that."

Helene took a deep breath. "I don't know if you really want to know everything about me, or the . . . things that I've been involved in. Or if you would want to marry me if you did."

He shook his head. "I want to marry you, Helene. There isn't any doubt in my mind about that."

"But am I going to be a good constable's wife?" she asked. "Those ladies at the stationhouse, they're a very certain kind of woman, right and true and proper, while I'm . . ."

She almost said "robbing museums" before she caught herself.

"I'm very different."

"Very different is what I love," Covrane said. "You have been through a lot in these past few days, and I've seen . . ." He shook his head for a moment. "I'm not sure what I've seen, other than official records telling me things that are clearly untrue. I don't need to know the things you've done—even the things you did today, Helene— because so much of what's . . ." His face looked like he couldn't even find the words.

"What's right and true and proper?" she offered.

"The only thing I know that's right and true and proper is what I feel here," he said, taking her hand and putting it over his heart. "Please tell me you still feel the same."

"I do," she said, with an intensity she didn't even realize she felt until the words came. "If you can feel that way, even after all this . . ."

"After all this. Your secrets don't matter to me, only you."

"I'll never be the sort of wife like those ladies in the stationhouse."

"Thank the saints for that."

"Then it's settled," she said, kissing him again. "Tomorrow, Julien and I will have dinner at your mother's, and we will find our way to Saint Bridget's on the first of the month."

"That's just seven days away."

"I don't wait to take my shot, Lieutenant," she said. "Let me say some goodbyes, and then it's time for us to run, darling."

"Go on, I'll wait by the door. I think I make your friends nervous."

"I won't be long at all," she said, kissing him again.

And she was surprised by how much she meant it.

MILA STOOD NEAR THE ENTRYWAY OF THE TAPROOM AS HELENE returned.

"Everything all right?" she asked.

"Everything is a delight," Helene said. "And you shouldn't spy."

"Just having your back."

"Well, have my back on the first of Nalithan, hmm? Someone needs to stand at my hip."

Mila thought Helene was having a joke with her, but then her eyes told a different story. "Really, you want me?"

"It's you or Lady Melania, and that might invite some odd questions."

"You want me?" Mila asked again, shocked that Helene would think of her.

"Want her for what?" Raych said, coming up with Jhoqull.

"She wants me to hold her bracelet," Mila said.

"So this is happening?" Raych asked, excited.

"I want it on the first," Helene said. "Celebrate a new beginning, perhaps?"

"An excellent day," Jhoqull said.

"Helene," Raych said. "All of you, I just . . . well, we didn't need to go through what we did to get the boys free, but . . . I'm glad we got to do it together. And not die or get arrested."

"That would be very hard to explain to my intended," Helene said. "But I am going to go. I've spent too many nights sleeping next to one of you."

"Agreed," Raych said.

"Be with your man," Jhoqull added. "We all deserve to relax, I think. In fact, I should take Kennith out of here to someplace more private."

"Wisdom all around," Raych said.

Mila chuckled at that, but she would be going back to the dorm with her two roommates after this. Whatever ill-defined romance she had started with Veranix at the beginning of the semester, it hadn't cooled from the initial ardor, but . . . it was still ill-defined. She wondered if it was time to put some definition on that.

"In the meantime," Helene said. "You all make sure Asti knows— and I know he's still got something planned—but whatever it is, I'm still here for whatever he needs."

"Even as a constable's wife?"

"Family is still family," Helene said. "Julien told me everything Verci did, and . . . just tell them, I'm still here for them."

"Will do," Mila said. "Get out of here."

"Happily," Helene said, and she went off into the night.

Raych sighed. "I still need to get the full story out of Verci. And Asti."

"Asti will not tell you," Mila said.

"Probably not," Raych said. She glanced over at him, and then back to Mila. "So what about you?"

"I should get back to campus soon," Mila said. Glancing over to the table in the back. "And also rescue Kaiana from your very drunk sister and get her back as well."

"Blessed prophets, Lian is really in it, isn't she?" Raych said, laughing. "I'll go peel her off Kai."

Jhoqull clapped Raych and Mila on the arms. "And I will gather up Kennith and bring him home. But . . . I cannot speak for Kennith, but I say for me, that House Gheqham is united with House Rynax. You need us, we will come."

"Am I part of House Rynax?" Mila asked.

"Without question," Asti said, as he had come quietly come over to them. Raych and Jhoqull both used this as a moment to move away. His attention was on Mila. "I hear you had a very good plan."

"I had help," she said. "And I had a few good teachers."

He chuckled ruefully. "Blazes, I'm going to miss Pilsen."

"Same."

"But you, young lady, I want to keep missing. More at school and less finding your way back here."

"Not my fault you keep needing me," Mila said.

"By every saint, I wish we didn't," he said. "But I'm very glad you were here for Raych. I'm just hoping you can quietly stay over there without further trouble."

"It's not been all quiet for me there, you know."

"It should be, so make a point of it," Asti said. "Also, you should know that Grieson is dead."

That was troubling. "What does that mean for me?"

"I don't think it should affect whatever strings he pulled to get you in there. That should be fine. But it might mean whatever accounts were paying your tuition and fees could dry up."

"I still have money if it comes to that."

"If it does, let me know," Asti said. "You shouldn't have to handle that alone."

"I'll stay in touch," she said. "Whatever you have planned, everyone here is with you."

"No," Asti said. "I can't ask anyone—"

"Helene wanted me to tell you that she's in. And so am I. And I'm telling you, I see everyone here. You need us, we're here."

"What I want," he said quietly, "is to not have to need you. But I don't get what I want. So the sentiment is very appreciated."

"Like Jhoqull said," Mila said, "House Rynax."

Kaiana came over to them. "We should get to campus before curfew bells. At least you should."

"Right," Mila said.

"Thank you for your part in this," Asti said to Kaiana. "And tell the Thorn to keep his guard up. The Brotherhood is apparently still out there making noise."

"He's not the Thorn anymore," Kaiana said.

"And I was retired from the game and running a shop, and this happened," Asti said. "We don't always have the luxury of choice. I hope he doesn't have to deal with it, but they might come for him."

"We're very familiar with that," Mila said. She looked over Asti. As usual, there was something broken about him, but with that there was a new sense. For the first time in the months she had known him, he seemed . . . lighter. "But we appreciate the warning."

"Come on," Kaiana said, and they left Kimber's for the long walk back to campus.

CHAPTER THIRTY-ONE

The night went on, and friends all went their own way. Asti was happy to see each of them here, and see each of them leave, until it was just him and Verci, and Raych and her sister, and Kimber patiently tending to them.

"I would like to see you here first thing in the morning," Kimber said to Asti. "That is if you don't want a room upstairs."

"To go to morning services with you?" Asti said. "I'd like that."

"That actually wasn't why, but I'm very happy you want to."

"In the midst of all this I had an experience that I can only describe as miraculous," Asti said. "So I think I could stand a bit of . . . clarity."

"I'm always here for you for clarity," she said, taking his hand. "But I want you in the morning because the boy you sent here to learn how to knife fight will be here."

"That kid!" Asti said with a laugh. "He came?"

"He came and I've been putting him to work all week. But I need you to step up with him."

"You want me to teach him how to fight?"

"I want you to be there for him, in whatever way you can."

Asti nodded. "Of course."

"Good."

Verci clapped him on the shoulder. "We should be heading out, and get Lian to her house. Where are you going to be?"

Asti looked up. "I'll walk with you all. Least I can do is help you all keep Lian upright."

"Appreciated," Verci said.

They made their way down to Colt Street, though Lian ended up draping herself over Verci. Asti walked in front of them for a while, and Raych came up and matched pace silently for a couple blocks.

"I need to tell you something," she said quietly. "When . . . when I was trying to figure things out, I . . . I looked through your journals."

"Oh," Asti said. He wasn't sure how even to respond to that. "Did they help?"

"Not really, but I . . . I want you to know, I don't really understand everything you've gone through, but . . . after everything, I'm . . . I want you know I am your sister here."

"I know," he said. "Saints, you certainly proved yourself a Rynax tonight." He chuckled. "The Druth History Museum. Bold, Raychelle, bold."

"I did what I had to," she said. "Which is why I understand why you've done the things you've done."

"I don't know if I understand myself most of the time," Asti said. "But . . . it's good to hear you say that."

"Is . . . I mean . . . can you hear Liora now?" she asked gingerly. "Is she here?"

"She's not," Asti said. "Something happened while I was being tortured, and Sholiar sprayed me with something which must have messed with my head further, and I saw . . . it doesn't matter. But I think in all that, Liora got locked behind a door in my mind. She's been gone since."

"That's good, right?" Raych asked.

"If it lasts," Asti said. "But I'll take the quiet for now." And it was all quiet in his head. The beast was . . . it was there still, but it was . . . content.

"Oh," Raych said. "I should probably warn you, that Poasian merchant was trying to find you. He was very insistent."

"He came to find you?" Asti said. "He came over to Kimber's the night of the party, I agreed to talk to him in the morning, and, well . . . I wonder what that's about."

Raych reached into one of her pockets. "This morning, he gave me this to give to you." She handed him a piece of paper. Asti glanced at the Poasian script, and suddenly there was a click in his head.

Like a different door opened just a little bit.

"What is it?" Raych asked.

"Asti?" Verci asked, now outright carrying Lian, who was dozing in his arms. "You all right?"

Asti rubbed at his temples, suddenly dizzy. There was suddenly something on the edge of his memory, reading a list of names, but . . . he couldn't make out any of the names on the list.

"I don't know," Asti said. "That Poasian word triggered something, but . . ."

"I'm so sorry, I had no idea—"

"Not your fault," Asti said, stepping away as he found his equilibrium. "It's Nafath's. He must . . . what did Grieson tell us?"

"That something important was inside your skull," Verci said.

"And Nafath must think he can get at it."

"Should we pay him a visit?" Verci asked. "Maybe one with knives?"

For once, Asti felt a distinct need for caution. "No. I think . . . I think it's better that whatever is in my head stays locked down as possible. Any further engagement with him might unlock it. We stay clear."

"If you say," Verci said.

"I don't even want to risk it until we know more," Asti said. "So for now—"

Asti didn't get to finish that thought, as his attention went to the plumes of smoke coming from above the buildings ahead of them. The flash and flicker of flames beneath that.

"That's Colt Street," he said, and started to run.

RAYCH RAN AFTER ASTI, HER HEART POUNDING, FEAR RISING, TERRIFIED by the idea that she didn't dare think was true. It couldn't be true. It mustn't be true. But as she rounded the corner, she saw it absolutely was.

Hal and Lian's house was on fire.

Corsi was in there.

Asti didn't hesitate. He ran right up the stoop, kicked the door in, and charged inside.

Verci was right behind, and he deposited Lian onto her feet, handing her over to Raych. "Call Brigade, call anyone," he said. He shouted those same instructions to the handful of onlookers on the street. All of them just standing and gawking.

Verci looked back at her. "Corsi's in there."

"Go!" she shouted, and he was off like an arrow into the house.

Black smoke billowed out of the windows, the flames crackling louder. Someone must have gone to a whistlebox, because Raych heard a fire call in the distance Not that it mattered, the house was engulfed. At most, the Brigade could prevent it from spreading to its neighbors. Even across the street, Raych could feel the heat on her face. How long had Asti and Verci been in there? It felt like eternity. Lian woozily opened her eyes and saw what was happening to her house.

"What is . . . how . . ." she stammered. "No! No!" She stumbled forward, like she was going to run inside, but Raych held her back.

"Nothing you can do," Raych said.

"Hal!" Lian screamed, her voice expressing all the terror Raych was keeping inside. Her son was in there, now Verci and Asti were as well. She had just gotten her husband back, if he was killed here and now, she . . . she didn't know if she could bear that. But she let Lian scream for her right now.

"Hal! Hal!"

Asti came out the door, carrying someone over his shoulder. He got to the street and dropped to his knees, and Lian raced up to him, Raych right behind her.

"Hal, Hal," Lian said as Asti put the body down. He fell over, coughing.

The man Asti had carried out wasn't Hal. Raych didn't know who he was.

"Who is this?" Lian screeched. "Where is Hal? Where's my husband?"

"He's all I found," Asti wheezed out between coughs. "Didn't find anyone else."

"But Verci?" Raych asked. "Corsi?"

Determination set in Asti's eyes, and he got to his feet, even as another round of hacking coughs tried to stop him. He was about to move when one of the windows on the upper floor shattered and Verci came leaping out. Even in this moment, Raych was astounded by how effortless he made jumping down from a second floor to an awning to the ground.

"Where's Hal?" Lian asked.

"Where's Corsi?" Raych pressed, grabbing on to Verci, part of her wanting to be sure he was really there, really still alive.

Verci shook his head. "I looked everywhere. There . . . there's no sign of them."

"Are you sure?" Raych asked. "Maybe they were—"

"Gone," the man on the ground coughed out. "They're gone."

"Who is this man?" Lian asked. "Where is Hal?"

Verci looked down at the man. "I think . . . I think he's our lawyer."

"What?" Asti asked.

Verci was on his knees. "Mister Cheever, are you all right?"

"I . . . I couldn't . . ." The poor man's voice was a rasp, his face and arms were covered in burns, and there was a horrific welt on his forehead.

Lian had lost all composure, wailing on the ground, and it took every ounce of strength Raych had not to join her. "Asti, get some water. There's a pump over there."

"Make a Yellowshield call!" Asti yelled at someone as he went for the water.

"Easy, easy," Verci said. "Can you hear me?"

Cheever opened his eyes. "Mister Rynax. Good to see you at liberty."

"Good to see you," Verci said. Asti came over with a handful of water and brought it to Cheever's lips.

"What's going on?" Asti asked. "Who is he?"

"Cheed Cheever, from the Justice Advocate Office," Verci said. "He was helping me and . . ."

"I came to check on your claim, with your brother-in-law, Mister Elman," Cheever said.

"What happened?" Raych asked. "Where is he? Where's my son?"

Cheever tried to sit up, but that seemed to be too much strain for him. "We had been talking about your case, and it had gone on for some time as he was struggling with the young lad. I was advising him on securing the nappy when . . . when . . ."

"When what?" Raych asked. Asti had returned again with more water, this time in a proper cup.

"A number of rough gentlemen forced their way into the house," Cheever said. "They made a number of threats regarding you and your brother—is this your brother?"

"Go on, sir," Asti said.

"Pleased to make your acquaintance, and to see you at liberty. Very sorry I wasn't more helpful."

"What happened with these men?" Verci pressed.

"They were quite put out by you, saying you needed to stop, and they needed to send a message."

"A message?"

"When I tried to stop them, they knocked me to the floor," Cheever said. "And said, 'you tell those Rynaxes, this is what happens when you mess with the order of things.'"

"What?" Asti asked.

"Hal and the baby?" Raych pressed.

"They took them, and then started the fire," Cheever said. "They said, 'collateral until the Rynax boys learn who owns these streets and what's beneath them.'"

Raych wanted to feel relief. Her son was still alive. Hal was still alive. But these monsters took them, and burned down her sister's house on top of that. And for what?

"What does that even mean?" she asked Verci.

Verci looked to Asti. "I'm not sure."

"I'm not either," he said, looking up as he waved approaching Yellowshields and Fire Brigade over. "But you get your sister to the Gadgeterium, get her safe."

"What are you going to do?" she asked.

Verci and Asti looked at each other, a silent understanding passed between them.

"We don't know who did this," Verci said. "But we have a very good idea who to ask."

JOSIE HAD LET THE LAMPS GO LOW. SHE HAD SPENT TOO MANY HOURS sipping at her stash of *volsaka*, the clear Fuergan liquor that she had grown more than a little too fond of, while admiring her new acquisition.

She'd have to get the canvases reframed, but that wasn't a problem. If that was the mild inconvenience for getting these treasures back, more than acceptable.

But she had let it grow late, and she should find her way to her bed now.

She pulled herself out of her chair, took her cane, and made her way to the niche that opened the secret latch to the door to her bedroom. Circumstance and practicality had forced her to abandon most of her secrecy in the past months—no more living in hidden bunkers and never seeing the light of day—but she would never be able to sleep properly in a room that had an obvious door.

Fortunately she still had enough clout and resources to have the offices she claimed at the Elk Road Shack and the Honey Hut—her new centers of power—made with a proper hidden door to her beds. Tonight was an Elk Road night, as most were. She didn't have the strength to move back and forth as much anymore, not without Ia by her side.

Where was that infuriating Bardinic woman?

Josie put her hands on the piece of molding on the niche that opened the door, but she could never get a grip on it anymore. Hands didn't work like they used to.

"Ia!" she called out. "Get in here!"

No response.

She worked her way to the office door. "Ia! Where are you?"

It wasn't like that girl to ignore her, but Ia had been busy all day. What was the name of that fellow who guarded the back hallway?

"Sommick!" she called out. "Get in here!"

She realized the Elk Road Shack sounded far quieter than usual. Even this late, there were usually quite a few drunken hooligans and a few Scratch Cats making some noise. But right now, no one.

"Sommick!"

The door to her office flew open, and Asti Rynax came in like a summer storm. He looked like he had already fought every sinner in the canon: his face and arms streaked with blood and ash, knives in his hands, ice in his eyes.

"Sommick isn't coming."

"Asti," she said cautiously. "Glad to see you're out, but . . ."

His voice was calm, even, as he said, "My brother has a question for you."

"Verci, what—"

Verci walked in the door, and he was a terror, absolute rage on his face.

"Where is my son?" he growled.

"Your what?"

"Where is my son?" he shouted, and he jumped at her, kicking her cane out from under her. She had no doubt he had come to kill.

"I don't know, what are you talking about—"

"Don't lie to me!" His blade came to her throat.

"Verci, I swear to you I'm not," she said. "I have done some horrendous things, including to you boys, but I would never, *never*, hurt a baby."

Asti stepped forward, putting his hand on Verci's. "Someone burned down Raych's sister's house. They took her husband and Corsi. If you know anything . . ."

"What do you know?" Josie asked.

"There was a message that we 'messed with the order of things,'" Asti said.

"And that my son was taken as 'collateral' until we learn the order of things on the street."

"And what's beneath them."

Josie stepped away and fell into her chair. "Rutting blazes."

"What do you know?"

"That the message was as much to me as to you," she said. "I'm very sorry, boys."

"What did you do?" Verci snarled, moving in close to her.

Josie wasn't going to have any of that, staring him down. "I had the audacity to try to hold on to my streets when other folks wanted to take it. All of it, boys, all of it comes down to the same folks— the ones building the Andrendon, the ones who burned out the alley, the ones chipping away at me—and surely the ones who did this. They're sending a message."

"Why now?" Asti asked. "This can't be connected to what threw us into Quarrygate."

"No. But it's probably connected to what Raych did today."

"The paintings?" Verci asked.

"I told Raych one reason I wanted the paintings—a very personal one for my family. But there was another reason. Those paintings were at the museum on loan from their owners, with that loan insured by a goldsmith house. Neville House."

The looks on the boys' faces told her they knew exactly what that meant.

"One of the three houses backing the Andrendon," Asti said.

"And the loss of the paintings will cripple them," she said. "That was the point, and clearly that point was heard by the folks behind it, and they enlisted their people on the ground."

"Who?"

"Someone powerful, I've been trying to find out. The crime bosses in the city are in chaos since Fenmere died. It could go as high as Gemmen for all I know."

"So who has Corsi?" Asti asked.

"I don't know," Josie said. "I swear to you, I don't. But as much as you don't trust me, as much as you hate me, believe that I am with you on this. I have always been with you."

"You betrayed us!"

"I was working a different angle, and had to secure my own position in this neighborhood. But now I am telling you, we need each other. We are together on this."

"On what?" Verci asked.

"On making the bastards who are behind it all—the Andrendon, the fires, taking your son—making them all pay."

"We've been working on a plan," Asti said. "This business with the paintings and Neville House tipped your hand, and I'm not sure if our plan can still work."

"What kind of plan?" she asked.

"It was a long-game plan, with just the two of us," Asti said. "But now that'll have to change."

She could see it in his eyes, the gears were clicking together.

"If we're together on this, we can make it all work. Stop them and save Corsi."

Verci shook his head. "If this turns left like so many other things have, if Corsi—"

"The plan needs to be perfect," Asti said. "It'll need time, it'll need us keeping up appearances. We need to look like we're behaving."

"So they are willing to give Corsi back," Verci said.

"So they won't suspect it when we move," Asti said. "And I swear to you, brother, we will get him back. Even if I have to burn this whole city to the ground for him."

Good. Josie wanted them back in the fold, and even if the reasons why were horrifying, if it got her the Rynax boys back, that was good. And she'd make sure whoever took the baby was suitably punished. There were rules to this game, and babies were off limits.

"Whatever you need, if I have it, it's yours," Josie said.

"Good," Asti said. "Because we're going to need time, we're going to need space, and we're going to need money."

"I can do that," Josie said.

"And we're going to need everyone."

"What do you mean, 'everyone'?" Verci said.

"I mean every damn friend, ally, rival, and enemy we've got in North Seleth," Asti said. "Everyone."

TO BE CONCLUDED IN

THE ANDRENDON PLAN

ACKNOWLEDGMENTS

And here we are, back to Maradaine, back to the Rynax family. And as cliché as it can be for heist stories evolve into found families, the Rynaxes and their extended friends and allies really are one to me.

But I'll still do the horrible things to them. It's in the job description.

Years ago, when I knew how I would be breaking up the phases of the saga, one phrase kept drumming in my head for Phase Two: ***Autumn in Maradaine, everything will fall.*** This is definitely true here, as we put Asti, Verci & Raych through a lot of hardship. And, as you can see at the end, I intend to continue to do that.

Everything with Maradaine is improved and strengthened by the work I've been doing on my podcast *Worldbuilding for Masochists,* and I can't express how much my co-hosts, Rowenna Miller and Cass Morris, are just the best people to work with. Brilliant, creative minds, and incredible anchors of support. More support came from patrons and fans, like Brian Yost, Nina Mulligan and Ember Randall.

Also instrumental were my usual sounding boards: Daniel Fawcett, forever my absolute rock when it comes to every element of this saga; and Miriam Robinson Gould, the best first reader I could ask for.

Of course, as usual, I relied heavily on my publishing team, including my editor Sheila Gilbert, and everyone at DAW and Astra: Betsy, Katie, Josh, Leah, Alexis, and Stephanie, plus countless others whose names I don't know.

On top of that, my family remains a source of strength and inspiration. This includes my parents Nancy and Lou, and my mother-in-law Kateri. And, of course, my son Nicholas and wife Deidre, who have continued to put up with me during this incredible journey through Maradaine and beyond.

And thank you, dear reader, who hopefully just read the last words of this book, and are eagerly awaiting the promise that it holds. I am equally excited to deliver on that promise.

-Marshall Ryan Maresca
October 2022

ABOUT THE AUTHOR

Marshall Ryan Maresca is a fantasy and science-fiction writer, author of the Maradaine Saga: Four braided series set amid the bustling streets and crime-ridden districts of the exotic city called Maradaine, which includes The ***Thorn of Dentonhill, A Murder of Mages, The Holver Alley Crew*** and ***The Way of the Shield***, as well as the dieselpunk fantasy, ***The Velocity of Revolution***. He is also the co-host of the Hugo-nominated, Stabby-winning podcast **Worldbuilding for Masochists**, and has been a playwright, an actor, a delivery driver and an amateur chef. He lives in Austin, Texas with his family.